The Cathar Legacy

By

Nita Hughes

This book is a work of fiction. Places, events, and situations in this story are purely fictional. Any resemblance to actual persons, living or dead, is coincidental.

ISBN: 1-4116-6430-2

Pyradice Publishing markets products and services that focus on educational and inspirational topics (visit: www.pyradice.com).

This book is printed by Lulu (visit: www.lulu.com/nitahughes) on recycled paper.

ACKNOWLEDGEMENTS

The author wishes to gratefully acknowledge the energy, encouragement and professional diligence of my dream agent, Gabriella Ambrosioni. Her faith echoed that of my beloved spouse, Douglas Hughes, whose creativity was instrumental in preparing this manuscript for publication.

Thanks also go to my dear friends, Mara and David Snaith, Rob Riebling, Odette Carothers, Shasta Rose, Richard Neumeyer, Rocky, Annie and the Butler clan, as well as to my children, Kim Brady and Kris Gerbracht for their generous aid in editing.

As to inspiration, my Mother, Audrey Davis, implanted it and waters it always with her love.

ONE

Mon Dieu! Let it be so! Pierre de Lahille's silent mantra strengthened with every cautious step. An icy chill ran down his spine at the magnitude of their hidden treasure, described in the records of the Inquisition as: "…so powerful as to transform the world." Shouldering a hunting rifle which was too massive for his diminutive form, he glanced around before nearing his destination. One hand shielded the misty glare of the watery-gray dawn as he scrutinized the landscape. As with much of France's Department of Aude, profuse outcrops of rock, like the granite ribs of massive dinosaurs, dotted a land barren of all but an isolated tree, thorny shrubs and silent hills. Pierre remained motionless until he felt assured that no human, no movement, no sounds, nothing but the sigh of his own breath penetrated the area surrounding his sanctuary.

Before his final approach, he turned, allowing a smug grin of satisfaction in acknowledgement of his tactics. His careful steps atop brambles and brush effectively obscured his footprints. He shrugged as if to dismiss the irony in assuming such tactics. *How was it,* he wondered, *that a quiet research scientist, an aging academic whose physical pursuits rarely ventured beyond turning the pages of a book or petting his arthritic cat, should be traipsing the countryside like Inspector Poirot on a dangerous mission?*

Entering a stand of shrubbery, he made his way through the spindly trees and knotted tangle of berry canes. Careful not to break a twig, he parted what appeared to be an impenetrable thicket which concealed a pile of boulders. Exercising great care, he moved the largest one, giving thanks for his anemic frame as he lowered himself into the stygian depths of his secret sanctuary.

As he landed on the floor of the cave, he shed his cumbersome raincoat and his gun. In spite of the damp chill of the cavern, rivulets of sweat, like stalactites weeping, dripped relentlessly down his face, triggered by the realization that, God willing, his discovery could result in the world's most critical turning point. So honored was he to be part of such an undertaking, that he rarely allowed himself time to dwell on the inherent dangers.

He shook his head, as if to release a disquieting uneasiness, stopping for a moment to aim his flashlight at all sides of the cavern. Seeing nothing but the granite folds of millennia of geologic upheavals which had formed impenetrable fortress walls, he felt reassured. His breathing slowed to match the silence of centuries, confident that, even in an area known to be honey-combed with caves, no one knew of this unique subterranean universe.

Its location, deep in the south of France in a section of Aude not yet given over to grapevines, was secluded enough that even long time residents of neighboring villages hadn't discovered it. To avoid exciting any curiosity, Pierre had taken great care to disguise his wanderings by carrying a hunting rifle and bringing home proof of his pseudo-avocation.

Diligence was second nature to him, honed to such a degree that he knew his colleagues described him as anal. His focus on precision, however, had always assured success in all he undertook. Today was different. The knowledge of how close he was to unveiling something phenomenal had eroded his certainty that he had prepared for every possible contingency. A nature so long imbedded in scholarly deliberation, leading to precise conclusions, obviously hadn't provided immunity to the corrosive impact of fear. Hyperventilating, his clammy hands underscored his apprehension.

To quell such emotions, he turned his thoughts to his team, letting out a sigh of relief as he anticipated their excitement when he disclosed his discovery. Comparisons of his manuscript with the other three manuscripts—one per team-member—should provide the litmus test as to whether his discovery was the linchpin that would unlock their message. Much of the text of his manuscript had seemed meaningless until he found a tracery of the word "light" threaded throughout.

Thinking of his teammates surprised reaction to such 'enlightenment' brought each of their personalities to mind. He smiled, remembering the skepticism he had felt at such disparate individuals ever having come together. Dana Palmer, feisty American photographer; Eric Taylor, reserved British writer; Professor William Marty, respected French historian; and Veronique Alexandre, brilliant archeological researcher at the University of Toulouse. On the surface, all had certain logical credentials. But logic had played no part in their discovery of the manuscripts.

An explosive guffaw escaped as it dawned on Pierre that, as earth-shattering as the news of the treasure would be, the treasure hunters' provenance would be equally beyond belief. Should they—could they— reveal their thirteenth century commitment to return in the twenty-first century to unearth the secret of the Cathars? Pierre's reclusive soul hoped they would never have to explain how they had succeeded when six hundred years of the Catholic Church's zealous efforts to find the treasure had come to naught. Revealing what they found and who found it would stretch the limits of rational explanation.

Certainly it had required more than logic to erode his resistance to accepting what Dana described as "woo-woo". Ultimately each, in their own way, had experienced a dramatic recall of their Thirteenth Century lives as Cathars. A Christian group—whose practices emulated the teachings of Christ— the Cathars were labeled "heretics" by the Catholic Church and destroyed.

Each of the team members had vowed to protect the treasure—then and now. Ultimately, the serendipity of their team's reunion and their improbable success in finding the treasure had extinguished Pierre's lingering skepticism.

So perilous had been their discovery of the four scrolls that, once achieved, their elation had known no bounds. An initial impulse of: "wow, let's get this into the hands of the world's best scientists fast," was paramount until Veronique extinguished their excitement. "Do you really believe, now that we have possession of the manuscripts, that we, or they, are in any less danger?"

Pierre shivered, not from the impact of the cavern, but from the chilling images of the Inquisition. Given the Church's 600 year vendetta to eradicate heretics and locate their treasure, what methods would they use now to possess it? Fear threatened to overcome him at the recognition that, rather than a folie a deaux, theirs was a folie a cinq: the belief that five people could prevail against the power of such an adversary. The Vatican's massive resources, unlimited wealth and powerful alignments created such a formidable foe as to make any optimism on the part of their team seem juvenile.

Pierre felt his esophagus tighten, sealing away his breath at the knowledge that they had no alternative but to proceed with a quest that went beyond time and beyond rationality. As a gasp broke free, his airflow resumed and his thoughts sought a more reassuring avenue as he began a review of the safeguards they had chosen. .

Soon after the discovery of the four scrolls, as each closely examined the one assigned to them, they met with the same stumbling block: a complete inability to decipher meaning from their individual scroll. Pierre smiled as he recalled that it was Dana, the least analytical of the team, who felt the secret lay hidden within an enigmatic combination of all four manuscripts. Relief grew as they acknowledged her insight, but so did frustration. Heads shook in bewilderment as they labored to discover the mysterious lynchpin needed to decipher the manuscript's treasure.

It was this key that Pierre felt certain he had discovered. His "Eureka" moment had taken place as he'd recalled an old manuscript a scientist in Scotland had sent him. As was true for most ancient parchments, it turned out to be a "palimpsest", a parchment which had been overwritten by subsequent scholars eager to reuse the precious linen. Reading through the lines, so to speak, had painstakingly revealed the skeleton of many layers of overwritten parchment disguising the ancient wisdom of the Scotsman's original Druid text.

Immediately Pierre's thoughts had turned to: *Could their manuscripts have been overwritten, either randomly or with purpose? Might the connection come to light through a careful filtering of all overlaid lines? Would such close scrutiny—ideally with the aid of a particle accelerator—clearly reveal a message able to change the world?*

His team's dictum to keep their discovery hidden, limited his willingness to request the use of a particle accelerator. But, once again, it was a comment of Dana's that prompted him to consider something that he did have access to: the use of digital cameras, processing techniques, ultraviolet and infrared filters which could give some idea of whether or not such layering enshrouded the message. Even a limited application of such techniques to his manuscript alone was enough to hint at the enormity of the message contained in the combined scrolls.

Pierre's shoulders lifted and fell with each deeply drawn breath as he contemplated the bombshell the four manuscripts would reveal. Getting the four manuscripts together, however, would present a daunting task, given the teams' agreement that having it fall into the wrong hands was far too dangerous a risk. For now, each team-member had chosen a failsafe hiding place for "their" manuscript. Shining his flashlight behind him, each shadow deepened his awareness of how foolhardy such measures may prove.

And yet, destiny having dictated their success thus far convinced him of the logic that they would prevail. Girding his resolve, Pierre entered the largest cavern of the cave. His scrutiny reassured him that this vast space appeared to be a dead-end. It actually had a couple of rather obvious auxiliary tunnels which, should any pursuer investigate, would lead to dead-ends. Only he knew the cave's secrets. He moved to the far right-hand corner of the large cave and, with great effort, pushed away a large slab of stone that had completely concealed a miniscule crawlspace. Claustrophobic in dimension, entry could barely be traversed even by someone as slight as he. He recalled how painstaking his careful stocking of supplies—digital cameras, lenses, microscopes, notebooks, and lanterns—had been.

By far his most difficult task had been the delicate unfolding of the fragile parchment in order to create a digitized copy. Being able to examine the text on his computer had allowed for easier and repeated examination without destroying the original manuscript. Even so, he smiled, he couldn't resist a periodic examination of the original, as much to assure him that it was real as to inspire him to persevere with his soul's mission—to translate it for the world.

Repeating his practiced technique, he extended his flashlight safely in front of him as he crawled, belly flat against the ground, pushing his hunter's case carefully so as not to injure the laptop computer it contained. He knew by now the location of even the smallest protrusion of rock. He continued for approximately seven yards straight ahead, then one turn to the left and a drop down of about four feet to a flat area where he could stand. His flashlight illuminated a small cave within a cave, its circumference measuring approximately seven by ten feet, with a ceiling height of little more than five feet. He trusted that, should anyone ever discover the tunnel, none would explore an entry only navigable by one as diminutive as.... He smiled, remembering Dana's nickname for him: "Yoda". She confessed that, from the moment she met him, she thought of him as the elfish character in the Star Wars' films. Her comment was softened as she had assured him that it wasn't just his stature, but her awareness that within resided strength, wisdom and an element of eternal endurance.

He was glad Dana couldn't see how fragile such qualities felt as he anxiously darted his flashlight across the ground, searching for any sign that an intruder had penetrated his inner sanctum. The shallow coating of pristine dust restored his confidence. Pierre moved to the right hand edge of the confining space, an area he'd designated as his "office". He grasped a shard of rock, lifted it, and swept away the rubble and dust that covered a miniscule opening to his "vault", directly below. He gently drew out the second hunter's case which rested within. Empty of a brace of pheasants, it held an airtight canister which protected mysteries more seductive than any Holy Grail. He withdrew his manuscript from its enclosure, his gestures as loving as an embrace. It had become a ritual that, before he began work on the translation of the computerized version, he would bless the actual document, its mysterious author and his soul's special vow to protect it.

As he let his gaze linger, Pierre thought of how many so-called ancient treasures he had examined in his time. Most had turned out to be, at best, worthwhile relics of the past, now exhibited in the world's museums. His stare held a mix of adoration and bewilderment at the awareness that his manuscript, united with the other three, would reveal a message of far greater value than that of the Rosetta stone. The equipment he had sequestered beneath the canister facilitated a limited scrutiny of the barely legible text, a curious mix of Greek blended with something more akin to astrological signs. He sighed with satisfaction as he reconfirmed that elements within the text may lead to the manuscript's' long-sought translation breakthrough. .

However, a complete confirmation of the message seemed to require juxtaposition with the other three manuscripts. But how, he wondered? Having all four persons and four scrolls assembled in the same place would prove a perfect a target for their enemies. He sighed, remembering that the others had agreed to keep theirs under lock and key until he had completed his painstaking examination. What his manuscript offered thus far were tantalizing hints of the treasure's power along with their team's limitations.

He had started with his limited access to scientific methods of analysis, exploring a method of accomplishing even a basic translation of his manuscript's text. Stymied he'd turned to more esoteric methods—Gematria and other alchemical formula. His recent "ah ha" came at the confirmation that, to decipher the message, they would need all four manuscripts. He was eager to validate this theory.

As he opened his computer, inserted his crucial floppy disc and stared, his fear that it all might be a dream evaporated. His resounding "Yes!" filled the space so emphatically that he expected a rain of dust dislodged by the echo. The teasing footprints of references to 'light' were a clear indication; but they couldn't be fully understood without the other manuscripts. He scrupulously returned the scroll to its cylinder, relief at this first clue flooding him after weeks of muttering: "Merde!"

His cat-at-the-cream smile faded as his flashlight dimmed. Fading light or not, Pierre made certain the manuscript was well hidden and his disc and computer reinserted into its bubble wrap jacket inside the hunting case. He had completely disguised the entry, precise in replacing a jury-rigged trigger mechanism which guaranteed that, should anyone penetrate his miniscule sanctuary, their skeleton would remain to guard it. Confident of his manuscript's safety, he inched his way back through the narrow passageway, his thoughts grappling with the enigma of how they could compare all four parchments without compromising the scrolls—or their lives.

Emerging into the larger cavern, he put his boulder-sized issue aside to restore an actual boulder. Once in place, it revealed no hint of a continuation of the cave. Pierre donned his rain cloak, re-confirming that he'd obscured any trace of dusty footprints as he backtracked out of the large cavern and made his way toward the entry. Turning, he froze in place, held his breath and lowered his flashlight. He knew its fading light was too faint to account for the bright illumination in front of him. Pierre stared, disbelieving, at the thin stream of daylight piercing the bramble barrier that blocked the opening to the cave. His heart began to pound, knowing the pains he'd taken to draw the brush securely across the entry, cautious never to allow for a microscopic crack to betray the cave's presence.

He extinguished his dimming flashlight and strained to catch any sound. Making use of the light from the entry, he cautiously approached. He ran his palm across the wall until it met with the reassuring touch of his hunting rifle, propped a few feet inside the entry to the cave.

Allowing for what seemed ages—but was less than half an hour—and without any evidence of sound outside, he concluded that somehow he hadn't replaced the cave's covering securely, or that a strong gust of wind had blown just enough brush aside to allow for the shaft of light to enter the cave. Even so, gun cocked and ready for the unexpected, he made his cautious exit.

Using one hand to balance the rifle and the other to shield his eyes from the glare of daylight, he eased through the brush covering the entrance, and raised his head—only to be met with a blow that propelled him into darkness far more impenetrable than that of the deepest cave.

TWO

Alberto Vicenzo, formally known as Cardinal Vicenzo, was pacing his luxurious quarters in the Vatican, impatient to leave its far too visible location in Rome behind. His plans were to depart tomorrow for the south of France, where—known only as "the Overseer"—he could administer the "Q" Project" in a secret location conducive to assuring the Church's critical success. He, who had never known any situation to cause him to break into a sweat, felt his brow starting to form a glaze at the intensity of his current undertaking. It was the most ambitious gamble of his lifetime.

As an ecclesiastical minister to the Most High, he waited discreetly in the anteroom of the ancient cloister which housed his residence. His demeanor was stern, conditioned by a deeply judgmental nature and enhanced by years of practicing celibacy and mortification of the body. As a numerary of the Opus Dei, he had always been immune to the pride that others might feel in undertaking this most critical of tasks. The magnitude of his current undertaking—the "Q Project"—was such that, if successful, the Church may never become aware of.

Down through millennia, the Church had searched for certain ancient texts reputed to have the power to change the world. The Overseer looked over at the door as he waited for the arrival of

Benjamin Carter, who swore he had found these scrolls, only to have them reclaimed by others.

The Overseer savored his role in devising new methods to guarantee that the Church shall, at last, possess the manuscripts. By forming the Q Project, its status level ultra-secret, it allowed him unlimited use of all of the sophisticated Vatican resources needed to aid Benjamin Carter in delivering the scrolls.

A frown revealed the Overseer's steely disdain for Benjamin's vainglorious egocentricity. Still, Benjamin's claim to know who controlled the scrolls, and how they could be made to surrender them, made dealing with a man so vain, so vindictive and so venal, worthwhile—at least as long as such an association proved necessary.

The Overseer looked through one of several secret peepholes to observe the entrance protocols that demanded special identification. His assistant was scrupulous in vetting anyone entering the Overseer's sanctum sanctorum. He'd already notified the Overseer that a limousine delivering "Mr. Adam" had entered the grounds. A hint of what might, in ordinary humans, be called a smile surfaced as the Overseer looked around. His gaze absorbed the sophistication of the protective measures taken to safeguard all important areas of the Vatican. One of the more elementary ones was to assign to Benjamin Carter—presumed to have died in a fall from the ramparts of the ancient castle of Montsegur—the code name "Adam".

But his real pleasure came from the enhanced protection he'd recently established for his most significant project: "Q". So ultra-secret was such a project as to have a "Need to know" list which consisted only of himself. All critical communications were directed through a department in Rome controlled by him. All staff related to the Q Project—a title unknown to them—were enthusiastic supporters of what they knew as The Alliance of Faiths Project. They worked on-site in the Alliance office, coordinating with the Vatican Library. Detailed research, reports and allocations for sophisticated detection devices were vetted via a special group nestled within an innocuous building staffed by Church officials involved in the more mundane tasks of the Church. To all intents and purposes, the project was one of several whose purpose was to, if not unite, promote a closer understanding between the Catholic Church and other faiths.

The Overseer was never associated with such elementary projects. However the name and purpose served as a perfect cover for his far more critical undertaking. His value to the Church had always lain as much in his ephemeral duties and obscure identity as in his scrupulous efficiency and allegiance to the Church. Sometimes, but not always, such allegiance had included the Pope. Always, however, his own function remained unknown and undefined, instilling in him the powerful confidence that neither he nor his endeavors, would ever be questioned.

In order to implement the crowning achievement of his lifetime, he chose to be geographically near to the project's resolution. He would leave tomorrow for the South of France, sequestered as far from Rome as possible, and yet choosing a secure location within a heartbeat of his target. He let out a long sigh as he waited. He didn't trust Benjamin Carter, although his involvement would prove essential—as long as it produced results.

A discreet knock on the door was followed by a subservient bow on the part of his aide who entered and announced: "Mr. Adam is here to see you, your Excellency."

"Show him in, Brother Bernowski."

Although he had faced Benjamin Carter before, the Overseer was unable to fully contain a fleeting look of revulsion as the man entered. The man's grotesque features were a legacy of his fall, the mangled mass of gnarled facial skin almost obscuring his hooded eyes. Benjamin missed the Overseer's reaction. He rose from his deep genuflection of honor in time for the Overseer to have restored his inscrutable demeanor.

"Please take a chair." The Overseer pointed to one opposite his massive mahogany desk. "You've been assigned to deliver that which you assured me you were capable of delivering: the manuscripts the Church has searched for through the centuries. I expect nothing less than a complete account."

Benjamin, with little sign remaining of his once arrogantly handsome and self-assured persona, managed to detect the chilling "or else" implicit in the Overseer's words. "As mentioned, I have every reason to believe that Eric Taylor and Dana Palmer have the manuscripts." He nearly choked on his next words. "They discovered them in a web of caverns that honey-comb the area surrounding Montsegur. I did my best to assure that Taylor and Palmer would remain entombed in those very caves. But…"

"Yes. Quite so. *But* they out-maneuvered you, somehow prompting your fall over the steep cliff to your presumed "death."

Benjamin ran a hand over his phantasmagoric features. "Better if it had been death."

"No. Better you survived and they think you dead. With your knowledge, those manuscripts will end up where they belong. " The Overseer hesitated, his expression betraying none of the anticipation he felt. "Tell me about these two. The more that is known, the better strategies I shall apply to outwit them."

"I'll begin with the facts. Eric Taylor was once a priest. Having lost his sense of it being his true calling, he left the Church eight years ago and returned to university to study journalism. He's since become well-known as a writer whose work increasingly focuses on spirituality. It was his Cathar series for International Travel that brought us together. He consulted with me—even stayed with Dana at my home—when he began doing research on the Cathars and their treasure." Benjamin paused, unable to keep the bile from rising, both in his throat and in his words. "The damn meddler showed up just after I'd discovered one of the manuscripts and was on the trail of the others." He shook his head, his words etched in acid. "Somehow he got wind of it."

"That word "somehow" must never appear in use again." The Overseer's stare punctuated its message, bullet-like, into Benjamin's soul. "Facts and results are all that is of importance."

"Quite so, your Excellency. But you must understand the non-logical part. Their discovery of the manuscripts was uncanny, going beyond that of any writer and photographer skills. Dana Palmer, the photographer, is less a photographer than a witch." Benjamin rushed to explain. "I mean, she "knows" things she shouldn't know. During the time I was bedding her best friend, Evie, I learned that Dana's obsession with the Cathars had stemmed from her having recalled her life as a Cathar during the thirteenth century." Benjamin shrugged as he rushed to bridge the stiletto stare of the Overseer. "Sounds daft, I know, but she isn't the only one who claims a life as a Cathar. Eric does as well." He threw up his hands. "God knows how many of their pals may subscribe to the same balderdash."

"Whatever their beliefs, Mr. Adam, the Church destroyed the Cathars once. I trust, should the "Good Men" have truly reincarnated, their current souls are equally gentle and open to a swift death." The Overseer walked over to the window and stared out before turning back, his demeanor sending a chill down Benjamin's spine. "Your mission is to mop up any remaining such souls and claim their manuscripts." The Overseer paused as he studied the ruined face of his minion. "Are you completely committed to producing these documents?"

Benjamin knew not to rush his assurances. His face may be mangled, but he had faith that his skills at maneuvering a situation to his own ends had remained intact. "In answer to your question: I am totally dedicated to outwitting Eric and Dana, both as revenge for this—he ran a hand across what was once a face—as well as for possessing the manuscripts."

"I have no interest in your first rationale, except as to its motivational uses. Returning to the most important outcome—possession of the manuscripts—how will you accomplish this?"

"I've targeted the logical *experts*—his tone revealed his contempt—and am convinced that Eric and Dana's only hope for translating such manuscripts will require more than one expert." Benjamin paused, taking note of the question in the Overseer's eyes. "In the South of France, one of the best is Pierre de Lahille." Drawing a deep breath, he played his high card. "I've already assigned a someone to follow him, trusting Pierre will lead them to the manuscripts."

"Very good. But in future all such arrangements are to be implemented through me." His voice heightened its tone, startling Benjamin. "Do you understand?"

"Yes, your Excellency. I was anxious to have him followed in case the manuscripts were leaving the country." Benjamin's obsequious follow through, while oily, was heavy with earnestness. "I am dedicated to placing those manuscripts in your hand, Your Excellency. It will restore my face, both literally—with your generous offer of the world's finest surgeons—and academically."

He hesitated. "And, of course, earn the undying gratitude of the Church. I know the Pope will be most appreciative."

"Yes, well, I too trust you will not end up losing face, Mr. Carter." The Overseer moved toward the door, his steps matching the firmness of his words. "I expect much closer involvement, with all such actions and decisions reviewed on-site at my new headquarters. Tomorrow I leave for the Abbey Fontfroide and will be housed in a building removed from the main part of the property. I will contact you regarding your next steps and shall expect to hear of your success in having Pierre de Lahille followed.

After Brother Bernowski led "Mr. Adam" away and the door closed securely behind him, the Overseer returned to the window, gazing out with resolute assurance as he replayed some of the more difficult situations he had previously overseen—unknown to the Church, as was this current one—but all for the greater good of Mother Church. The death of Pope John Paul I after 33 days in office; the attempted assassination of his successor, John Paul II; all delicate matters but all situations whose outcome ultimately benefited the Church. Whatever was required, whenever and however, his highest ambition was to continue his role on behalf of the best interests of the Church. It was never more critical than his current situation, he thought. He would obtain the manuscripts and, after analysis, determine how best to deal with them. He allowed a ghost of a smile to briefly cross his lips, prompted by the knowledge that none of his activities need concern the Pope. Secrecy was only one in an arsenal of skills designed to assure that not even a breath of such a project as "Q" would ever reach the ears of the Pope.

THREE

Dana Palmer surveyed her surroundings. At ten minutes to nine on a lovely May morning, she felt delighted by the gentle mist that hung in the luminous country air of the south of France. The quiet was complete, the setting rich with images of the past.

Perfect, she thought, *no modern distractions that needed to be shielded from the camera.* It strengthened her confidence in capturing the exact shots needed to illustrate their article on the Templar-Cathar connection. Her writer partner, Eric Taylor, had nearly perfected the text, but she felt it needed a few more photos of Templar ruins

A sigh escaped her, scarcely breaking the stillness. The absence of any evidence of the twenty-first century, coupled with complete silence, emphasized the timeless aura of the landscape. It was just that characteristic that prompted her to extend her arms and twirl around with a sense of joy and freedom, reveling in the sense that *all* was remote: time, tension, deadlines and most of all, fear.

She and Eric and their Cathar Clan, as she thought of them, had only a brief celebration of their success at their soul's mission: to return in the twenty-first century to reclaim the Cathar treasure. The heightened danger inherent in accomplishing the translation of the four scrolls was proving to be more daunting than finding them.

She shook her head so briskly that her long, dark hair swirled across her face, covering her vision and brushing away such thoughts. Smiling, she returned to her focus: the grass-covered ruins—deep in the Languedoc hills—of a Templar commanderie.

Even the minimal ruins remaining retained a message of the power the Knights once held. The very air that surrounded Vaour seemed to veil images that lay in wait for her camera to penetrate. Dana marveled at finding herself alone in such a setting. Located on the river Aveyron's right bank, the command post of the Templars—once bustling with activity—was all hers.

A skylark warbled its cautionary call as Dana, cheeks flushed and hazel eyes opened wide, eagerly set up her tripod. She took endless time to position and focus her professional Nikon digital camera. She hesitated periodically, chewing at her right fingernail, anxious that the angles be ideal and the images indelible. A memory of her mother's chiding, "For God's sake, Dana, just stay with it and you will be perfect!" The words were sharper than any lens could focus.

She frowned. It wasn't perfection she was aiming at as much as it was assurance that she wouldn't be considered a 'flash in the pan'. The branding phrase had imbedded itself at a very young age, uttered with power and malice by her revered father, initially when she ceased her rigorous training in gymnastics and dashed their dreams of a gold medal in the Olympics. Her mothers' tears added a painful accompaniment to her father's wrath. "How could you, my little acrobat." Such histrionics were replayed when Dana forfeited her degree in finance in order to pursue photography. The pain of their accursed label left a mark so indelible that no amount of success could permanently erase her fear that, at the next important undertaking, she would once again disappoint.

If such a fear had ever truly waned, her current assignment resurrected it—like a Phoenix from the ashes—with an outcome so crucial as to stir acute trepidation. She drew a deep breath, shaking off such thoughts. Leaping from one stone wall to another, she stubbornly called out a challenge to her father's departed soul: "I *won't* fail this mission."

Startled by her echo reverberating through the silent remains of what was once a solemn setting for the mighty Templars, she looked around, relieved to see only her professional gear, arrayed like futuristic debris from space that had landed in Medieval France.

She closed her eyes, trying to feel the energy of the place. Recollections of her earlier assignment to photograph an article entitled, "Why the Resurgence of Interest in the Cathars?", plunged her back into a rich world of intuitions and images of the past. Such outré experiences had proven of greater weight than any in this lifetime. That there was such a thing as reincarnation—once not even considered—Dana now knew without question to be true.

Each member of their team: she and Eric, Pierre, Professor Marty and Veronique, all had recalled lives in thirteenth century France as Cathars. The power of their souls' mission was indelible. Their role in the past had been to hide the Cathar treasure, agreeing to return in the twenty-first century to reclaim it. Dana's shoulders rose and fell with her deep sigh of certainty. '*Flash in the pan'*, she mused, *simply wasn't an option for a mission of such magnitude that the fate of the world hung in the balance*."

In an attempt to restore her earlier peace of mind, she scrambled confidently up to the top of one of the larger ruins, eagerly addressing the task at hand: to get some dynamite photos. She took her time scanning for the most perfect angles, focusing and refocusing until she'd found them. Once confident she understood the general layout of the exterior and interior courtyards, the farm buildings, store, chapel, stables and general quarters, she paused, smiled and fell silent, trusting her photos to recapture the power of the Templars.

After endless shots taken of every conceivable angle and ruin, she hoped she'd captured even one perfect photo that would reveal the soul of the Templars. She sat down on a ruined wall, her right hand forming a fist which went to her lips, sealing away any doubt that her photos might reflect her lack of clarity about the Templars. *What exactly, she wondered, was their connection— if any— to the Cathars?*

Eric's text for their second article, "Cathar Treasure—Templar Wealth?" did justice to their power. Historically, she knew the facts. The Knights Templar began with a small group of impoverished monk- warriors, devoted to the Church and to the protection of pilgrims traveling to and from Jerusalem. King

Baldwin II provided them with lodging in the al-Aqsa mosque built near, or as some claimed, on top of, the former Temple of Solomon. Their rise to seemingly unlimited power and vast wealth in such a short period of time was a major mystery. Some attributed it to large donations which supported their religious zeal or to the decree that exempted them from all taxes and any authority save that of the Pope. Conjecture had it that the real source of their great power and vast fortune was due to their having discovered the Cathar treasure. If not discovering it, speculation suggested that the Templars may have been asked by a noted Languedoc personage, Godfroi de Bouillon, to protect the parchments.

Although Godfroi was never a Cathar, the de Bouillon family had relatives who were. Godfroi's fame came from having formed the Priory of Sion, sponsoring its loyal soldiers—the Knights Templar—to faithfully guard the treasure. Whatever the source of their wealth, the Templars became so powerful that, within a generation of the Cathars extinction, the Church turned their indictment of "heresy" toward the Knights Templar.

Many scattered to England and Scotland, where their wealth was confiscated and their order decimated. All that remained was a splinter group known as the Knights of the Rosy Cross, later Rosicrucian's, who established themselves on the island of Malta. Beyond the facts there remained mind-shattering, down-through-the-ages, speculation.

Dana had to admit that the Cathar-Templar-treasure connection was strengthened by the fact that many of the original Knights Templar came from families in the Languedoc area, as did the Cathars. Although logic attested to a possible connection, Dana felt a resistance to such a conclusion. She suspected it stemmed from her fierce allegiance to the gentle Cathars.

The Templars' focus on war and wealth was, in her estimation, completely antithetical to the Cathars' loving, Christ-centered existence. Until recently she'd firmly discounted any likelihood of the Cathars having entrusted the Templars with their treasure. But Eric suggested she read some extraordinary research material that shed quite a different light on the Templars and what may have been their connection to the Cathar treasure.

Fragments of her reading returned, the facts eye-opening: a British team of military engineers had unearthed the underground complex of King Solomon, only to discover a Templar cross, Templar swords and other evidence of the Templars occupancy during the eleventh century. If they had confiscated the incredible wealth of King Solomon's Temple, such "seed" money could have provided the means to become the most powerful financial organization in the world, an organization so wealthy that it engaged in widespread lending to kings, popes and landed gentry.

But it wasn't only their presumed possession of King Solomon's gold, Dana learned, the Ark of the Covenant was said to have been entrusted to their care, as well as the relics of Mary Magdalene. It was on the latter point that Dana succumbed to information overload. As stubbornly as she had previously resisted a Templar-Cathar connection, she felt almost as equally resistant to considering a Templar-Mary Magdalene link. Dana scanned the remaining ruins, teeth clamped at her silent indictment: *Damn you. Warriors and wealth couldn't have, shouldn't have any connection with the Cathars or the Magdalene!*

Looking around as a breeze rattled the boughs of a nearby tree, she sensed the Templars enveloping her in their greater mystery, forcing her to consider new information that cast doubts on her earlier conviction that the Templars were purely venal. The Templars returned from the Far East with skills in the hermetic arts, intrigued by the possibility of discovering the Philosopher's Stone. The acquisition of such alchemical skills could also account for their wealth. But beyond wealth, their hermetic skills were believed to have been incorporated into the creation of the magnificent thirteenth century windows of Chartres Cathedral—as well as the famous labyrinth at Chartres.

And now there was Mary Magdalene to consider. Dana balked in spite of the accounts which seemingly connected the Templars with the Magdalene. In 1129, at the Council of Troyes, Bernard de Clairvaux, the French Cistercian Abbot, undertook the formal indoctrination ceremonies creating the Order of The Knights Templars. But it was to whom they were dedicated that astounded Dana—their Oath of Allegiance was to Mary Magdalene!

Her credulity was tested even further on learning that, during a raging conflict over their proper resting place, Mary Magdalene's relics—her skull encased in gold, as well as bones contained in a crystal casket supported by four lions—were entrusted for safe-guarding—*to the Templars!* Many questions raced through her thoughts, but the most prominent puzzle was: *How and why did the remains of a woman who lived in Jerusalem come to be sequestered in the south of France?*

Posing that question to Eric had unleashed a pile of books and endless conversations, all purportedly showing evidence supporting the account of Mary having arrived by boat in a small harbor village in the south of France in approximately AD42. The village, named Les Saintes-Maries-de-la-Mer— the Saints Mary's of the Seas—saw her living and teaching just west of Marseilles, not far from the Languedoc area.

And that was just the tip of the iceberg. Dana's brain fogged with all she had read last night; unable, or unwilling, to entertain a Templar-Mary Magdalene connection. She'd return to it, she decided, when she was shooting their third article dealing with the Cathar-Mary Magdalene connection. She shook her head, determined to release this subject which, like a flock of birds—*doves no doubt*—flew through her mind.

With a grin of irony at the relief she felt in returning to the Templar landscape, she gazed around, analyzing her sequence of photos. *How the mighty had fallen,* Dana thought as she studied the bare ruins that remained of their commanderie. If there was indeed a Cathar—Templar connection, the only one she was willing to accept was that of King Phillip IV, who proved to be the butcher of both. His success in destroying the Cathars was soon also unleashed on the Templars.

King Phillip was deeply in debt to the Templars and bitterly resented Pope Boniface VIII for entrusting Mary's relics to the Templars instead of to him. Such a slight fueled his longing for the Templars' destruction. His venality anticipated possessing all they had –and all they knew.

It required the murder of two Popes before Phillip was able to hand-pick the next Pope, one who would allow him to exercise the Inquisitions' power to brand the Templars as heretics and subsequently subject them to torture and death.

Dana shook her head and turned to the task of repacking her photographic equipment, trusting her photos had captured the soul behind the still powerful ruins: the bunk houses of the Knights, the stable and kitchen, the guest quarters for visiting dignitaries, and a rather sophisticated lavatory. *But, will such photos reveal any sense of the Templars*? She wondered. Sighing, she removed her fifth roll of film and began positioning her gear in the trunk of her car.

She gave one long last look at the ruined Templar commanderie. Its message, she felt, remained enshrouded in an element of tristesse, veiling the grey skeletons of ancient rock walls. A sigh escaped as she drove slowly through the haunted landscape. At the exit she stopped, reached for her small hand camera, and took one last shot of an abandoned cistern. Capped and overgrown with vines, its farewell image seemed to resonate a warning: *Our Templar secrets are equally sealed—and far more impenetrable.*

FOUR

As she drove away, Dana remembered hearing of a dolmen dating from 2000 B.C. in the area, somewhere close to an ancient village nearby. Trusting the site may shed further light on the Templars, she braked to a stop, glanced at her map, and located the village. It was marked with a mound of boulders indicating ruins. She turned the car around to head in that direction, thinking, *If the village existed during the Templar days, there may be a museum nearby.*

Two kilometers later, she spotted a sign, scarcely visible and buried deep in overgrown grass. It pointed to a path that led up a little hill. She parked in a clearing, took her digital camera and began the climb. A near slide on the mud-slick trail stirred resolve that should she not see any sign of a ruin when she reached the top of the hill, she'd return to her car.

She took a moment to catch her breath as she reached the ridge. The view of the valley below was well worth photographing, even with no signs of any dolmen. She took a series of shots from as close as possible to the precipitous edge of the cliff.

A return of light rain prompted her to return her camera to its case, gather up her gear and head back to her car. As she buckled her backpack firmly she startled at a sudden sound. A blow—*from a rock, a tree limb, a person, or…*It was her last thought before she opened her eyes to find herself tangled in brier bushes half way down the hill.

Never make a move without foresight, she remembered her gymnastics instructor saying as she carefully reached to wipe a stream of blood from her forehead. There was no indication of whatever—whoever—had sent her tumbling headlong down the hill. The wrong side of the hill at that.

Coming to a stop mid-way, wedged against a sapling, she took a cautious inventory. Her right arm looked awful. Its red streaks of scratches and bleeding scrapes were fierce, but the greater pain came from the back of her head. Although blood-streaked, the gash didn't seem the "must have stitches" type and the bleeding had already stopped. *How long had she been out,* she wondered. She moved her hand to look at her watch, surprised at the shredded pad of the hand. *Over an hour!* she thought as she carefully flexed her fingers and gingerly moved each leg. "Ouch," she cried as her battered right knee protested..

Like the hand, she decided it looked worse than it was. Grasping a bough of the sapling, she pulled herself upright, testing her leg's ability to support her. It did, but not without protest. Surveying her surroundings through a misty rain, she spotted her camera case and backpack caught in the shrubs below. *God willing, my camera is intact*, she thought as she scanned for the safest route down to retrieve it.

Eric's parting words echoed: "*I don't like the thought of you heading off alone. It's too remote. What if...?*" She knew his fear was more than that of her solitary sojourn to photograph the ruins of a remote Templar site. They'd agreed that it was important to continue their 'normal' lives as a writer and a photographer. Agreement, however, didn't erase anxiety. Nor did the knowledge that their careers had played a role—and had yet to play a bigger role—in the success of a higher goal. A deep sigh escaped as she examined the magnitude of their task—to unveil a treasure capable of *transforming the world.*

As she touched her throbbing head she suddenly *knew,* first-hand, that they weren't the only ones focused on the treasure. Concerned that she may have experience a slight concussion, she turned her focus on getting back to her car, regretting the foolishness of her solitary climb. Alone *in the hinterlands,* she thought, *went beyond irrational to dangerously vulnerable.* Forgetting, even for a moment, that each member of their team was prey, was inexcusable. Their predators would never be so cavalier.

Get a grip, Dana, literally and figuratively, and get down this hill and back to your car. She shook all but immediate concerns from her mind as she scanned her path downward.

Grateful for the cessation of the light rain, she could make out a pastoral stretch of farmland dotted with young shoots of grain, green meadows and a herd of sheep grazing in the distance. She listened, hearing only the cry of a bird scolding her as the interloper. To descend seemed formidable, but she wasn't about to climb back up. Resting against a tree, she studied the safest route down. The hillside, lined with a coating of wet leaves ready to toboggan her down the slope, made her grateful for a few saplings that provided handholds. Dark clouds gathered, hinting at more of a storm. *She must get down***,** she thought*, before any deluge.*

Dana worried about ending up farther away from her car. She'd parked it in an open area alongside of a field, but on the *other* side of the hill. *Even so,* she thought*, down would prove to be, if not the nearest, certainly the most expeditious path to it.* She began a tentative descent, careful of her footing, both the need to secure it and the pain it brought. Relief filled her when she reached her camera bag and found both camera and case unscathed other than having a coating of mud..

Hesitating before hoisting them onto her left shoulder to keep her right hand free for grasping boughs, she registered her knee screaming: "Stop!" A faithful practitioner of yoga and chi gong, she began to breathe in a certain way designed to draw healing energies to her hands. Making sure she was well braced, she directed warmth to her knee, finding that the pain of her abraded palm seemed to benefit as well.

A strengthening wind urged her to press on. She glanced at her watch, relieved to find it still worked. One thirty—over five hours since she had driven away—too long to avoid alarming Eric.

All thought turned to her next handhold as she took cautious sideward-steps to provide greater purchase down the moist slope. Nearing the bottom of the hill, Dana leaned against a rock outcrop, thinking: *Which direction to reach my car? Let me make the right choice.*

Squaring her shoulders, she resumed her steps, trusting they would lead to her car. Too eager, her knee protested and gave way, her stumble creating a fall of loose rocks down a slight incline. Their rattling seemed magnified, breaking the silence with a resounding response.

A sharp bark filled the air, continuing in a more menacing tone as it neared. *Oh no, not a dog!* Dana froze in place, discarding the notion of raising her camera bag as a weapon. She remained motionless, resisting meeting the dog's eyes as the large golden mass of animal neared. Its' bark was so loud as to almost erase an accompanying human cry. "Gabriel! Halte!"

The dogs' cries changed to a pleading whine as he reluctantly halted, ears cocked, tail briskly sweeping the air, waiting reluctantly for his master to give him the signal to disembowel this certain-to-be-a-sheep-thief.

Dana let out a sigh of relief at the sight of another human. Briskly approaching the animal, the old man cinched a leash to the dog's collar. His bushy white eyebrows arched in puzzlement and concern as he turned from his dog to face Dana. "Bonjour madame. Comment allez-vous—la jambe?" he asked, his sweeping gesture taking in her battered knee.

Dana cobbled pidgin-French phrases together to assure him her injuries were minor and that she must reach her car.

"Une voiture—c'est rouge?" He smiled at her nod and pointed off in the distance before taking her arm. "Courage! L'homme attendez por vous." Dana felt relief turn to fear as the meaning of his last words registered: *"Take heart. A man awaits you there."* A man? What man? Her thoughts raced. It couldn't be Eric. No one knew where she was going. She deliberated over asking the farmer to describe the man. Alarming questions surfaced as to his having been the perpetrator of her plunge. Any hope that she'd not been targeted as part of the team with the treasure, evaporated.

Who awaits me and what is his purpose filled her thoughts as she gave her attendant a questioning glance. Given her minimal French, she opted for a literal, one-step-at-a-time solution, letting the man take her arm and lead her to who and what waited.

The farmer's strength belied his white hair. His muscled arm firmly bracing hers, they pressed on until rounding a hill and carefully navigating its incline. He stopped and motioned into the distance. Relief and fear filled her at the sight of her rental car beaming its presence via its lipstick-red veneer. She squinted, her laser-like focus scanning for sight of another human silhouetted against the flat expanse of ground surrounding her car.

As they neared the car, her caution grew. She expanded her scrutiny to take in a broader radius. No sign of anyone. As to someone actually being within the vehicle, they would have had to break in. Her car keys remained securely within her camera case.

Dana's confidence grew with the knowledge that her rescuer, Monsieur Dissell, not only had a strong grip on her arm and a fierce dog accompanying him, but a hunting rifle as well. She kept her focus steady, readying herself for whatever waited.

Monsieur Dissell guided his invalid cautiously until they reached her car. He looked puzzled, muttering something about "c'est homme" having "disparaitre".

Vanished yes, Dana thought, *but not before ransacking her car*. The door stood open, the visible damage to the lock of little concern. Ignoring the protest from her sore knee, she hurried to the rear of the car and threw open the trunk. Her other digital camera and lenses had been scattered. A quick survey revealed that an earlier disc, one she had yet to upload to her computer for editing, had been taken. As she gathered up the debris remaining, she let out a sigh of relief at the sight of her beloved Leica. Rarely used and kept more from sentimental attachment, it had been tossed in the back, unscathed apart from a missing roll of film. That, and the knowledge that she had her brand new, state of the art, break the budget, $5000 digital camera with her—memory disc enclosed—prompted a sigh of relief. She felt reassured that she'd taken ample shots of the Templar site. Until she spotted her briefcase.

Rage intensified at the sight of its broken lock and missing pages, primarily notes on the photographs for her assignment. She turned to find a puzzled Monsieur Dissell studying her as she looked away from the violated trunk to the muddy ground. His dog was sniffing at a third set of footprints that led from the car, across the parking area and into a distant stand of trees.

Dana's heart began to race as the illusion of the last few months—no overt signs of pursuit—burst like a soap bubble. She tried to disguise her fear as she met her rescuer's gaze. His expression mirrored her puzzled look. With a shrug, a smile and a few French phrases, she dismissed the state of her car and the missing man, assuring her guide that she was able to drive. Her only thought was: *I must get away.* To counter his worried look, she increased her protestations that she was capable of driving such a short distance, even with her injuries.

Reluctantly, he accepted her effusive "Merci beaucoup-adieu's". Nevertheless, he remained a solid presence in her rear view mirror as she drove away. Anxious that someone may appear out of the woods at the sound of her car's departure, she felt grateful for his stalwart stance. Even as Monsieur Dissell's figure diminished, he remained resolute until she turned her car onto the paved road.

The route back was swift, blurred by a mix of heightened apprehension and pain. Constant looks in her rear view mirror confirmed that no one followed. Her firm pressure on the accelerator exacerbated the pain in her right knee, making her feel woozy and attesting to what Monsieur Dissell thought: she was concussed and in shock, both physical and mental.

She ignored such things, thinking only of who had followed her and why they let her get away. She'd been so careful. They'd all been careful. But after months of calm—spent partly on deciphering the manuscripts but also on the joy of rediscovering one another—she'd eased up on her vigilance. Or at least it had no longer carried the super-alert charge of eight months ago when they found the scrolls.

After overcoming phenomenal odds to discover the scrolls, they were consumed with safeguarding them as they tried to translate their message to the world.

Recalling her stolen notes, she tried to account for every line, analyzing just how revelatory and damaging they might be. A sigh of relief escaped, knowing how scrupulous she and each member of their team were in not putting anything significant in writing. Her notes were simple references to their assignment, along with descriptions of some of the photos she had taken for their article.

That and nothing more. Today's debacle angered her as a greater sense of fear blossomed.

The danger surrounding their discovery of the manuscripts had left each team member with varying degrees of paranoia. *Obviously eased as the month's went by*, she thought. Hers had always been less acute, due to her delusion that somehow she and Eric might be classified as meddlers—media types—with no significant role to play in discovering the Cathar treasure, let alone in deciphering its meaning. *The only person certain of the degree of their involvement was Benjamin Carter—who was dead. He was, wasn't he? A foolish question,* she thought. But much less foolish was her sudden ripple of raw fear.

FIVE

How dare Eric let me remain in such a fool's paradise of denial. She shook her head at the thought, tenderness stirring at an awareness of the depth of anxiety Eric had had to conceal. Her eagerness to reach what Eric called their "granny flat" and the French called a "gite", intensified.

Her desire to be with him still took her by surprise That they'd ever been—or ever would be—deeply connected, was 180 degrees from any emotion she would ever have thought possible in regards to Eric Taylor.

As a balm to ward off fear she chose to recall their first meeting eight months ago. A rush of memories surfaced, flooding her with images. Newly arrived in the south of France, she was excited at her assignment to photograph a series of articles on the resurgence of interest in the Cathars. Her eagerness to meet her writer half, Eric Taylor, had faded as she waited at their agreed upon meeting place—and waited—and waited. Given her long flight, no sleep, and barely three hours since disembarking, she was exhausted and growing cranky.

Despite the hotel's charms—its little café and its strong French coffee—with every passing moment she had fought back irritation, longing only for the comfort of her hotel bed. After more than an hour and no sign of her writer-partner, she had begun rehearsing a choice of increasingly acid greetings. When he had finally appeared, casual grin in place, with his light account of car problems, one glance confirmed her verdict: a first-class prig.

Everything about him, she recalled, was too self-contained, self-assured, self-involved—too, too Self with a capital S. Mid-forties she'd guessed, but disguised in youthful garb—perfectly pressed tan pants, blue shirt with horse and rider logo, cashmere sweater over his shoulders, sandy hair casually brushed aside from deep set hazel eyes, a too confident grin and a to-the-manor-born British accent tinged with a Scottish burr. All seemed artificial and had set her teeth on edge.

Eventually she was to revise her initial judgment, chalking up her first impressions to a combination of her exhaustion, his British-ness and her fear of responding favorably to anyone of the male sex. Her breakup with her fiancée prior to leaving for France—triggered by the pain of his secret affair—had left her antennae aimed at deception.

In time she would discover that Eric Taylor hid behind his clothing as dedicatedly as she did behind her camera's lens. Disenchanted with his years in the priesthood, embittered by his subsequent deceitful marriage, Eric ultimately admitted to his deep-seated fear of trust.

Regardless of appearance, Eric's credentials as a writer were exemplary. The only lingering doubt she'd felt was whether he might skew his story in a way that proved antithetical to the Cathars. She could never partner with a writer whose intent was to discount them. The incidents propelling her to France were far too extraordinary to have left her neutral where the Cathars were concerned.

Even now, she still felt awe at the uncanny episodes that introduced her to the Cathars, incidents so inexplicable that she had long kept secret what she thought of as major "woo-woo" experiences. So crazy-making were they that she even withheld sharing them with her closest confidante, fearing Evie—a life-long best friend whose passion was psychology—would brand her as "certifiable".

Out of nowhere, her dreams were all of Cathars, a group she'd never heard of before. She turned to history books, but her compulsive search produced little in English and that which she did find only increased her alarm. A Christian group—known as the Good Men for their selfless aid to others—practiced beliefs originating from the Gnostic teachings of Christ. Their impact increasingly won converts from the debauched Catholic priests of the time.

As she read, she felt that she "knew" the people, the castles and the villages mentioned. Even more convincing were her emotions. Waves of anger consumed her at the Inquisition's complete destruction of every last Cathar Perfecti and Credente—priests and followers. Inconsolable grief surfaced, along with a deep sense of loss of something or someone.

The final bit of 'woo-woo' that convinced even her friend, Evie, with whom she had finally shared her secret, was beyond coincidence. Her agent called with what she fully expected would be an assignment to photograph yet another stately southern manse. She'd long given up on his finding any different jobs for her. Dumbfounded at his mention of Cathars, she had fallen silent, fearing it was one more surreal incident that she was imagining.

"Well, do you want it or not?" he'd shouted in response to her silence. "International Travel Magazine wants you to go to France to photograph a series of articles on the Cathars." She smiled as she recalled her startled "Yes," but even more vivid was the memory of her manic laughter in response to his follow-up question: "Have you ever heard of the Cathars?"

As excited as she was at such an assignment, she'd been primed for battle if her writer partner, Eric Taylor, showed any intent to discount the Cathar role in history. Her fears had deepened when she saw him in a secret meeting with two men in full regalia - one a Bishop and the other a Priest. When his visitors drove away a powerful queasiness had consumed her at the sight of the Vatican insignia on their car. In response to her questions, Eric revealed his years as a priest, expressing bitterness at his inability to trust love—of God, women, humanity—of even himself.

Early emotions regarding her writer partner had segued from dislike to distrust and ultimately, to destruction of all that she had ever believed real. Memories returned with every Cathar village and castle she photographed. She "knew" their Lords, but more importantly she remembered her 13th Century name, "Clotilde". Ultimately, she knew Eric to have been her husband "Jean".

Moreover, they both had recalled the dramatic past life they once had shared, including her death on a flaming pyre at the base of Montsegur and Jean's escape with three other Cathars to hide the Cathar treasure. Even more earth-shattering was a revelation—unthinkable to absorb—of their soul's agreement to return early in the twenty-first century to reclaim the treasure.

Could love assure their success? Dana wasn't convinced. They had loved before—each other and their Cathar faith—and they died for it. They loved again. *But with any greater ability to have such love prevail*? she wondered, given that love wasn't the only thing that followed them from the past. Along with it came fear, his fear of trust—his brother had betrayed him—and her fear of failure over having tried unsuccessfully to protect those she loved.

As she neared their gite and her pain increased, Dana kept her focus on thoughts of Eric and a more positive evaluation of their partnership—then and now. Their task in the present seemed insurmountable—to aid in translating the manuscripts revelations before humanity met with destruction. *A formidable fate,* she thought. *But surely one which their souls would not have been entrusted if they weren't predestined to succeed.* She let loose a long sigh of relief as her logic restored her confidence.

Whatever their ultimate destiny, she knew that the Church, then and now, would increase their efforts to get the manuscripts. Why they hadn't brought their biggest guns to bear before now stymied her. Whatever the reason, obviously their gloves were now off. She had to let the others know that any assumptions of having the luxury of time had evaporated.

Fear returned, superseding her pain. It was an icy, paralytic fear at her actions—or inactions. Convinced of the eternal nature of the soul, she was fearless for her own fate. But she dare not make a false step that could result in the manuscripts, or any of their team—*let alone the world*—being destroyed.

SIX

Relief enveloped her as she drove though the ancient rock-walled entry enclosing the large chateau with its small gite. A sense of arriving within a secret garden which dissolved all care descended, leaving her feeling, if only for a moment, safe within its serene and sequestered sanctuary. The gite's wisteria-covered walls—French blue shutters opened wide—sparked anticipation of Eric waiting behind them.

Ignoring her pain, she flung open the door, shouted "Eric!", and headed for his second floor work space. Whether it was the relief at returning or the rage ignited by the day's drama, determination intensified as she silently repeated her vow to let nothing stand in the way of fulfilling her soul's purpose.

"What happened?" Eric leapt from his computer in alarm, supporting her as he led her to a chair. "Sit while I get some antiseptic." Returning with a tube of ointment in his hand, his forehead furrowed as he knelt to apply it to her injured arm and leg. "OK, let's have it. Who did this to you?"

Dana rushed her words. "Something struck me into a nasty spill down a hill. I was unconscious for over an hour before I came to near the base of the hill. But I was lucky. A farmer came by and helped me back to my car." She hesitated, letting out a long sigh before resuming. "Only then did fear really hit me."

Eric's jaw clamped tighter at the tension in her words and eyes. "Go on." He stared and waited.

Dana began a full account, starting with her filming of the Templar site, her decision to find a nearby village, her fall while climbing a hill, her rescue by Monsieur Dissell, his peculiar comment about a man waiting at her car and her panic at the discovery of the break-in and theft.

"Did you get a look at the man? Were you followed?" No sooner than the question left his mouth, Eric walked over to the window, pushed wide the shutters and leaned out to survey the landscape. He returned, forehead furrowed. "I'd hoped you weren't considered a target." His eyes held a mix of anger and resolve as he swept her into his arms. "I swear I'll not risk any harm to you this time around— the scrolls be damned!"

Dana looked stunned as she wriggled out of his embrace. "You can't mean 'the scrolls be damned'. That's why we're here, then and now. And I'm fine." She illustrated it by standing even taller as she put her full weight on both legs—only to reach for his arm, wince and hobble over to the bed.

"Lie down. I'll bring you some aspirin." He grabbed the extra pillows and gently eased them under her leg. After a long study of head wound and her pupils, he doubted the likelihood of a serious concussion. But he shook his head in impatience. "Obviously it's time to consider calling for a doctor."

Dana attempted to rise. "No. I'm fine, you'll see. A little arnica, aspirin and rest and I'll be tip-top."

"If not..." His words faded but returned with vigor. "I've been planning ways to keep ahead of them." He gently eased her back onto the pillow. "But they can wait until you're mended."

"I'll be fine after a bit of rest." As Dana spoke she felt pain, fear, exhaustion and delayed shock overtake her. To shake it away she began to babble. "My missing notes aren't revealing."

Eric nodded, headed for the bathroom and returned with a glass of water, a bottle of aspirin and a tube of ointment. "That can wait. Take these and get some rest. You'll need your full energies for our visit to Rennes le Chateau." He waited until she swallowed the pills before continuing. "The magazine e-mailed us today. They love the draft of the Templar article, made a few edits and are looking forward to a grand finale segment on Mary Magdalene."

"'*Grand finale'* meaning 'outrageous', I'm afraid." Dana frowned before returning to a more positive focus. "You did a great job of leaving the Cathar-Templar connection open to conjecture."

Eric knelt beside her and planted a light kiss. "I'm glad you approve. I know your doubts about their alliance."

Dana winced as she shook her head. "The pairing of the Templars with the Cathars feels about as likely as that of Osama bin Laden and Mother Teresa."

Eric smiled as he pulled the coverlet around her, watching for signs of her body's willingness to let go and sleep. His words were soft, more an incantation than a dialogue. "Goodness knows what you'll come up with when we get going on the Cathar treasure and Mary Magdalene."

Dana's words came from far away. Her look was more through him than at him, causing Eric to glance behind him. "The Magdalene beckons me," Dana murmured as she gave a wan smile. "So strange. I'm not Catholic, don't know about the Mary's and..." She sighed and closed her eyes.

Eric began a gentle rubbing of ointment over her bruises. "Don't try to explain." He whispered. "I've learned not to discount your intuition." As soon as her eyelids remained closed Eric gently removed his hand, disconnected his computer and tiptoed downstairs

It seemed ages until she came around, Dana thought as she struggled to separate from a heavy dream of being pursued, one where she had to get somewhere. Just when she felt she was getting somewhere, something or someone tried to pull her back. She glanced toward the fading light etched beneath the closed shutters. She shook off the residue of her dream and eased her feet over the edge of the bed, wincing at her knees protest. Memories returned with every tentative step she took toward the stairway. Along with the memory of how she had injured her knee came images of the break-in of her car. Anger infused her.

"Eric?" She called out as she descended, concerned that the house seemed too silent and too dark. As she switched on a light she saw that Eric was sitting at the table, oblivious to nightfall, lost in the dim light of his laptop as his fingers flew across the keyboard. Startled by her hand on his shoulder, he rose and drew a chair over close to the fireplace.

"I didn't hear you. Sit down here by the fire. How do you feel?" The instant she murmured "Better", he returned his focus to the computer.

"You're lost in cyberspace." Dana smiled, knowing the odds were less than 50-50 that he registered her comment. Raising her voice, she added: "Are you working on revisions to the Templar article?"

Eric turned, looking like a fish out of water as he tried to acclimate. "No. I'll put the final draft of the Templar article alongside the bed for you to read." He turned back to the screen, his voice carrying frustrated overtones of anger. "We've been spinning our wheels, spending months lost in the quagmire of four manuscripts needing to be translated in conjunction with one another without jeopardizing them or their translators. It's well nigh paralyzed us into hiding them away while Pierre works on his to determine what comes next." He scrolled down on the screen, a series of bullet points drawing her near. "I've come up with what should have been obvious early on."

"Wow; you have been working!" Dana began a closer examination of the text on the screen, surprised at the number of pages as he scrolled back. As curious as she was, she felt suddenly famished as she spotted the remnants of Eric's meal. "Before I can digest all that, how about some of that cheese and bread? I'm starved. A glass of wine would be great, too."

"Sorry, Dana. I'd forgotten that you couldn't have eaten." He stood, opened their little fridge and exclaimed, "Voila, les soupe! I'll fix you some of the soup Barry brought us last night."

Dana nodded a vigorous yes, her taste buds reliving the richness of what was less a soup and more a delectable cassoulet. Barry Dickenson, their landlord and superior cook, lived in the old chateau situated near the property's entrance, their gite having been tucked at the far corner of his estate.

Although very British, Barry was also very French. He'd lived in the Languedoc area for over fifteen years and spoke the language as well as a native. A pianist of some renown, they could sometimes hear faint strains as he played. As a landlord, he was the soul of generosity, informing them of places, people and events in the area, as well as leaving them alone to enjoy the solitude.

Barry's gite was just one of many in a long line of charming hideaways, Dana thought, recalling she and Eric's first gite—actually two separate gites—their relationship coolly professional. The gite was magical, providing the perfect sanctuary during the early days of creating the article exploring the resurgence of interest in the Cathars. Madeline Villar proved to be not only the owner of their hideaway deep in the heart of Cathar Country, but a kindred soul in every sense of the word.

As was Madeline's bombastic father, Professor William Marty, archaeologist, linguist, and as pro-Cathar as if they still lived. The gite had proved to be a rendezvous point for many kindred souls. Professor Marty and Pierre were longtime friends and fellow professionals. Although physically opposite—Professor Marty Falstaffian in his height and girth, and Pierre so slight as to be able to walk under one of the Professor's arms—both enjoyed teasing the other with comments such as, "Let me accede to the learned Professor,"

Not surprisingly, as was the case with Pierre and Veronique, Professor Marty was destined, past and present, to be a valuable member of their team. Dana grinned as she pictured the Professor toiling over the translation of his scroll, his passion spurring his commitment. Pierre and the Professor's knowledge of the Occitan language were formidable enough. But both, because of their research into the history and archeology of Jerusalem and the Crusades, had learned Hebrew, Greek and Aramaic. They also had experience in translating the ancient texts of the Essenes, a Gnostic group of Christians rumored to have inspired much of Christ's wisdom teachings.

Once again Dana thought of what a powerful team they made, using such thoughts to rekindle her faith in their ultimate success. Veronique's background as chief researcher and analyst for Benjamin Carter—having access daily to a workplace filled with state-of-the-art analytical tools—played a crucial role in the elegant assemblage of, not only souls, but special minds coming together at a special time in history.

Three of the manuscripts had one person each assigned to analyze them—Pierre de Lahille, Professor Marty, and Veronique. All had been involved with the ultimate discovery of the four manuscripts hidden in the caverns surrounding Montsegur. These three were the logical experts when it came to their translation. Eric and Dana combined as the fourth manuscript's caretakers. Dana felt frustrated at her inability to aid in the translations, although she had worked on ideas to safeguard them. *Apparently not secure enough given her experience today,* she thought. As the soup worked its magic in restoring her, she wondered what Eric had come up with to improve on their existing approach.

Selecting four safe sanctuaries had proven challenging. She and Eric had narrowed it down to two choices, each able to house a "rare manuscript." Both hideaways were secure and both would give them access to the manuscripts at any time. The first option was a Cistercian Abbey whose owner had designed a section of the building that served as his wine cellar to include a storehouse for his rare collection of antique books. The other was a bookstore in Montolieu. Professor Marty had vast confidence in the owner's integrity and great envy at his climate-controlled vault used for storing old manuscripts. And yet Professor Marty had not used such a site, preferring a solid safe deposit box, saying, "Closer to home where I can examine it when I make bank deposits."

Veronique had considered the climate-controlled vault in St. Sernin's underground housing ancient relics, paintings, manuscripts, etc. Her original idea was that, since her office was in Toulouse and often required her to interface with projects at the cathedral, she could visit her manuscript regularly. When she was promoted and transferred to a special project in the village of Vals, she had opted to place hers in a safe-deposit box.

As difficult as Dana and Eric's choice between the two locations became, equally challenging was deciding whether both should know its location. Dana remembered many late-night discussions of all the issues. If one was captured and that person was unaware of the manuscript's location, no revelation could take place. On the other hand, if the one that did know was captured, they could be forced to reveal its location under duress. At the same time, having the other one kept in the dark meant they would be unable to safeguard it.

For those reasons they passed on the two offers and, for the time being had chosen a safe deposit box, satisfied that access requirements were so stringent that, kidnapped or not, only the authorized signers could obtain access. The bank proved to be the same one chosen by Veronique, a major institution in Toulouse and a half hour's trip from their gite. Eric regularly made the drive, combining research in the University, or at the Basilica of St. Sernin, with a visit to his bank for scrutiny of their manuscripts. Frustrated by his limited, but slowly growing, knowledge of Greek, neither he, nor his teammates had surfaced any revelations.

Eric's role in deciphering the manuscripts was more one of applying his knowledge of religions—modern, traditional, ancient and esoteric. At the moment he was fascinated with applying his long time love of codes in an attempt to decipher the alchemical mix the manuscripts text seemed buried in. His manuscript, as well as the other three, were rife with recurring arcane symbols.

Dana fixed her gaze on Eric, as if such intense focus could prompt a response to a question that had begun to haunt her: *What role do I play*? He'd decided she needed more than soup and was lost in his culinary preparations, leaving her to ponder the answer. She reviewed their role during the 13th century. Clearly Eric was critical to the success of their mission—then and now. As Jean de Mirepoix, he was one of the four Cathars that hid the scrolls, agreeing to return and reclaim them during the twenty-first century. She had no doubts over her contribution in the past. As Clotilde de Mirepoix, she supported her fellow Cathars at Montsegur, fighting to protect them, but destined to join them on the pyre's inferno.

Her role in the present puzzled her. The nagging question hadn't surfaced during their perilous search for the manuscripts. She'd been crucial during that period. But now that the manuscripts were in their possession she was at a loss to feel of any further value. Acute frustration was growing at her sense of inadequacy. Her involvement seemed fruitless. With no knowledge of ancient languages, codes or customs, she felt impotent in serving the team.

A twinge in her knee underscored her awareness that the pain of feeling useless was much greater than her physical pain. A sudden rush of what a Hawaiian friend called "chicken skin" overcame her, leaving her arm hairs standing on end. It was accompanied by an interior prompt. *"It is for you to discover what role you are to fulfill.*" So emphatic was its edict that she startled as Eric placed a heaping bowl of soup under her nose.

"Here, eat!" He added a tray of cheese, veggies and bread. "I'll join you." As she dutifully took a wedge of cheese, she stared into the distance.

Eric moved her hand back down to the tray, giving her his teasing Scottish grin. "It seems I've infected you with my "staring-off-into-space" disease. Where did you go?"

Dana felt encouraged at the warm burr in his tone and the sparkle in eyes softly edged in humor at the human condition. The combination held a subtle, teasing insouciance that was part of what had charmed her. She'd rarely seen signs of it of late, so eroded had it been by a frowning intensity at the gravity of their mission.

Her reply was measured and slow. "I've been trying to understand where I fit in now. I can't help translate or such. Although I enjoy photographing the Templar article and look forward to filming the one on Mary Magdalene, I can't see how my efforts aid in deciphering the manuscripts."

"How could you ever question where *you* fit into this?" Eric looked dumbfounded. "It's my turn to get metaphysical. As best as I can express it, you, my love, somehow hold the key to the treasure. That much I'm convinced of. It has nothing to do with any pragmatic "doing" of anything, or even directly connected to your extrasensory gifts." Assuming her silence discounted his attempt at an explanation, he tried a more graphic approach. "Imagine—since we're about to enter her territory—your reply if someone were to say: "What influence did Mary Magdalene have on Christ's teachings?" He reached over to place Dana's bit of cheese and bread back in her hand. "Chew on that thought while you get a little more food into you. Trust me. You are, and will continue to be, crucial to this mission."

"Fair enough." Dana said as she savored the gruyere cheese and reached for her glass of wine. "I'll drop it for now. When I've finished eating, I want to see what you've come up with."

Not until the last bit of soup was swept up by the last crust of bread, did both begin to speak at once. Smiling, they lifted their glasses and headed for the computer. "Now to show you what I've come up with." Eric's voice deepened to match his solemn look as he restored the program he'd been working on. "Pull up a chair." Dana felt enlivened by his confident tone as he turned the printer on and sheaves of pages began spilling around them. Excitedly, he handed them to her. "It's easier to describe in print. This is just one example of your importance. I need your take on whether I've covered all bases." Eric began to put the pages in sequence. "Begin with a review of the Objectives section.."

As Dana began to study Eric's detailed list, a knock sounded. "Drat!" Eric muttered as he hastily grabbed the pages, turned them over and placed books on top before opening the door.

Dana's intake of air was wrapped in a cloak of anxiety that had notched up considerably since her experience this morning. 'Who could it be' thoughts matched her racing heartbeat and brought a new level of fear.

"Professor Marty!" Eric's shock was matched by Dana's rushed words.

"What brings you here? isn't it too dangerous? Are you alright?" Her questions met with no response as the professor staggered into the room. One look at his expression, forehead furrowed, eyes filled with sorrow and face shattered in fear, told them even more than his halting words.

"Pierre is missing!"

SEVEN

Like a dirigible suddenly deflated, Professor William Marty's confident direction and enduring composure—a blend of former rugby player and respected college Dean—completely evaporated. A crumpled, hollow man sat before them, rubbing his eyes as if he could obliterate the reality of his declaration.

Freeing herself from a frozen state of disbelief, Dana headed for the liquor tray. A glass of Armagnac, she decided, would numb the shock that fixed both Eric and the Professor into a strange tableau. One of Eric's hands rested on his forehead while the other supported him against the table, his eyes filled with terror. Professor Marty had ceased any movement, head slumped forward against his chest like an abandoned marionette. Their rigid stillness reminded her of a pageant that posed real people to represent paintings. Theirs could only represent the sorrow-filled image of Job's suffering.

Dana's return with a tray of drinks broke their paralysis. Eric said, "Let me help you with that." He poured with an unsteady hand, pushing the small, overflowing glass into the Professor's hands. "Here, don't talk until it's empty." Following his own dictum, he sat alongside the Professor, drained his own glass and refilled it. "When did you last speak with Pierre? Did he mention where he might have gone?" Before the Professor could reply, Eric sprang up and rushed to the door, looking back in fear. “Were you followed?”

Professor Marty joined Eric. Dana’s instinct was to accompany them until her gaze settled on Eric’s critical pages. She remained as guardian-in-waiting until they returned.

Eric double-locked the doors and shutters before turning to address Professor Marty. “I can’t see any signs that you were followed; but we can’t be too careful.” As they resumed their chairs alongside Dana, Eric looked from one to the other. “It’s dangerous having us gathered together. We could just as surely vanish as Pierre.” Their stunned silence was broken by the clink of bottle to glass as Eric topped off the Professor’s drink, his expression filled with a mix of anger and concern. “I’m afraid, Professor, that you made a rash decision in coming here.”

The Professor held his head down as he let out a long sigh. “Perhaps, he said—but not necessarily.” He seemed re-infused with energy as he continued. “Hear me out. I considered all of the actions and involvements of each member of our team, calculating the likelihood of our adversaries connecting us.” His expression seemed restored to life as he rose and began to pace the room, motioning Eric, who was about to interrupt, to a halt. “Furthermore, although they doubtless suspect the treasure consists of more than one manuscript, it’s unlikely they know that there are four—and certainly not that all need to be interpreted together.” He shrugged. “I’ve discarded any notion of their belief that the treasure is the Holy Grail or any such physical entity.”

Eric pursed his lips in deliberation before replying. “Given Benjamin’s focus on finding the treasure, we know he was clearly aware of its being one or more manuscripts. The only question is how much Professor Carter had shared with the Vatican before his death.” Eric fell silent, his look pensive.

“I agree that they’ve no illusions as to the true nature of the treasure. As for the number of manuscripts, I think we may be ahead of the game.” The Professor fell silent, joining Eric in a deep deliberation.

Dana shattered their reveries. “Whether they suspect the existence of more than one manuscript, they have definitely increased their surveillance.” She recounted her earlier adventure.

"Eric is right. Your visit is risky, Professor, and apt to put you on their list of suspects." She looked at Eric. "Prior to his death, Benjamin would almost certainly have informed them of our involvement." Dana paused, her raised eyebrows revealing her racing review of who else was on their list.

Eric continued her train of thought. "True, we are definitely in the running. But, logically, even if Benjamin Carter was beginning to suspect Veronique or Pierre, he may not have had time to share such suspicions before he died." Eric shook his head. "Until tonight, no one would have suspected you, Professor."

Eric's reassurance was punctured by Professor Marty's response. "Not true. You and Dana stayed at Benjamin's home, so he not only knew of your involvement but he also knew who you had met and much of what was said." He looked from Eric to Dana whose grim expression spoke volumes in response.

The Professor kept his focus on Dana. "And that which wasn't shared with Benjamin was surely mentioned to your friend, Evie, who was staying at Benjamin's home." Professor Marty rose and began to pace the room, his tone of voice reflecting his anxiety. "Given Evie's intimacy with Benjamin and the fact that it was she who revealed to us the fact that Benjamin possessed a strange manuscript…" Professor Marty held out his hands. "We must assume that any such speculation as to who may be involved would likely have been shared with Rome." He paused, stroked his beard and slowly added, "Unless, that is, he wanted—Benjamin-style—to grab the treasure and the glory himself."

As the Professor returned to his chair, Dana nodded, her wry response turning solemn. "That's a distinctly probable conclusion, Professor. However, for safety's sake, we must assume that we are all suspects."

A stunned silence filled the room as the Professor fished into an inside pocket for his pipe. After lighting it and inhaling, he seemed calmer. "The only doubt remaining is whether Benjamin had time to share his suspicions that there were other manuscripts. As to the certain identification of all members of our team, I still hold that they may yet remain unclear as to my involvement. They are suspicious of Veronique and are certain about you two. But as to Pierre, well…"

Eric picked up the thread. “With their knowledge of Benjamin’s possession of a rare manuscript, logic would lead them to suspect the only local expert qualified to translate such a document would be Pierre.”

“Who has vanished.” Eric stared at the Professor. “From his office or …?”

“Presumably from his home. I called earlier today, ostensibly to meet to discuss a document on the French Revolution. But actually to brainstorm a safe method to compare notes. His housekeeper said he had left to go hunting early yesterday. She seemed bewildered as she mentioned that he hates hunting, it wasn’t hunting season and he didn’t say how long he’d be gone.” Before an anxious Dana, mouth open, could speak, he added, “She said a neighbor spotted him yesterday at a petrol station at the intersection of the road between Arques and Rennes le Chateau.”

Dana’s eagerness faded into silence, the slight biting down of her lower lip a clue to the intensity of her pondering. Suddenly roused, she grabbed for Eric. “Do you remember our first lunch with Pierre? He took us to a little café outside of Coustaussa, midway between Arques and Rennes. Pierre claimed that area was riddled with caves, discovered and undiscovered. I felt it to be more than just a casual comment. It came back to me when we were discussing the importance of hiding each of the four manuscripts in a secure location.” She stared at Eric. “Remember how Pierre smiled, saying his would vanish off the face of the earth?”

“Right, and never revealed where he’d chosen to hide it.”

“Quite so." Professor Marty rejoined. "Knowing Pierre, he would choose a cave, given that all four manuscripts shared such a hiding place and remained lost through the ages.” The Professor tapped his pipe against the side of an ashtray and continued in a voice heavy with defeat. “The Departments of Aude and Ariage are honey-combed with caves. Only by following Pierre could anyone discover the specific cave where his manuscript is hidden.”

Eric slammed his fist on the table. “Pierre would do everything possible to prevent anyone trailing him.”

Dana nodded. “No one could outmaneuver Pierre. His senses are superhuman. He could spot a butterfly on a bush a mile away.”

Professor Marty rejoined. "True. Pierre is wily enough to spot any stalker, but only if that person were actually there." . "Never underestimate the power of our adversaries. What if Pierre was bugged—his equipment, his jacket, his phone, his car or...?" The Professor paused, knowing the most technical one in the room, Eric, would rise to the bait.

"The Vatican has the most sophisticated technology. A simple micro-transmitter, picking up a broadcast from a satellite positioning station, could track him with no one in sight. They then pinpoint his destination and wait to ambush him." Professor Marty nodded as he stared pointedly around the room, a muttered expletive attesting to his fear that they too may similarly be bugged.

"God help us." Dana let out a long breath, trying to keep censure out of her voice. "That being the case, Professor, you should have considered that they could have followed you and even now be recording our every word."

Eric glanced over at his computer and the sheaves of papers weighted down with books. "Never doubt their capabilities." Eric walked over to take up the pages. "This...he riffled through the pages. "...and that...he pointed at the computer, are too dangerous for what and who we are dealing with. Gather round Professor. Since you're here, I can go over this with both of you." He shook his head. "We've been pretty sophomoric up to now in our belief that we could each keep a manuscript sequestered for study." Dana studied his look of exasperation at his ever having considered, even for a moment, such a solution.

"The safety of each manuscript is much more critical than our safety." Eric's look dismissed the 'But' that tried to issue from the Professor's lips. "God knows, even with greater due diligence, we may be too late now that Pierre's gone missing." A shudder accompanied the unthinkable. "If his manuscript is ...." Eric shook his head, unable to envision such an outcome. "We must immediately take steps to protect our remaining three manuscripts." Eric positioned the pages between Dana and the Professor. "Follow along while I explain our crucial next steps."

"One, we complete the painstaking task of getting the ancient parchments 'unfolded'. Thanks to Veronique's lab and its sophisticated tools, we've succeeded with that delicate procedure.

The next step is urgent. We digitally photograph and create CD copies of each manuscript."

"That explains your numerous visits to the safe deposit box lately," Dana interjected

"Right, Dana. With Veronique's painstaking efforts in unfolding the parchment, I filmed the text. Since hers resides in the same bank vault, we'd just begun working on filming hers. But as to having them on my computer, or any computer for that matter, it dawned on me just how risky—password protected or not—that would be .

"That leads me to step three." Eric reached for his briefcase and drew out a small object about the size of a Swiss Army Knife. "Once an exact digital copy is made of all four manuscripts, should any manuscript be stolen or destroyed, we will possess carefully encrypted copies of their contents." Eric waved the object in the air.

The Professor shook his head and muttered, "Not in that little thing? "

Eric continued. "Precisely! We store them all—not on anyone's computer—but on this flash drive."

The Professor shook his head. "Even if I can imagine such a thing, wouldn't it be easier to steal these little things than a manuscript or a computer?"

Eric grinned as he watched Dana nod her agreement. "Even if found, the flash drives will each be password protected and incapable of being read. That leads us back to the actual manuscripts.

"Finally, once digitized and encrypted, all of the original manuscripts must be returned to separate safe deposit boxes." He turned toward Dana. "We'll have to brainstorm having someone possess copies of the keys and information." Eric looked from Dana to the Professor, anticipating their reaction.

"All four manuscripts, you say. But we now only have three. Sort of locking the door after the fact, I'd say."

"Right. Had I gone ahead with this sooner..." Eric's voice matched the remorse in his eyes. He gave himself a little shake returning to what was and not what might have been. "Three or four, their translation may be beyond our capabilities. At some point we may decide to enlist the scientific world in their full translation." An audible gasp filled the room.

"But the Vatican..." Dana looked shocked as she fell speechless.

Eric reached to take her hand. "We'll continue to do all in our power to keep the manuscripts, all copies and everyone involved, protected. But, let's face it, if what I'm beginning to suspect is true, at some point we'll likely need the highest technology, the greatest brains and the most intense effort, not only to accomplish their full translation, but to design a way to unveil their message to the world."

The Professor waved the last sheet of pages at Eric. "Thank God, that isn't something we need to deal with now."

"No, it isn't, but we have to move fast with what is on our list." Eric picked up the pages, removed his lighter and aimed its flame at the collection of pages he'd tossed into the empty kitchen sink. "I'm going to brainstorm communicating with the others, certainly with Veronique. She is the one most likely to be able to get Steps Two and Three accomplished with the remaining manuscripts."

The Professor firmly shook his head. "Right, and I assume that means mine, since Pierre's is God knows where. So how do we safely go about filming and encoding my manuscript? I'm certainly going to need lessons in..." He pointed to the little gadget still dangling from Eric's fingers. "These gadgets and how to use them."

"You're going to love their simplicity. And we should set a safe place—before you leave here—to rendezvous and get your manuscript encoded. How about..." Eric startled as Dana leapt up with the look of a wounded bear.

"What's wrong? Have I over looked anything?"

"Pierre! Now that steps to protect the manuscripts are in place, can we return to the human element—a teammate who is missing?" Her eyes flicked away a sheen of tears, rage replacing them as her hand formed a fist. "How can we blithely discuss the importance of documents and overlook Pierre. He could be dead for all we know, but..."

Professor Marty's explosive retort penetrated Eric's shock at Dana's charge. "*But*" is right, Eric. We're overlooking the most important step: Pierre. Apart from being a teammate in trouble, if he never shows up and, therefore, no one knows the whereabouts of his manuscript, we are all scr ….excuse my English…diddled—but definitely."

Eric's concern at the pain in Dana's eyes superceded any response to the Professor as he put his arm around her. "Look, my love, we will do everything to find Pierre. He could be perfectly safe. You know how involved he gets when he's into something—oblivious to where he is, how long he's away or who might be worried." He drew a deep breath as her hands unclenched and her shoulders lowered to accept his embrace and his arguments.

Her response was so abrupt that an image of a mouse confronting a tiger filled him. She reached for their cell phone. "Right! Pierre may be back. Let's try to reach him."

Eric hesitated, but the look in her eyes didn't broach any delay. "OK, we'll use the cell phone, but we risk it being tapped." He lifted the receiver, dialed Pierre's office and waited. "Too late. I'll try his home." Dana held her breath, willing Eric to smile and say "Hello", but Eric's expression extinguished any such hope. The tension in the room deepened as he closed the cell phone and shook his head. "No connection."

Dana began to pace and Eric knew to not make the mistake of rushing to her side. Professor Marty observed them both before commenting. "It's not like Pierre," he whispered. "As consumed as he gets, he wouldn't vanish for days without notifying us." The Professor joined them in falling silent for a few moments before looking up, his expression animated and his tone of voice authoritarian. "Now here's *my* list: One—Pierre is fine and will contact us soon. Meanwhile, however, we drive down to the Coustaussa-Rennes area and search for his car. Two—he was discovered and his manuscript taken from him, his captors deciding to keep him alive for his help in translating the scroll. Three—they found Pierre; he wouldn't divulge the location of the manuscript and…" The Professor halted at a scream forming as Dana turned.

"They'd torture him." Her tone bristled with horror and rage.

"Easy there," Eric said. "Pierre's a shrewd bugger. I think he's alright."

Dana took his words in and nodded as she turned to Professor Marty. “Eric’s right. We all know that Pierre would fight like a badger to escape, hide in a cave, or….”

“Right; but sitting around waiting isn’t an option.” The Professor began pacing, a look of clarity in his eyes as he turned to the others. “We must agree on a strategy to find Pierre as well as, should any of us vanish, to know where each manuscript is.”

Eric nodded. “Exactly. Getting my plan in place—he pointed to the ashes in the sink—is imperative. What about your meeting me at the bank in Toulouse? Can you safely transport your manuscript?”

“Too dangerous and too cumbersome. Best you bring your digital camera and encryption device to me, ideally at my bank in Durban.” The Professor pursed his lips. “Or better yet, if Veronique can encrypt it, I’m meeting her tomorrow afternoon at four o’clock”

“I think she can. I’ll call her tomorrow before heading off on our search for Pierre.”

Professor Marty’s quick retort broached no such thing. “It has to be me that does the search. You both agreed that it’s unlikely they’ve connected me with the treasure. “

Dana shook her head. “That’s even more reason not to tip their hand by snooping around Pierre’s area. They may connect our stay at Madeline’s gite. If so, not only you, but your daughter may fall under suspicion.”

Eric nodded. “Right. We don’t want to blow your cover if there is any chance remaining that they haven’t targeted you.”

“My point exactly. The fact that they don’t suspect me is even more reason that I begin the search. With utmost discretion, of course.”

“Discretion or not, you risk blowing your anonymity, Professor.” Eric stifled the Professor’s open-mouthed attempt at a rebuttal. “Hear me out. Dana and I are about to begin an article on Mary Magdalene by heading to Rennes le Chateau. It’s logical that we should investigate. We’ll be all over Pierre’s territory, taking photos, interviewing the museum’s caretaker, the mayor and others.”

“But at no less risk than Pierre, given their certainty that you two are involved. That still leaves me.” The Professor’s tone broached no argument.

"Maybe you're right." Eric's sudden agreement took Dana and the Professor by surprise. "We won't know until you leave here." The Professor's look segued into puzzlement.

"They know we are involved and they know we are here in this gite. If they are watching the place, they would have seen your car." Eric's sigh spoke volumes, as did his words. "So they now suspect your involvement."

The Professor seemed nonplussed, but only for a moment. "Pure speculation. What's reality is that I must take my leave. If anyone *is* watching, they will begin to question the length of my stay." His smug smile showed how pleased he felt at his plan. "I've one card to play that may throw them off. As a closet thespian, I shall dissemble at the doorway, chattering loudly about stopping by as a favor to my daughter, who insists you stay at her gite." He looked from Eric to Dana as he shrugged. "They may write off my visit as inconsequential. It's worth a try, anyway."

"Granted." Eric's response took both Dana and the Professor by surprise. "But not if you head for Rennes tomorrow and snoop around. We'll handle the sleuthing under the guise of researching our article. What you *can* do is to come up with a strategy to safely convene the team and communicate our critical next steps." He gave the Professor a little salute. "How 'bout it partner? That's a tall order. Are you up for it?"

Eric watched the Professor's excitement return. "Unveiling this treasure while safeguarding it is as daunting as translating the Rosetta stone. Impossible as it seems, I agree to give it a go."

"I'm counting on you to come up with a solution to convene without risk." Eric watched as the Professor squared his shoulders, reached the door and turned with a wry grin.

"That just leaves one thing that I'm confident I can do: the delivery of my exit scene, full volume for the benefit of any eavesdropper."

Eric gave a brisk nod. "We'll notify the others that Pierre's gone missing. Meantime, please be extra careful. "

The Professor frowned. "I'll be on tenterhooks until I design a safe means to convene our team. We'll all be anxious to learn what you turn up on your search for Pierre." His expression lightened. "I have an idea. You mentioned stopping at the museum in Arques. I can call the curator and ask to have my assistant, Francois, pick up some books." The Professor looked from Eric to Dana. "You can insert an oblique message regarding "P. OK" or the like inside one of them."

"Agreed. Give me a book title." Eric reached for a pen.

"Hmm…Ask the director to let you peruse "Foxes' Christian Martyrs of the World."

"Will do." Eric said as he opened the door.

The Professor said a loud goodnight as he exited, raising his voice as he added, "My daughter will be disappointed that I couldn't convince you to move to her gite." He gave a Gallic shrug, one whose overblown image of dismay matched the volume of his words. "It's been a slow season for the gite business."

"Sorry, old chap. Seems you stopped for nothing. But do give your daughter our regards." Eric's words rang on the air.

"I shall. Bonsoir!" A brisk tap of the brim of his hat and the Professor entered his car and drove away.

Eric remained at the opened door until the Professor's car had vanished from sight. His gaze turned from the veil of dust dispersing in the aftermath of Professor Marty's departure to something even more intangible, but no less penetrating. He froze in place, listening to the silence as he tried to identify any sound, sight, or suggestion of their having been observed. The emptiness on the air was deceptive, like that of children playing hide and seek—muffling their whereabouts.

EIGHT

The Overseer took pride in his thoroughness. It was deep into the night—nearly morning—but still he remained as alertly focused on his objective as an Olympic skier on his technique. He painstakingly reviewed his strategy. Benjamin was among his chief concerns. He knew that anyone that egocentric, impulsive and vengeful was apt to emulate a bull in a china shop and bring chaos and destruction to the Q Project.

"I won't let that happen." He murmured as he pulled his weather-worn diary closer under the light. He'd spent considerable time in analyzing other projects he'd successfully accomplished, paying particular attention to his victorious moves with two of the most delicate and dangerous of his many accomplishments.

As he replayed the delicate series of moves he'd orchestrated with one of his most sensitive challenges—the turmoil of Pope John Paul I's brief tenure—he smiled. It certainly had more than one egocentric rebel involved. *Fortunately I did the best thing for the church in returning it to its conservative focus,* he thought. He scowled as he recalled the rash actions of the newly elected Pope: his plunge into revising the Code of Canon Law for the Latin and Orthodox Churches, promoting ecumenism and devising a strategy of outreach to all faiths were only a few of his undertakings in the first month of his reign. It was the his rash instituting of an investigation into the Vatican Bank scandal and its links to the Banco Ambrosiano in Milan that was the final nail in his coffin. Literally as the bold man unexpectedly and fatally suffered a heart attack after only thirty three days into his reign..

Force of habit had the Overseer glancing to the Heavens and sending a silent benediction to his late hoped-to-be-great colleague.

It was a delicate time, he thought, *but no less challenging than the Q Project.* "Q" for Quest, a quest that had gone on for centuries. One so critical to the well-being of the Church that it drove the Inquisition to eradicate any and all heretics, trusting that through such terrifying tactics they would succeed—if not in possessing the powerful manuscripts at least curtailing those who knew of them and any rash attempts to reveal their secrets.

The Overseer let out a long sigh as he recalled the only challenge he couldn't erase was the pervasive curse of the modern age. Curtailing an individuals actions or going after a tangible treasure, as daunting as such challenges can be, proved to be far more straightforward than trying to extinguish a widespread blight such as that of the sexual abuse of young people by their trusted priests.

He spat his fury into the whitest of white handkerchiefs, muttering, "But as for allowing priests to marry or women to apply contraception, not while I am the Overseer. It is the Church's role to maintain the strength of such dictates."

Feeling his energy surge he felt surprisingly virile for one who would soon reach his 75th birthday. There was so much yet for him to accomplish before his 80th when he would no longer be able to exercise his ecumenical voting rights in the conclave.

He would go out with a monumental victory—unknown or not—on behalf of the Church. Reclaiming the Cathar treasure would truly be his crowning achievement. The Church had long known the power it would unleash—to transform the world and thereby remove the underpinnings of the Mother Church. *Such an event is unthinkable. I have the power and I will use it,* he thought.

Thinking of power returned him to his reserve strategies. Unknown to Benjamin, he had prepared a skilled team which lay waiting in the wings. More secret than the deepest mole in the CIA, they were definitely more finely tuned in sophisticated destructive techniques.

Let Benjamin the buffoon do his best. I'll give him a little more time, but only a little more time before I blow the whistle.

An image filled his thoughts, one of silvery sleek piranhas flashing their fangs, stripping away the flesh and vanishing as if they'd never existed.

Dana and Eric are children, he thought, *rashly playing in a world of approaching danger of a magnitude never seen before or since.*

NINE

Eric felt concern at Dana's silent gloom on their drive to Rennes. He knew that Dana's love of nature was as intense as that of photographing it. But neither the cessation of rain, nor the beautiful May morning had changed her mood.

Dana registered Eric's glances but her focus remained on thoughts of Pierre. A stream of scenarios, one more frightening than the other, colored her thoughts. After chasing her thoughts in circles with no conclusion, she forced her attention back to her photo shoot for the day.

Her friend Evie claimed that Dana escaped behind the lens to safely capture reality while being isolated from it. If so, it was especially true today. She looked forward to the oblivion of an intense focus on photography to blur her anxiety over Pierre.

Anxious for such an escape, she turned to Eric. "How do you see the day going?" Dana's question was slow to prompt a response. His eyes were fixed on the road but clearly his thoughts were as remote as hers. Repeating her question at higher volume prompted his acknowledgement but one edged with a distant quality.

"Business as usual. I'll interview the museum director at Rennes while you take your photographs." His tone heightened as she stared and waited. "Rest assured, I'll ask about Pierre." At still no response, he pressed on. "What say we rendezvous back at the museum after you're through with your photo shoot? You'll probably want to get some shots of the director."

"Sure, but…" She shook her head, exasperation in her reply. "When and how do we begin an actual search for Pierre?" Dana's expression darkened as she abruptly turned to glance out the back window. "I can't believe it! I've been so lost in thought that I forgot to look for his car."

"Rest assured. Pierre wouldn't have abandoned his car on a main road. Assuming his destination was a cave, he'd opt for out-of-the-way country roads."

Dana pointed wildly at a dusty country road as they passed. "Like that one!" Eric slowed the car but didn't stop.

"Aren't we going to check it out?" The dismay in her voice heightened as she tried to keep sight of the diminishing road.

"Not now. I say we get to Rennes first and make some inquiries about where such roads lead."

"It makes sense, I suppose…" Her disappointment showed in her bleak expression. "But finding Pierre is all I can think of."

Eric reached over and squeezed her hand. "I understand. But we can search more efficiently with an insider's advice before driving willy-nilly down cow paths."

"That road seemed more than a cow path." Dana reached for her notepad and began to sketch a map showing the roads relationship to their departure point. "I'll indicate any likely roads we pass, showing the distance from the intersection at Coustaussa."

"Good. Make it six for that one." He glanced over at her hand-drawn map and smiled. "Excellent. I can use it to ask the museum director at Rennes where each road leads."

Dana twirled her pen back and forth like a metronome. "It's a start, anyway. We need to talk to Pierre's neighbor and get more information on where he last saw him." She sighed heavily as she underscored her mileage notation.

"That's another reason to stop at Rennes first. We'll make our phone calls, including Pierre's housekeeper and the neighbor who last saw him. With their input, along with the museum director's, we'll be better prepared to conduct our search."

"Let's hope so." Dana turned abruptly away to stare out the window.

Eric tried to lighten her heaviness. "Stiff upper lip, my love. If Pierre's destination wasn't too far from where his neighbor spotted him, we have a good chance of covering the territory."

Dana reached for the Michelin map and began to study it. "Let's hope he wasn't headed further a field. Beyond Rennes he could go anywhere—south to the Pyrenees, east to Durban, or west to Montsegur." She tossed her map aside. "Knowing Pierre, his hideaway is probably a cave and closer to his home." She glanced up, her tone rising in forced optimism. "It has to be."

Eric smiled. "Stay with those feelings. Look, there's another road up ahead." Dana did a fast sketch of this second road, indicting 10 kilometers since the Coustaussa turnoff.

"These two roads should give us a starting point." She looked over at Eric, excitement in her voice. "They're close enough to Pierre's home in Arques." Dana glanced back at the second dirt road. Only the slight biting down of the corner of her lower lip revealed her pensiveness as she spoke. "I agree. Pierre wouldn't leave his car on a main road. He'd park his car out of sight and headed for his cave in a roundabout way. Given the neighbor last saw him in the area between Coustaussa and Rennes, we should explore those roads for signs of his car."

"Agreed, but first things first." Eric pointed to a sign. "Rennes is only 4 kilometers. How about we make our phone calls, interview the museum director and you take your photos? If exploring your roads seems to make sense, we'll return to them."

"Good. But let's call the housekeeper first. She's the one more likely to have news of Pierre and where he may have gone."

Eric smiled as Dana's expression moved from impatient to hopeful. "We'll press on until we find him, my love. But I need to call Veronique first and confirm her ability to encrypt hers and the Professor's manuscripts."

"Rennes must have more than one public phone. While you phone Veronique I'll call the housekeeper and the neighbor.." Dana's resolve was echoed in her firm closing of the notebook.

"Righto partner. And if no leads come from them, I'm sure Professor Marty will soon ferret out some information."

Dana tried to control the catch in her voice. “It’s *how* we find him that’s the problem. As hard as I try, I don’t *see* anything.” Dana blinked away the threat of tears.

Eric reached over and took her hand. “Apprehension always blocks your intuition. Relaxing gets you beyond it. So breathe.” Eric swung the car hard right into an intersecting road. “There’s the Magdala Tower and Rennes up ahead. Our phone calls will dictate our actions. If Pierre is safe, it’s business as usual. If not, we begin a targeted hunt.“

“Agreed. But with ’business as usual’ my choice.”

Eric slowed the car as they entered the village of Rennes. Scarcely a soul stirred, apart from a dog ambling his way to the boulangerie. The scent of warm bread filled the air as they drove slowly through the ancient streets of the little village and headed up the hill to the Magdala Tower and the Church Square. It was there they would find all the activity absent in the town.

Turning onto a cobbled road, they passed a few small shops and larger storage buildings before nearing the central square. Dana drew a deep breath, resisting a bombardment of energies as she thought: *Rennes le Chateau contains deeper mysteries than almost any other area on the planet,* she thought. Its malevolent magnetism had pulled them during their work on their earlier article “Why the Resurgence of Interest in the Cathars?”

She smiled at the memory. It was well before she and Eric had understood their connection from the past, let alone their purpose in the present. Pierre was the one who had deflected them away from the seductive lures of Rennes. “Save Rennes for when you’re doing an article on the Templars—or Mary Magdalene.”

Well, that time is now, she thought. She quelled an urge to escape by focusing on her upcoming task of taking shots for the article on Mary Magdalene. As they neared the Tour de Magdala, dedicated to the mysterious Lady, she shivered. Her emotion wasn’t fear as much as surprise at her sudden draw to the Magdalene.

She stared at the tower as they neared. Misted in cloud, it seemed wrapped in a cloak of layered emotions that enshrouded the sorrow within. Regardless of Rennes’ association with Mary Magdalene, its predominant energy felt dangerous, leaving an imprint as viscous and destructive as walking into a tar pit.

Before she could adjust, assimilate or avoid such threatening energies, Eric had parked near *two* phone booths. After he'd removed the camera equipment, he lifted his briefcase out of the "boot", as he called it, locked the car and turned to Dana. "One look tells me you're under Rennes spell." He shivered as he stared at the Magdala Tower. "It's impossible, even for me, to avoid it."

As Dana followed his gaze she fell into a well of silence, hypnotically transfixed. Her response seemed to come from beyond her as her voice deepened. "That which was put in place to guard Rennes secrets is waiting to be revealed." Eric's puzzled look prompted her normal voice to return. "I refuse to let Rennes suck me into morbid dead-ends. Let's get to the phone."

"Right." Eric headed for the phone booth. "Hopefully, we'll begin our day with good news."

Dana entered the other booth and dialed the housekeeper. She closed her eyes, praying for a positive response.

The housekeeper's reply that she had not heard any word from Pierre punctured Dana's hopes. Dana mentioned calling the neighbor.

"The neighbor has gone to market."

"Yes; I understand. But we need to ask him the exact place where he last saw Pierre." She held the receiver tighter as Beatrice assured her that the neighbor would return later this afternoon but that his English wasn't very good.

"I could ask him exactly where he saw Pierre and call you back", Beatrice said. "Or I'll invite the neighbor over for four o'clock tea and you could come by then."

Dana released a long breath. "Four o'clock tea sounds good. Merci Madame. See you then. Au revoir."

As she turned to tell Eric she heard him say to Veronique, "The number here is 63556294. A bientôt."

Dana raised her eyebrows. "What's up?"

"She'll call me back from a public phone."

Both jumped when the phone rang. Eric lifted the receiver. "Veronique; bon! Pierre's missing. Have you any news?"

Eric's silence seemed to go on forever. Deep exhalations accompanied several "I see" and "Are you sure?" replies. Dana's impatience mounted. After a final, "No. Don't risk it. I'll try to reach you as suggested." Eric reviewed his action steps to protect the manuscripts. From the nod of his head and the relief transparent in his voice, Dana assumed Veronique could do the encryption of her manuscript. The conversation diverted. "We've got to get the team together to have any hope of translating the manuscripts. Can you brainstorm a suitable place that would be safe?" A long silence prompted the return of frown lines in Eric's forehead. He finally replaced the receiver and turned to Dana.

"Pierre's absence alarmed Veronique. She agreed to act immediately to get hers and the Professor's manuscripts onto flash drives and the originals into safe-deposit boxes." Eric frowned, his words heavy with disbelief. "I couldn't believe my ears. She agreed we need a safe place to work on the scrolls but urged extreme caution." Eric drew a long breath. "Veronique swears Benjamin Carter is alive and involved."

"Benjamin!" Dana shook her head. "He couldn't possibly have survived such a fall."

"My thoughts exactly. But knowing that Veronique doesn't deal in conjecture, I listened to her explanation." Eric drew a deep breath. "She's had inquiries at the University—more than inquiries—specific requests for files relating to Benjamin's work before his death."

"Of course, the Vatican would leave no trail unexamined. But that doesn't mean Benjamin's alive."

"As his assistant, Veronique was the only other person who knew Benjamin's secret password for his special projects. Remember his announcement of discovering the Holy Grail?" Eric's tone deepened. "The recent requests bear his private code. Veronique thinks he could have survived the fall, taking the last eight months to recover."

"No!" Dana's face fell. "He could have shared his password with someone." She drew a deep breath. "How is Veronique dealing with such requests?"

"Very cautiously. If Benjamin lives, she is certain to be under suspicion. Meanwhile, she returns the Vatican's requests with a firm reply that Benjamin Carter's files are the sealed property of the University."

"And Pierre? Did she suggest where he could be?"

"No. But I could tell by her voice how uneasy she felt at the news of his disappearance." Eric raised his eyebrow. "She suggested we meet to discuss means of getting the remaining team together. Her rendezvous plan seemed a bit farfetched. I told her I'd have to think it through before confirming."

"Out with it, Eric. What did she suggest?"

"She suggested we meet at the cathedral at Albi during high mass, with me in *priest's* disguise and she as a little old lady." He smiled. "It seems her partner, Claudia, has experience in the theater and can do a brilliant job with costume and make-up." Eric fell silent, a frown revealing his doubt.

"Don't discard it too fast." Dana grinned. "At the very least it would give me a chance to see you in priest garb."

"Right…" His assurance didn't match the look on his face. "Such cops and robbers techniques are pretty primitive—like fighting missiles with stone axes."

"I know what you mean. But remember Goliath." Dana tried to erase the fear in his voice.

Eric's frown and set jaw remained. "You realize that if Benjamin lives, there goes any likelihood of Veronique remaining incognito. And as for Pierre…"

The enormity of his statement was broken by the crunching sound of footsteps on gravel. Dana startled as a man veered away from the phones and headed for the museum's entrance.

Eric shook his head. "How about your call to Pierre's housekeeper? Did she have any new information about Pierre?"

"No. But she said her neighbor might. She suggested we join them at Pierre's house at four o'clock to discuss the matter."

Eric checked his watch. "Of course."

"Good. When we pass the intersection where Pierre last was seen, maybe we can pick up some clues." Dana looked at her watch. "Four hours from now seems too long."

"With research, photos, interviews and the like, we can easily spend two hours in Rennes." When Dana hesitated, he added what he hoped would get her agreement. "Lunch in a local café and a thorough exploration of the two roads will more than fill up the extra time until 4 PM."

Dana shrugged. “I vote we pass on lunch and spend more time investigating those roads.” A heavy sigh punctuated her words.

Eric reached out and tilted her chin up. “I understand. Let’s go get the museum director’s input on those roads of yours.”

Dana grinned, outpacing Eric as she rushed ahead. In their haste, neither one took any notice of the old man who ceased feeding the pigeons and limped after them.

TEN

"Let's strategize before we corner the lion in his den" Eric said as they neared the museum caretaker's office and took note of the name on the door: 'Monsieur Morrel'. "Good. It's the same chap I spoke with on our first assignment. Never did come out here to meet him, though. I'll chat him up a bit about our new assignment, get his advice on research options and the like before leading into Pierre's likely whereabouts. You should meet him, maybe take a few shots of the Administrator in his office?"

"Of course I'll come in." She held out her hand-drawn map. "I want to get his input on these and other roads in the area." She whispered as they entered the museum director's office.

Monsieur Morrel seemed as amiable in person as on the phone. He smiled broadly as introductions were made, the administrator shaking Eric's hand effusively. "Ah, Monsieur Taylor, the writer; we spoke some months back. I'm pleased to have the opportunity to meet you." He offered his hand to Dana. "And your lovely cohort, Dana Palmer. I must say I was captivated by your photos. Perhaps Rennes may be the focus of another article?"

"But of course, especially since our current articles deal with the Templars and Mary Magdalene." As the curator expressed his excitement, Eric rushed on. "But before I ask for your suggestions, I need your advice concerning one of our research experts that we were to consult today. When we called to set up a meeting with Pierre at the Marie in Arques, we were told he's gone missing and was last seen in this area."

"That would explain it!" Monsieur Morrel slapped his hand across his forehead. "Your Pierre must be the same as our Pierre if his office is in the Marie in Arques." At Eric's astonished nod, the director frowned. "Old Pierre hasn't been around for days. I used to be able to set my watch by him. He'd spend hours pottering around here. He often brought his lunch and stopped off for a chat before leaving. But it's been several days since I last saw him."

Dana rushed her map forward. "His neighbor thought he may be headed on a hunting trip, perhaps driving down some country roads in the area—like these. Maybe he had car trouble?"

Monsieur Morrel studied her map, removing a more detailed area map from his desk for comparison. "As to hunting, such a thing seems impossible. I never knew Pierre to hunt." He pointed to Dana's hand drawn map. "Pierre knows this area well and would never have headed down these roads. They lead to dead ends. One arrives at a large farm with a particularly grouchy family standing guard. The other ends in a cattle yard blocked by steel gates." He looked up in response to Dana's groan. "Pierre is well-known in the area. If he went anywhere around here, for whatever purpose, and had car trouble, I would know. His jaunt would be commented upon, good Samaritans ready at every turn and quick to tell their tale."

Dana looked over at Eric, her expression crestfallen. "It looks like we won't have to check these roads after all."

"No… But perhaps Monsieur Morrel could keep us informed if he hears of anything." Eric extended his business card with his cell phone number.

"But of course." He pocketed the card as he grinned. "I prediction that Pierre is off doing research and will soon return, surprised to learn that anyone missed him." He reached behind his desk, pulling out a book on Mary Magdalene. "Now, as for your new articles, Monsieur Taylor, I would recommend your research include a look at this. It is a most comprehensive and provocative account of the mysterious Mary." He held it out. "A loan."

"Thank you. We'll treat it kindly. For now, if you have some time, I'd like to get your opinion on other aspects of my research." He turned to Dana. "How much time will you need for photos?"

"I'll meet you back here at three o'clock." Dana's neutral tones covered what Eric knew was keen disappointment.

"Perfect. That should give me more than enough time." He smiled as he turned to the director. "That is, if you can allow such time, it would be most helpful with my research."

The Director smiled over at Dana. "Certainly, assuming you agree to share lunch with us." He looked down at his watch. "One o'clock?"

Eric looked at Dana. "Do consider it if possible."

Monsieur Morrel smiled as he added, "If not, I'll save a sandwich for you."

Dana graciously declined, thanking Monsieur Morrel as she turned to leave.

Eric whispered as he held the door. "I'll be ready when you show up. We'll head for Arques."

Dana nodded, strode out the door, through the museum and into fresh air. She released a deep sigh of disappointment at the director's response to the roads she'd drawn. Feeling the wind gone out of her sails, she headed for the church. The square was filled with tourists, children running to and fro, camera's flashing, picnics being readied for lunch and an old man feeding the birds.

Dana skirted them all, determined to ward off an ominous sense that grew with every step. She resurrected a meditative exercise that had always proven helpful. W*ith each step I clarify my focus on this assignment*. The repetition seemed to override all else with its pragmatic dictate—until she neared the infamous church.

Steady on, Dana, she counseled herself as it loomed ahead. Resistant to entering, she took a seat on a bench near the church's entry, deciding to review the history of Rennes Le Chateau.

The village was ancient, going back to pre-history, where artifacts indicate it had been used as a campground by early man, to a Roman settlement, a Visigoth community, a Christian church and, currently, a playground for multiple conspiracy contingents.

Some of whom she spotted up ahead, their excitement floating in their wake. By far the largest percentage of people gathered at Rennes—today and every day—consisted of seekers of Visigoth gold, the Holy Grail, hermetic manuscripts, the bloodline of Christ or the key to deciphering the forty square miles of sacred geometry surrounding Rennes.

Dana slowed her approach as she neared the entry to the church. A loner by nature, today more than ever, she resisted any mingling with the crowd. Especially the sort her role as photojournalist would attract. She decided to take exterior shots before entering the church. Tripod, camera and lenses ready, she paused to take in the lay-out of the square. Every structure surrounding it cried out its importance, if not in all of history, certainly in the lifetime of its notorious priest, Berenger Sauniere. *Could any photograph*, she wondered as she took numerous shots of his universe, *possibly capture Sauniere's secret?*

Berenger Sauniere, a poor young priest, took up residence in the tiny precinct of Rennes le Chateau in 1885. He took lengthy walks, ostensibly gathering stones to use in remodeling the decaying church. Soon after taking up residence, he became unaccountably wealthy, spending so lavishly as to stir questions concerning the source of riches great enough to not only reconstruct the church, but build the elaborate Villa Bethania and the Magdala Tower as well.

Speculation as to the source of his instant and incalculable wealth ran the gamut: he'd discovered the wealth of the Templars; the treasure hidden by the Cathars; buried Visigoth gold; the Ark of the Covenant; the Grail and/or the treasures of the Temple in Jerusalem. Or was he blackmailing the Catholic Church with a secret so earthshaking as to threaten their power?

Whatever the treasure, suspicions grew. During the year 1891, Sauniere dismantled the church's alter and, rumor has it, unearthed several parchments whose enigmatic text must have been deciphered by the Priest, at least successfully enough to allow him to manifest considerable wealth.

The mysteries continued. A number of heinous murders took place, including that of Sauniere's cohort, an old priest near Coustaussa—Jean Antoine Maurice Gelis. Gelis, a recluse whose paranoia caused him to lock his home to all but a niece who brought him food, granted entry to someone on All Saints Eve in 1897. That person smashed his head with fire irons and laid out the body with great care, positioning the corpse in a stately pose, hands crossed over the chest, identical to that which another priest would do. Although the house was completely ransacked, Gelis' money remained untouched.

More murders surfaced when, fifty years ago, researchers discovered three corpses in Sauniere's garden. All had been shot. In addition, Noel Corbu, who cared for Sauniere's ailing housekeeper, Marie Denarnaud, after the Priest's death, died in a car crash that many suspected was not an accident. Corbu's closeness to the housekeeper, presumed to know Sauniere's secrets, prompted rumors that she had shared such secrets with Corbu before she died.

Further feeding the rumors, Sauniere, a lowly priest, made many visits to Paris where he met with senior members of the Catholic Church, as well as with the King's Chancellor of the Exchequer. Whatever their discussions entailed, the end result was that Sauniere's wealth continued to expand.

Prior to Sauniere's fatal "heart attack", he had met with his confessor, who, after hearing his confession, reacted in an unthinkable way. He refused to give Sauniere either penance or absolution. Sauniere's death, on January seventeenth, was highly suspicious, his coffin having been ordered, not by him, in advance.

Dana took a deep breath, feeling leaden at such a heavy litany. The air hummed, like locusts, with sinister forces. Undaunted, she attached her telephoto lens and focused on the Hautpoul estate.

The once-graceful building reminded her of the Southern mansions she once photographed. Not the architecture, but the atmosphere of ethereal shadows from the past hovering around the decaying Hautpoul manse's once-luxurious façade. The grounds of the estate held many mysteries, not the least of which was the unusual tomb of Marie de Negre-Hautpoul, last of the legendary Blanchfort line. The above-ground tomb had inscribed on it what was reputed to be a portion of the parchment's enigmatic text.

Before vandals destroyed the tomb's inscription—as recently as the 1980's—Lionel Fanthorpe, using a logic puzzle known as the "knight's tour", claimed to have translated the tomb's inscription, but only compounded the enigma. The bizarre phrase—"Blue Apples at Noon"—baffled researchers and prompted even greater hoards of treasure seekers drawn to the tomb. With its arcane inscription, it became a magnet, heightened by the artist's rendition of the tomb in the famous painting, "Les Bergers d'Arcadie, by Nicolas Poussin. Speculation grew, not only over the symmetry of the figures posed around the tomb and against the background of Rennes sacred geometry, but over the revelation that Poussin was listed as a member of the secret society called the Priory of Sion.

Dana could feel a headache coming on, a combination of too many mysteries pointing in too many directions—or misdirection's, she thought. She took a few more shots, wondering if the camera could penetrate the miasma of secrets. After numerous shots she packed away her new digital camera, shouldered her tripod and prepared herself for taking photos inside the church.

While sorting her gear, a lens cap escaped. It began to travel down a declination in the path, heading for a bench where an old man sat feeding the birds. She shouted: "Monsieur, mon pellicue, si'l vous plait!"

Fully expecting the man to halt the lens cap, she was shocked when he bolted upright, ignored it and ran down the path toward the Villa d'Hautpoul. His gait, although far too swift for anyone elderly, held a subtle hitch, giving the impression that one leg may be injured. But it was the fleeting glimpse of his Quasimodo-like face that caused her to cringe. She stared in surprise as his collapsed posture unfolded to over six feet tall.

Dana's shock was so great that her attention left the flight of the lens cap to observe the flight of the man. She deliberated over following him, but retrieved her lens cap before giving one last glance to confirm the man had disappeared. So swiftly had the incident occurred as to make her doubt its reality. She shook her head and headed for the church, eager to finish with filming and Rennes.

On entering the church, Dana was struck by the inscription over the door: *terribilis est locus iste* (this place is terrible). *What,* she wondered, *was the inception of the terror that overpowered the cloying scent of ages of worship?* Dana had read that the ancient church, dedicated in 1059, had been built over a Visigoth foundation, which in turn was built atop a pagan temple, ad infinitum. Always a place of power, theories abounded as to Rennes strange energies. The current favorites were: it was caused by telluric forces, astrological influences or visitors from other planets.

Which theory, its guardian wasn't saying. She grimaced as she entered and met his loathsome gaze. A hideous demon, Asmodeus, the reputed guardian of Solomon's treasure in Jerusalem, stared down at her. *What have you seen* she wondered as she stared at the diabolical visage of the grotesque figure? After taking a series of photos in the hopes of capturing a visual response, she turned her focus to the church's cold interior. *How is it,* she wondered, *that such a sinister church was dedicated to Mary Magdalene?*

The church's carnival atmosphere held a smaller than usual crowd that milled about, examining every notorious decoration with intensity, their theories reverberating on the air. A scanty crowd, she thought, due to France's extended lunch time. Those who remained were much too absorbed to pay attention to her. Her eyes dismissed the occupants as she decided on her next shots.

The church walls extended the building's unorthodoxy with bizarre incongruities in the Stations of the Cross. The murals, statues and stained glass windows all had been installed by Sauniere and all were equally puzzling as religious art. Two commanding statues—one presumably that of Mary and the Christ Child, the other of Joseph and the baby Jesus—contained features commonly ascribed to the Magdalene and Jesus. As Dana focused and took a series of shots, each angle reinforced the overall impression that the adornments, although religious in that they represented holy figures, screamed a message that was the antithesis of that of a traditional Catholic Church. Furthermore, it seemed to shout a challenge to any who would denounce the church's design or attempt to decipher its mysteries: *Beware or Be Destroyed.*

At every turn the feeling deepened that she was in a Grimm's fairy tale world, a witch's bubbling cauldron waiting somewhere in the wings. She forced a return to a more professional state of mind as she began setting up shots of the infamous altar.

A key feature of Rennes' mysteries, it required more time and a great many more shots to try to capture what was considered the doorway to Sauniere's wealth. Legend had it that Sauniere, in his nightly digs around the church, saw fit to excavate beneath the altar. It was there he discovered the baffling parchments which, theory suggests may have been buried by the former cleric, Abbe Antoine Bigou, Sauniere's predecessor, priest and confessor to Marie d'Hautpoul. Marie, the lady of the tomb, was believed to have been privy, via her closeness to the Abbe, to the parchment's secrets. But it was Bigou himself who considered them so profane as to require a burial in what he considered an inviolate and sanctified hideaway.

Such a straightforward account of the parchments and their discovery, Dana thought, was the last bit of anything resembling fact as concerned Sauniere's tenure in Rennes. Henceforth all was to be layered enigmas—not the least of which was the bizarre cipher etched upon Madame Marie's tombstone.

Before the tomb's inexplicable destruction, and in spite of all the effort experts brought to solve the inscription's mystery, somehow only Sauniere seemed to have the solution. One which he never shared with anyone. Except perhaps his housekeeper, whose deteriorating condition erased her ability to recount his secrets.

But why then, Dana wondered, *did he feel the need to leave peculiar clues imbedded in the redesign of his church, as well as in the other buildings he had so carefully constructed?* Beyond such lavish structures—improbably and dangerously positioned at the edge of a precipitous cliff—lay miles of a less tangible mystery: sacred geometry. Completing her shots of the church's interior, Dana packed up her gear and escaped its haunted confines. *I need a breath of fresh air,* she thought as she breathed deeply—*even if it carried mystery on every breeze.*

She walked across the courtyard to the base of the Magdala Tower. The tower of the Magdalene, her very name translating as 'Watchtower'. She paused at the edge of the cliff and stared up at its crenellated top layer, feeling a slight nausea. Clouds drifted above, grey wisps encircling the structure like sentinels whose mission was to obscure. *Anyone in that tower*, she thought, *would have a front row view of all the mysteries of Rennes, including the hills and valley that comprised its sacred geometry.* More than just a scenic backdrop, or the skillful incorporation of the Golden Mean as reflected in two of Poussin's famous paintings, this natural composition, if examined by the skilled eye, was said to communicate a deeper mystery. *If so*, she thought, *it was far more difficult to translate than 'et in Arcadia ego', the inscription appearing on the Tomb in Poussin's painting.*

How was Poussin connected, over two hundred years before Sauniere, to the hidden mysteries of Rennes le Chateau? Dana wondered as she completed her photographs of what, to her eyes, appeared as a spring-green background of meadows and hills.

Dana willed her lenses to penetrate their hidden message. *Whatever mystery such scenery stubbornly concealed,* she thought as she shot numerous angles, *there were rumored to be an elite few who understood. The painter, Poussin, was among them.* Accepting her inability to decipher sacred geometry's message, she completed her outdoor photos, collapsed her tripod and returned to contemplating what intrigued her more: Rennes hidden parchments.

Were they the same parchments as the Cathar treasure? She and Eric had examined that question thoroughly, arriving at a resounding "No". Far more likely was the theory that it was Visigoth treasure from their sacking of Rome. Many of Solomon's temple treasures ended up in Rome, only to vanish after being conquered by the invading Visigoths. Another alternative was that the treasure had to do with the secret bloodline of Christ—the *Sangreal*—the Holy Grail. Its chalice consisted of Mary Magdalene herself, by virtue of marriage to Jesus and the birth of children, she assured the safety of the royal blood by her flight to France, where the lineage perpetuated the House of David via the Merovingian dynasty. Sauniere may have been paid richly to hide such a secret. If revealed, it could destroy the Catholic Church.

The translation of the tomb's message, however, pointed to its being Visigoth treasure. Whatever the parchments were, Dana longed to know how Sauniere had deciphered them, suspecting that his method may be the same formula their team labored to learn.

If Visigoth treasure, what was the nature of the wealth it offered Sauniere? The Ark of the Covenant, the Treasures of Jerusalem, or…? That secret remained unknown in spite of the touted translation of the tombstone's enigmatic inscription. Commonly known as the "Blue Apple" message, it overjoyed the mystery hunters who hoped they'd found the key to the mystery. She drew her notebook from her camera case and reread the strange translation of the tomb's inscription:

This treasure belongs to Dagobert 11 King and to Sion and he is there dead. Shepardess no temptation that Poussin Teniers hold the key peace 681by the cross and the horse of God I complete this Daemon guardian at midday blue apples. .

Even a brief contemplation of the message had increased Dana's confusion. She knew that the Dagobert II reference was to that of a real person—the last of the Merovingian Dynasty's Priest-Kings. Many of the mystery seekers held fast to the theory that the Merovingian line—descendants of the House of David via Jesus and Mary Magdalene—must be restored to the throne of France.

Dana remembered the book she'd been reading before she fell asleep last night. Merovingians, Carolingians, Mary Magdalene in the South of France, their magnetic currents resonated throughout her dreams and returned to captivate her now.

It's the energy in this place, she thought, shaking her head. It felt like stepping off a carnival ride. To short-circuit her dizziness, she glanced at her watch, surprised to discover she'd already overshot her agreed upon meeting time by ten minutes. Quickening her pace, she headed for the museum, not stopping to look back and discover the old man had returned and was following her.

ELEVEN

The entry area of the museum—administered by the Terre de Rhedae Association—dated back to the Neolithic area when the Celts first arrived in the fourth century BC. The structure was called an "oppidium", once serving as an underground stronghold for safety. Most of the museum, Dana knew, was located in the former presbytery, a section that once served as Sauniere's home.

Chalking it up to the chill of entering Sauniere's old home, Dana shivered as she neared the steps to the museum. Her sense was that of being trapped. It was so keen that she turned, expecting to see someone—or something—following. No one or nothing unusual came in view. Only a group of children gathered around a man who had stooped to draw a figure in the dirt. She took the steps two at a time until she reached the doorway.

On entering, she almost collided with the after-lunch crowd of visitors paging through books, postcards and pamphlets detailing the mysteries of Rennes le Chateau. Added fuel for the fire, she noticed, was a new pamphlet with a catchy title: "The Key to the Mystery— Mary Magdalene and the Bloodline of Christ"

She'd resisted connecting Rennes' mysteries to Mary Magdalene. Although she wasn't a Catholic, Dana found it difficult to put into words how much she didn't want Mary Magdalene associated with this diabolical place. And yet, despite Rennes heavy atmosphere, she felt the energy of the Magdalene around her. For several months now the Magdalene had insinuated herself in Dana's thoughts and dreams. Both awake and asleep she felt her heart stir with a growing emotion of protectiveness. She wasn't clear whether it came from her to the Magdalene—or vice versa. Dana scowled as she reached for the provocative pamphlet, gave it a cursory look and stuffed in her briefcase.

She recalled her initial antipathy on learning that International Living Magazine wanted them to devote a segment of their series not only to the Cathar-Templar connection but to include a third segment which would focus on the Mary Magdalene connection. Dana resisted what she felt might be a once-over-lightly treatment of the subject. Her agreement to undertake the assignment was prompted by Eric's assurance that their story would do justice to the Magdalene by offering the chance to counter the image of a woman so long discounted and reveal her power and wisdom as a primary disciple.

A tourist, seemingly oblivious to Rennes negative vibes, placed a book, "The Cathars" by Rene Nelli, on the counter. She smiled, long a fan of Nelli and totally in favor of the abundance of his literature on the Cathars in the Languedoc area. Although scattered throughout Italy, Spain and Eastern Europe, France's Languedoc area seemed to represent the womb of Cathar history as well as its grave.

Dana sighed, remembering how hard she and Eric had worked on their first article, trying to avoid any once-over-lightly treatment of the Cathars. Also known as the Bonshommes, or the Good Men, she was taken by how closely their religion exemplified the original teachings of Christ. Cathars lived simply, helped others, and honored their connection to Spirit, avoiding those physical representations—the eating of animal products, engaging in sex, a focus on wealth—which drew mankind away from the spiritual realm of connectedness to God. Although Christians, their extinction was prompted by Rome's fear of their growing favor with the populace, as well as the potential danger from all that the Cathars actually represented—and reputedly possessed. The Cathar treasure, described in the records of the Inquisition as "...so powerful as to transform the world", prompted the Church to institute the Inquisition, label them "heretics", kill them and possess the treasure.

A rush of sorrow and anger surged through Dana at their fate, along with six hundred years of the Inquisition's imprisoning or destroying any and all "heretics". Such emotions served to fuel her resolve, not only to reveal why the Cathars left such an indelible mark, but more importantly, to succeed with their team's efforts to translate their powerful treasure. So lost was she in the magnitude of their mission, that she jumped as Eric spun her around.

"Wow, he said as he studied her expression. Rennes is really getting to you. You have such a strange look." He took her by the arm. "What say we get out of here? I've had a good interview with the curator and picked up some ideas which we can discuss on the way to the car." He gave her a flash of his saucy Scots grin as he extended a small bag as they neared the car. "Hang on to this. It's the sandwich Morrel mentioned. You can eat it on the way."

Dana took it, her hunger suddenly acknowledged. "Any more mention of Pierre?" At his hesitation, Dana felt her heart sink.

"He assured me he would ask around and believes Pierre will show up soon." He felt the heaviness in her silence. "I support that outcome. You know Pierre is much too wily not to have covered his tracks." Eric gently put a hand under her down-turned chin and lifted it. "Chin up and soldier on—with faith that *all* things work together for good."

"Was that a taste of your priestly advice?" She lightened her teasing words. "You're right, Eric. I owe it to Pierre not to fall apart." If not a smile, a solemn confidence colored her tones as she turned to a neutral topic after finishing her sandwich.. "How did your interview with the curator of the museum go?"

"Actually, quite well. He was generous with his time and information—as well as with that croque monsieur you just devoured. His parting words were: "Call on me anytime. We don't want you international writers to overlook Rennes."

Dana's acknowledgement was minimal, her focus on subliminal messages that surfaced as they stood at the door of their car. A prickling uneasiness filled her as she glanced back at the courtyard. Her eyes instinctively went to the bench where the old man had been sitting. She deliberated at describing the man and his strange actions to Eric, but decided such conjecture would only deepen her malaise and his concern.

Film, camera gear and briefcases securely stored in the trunk, Eric checked their timing. "We'll arrive a bit early, but let's press on to Pierre's home. I'm eager to meet this neighbor and grill him."

Dana's brisk nod matched an added alertness as they pulled out of the parking lot. She scrutinized every car and every lane they passed. Eric smiled as he reached over and patted her hand. "Come on now. It's obvious that Pierre's car would have been spotted and reported if it were anywhere around here."

She hesitated before responding. "I know. But, since it hasn't been, where is it?"

"True." Eric frowned. "Probably closer to his home. I'm beginning to buy into the idea of Pierre's cave being somewhere close to his own neighborhood, with his car well hidden in a local hideaway."

"Right. He'd know the areas' safest places—an abandoned garage—somewhere it wouldn't attract attention." Dana raised an eyebrow. "If, that is, he even needed the car at all."

"Lost in his own backyard, so to speak." Eric pursed his lips, starring off into the farthest reaches of the road ahead. "That would explain his comment when we first had lunch with him and discussed a visit to Rennes. He insisted that there were even more significant mysteries near Coustaussa."

Dana perked up as they approached the first of the side-roads. "I know we're not going to explore these, but I'll still indicate any others I may have missed on the way here. Car or no car, we can't rule out that Pierre may yet be somewhere around here." Dana retrieved her tablet. Opening it, she felt uncertain as to whether the upcoming intersection was the one she'd already indicated. She turned around to view it from the angle of their original approach.

She let out a cry, quickly turned back and sank low into the passenger seat, her voice iced in fear. "There's a car following us—a black sedan, but ..."

Eric slowed and checked his rear view mirrors, not wanting to meet up with a French agent de police. "It's going far too fast. I'm going to slow even further to allow him to pass. Try to catch sight of the driver and the license plate as he does."

Their little Twingo had nearly slowed to a full stop as Eric moved over to the far right side of the road. With no traffic coming the other way, the sedan showed little interest in passing them.

Dana reached for her little Nikon camera. "The car is deliberately avoiding getting any closer. I'm going to try to make out the license plate with a telephoto lens." As she attached it and kneeled across the seat to take a series of shots, she muttered: "*Vatican City/Rome* by the markings. If only the windows weren't blackened, I could see who's in the car." No sooner had the words left her mouth than the car accelerated, pulling out and around them as it sped through the stop-sign in the direction of Arques.

"Damn! I'd swear they heard me. And I'm certain they could see me."

"Seat belt back on, Dana," Eric said as he swung the car around and, in an attempt to keep pace, followed as fast as their little car could go. Within less than two kilometers he realized the futility of thinking they could catch the black Mercedes. In a hail of dust and gravel, he pulled over to the side of the road. A wide-eyed Dana was craning to catch any lingering sight of the sedan as Eric turned off the ignition. "Sorry for the impetuous move. As foolish as it was to try to match his speed, I'm damned if I'll put up with being at their mercy." Dana was shocked, not by his words, but at a jaw set so tight as to threaten to crack the veneer of his teeth.

"I agree, my love; better proactive than reactive. Something occurred to me as the car passed us." Dana stared into his eyes. "Do you think what I think?" She waited for his response.

"Maybe. If what you're thinking is that this car reminded you of the Vatican car that sped away from Montsegur after Benjamin's death."

"Exactly, except I'm now beginning to entertain the concept of Benjamin's "presumed death". We never saw the body or heard of funeral plans. Maybe we should consider Veronique's belief that he could have survived that fall?" Dana grimaced. "Except, given Benjamin's ego, his remaining out of sight all this time puts it beyond belief." She paused, staring off into space before adding, "Unless, as Veronique suggested, his injuries were so severe as to require eight months of rehabilitation."

"True, and/or that it combined with his intent to remain 'dead'." Eric's words were accompanied by a squeal of tires as he gunned the accelerator, sending their little car skipping back onto the asphalt and down the highway. "Whether Benjamin or not, there's no question we're under surveillance by someone—and a confident, cocky, no-where-to-run surveillance at that."

"We expected it so we mustn't get demoralized. They won't get the upper hand." Dana's "won't" bristled with rage, her voice fueled with determination. "I keep reminding myself that, whatever their power, we have destiny on our side."

Eric glanced over at her, his mouth turned down in a sardonic grin. "Such certainty could trip us up. We mustn't rely on pure faith."

Dana felt her assurance eroding at his words. "That philosophy sounds strange coming from a former priest." She tried to maintain some lightness, but her voice couldn't hold it. "All this is really getting to me. Not just the car following us, but..."She proceeded to describe her baffling encounter in the church courtyard, the wayward lens can and the old man who ran with the skill of an athlete. "I have a strange feeling that the person in the car that followed us could be the same man."

Eric shook his head. "You're right. This *is* getting to you." He glanced down at the clock in the dashboard. "What do you think? Given that we're being tailed—dare we proceed to our meeting with Pierre's housekeeper?" Eric's doubt was emphasized by the Twingo's slowing down.

Dana looked crestfallen. "You're right. That may be exactly what they expect—an obvious connection linking us to a search for Pierre." She waited but Eric's response was silence. "On the other hand, we could stay alert for the black sedan and, if no sign of its return, continue to Pierre's house." She finished with a question in her tone and in her eyes as she waited for Eric's reply.

"For now, let's reserve judgment. Keep your camera ready and your eyes sharp. If no sign of our pursuer, we could chance it." Eric hesitated. "I'll look for a hideaway place to park the car. At Dana's a smile of agreement Eric shook his head. "I know you, my psychic partner. Your ulterior motive goes beyond just a conversation with his neighbor. You want to be in his home to pick up signals of what may have become of him. Right?"

"You know me too well." Dana gave him a thumb's up signal. "So, let's try to pull it off." She turned to resume a scan for any vehicles following them.

"Seems our pursuer was simply keeping us under surveillance." Eric hesitated, his forehead creased as he turned to Dana. "...and yet?" At no response, Eric noticed that Dana was fixated on something that etched matching frown marks on her forehead. Eric brushed a lock of dark hair away from her brow before returning his attention to his driving. "Where did you go?"

Dana looked up, her expression haunted. "I keep returning to the old man in Rennes. The more I recall the incident, the more uneasy it makes me. Something in his build, his height....there was something about him that reminded me of Benjamin." She closed her eyes, squeezing them tight as if to restore the image. As she opened her eyes Eric was struck by the tenacity in her look

Eric slowed the car, pulled over and braked to a halt. "No way, as you Yanks say, that you could be certain. May I suggest that it's really Rennes that is getting to you."

"Not to mention being followed by a Vatican vehicle." Dana gave him a wry grin.

"Yeah well, both compounds our paranoia." He reached over to take her hand. "It must have been Veronique's mention of Benjamin that triggered your thoughts of the old man in Rennes. For all her academic, ultra-rational disposition, she can't actually believe Benjamin could have survived." His emphasis on the illogic behind such a conclusion met with silence, causing his voice to rise on his final bit of reason. "Come on now. I know the secret code convinced her, but Benjamin probably shared it with someone in the Vatican. You can't possibly buy into the theory that Benjamin survived a 3000 feet plunge down a cliff. It would be like falling from a plane without a parachute." Eric paused, aware that Dana wasn't buying it.. "Think it through. *If* Benjamin Carter somehow managed to survive, that old man couldn't possibly be what's left of him."

Dana's tone broached no rebuttal. "But he *can.* I know— and I suddenly recalled why. I keep coming back to my brief glimpse of his eyes. Benjamin had the most diabolical cast in his deep-black eyes. They leapt with flashes of equal parts ego and evil. Remember my commenting that I couldn't bear to focus on them, but once having done so, would never forget them?" She shook her head. "Brief glimpse or not, my instincts say that the not-really-old man was and *is*— Benjamin Carter"

"Hold on. I suggest your theory is based on worry over Pierre and the weirdness of Rennes. Promise me you'll reserve judgment for now." Eric's earnestness softened her response.

Dana gave him a wry grin. "Agreed. At least until I get a closer look at him. At which time I'll expect your humble apology." She resumed staring out the window as he drove on in silence, glancing in his rear view mirror. Apart from a couple of farm trucks going the other direction, the road remained empty.

Eric made a slow turn to the right as they entered the outskirts of Arques. "Although the sedan isn't following now, I'm convinced our every move is being scrutinized, if not anticipated."

"That would explain why they showed little interest in corralling us. They seem to know the outcome." Dana's voice held less disappointment than Eric had expected. "It's their advance scouting that puzzles me. Why not scoop us up now?" With those words, she fell silent, her gaze returning to an inner landscape.

As they entered the center of Arques, Eric checked his watch. "Keep an eye out for an appropriate spot, someplace out of view. Are you prepared to go ahead with this meeting?" Her slowness at a reply prompted a firmer question. "I mean really ready? That sedan is fixated on our destination. They could be waiting at Pierre's, complete with a lethal calling card."

TWELVE

Dana shuddered. "Not a pleasant arrival scenario. But the fact of their tailing us means they don't know where Pierre is."

"If they don't know, then..." Eric's raised voice and eyebrow revealed his teetering on the brink of an 'ah hah'. "Hear me out, Dana. Their following us suggests Pierre discovered he was being followed and disappeared on his own for a few days until he felt it safe to return. Ergo, the limo watches us to determine where he is." He waited for Dana's response.

"Sounds plausible, but my guess is that they picked up Pierre's trail and somehow lost it." Dana paused before adding her conclusion. "I don't think whoever—*if* ever—someone caught up with Pierre, they would kill him. I know it as well as. I know Pierre would never reveal the manuscript. They'd have to keep him alive to decipher it." She drew a breath. "As to the limo's interest in us, obviously the Vatican had already earmarked us prior to Benjamin's death." Dana fell silent as she thought: *If Benjamin lives, he'd remain in league with the Vatican, suspecting us as to be, not only in possession of the manuscripts, but in league with Pierre.*

Eric slowed the car as they neared the road leading to Pierre's house. He looked over at Dana. "I can read you like a book, my love. So...we add a 'Benjamin lives' theory to the mix. But for now we need to put aside speculation in favor of clues to Pierre's whereabouts. Let's assume they don't know where he is either."

A mix of hope and anxiety colored Dana's reply. "We have to find him before they do."

Eric nodded. "His neighbor's information may help us. We're about there. Watch for a place to park our car."

"On the right there's a boulangerie set back from the road."

Eric pulled in, pleased to find the bakery closed and the area in back surrounded by trees..

"Good find. Let's head for Pierre's house while the coast is clear." Grabbing his briefcase and Dana's camera, they set off.

While their car may have remained out of view, they weren't. They met with interested stares from behind pulled-back curtains in several of the homes, as well as protective dogs barking along their route. Dana grinned as they neared Pierre's driveway. "The museum director is right. There is no way Pierre's car wouldn't be spotted."

As they neared the house, Dana stopped to survey the surroundings as keenly as she focused her camera shots. She scrutinized the foreground, observing the driveway leading to house, studying the pigeonaire for signs of activity, wondering at the car—an older Peugeot—probably the housekeepers she thought as she ended at an orange cat curled on the doorstep.

Fixing the foreground firmly in her mind, Dana expanded her scrutiny to take in the background. Massive urns of lavender blossoms swayed in the breeze, fig trees and a kitchen garden fronted a pond that lay off at a little distance, six geese adding to its bucolic setting. Satisfied with her surveillance, she turned.

"I've brought your gear." Eric said as he removed her camera bag from his shoulder. "Will you need both cameras ?"

Dana hesitated before deciding that, even with no intent to actually take photos, she wanted the option available. As he handed them to her, Pierre's front door opened and his housekeeper, Beatrice, walked out, calling a hearty greeting. "Bonjour!"

"Bonjour Madame", Dana responded, rushing up with a suggestion of how pleasant the garden was and could they sit outside for their conversation. At Eric's smiling nod, Beatrice motioned them to follow her around to the side of the house. As they neared a group of lounge chairs and a wicker table, she paused, saying "etre assis, sil vous plait", smiling as she repeated, in excellent English: "Please, sit here. Tea is ready."

Beatrice left, returning with a tray containing a pot of vervein tea, four sets of tea cups and saucers and an assortment of delectable looking pastries. "Our neighbor, Monsieur LaPlante, will be joining us," she said, smiling as a man approached like an actor having heard his cue.

After introductions, the genial neighbor took his seat. Not until tea cups were filled and raised did he speak. His English,. although halting, was a skill he took pride in. "You ask where I see Pierre." Fervent nods and rapt attention encouraged him. "I leave early for—he pointed to his mouth—dentiste." Dana thought that if teeth revealed age she would put Monsieur La Plante at around fifty. "Pierre, he wait for petrol at same station I stop."

"Where is that station?" Eric asked.

"Is one half kilometers down the road to Coustaussa." He frowned. "I not wonder to see Pierre early—his eyebrow raised—I very surprise to see gun in his car." He looked over at Beatrice. "Pierre hunting—non, jamais!" She shook her head in agreement, echoing his "Never."

"I ask what animal he hunts?" He say: "Lapin." I shake my head—no believe. But I must hurry away for dentiste. Pierre still at gas pump." Monsieur LaPlante shrugged as he reached for one of the pastries. "I not know which direction he go."

"Do you know of any roads around here where he may have parked his car to enter a woods for hunting?" Dana rushed the words forward, their confident French well-honed enroute.

Monsieur LaPlante hesitated, his eyes moving as rapidly as his thoughts. He turned to Beatrice. "Please for paper?"

Eric halted Beatrice's move for the doorway. "I have a tablet." She took his pad and pen and handed it to Andre.

He licked his lips, painstaking in his recreation of the intersecting roads in the areas. His precision included the gas station, the numbered roads as well as the unnumbered dirt roads, which he indicated by 1, 2, 3. Some of these he showed ending at houses and others ending with his careful drawing of trees and rocks. Finally, giving his artwork an approving study, he looked up and handed the tablet back to Dana. “I include all roads possible.” He looked over at Beatrice. “But someone see his car by now. All know Pierre’s car.”

“True; but no one has reported his car.” Beatrice shook her head, her expression filled with worry. “Could Pierre have driven beyond the Department, Andre?”

Monsieur LaPlante pondered before answering. “It is a mystery that he go hunting. But to go far to hunt", he shrugged, "…impossible." He looked from Dana to Eric and then to Beatrice. "He at stop for petrol, maybe fill car to travel far.” He gave a brisk shake of his head. “Not like Pierre.” He turned to Beatrice with an encouraging smile. His rapid French took a minute for Dana to translate to: “He will return soon, my dear Beatrice. You would have heard from someone by now.”

Dana could see Beatrice’s wavering smile threaten to end in tears. She reached out and placed a hand on hers. “Have faith. Pierre will return and be very happy to find that you are looking out for him.” As the words left her mouth, they were followed by an image. “Has anyone come by or called, inquiring of Pierre, requesting his books—or any strange behavior?”

Eric nodded. "Has a black sedan driven by?”

. The neighbor halted his pastry mid-way between table and mouth—his focus on Beatrice’s response.

She pursed her lips, her hands twisting her napkin tighter and tighter. “Yes. I noticed such a vehicle twice—yesterday and this morning.” She turned to Andre. “It did not stop, but it did slow down. I thought it might be looking for an address.” She smiled at the absurdity of such a thing. “It must be a stranger not to know that our homes are all known by names.”

“And the driver, Beatrice. Did you see him?” Dana’s question prompted a look in Andre’s eyes that suggested he could confirm Beatrice’s account.

“I could not see through the windows. They were dark. But once the car stopped and a man got out. I could not see him clearly, but he looked to be an old man.” She looked over at Andre. “Did you see the car?”

"Yes. I saw the car and same man this morning. I go out to ask if he was lost. He turn back to his car and drive fast to Coustaussa"

"Could you describe him?" Dana waited for Monsieur LaPlante's response.

"Wrinkled face, like old man—but, he boiter—limp, Beatrice explained—he too fast, not old man." He began to stroke his chin as he haltingly added, "His face many cicatrices?" He waited until Beatrice translated: "scars." "Yes, very bad. But more bad in man's eyes." He shivered. "They stare like serpent."

A silence descended, freezing everyone in a pose of pensive deliberation, broken only by Beatrice's rattling of the tea cups. Her expression matched her nervous arranging of the empty cups on the tray. "I don't understand. Is this strange man somehow connected with Pierre's disappearance? Should I call the police?"

Eric exchanged a look with Dana before replying. "Before notifying the police, let's give Pierre another few days to show up. Such strangers or strange cars may mean nothing, but until Pierre returns all such activity should be observed."

Dana smiled at Eric's comment and added what she felt would appeal to a quality she'd sensed in Beatrice—a 'nobody messes with Pierre and his home while under my care' attitude.

"Beatrice, please keep watch and let us know if the man in the car returns." As Beatrice's shoulders squared and chin firmed, Dana knew she was on the right track in acknowledging the housekeeper's strength. "Like Agatha Christie, Dana began—having noticed one of the author's detective novels on the bench alongside their table—your observations could be important."

Beatrice gave a firm nod, her voice strong as she responded: "You may depend on me. But how should I notify you of anything unusual?"

Dana, knowing phone calls to be dangerous and yet not wanting to alarm Beatrice, turned to Eric. "How should Beatrice contact us?" She waited while Eric considered.

"I wish Agatha Christie was here to answer that question. The best I can come up with is to have Beatrice leave word at Pierre's office in the Mairie in Arques."

Dana frowned and lowered her voice to a whisper. "Obviously Pierre's phone—home and office—is being tapped." Dana deliberated for a moment, reviewing the best solution. She drew a deep breath, letting out a long "hmmm" before continuing. "How about Beatrice leaves word at the museum across the street from Pierre's office?"

"That too is going to prompt attention, especially since we're using it already." Eric fell silent as he considered alternatives. Dana turned to Beatrice and Andre, both frowning as they tried to translate Dana and Eric's hasty whispering.

"Please understand, Beatrice, we are so often away from our phone. And we think you should remain 'undercover'." As the housekeeper nodded, she turned to Andre to explain in French. Dana waited until they finished.

"We were trying to figure out a way, other than phoning, to get information to us." Dana commented to Beatrice and Andre as Eric remained in thoughtful silence. "Any ideas anyone?"

Beatrice was quick to respond, her new role evident in her confident tone. "If you want private conversations, you are correct not to use the museum." She paused, her forehead pursed as she looked up. "I have an idea of a place to use. It is near the castle at Arques." She hesitated. "Please do not laugh. It is an abandoned bus stop." As Dana waited, her expression eager, Beatrice smiled, her eyes sparkling with pride in her choice, obviously reveling in her sleuth role. "Inside, there is a box attached to the ceiling." She turned to Andre. "Remember why they abandoned this bus stop?"

He nodded. "Absolutement! A plague of wasps sting the children. They try to destroy wasps, but fail."

Beatrice nodded. "True. It took Mother Nature to finally destroy them. The box is useless now. But it could make a perfect letter drop." She fell silent, lips pursed as she resumed her head-nodding cadence before continuing. "Any delivery should be done at night, Andre, so no one can observe." Her eyes widened as she envisioned what Agatha would do. "We prop up a large bit of wood as a signal." Beatrice gave Dana a sly smile. "You've Got Mail".

Eric broke into applause. "Merveilleux, Madame Agatha Christie! "He turned away from a grinning Beatrice to Dana. "Brilliant idea, don't you agree?"

"It's definitely worth a try." Dana said, reaching out to grasp Beatrice's hand. "Madame, you missed your calling. You would make a good sleuth." Beatrice beamed as she turned to Andre. Her rapid stream of French conveyed both her pleasure at assuming the role of detective as well as a cautionary edict for Andre to keep such roles private..

The comment brought a wide smile from Andre as he looked over at Eric, who was lost in thought. Dana knew he was considering all the ramifications.

His anxiety was transparent as he whispered. "I'll go along with that as a solution to finding Pierre. But I wonder how long it will take them to begin to worry at such secrecy." The intensity in Eric's lowered tones and the urgency as he looked at Dana prompted Eric to smile as he turned back to Beatrice. "Sorry, we've forgotten to ask about any caves in the area."

"Ask about caves" was understood and followed by an immediate response from Andre. "Many caves—some large, some small. You think Pierre put car in a cave?" His expression as he waited had "crazy Americans" written all over it.

"No, but…Dana said as she shoved the tablet to Andre and asked him to please try to draw a map of all the caves he knew of in the area. Andre raised his eyebrow, looking at Beatrice, whose expression wavered from that of duplicating Andre's puzzlement to one of solemn support for such an action.

"It could matter, Andre. Perhaps Pierre combined caving with his hunting trip." Her expression suddenly revealed her alarm. "He could be hurt or lost in one." She handed him the pen. "Draw all caves around here. Your map could help Monsieur Taylor and Mademoiselle Palmer find Pierre."

It took Andre a minute to agree to such a notion, offering a disclaimer at his lack of knowledge of all the caves. But as he began to draw, he seemed to take pleasure in his precision, notating distances and even names of caves.

As he drew, all fell silent. Dana noticed the look of alarm in Beatrice's face at the thought of Pierre being injured. She reached out and took her hand, whispering. "I know you worry, Beatrice. I worry too. But I know Pierre is alright." The look of doubt and indecision in Beatrice's eyes remained. "If our team can't find him over the next few days, then we shall call on the police. But, with all working together I know we'll find him." Dana waited until Beatrice squeezed her hand and nodded.

"Yes; we will." Her confidence blended with a different concern as she whispered, "And when he returns, don't let him know what a goose I'd been."

Eric gave Dana a puzzled look as she and Beatrice finished their private discussion and turned back to Andre. After twenty minutes of painstaking drawing, Andre looked up at Beatrice and sighed, couching his concerns in his native tongue. "Explain I cannot know all caves. If they go to caves I should go with them."

As he completed his request, Dana translated Andre's concerns to Eric, who replied, "Tell Andre too many people could draw attention to our search." Eric lowered his voice. "If we have no success, assure Andre we will turn to him—as well as to the police—for help in our search."

"We'd like to depend on you, Andre, if necessary." Dana began, explaining the need for discretion. She waited as both Andre and Beatrice clarified her words.

Eric pointed to the tablet. "Tell him we have confidence in his map. We will check the area out and call for his help when we locate a likely cave."

Dana did a quick translation, adding all the French niceties in appreciation of his offer as she assured him that they would seek him out if their search turned up anything. Both he and Beatrice smiled and gave their agreement, their expressions solemn as Dana added: "It is important you remain secret about our arrangements."

Beatrice turned to Andre, her earnest stream of French even more emphatic than Dana's English. "It is a serious commitment, one that cannot be discussed."

Andre drew himself to his full height, a touch of rooster in his assured posture as he responded in English. "To find Pierre, I keep secret and do my best."

"Bon! We will make a good team. Vrai, Inspector Poirot?" Beatrice took Andre's hand in a mock handshake. "We are both very good at keeping secrets."

Dana studied Andre's expression, surprised to see the man's cocky confidence overlaid by a tinge of embarrassment. But his action brought a smile to Beatrice's face as he gave her a little salute. "To our success at finding Pierre."

THIRTEEN

The Overseer smiled at the perfection of his new headquarters. The ancient building was part of the extensive property belong to the Abbey Fontfroide. Located well away from the actual abbey, its entry was inaccessible from the well-marked tourist trail. If anyone ever came upon the sheltered building, its guarded entry was locked and marked "Private: No Admittance" in several languages.

He counted on Fontfroide Abbey's beauty to deflect any curious visitors. Its charm was such that visitors were certain to be hypnotized by the peace and solitude of the Abbey's setting from the moment they exited the autoroute and neared its cypress-lined drive.

The Overseer appreciated that few safeguards had to be installed in his headquarters. Anything that would reveal the enormity of his mission was hidden in ultra secure areas, both within and outside of the Vatican. A master strategist and a fierce soldier of the Church, his was a thinker's role. Although he honored the new Pope, he rarely dealt directly with his Excellency, who trusted completely in Cardinal Vicenzo's handling of the Church's most important issues. Implicit in such trust was the need for complete discretion and secrecy. Even, as necessary, from the Pope himself.

Powerful, private and having access to unlimited resources, the Overseer's role gave him full access to the best talent in the world, all ready to assure the Church's enduring influence. His history of accomplishing the Church's best outcome had, at times, necessitated unconscionable actions. Like a chameleon, he would say, be and do whatever it took in any given situation to mold the outcome most favorable to the Church.

The Overseer himself was as cloaked in secrecy as his projects. Those who worked on his behalf did so in awe at his powers. Few knew of him at all. Those who did thought him super-human, attributing to him a reputation of one who never had and never would, undertake any mission and fail.

Nor would he enlist the aid of anyone who did not share such a focus. *It remained to be seen what the egocentric Benjamin Carter had produced, he thought,* steeled for any outcome as his servant approached and announced a visitor's arrival.

"Bring Mr. Adam up to my office, brother." As he hurried away, the Overseer drew a deep breath, anticipating the account of his visitor. He was prepared for any outcome, whether another account of Benjamin's insubordination in initiating actions not pre-approved, or to learn of the ultimate victory: success in that which was agreed upon—possession of the manuscripts.

As to Carter's effectiveness, the Overseer knew it was colored by the depth of hatred he felt toward Dana Palmer and Eric Taylor—a personal motive that could mean reckless impetuousness or success with this assignment. The Overseer stared at the chessboard positioned at the table near the window. Playing chess was not so much a hobby as a means to manipulate the microcosm of moves necessary in the macrocosm of his current 'game'. He studied the next movement of the Benjamin piece on the chessboard.

As to understanding, let alone sharing his religious zeal to protect the Church, Benjamin Carter did not and could not. It was given to few to dedicate their souls to the Church with the passion that consumed him. Fulfilling the "Q" project—as was true with his past accomplishments—would require keen observation, careful moves and relentless focus on right action for the Church, protecting it even before it could ever become aware of any danger. Once he could examine the manuscripts, he would completely defuse their power to impact the Church—without any repercussions that could shatter centuries of Catholicism's role in the world.

He would possess the Cathar treasure. Nothing could blind him to flaws in the likes of the Benjamin Carters of the world. As to Benjamin's claims of having critical information that would assure the return of the manuscripts to the Church, the Overseer awaited results. Up to, until and beyond, Benjamin Carter would continue to be observed more closely than Satan himself.

As if his name was spoken aloud, a door opened and the man himself entered, introduced as "Mr. Adam" by the servant who bowed and left. The Overseer studied him as he neared. There was never any shame or sense of apology in anything Benjamin had ever said or done. But the expression on his face, distorted as it was with mock confidence, revealed the news was not good.

Benjamin made a move to sit down. One look halted him, prompting a bow that, if not a genuflection, came as close to it as an atheist could attempt.

The target of his obeisance wasn't impressed. The expression on the Overseer's face never wavered, a skill he'd perfected partially through practice, but primarily due to an innate absence of emotion, a quality that had allowed him to meet the most dramatic of situations with a steely equanimity that shattered any adversary. As to friends, he'd never had one, nor ever wanted one. Like the most sophisticated of machines, his function was to operate with a perfection that assured the best interests of the Church.

Such stoic power impressed itself—on Benjamin as well as others—with a certainty that left no room to wheedle, explain, convince, impress or seduce. Knowing that the Overseer wanted only facts, outcomes and solutions, Benjamin still heard himself beginning with a defensive clause. "I've dogged them night and day with no indication of where Pierre is, or what became of our man."

"*Your* man, you mean. I trust his ineffectiveness has proven me out. Never act on your own." The Overseer's words were made of steel—sleek, sharp, simple and deadly. "Your assignment is to obtain the Cathar manuscripts. With all the resources available to you, are we to conclude you must be replaced?"

The Overseer's question sent a chill through Benjamin, greater even than that which he had felt at the first sight of his own face. For that, at some point, plastic surgery could correct. But "*to be replaced*", he knew, was to be terminated as if he'd never existed.

He hoped the mixture of fear and rage he felt didn't supercede the confidence in his reply. "I will place those manuscripts in your hand." His own hands began to sweat at the silence which followed. So suffocating was the stillness on the air that he rushed his strategy forward. "However, a task so critical, one which has taken centuries, dare not be pushed too quickly. Knowing these people as I do, they will stop at nothing to prevent our possessing the treasure." Benjamin paused, wanting to measure the listener's reaction. He may have spoken to a tree, he thought, except that this tree could destroy him without hesitation. "I have learned from my rashness that if we move impulsively we risk having the manuscripts lost, separated or destroyed."

"*The manuscripts?* Dou mean that you have arrived at an accurate number?" The Overseer waited.

"Yes, no—that is, I know with certainty that there are two. And I believe—if they're as history suggests—that there may be four in total."

"However many there are, when will we have all of them in our possession?"

"I had hoped to obtain at least one from Pierre. With his capture, Old Pierre, who is an expert translator, could be made to reveal the number and location of the others."

"*Could?* Is it not a fact that this Pierre has outwitted you?" The words were brief, but the question was iced in frost.

"Only temporarily, Excellency. I assure you that I shall find him soon. But I must proceed skillfully so as not to risk any actions that may result in their revealing the treasure to the world, hiding it once again—or destroying it." Benjamin's confidence grew, primed by fury at his having been outfoxed, an emotion he was careful not to betray to the Overseer. "I am confident that I shall soon learn Pierre's whereabouts. He will lead us to all of the manuscripts."

"As to having the treasure revealed, hidden or destroyed, should any such outcome transpire, you shall suffer the same fate—to be revealed, hidden and destroyed."

Every scarred furrow on Benjamin's face turned white as he stumbled over his response. "You have my word and…"

"I care naught for words, but only actions and outcomes. As proof of your competency, I shall expect tangible success. And it is to that end that I shall dictate your next actions. Rather than a focus on the elusive Pierre, I want you to bring Dana Palmer to me. Her capture would assure Eric Taylor, would follow. From your description of your untimely fall from Montsegur, they are the two critical pieces to the puzzle of the missing manuscripts."

"Of course, Your Excellency. I quite agree." Benjamin's words magnified his obsequious agreement.

"I expect to take possession of Miss Palmer within two weeks time." The Overseer swiftly encircled a date before tearing off a page of his desk calendar. "Notify me of the success of this assignment and I will coordinate the security surrounding your delivery of Dana Palmer. I accomplishment, not explanations."

Benjamin took the proffered calendar page, unable to vanquish his fear as the Overseer's implicit message rang with even greater intensity. *Or have that date appear on your tomb.*

FOURTEEN

Dana's delight rang in her words. "I loved Beatrice's idea to hide notes in an abandoned bus stop."

Eric turned, struck by the lightness in Dana's voice. The return of her smile—broad enough to show her dimple—once so familiar, but now rarely seen, prompted his own smile and a desire to freeze-frame the moment. They'd been so preoccupied with people, roads, cars and conjecture, that he'd forgotten how much her youthful charm and delight had eroded.

In the span of time it took him to look, smile and return his focus to the road—like the cloud that suddenly covered the sun—so had her joy faded. Her shoulders rose and sank as a long sigh escaped. "I think we should call Pierre's cousin, Giraud. Those two are so tight that he may have some ideas as to which cave may prove to be Pierre's hideaway." Her voice held urgency.

"True. If anyone, Giraud may know." Eric glanced out the window. "Watch for a phone."

Excitement returned in Dana's response. "I can't wait to hear his reaction. He may not officially be one of the four musketeers in terms of translating the manuscripts; but if it wasn't for Giraud's rescuing us from Benjamin on the top of Montsegur..." Dana stopped, her eyes wide. "My God, can you imagine Giraud's response to Veronique's theory that Benjamin may have survived?"

"Merde" will be his most subtle reaction. Since *he* shoved Benjamin to his death, he'll want to confirm such speculation, and, if necessary, finish the job." Eric winked. "Right?"

A reprise of her earlier smile flickered before returning to a frown. "Granted, but bear in mind that such a response would be redoubled by Benjamin. He's sure to seek vengeance." Her voice strengthened. "Theory or not, we must let Giraud know."

"Right. The sooner the better." Eric pointed up ahead as he slowed the car. "There's the phone-booth. We'll give him a call." He stopped, exited and dialed the museum at Montsegur, thinking of the Giraud- Montsegur connection—now and in 1244.

Dana studied Eric's expression, aware of his having Giraud on the line from the echoing response. Fragmented, vocal and salted with voluble expletives, she smiled at Giraud's vociferous determination to find Pierre and finish Benjamin off. Beyond the bluster—she learned when Eric passed the phone to her—lay hope.

"Right Giraud, Pierre could outfox all the Benjamin's." Dana grinned as she held the phone away from her ear so Eric could hear Giraud's response:

"As to Pierre hunting: impossible! Pierre wouldn't swat a mosquito." The phone fell silent except for a prolonged "hmm" before Giraud continued. "Let me think on this. I don't know all of Pierre's secrets—far from it. But we were children together and I remember some of his childhood hideaways. You can be certain that a cave would be his choice in hiding the manuscript. Eric says you have a map of caves in his area. Send me a copy to pinpoint his likely choices."

Eric listened closely as Giraud assured Dana she could safely fax the pages to him. He'd let them know his results when next they called. As the call ended, Dana looked far more confident.

Eric took the phone and dialed Veronique. Veronique replied with a "she'd call him back" response. He gave her the number and hung up. Meeting Dana's puzzled stare, he explained: "I decided she should get her manuscript digitized and encrypted immediately so we only have Professor Marty's to deal with."

"And Pierre's." Dana's tone held assurance.

"Right." Eric drew her close. Of course." The phone's ring broke their embrace. Eric's suggestion met with a loud laugh of disbelief from Veronique.

"I know, I know, Veronique." Eric grinned as he held the receiver where Dana could hear. "I should have known you'd have done it as a matter of course." He listened, nodding as he repeated: "Under glass and in a climate controlled environment. Of course, I agree. Bur our having all four on flash drives is only the first step. At some point we must get them such protection. rather than a safe deposit box, but..."Eric listened closely to her follow-up suggestion. "Great, that would help if you could encrypt Professor Marty's manuscript; but you're not thinking of contacting him at his home, are you? You'll what, where?" Eric's eyes widened as Dana held her ear as close as possible to the receiver. Eric repeated Veronique's words. "You'll leave word with his daughter to have him contact you regarding a lecture you're giving at the University of Toulouse?" Eric's expression as he held the phone and listened veered from surprise, to consideration.

"Quite right. You could arrange for the digitizing of his manuscript more efficiently and safely than we could. Once you have his manuscript on a flash drive—oh, and do put him through a crash course in using it on his computer—we'll have gone as far as we can until we have word of Pierre." He listened to her response. "I'm working on that now. But having us all convene is too visible a target. Any ideas, let me know. I'll get back to you. Adieu."

The atmosphere remained charged with a renewed sense of momentum, highlighted by the scattering of gravel as they sped away, headed for Revel, their nearest "big" town. In less than an hour they had copied and faxed the map of caves to Giraud.

As they neared their gite, Eric's tone of voice held renewed confidence. "As primitive as Andre's cave drawings may be, having it off to Giraud has boosted my faith in finding Pierre."

"Mine too." Dana sighed. "I was about to traipse the countryside exploring each cave. But I'll wait until Giraud's examined our map. Do you think he might know by tonight?"

Eric shook his head. "Let's give him until tomorrow before calling." He let out a sigh as they pulled into their driveway.

As soon as they had parked and were walking toward their gite, Dana hesitated. “Speaking of thoughts, mine keep running with question marks.”

Having reached the door, Eric looked around and took her hand. “OK; then let’s talk outside.” Dana followed him over to a bench under an arbor of wisteria. Eric frowned as he stared at their gite. “Even having de-bugged it, best we talk outside.”

“True.” Dana drew a deep breath of the spring scented air, feeling the softness of early evening—what the French called “l’heure bleu”—descending. Her impatience was softened by a sense of peace as she sat down. “OK Eric. Ready? ”

At his nod, she began. “So much of this business strikes me as strange. But I’m convinced they are as much in the dark as to Pierre’s whereabouts as we are.” She let her statement hang on the air as she gazed off with an intensity that suggested she expected Pierre to suddenly appear.

“Agreed.” Eric remained attentive.

“But if they don’t have Pierre…” She shook her head, puzzlement deepening. “If he did outfox them, where is he and why hasn’t he contacted us?” Her eyes reflected her dilemma.

Eric took awhile to respond. “He could be playing it safe. They may have followed him and he outwitted them. Or, they captured him and he got away from them.” He fell silent, pondering the outcome of each scenario. “Whichever, they are now stalking us until we lead them to his and the other manuscripts.”

”Pierre would never let them take his manuscript.” Dana jumped up from the bench and began to pace, scattering gravel as she spun back. “If Pierre is safe, why hasn’t he let us know?”

Eric’s only response was a shrug.

Dana ignored his silence. “I think he’s outwitted them. If anything had happened to Pierre, I would feel it—and I don’t. He’ll contact us somehow.” Her feisty spark rekindled as she continued. “Furthermore, they don’t have Pierre *or* his manuscript. If they did, they’d round us up in a heartbeat. That being the case, he’s out there somewhere, I know.” Her eyes—dark with determination—underscored her words.

"And other things are looking up." Relief filled Eric's words. "Veronique boosted my confidence that we'll soon have each remaining manuscript copied and protected."

"It's the map with *the* cave circled that will do the same for me. And of course..." Dana fell silent at the sound of footsteps.

"I say, may your host offer you an early evening cocktail?" Barry walked up, tray in hand, skillfully balancing three frosty martinis gleaming more provocatively than any advertisement as they echoed his welcome. His broad grin revealed perfect teeth; his casual cords and sneakers total comfort, and his abundant hair, only just starting to gray, leant a subtle sophistication. The sum total communicated a natural élan. As he lowered the tray to a table alongside their bench, he raised his eyes to meet theirs. "Wow! Am I prescient, or what? Down those drinks tout de suite!"

Dana attempted a look of "carefree photographer on assignment in the south of France" as she took the glass. Her shaking hand betrayed her. Barry held her glass and, like a father with a sick child, encouraged her to take a few long sips. "You look as though you'd seen a ghost."

Eric hesitated before responding. "It's more a case of a disappearing ghost."

Dana's eyes widened with an impulse to knock the tray of drinks onto Eric's lap before his martini could loosen his tongue any further. "It's alright, Dana." Eric said, turning away from Barry to give Dana a reassuring wink. "Barry can see our concern. We'd lined up an interview with a researcher in Arques and just returned empty-handed." Eric sighed as he reached for Dana's hand. "The chap seems to have disappeared under strange circumstances. He left a couple days ago, ostensibly to go hunting—something all who know him swear is unthinkable. So, we've just returned from our fruitless interview with the whereabouts of Pierre uncertain."

"They've notified the authorities, I trust?" Barry shrugged as they nodded. "Not that they are likely to find him before his neighbors do. There's not an inch of ground, especially French hunting ground, that isn't surveyed by every neighbor within miles of it." Barry picked up his glass, savoring the perfection of both the drink and his pronouncement. "If not him, his car will certainly be spotted." After taking another appreciative swallow, he replaced his glass and raised an eyebrow. "A researcher in Arques, you say? He's not the Pierre whose office is in the Mairie?"

Dana let out a sigh of relief. "Yes! Do you know him?"

"Not as a fellow hunter, you may be sure." He grinned. "Far from it. We belong to the same chess club." Barry frowned. "Pierre claims chess perfects his skills—although what it has to do with research beats me." Barry lifted Dana's untouched glass. "Come on now, lassie, drink up. It'll restore the sparkle in your eyes."

Dana took her glass, but before drinking, asked, "Did Pierre have any other hobbies, besides hunting, that you were aware of?"

Barry was adamant. "Not hunting. Apart from research and languages, his passion was history. He loved it the way another man would love a woman." He stared off into space. "How is it the quote goes? *"...with a passion put to use in his old days, and with his childhood's faith.*" Barry looked up at Eric. "I suppose I don't need to convince you that Pierre would have given a great interview. Cathars, Templars, Merovingian's—you name it, if it's history, especially French history, Pierre's your man." Dana smiled in agreement as she turned to Eric, who seemed lost in silent speculation. Oblivious to Eric's state, Barry continued: "About the only hobby Pierre seemed to indulge was chess."

"I thought you might say spelunking." Eric rallied, intent on gathering advice. "Since the south of France floats atop caves, we figured he might be the sort who would explore them."

"Well, yes, Pierre was known to explore caves as part of his research, especially the Aude and Ariage areas." He looked excited. "You must visit to the Lombrives Caverns. They've pictographs that go back as far back as 10,000 years."

"Small local caves interest us more. Any idea as to how best to explore them?"

Barry grimaced. "Carefully, I suppose. Spelunking is one pastime that doesn't interest me. I'm hopelessly claustrophobic. Concerts under the stars are quite another thing." He turned to Dana. "If you enjoy music, there's a concert this Saturday night in Bruniquel, my favorite medieval hill town. Be my guests."

Dana smiled, looking over at Eric. "It sounds heavenly; but we're confronting a deadline and..."

Eric nodded. "A 'due yesterday' kind of deadline. Can we take a rain-check until we've put this series to bed?"

"Of course, but not on a refill of my magic martinis, I trust?" Barry took their empty glasses as he awaited a response.

"No thanks." Eric seconded Dana's firm headshake. "It's tempting, but I've got at least six hours at the computer tonight. We return to Arques tomorrow to interview the museum director. I need to be sure I've got my ducks in order."

"The museum director, you say? He's rumored to be a dour soul and new at the job. Gossip has it he's open to flattery." His grin reversed direction as he continued. "No substitute for Pierre, mind you." Barry stood, reached down and took the tray, looking back to say, "Do let me know if there is anything you need. I'm off to the local farmer's market tomorrow morning."

Before Dana could respond, Barry motioned toward their quarters. "Think it over and stick a little list under your doormat. I'll have a delivery waiting for you." He'd barely turned when he stopped, lowered his drink tray and slapped his hand against his forehead. "Speaking of delivery—that's part of what prompted my visit. You had a visitor today, someone with a special delivery for you." Their frowns prompted his rush of reassurance. "I didn't let him in, of course. I'm a stickler for respecting my guest's privacy. In all the years, I've only once used my key to enter the gite when a visitor was in residence. And then only when prompted by blood curdling yells that still haunt my dreams." He gave a Gallic shrug, "All that for a spider!" .

Eric looked ashen. "Was the delivery from the local Poste?"

"No, I assumed the chap was a printer delivering copies of your article. He was most anxious to put whatever it was inside."

"You didn't let him in?" Eric's alarm startled Barry.

"Never. I insisted he release the parcel to me; even said I'd sign for the delivery." Barry paused. "He wouldn't hear of it. Gave me the evil eye and left in a huff." Barry paused and frowned. "Actually, more than a huff—for a moment there I thought he might rough me up and break in." He paused, his expression pensive. "I've no doubt his real intent was to get inside."

"Did you get a good look at him or the name on the delivery van?" Eric's question was seconded by an anxious Dana.

“Yes…” Barry hesitated. “ …a rough bloke with a face like a boxer who’d taken too many knockouts. Tall, but walked with a bit of a gimp. From a distance I thought, ”old”; but up close he seemed as dynamic as a bull. I wouldn’t want to run into him on a dark night.”

Eric’s glance at Dana confirmed the familiarity of the description. “And the company name, Barry?”

Barry pursed his lips. “It wasn’t a marked delivery van. It was a black sedan.“ He shook his head. “It was only after he’d pulled away that it dawned on me that, for all his protest that he had to deliver an important parcel, I never saw the parcel.” He shrugged and turned to go. “I’ll call the gendarmes should he return.”

After Barry left, they entered their gite, nervously scouring every inch. Assured nothing was out of place, they ate whatever leftovers their fridge held, exhausting the issue of the suspected identity of their mystery delivery man. Too wired to sleep, they returned to projects.

Dana lost herself in studying Andre’s map of the caves, eager for tomorrow morning’s call to Giraud.

Eric did one last review of his final draft of the Cathar-Templar article. When he got to the end, he held it out to her. “I know you haven’t had time to read the revised version. Have a look before it goes to the press.”

Dana began to read, eyebrows lifted as she reached the section that described how interconnected the Templars were to families in the Languedoc area—most passionate supporters of the Cathars. She glanced up, met Eric’s neutral glance and returned to the final pages. As she put the last page aside, she shook her head, her look mixed with confusion and disbelief. “I can’t understand. If the Templars were connected to the most powerful families in the area—all having Cathar members, some Parfaits—why didn’t they try to halt the extermination of the Cathars?”

Eric sighed as he took her hand. “My question exactly. But to their credit, they actively refused to fight against them when asked to by King Philip.”

Dana riffled back through his pages as though the answer remained within. “If they’d aligned with the Cathars, they could have saved them. Their power was so great.”

"Not so great that the Pope didn't brand them as heretics and subject them to the same fate as the Cathars." Eric interrupted Dana's reaction. "Don't say it serves them right." He pulled her onto his lap. "I just wanted you to see that I included some comparisons in writing of the Templar—Cathar connection." He pointed to his article's finale. "As to their treasure, I concluded with doubt that the Cathar and Templar treasures were one and the same. But I did mention the likelihood of the Templars having found the Cathar manuscript's hiding place."

"After you and the other three hid them in the caves around Montsegur?" Dana bounded up. "But that could mean that one of the four either was a traitor or revealed their hiding place to a family member who in turn was connected to the Templars, and…"

Eric swept her back onto his lap. "Enough already. We have the manuscripts and will soon be able to interpret the treasure, given we retrieve Pierre and his manuscript." Eric looked around the room with an expression that caused Dana to shiver as she followed his gaze. "We must move much faster with the manuscripts translation." Seeing her deepening frown, he pulled her onto his lap. "The fact that our 'delivery man' didn't succeed is encouraging."

Eric bounded up leaving. Dana slide to the floor. "What gives? Why such a strange look, Mr. Taylor?"

His response opened a Pandora's Box of unthinkable outcomes. "I just noticed…look…" He pointed to the bronze statue of a curled up cat that served as a doorstop at the back entry to their gite. "I always position the doorstop so that if anyone picked the lock and opened the door they'd be blocked by the cat. It's been moved." Eric immediately conducted a repeat search of every inch of the gite, including writings, clothing, cameras and film. His scrutiny for any new bugs having been planted even included the bathroom sponge. Assured that nothing seemed to be missing and no bugs evident didn't disperse the pall of gloom that hung in the air.

Dana suddenly sprang to alert. *Something,* Dana thought as she gave an audible sniff—*a subtle scent that she recognized.*

Taking another whiff, she cried out: "It's Giorgio Armani—Benjamin's classic signature scent. Oh my God, Eric. Benjamin is not only alive—but he's been in our house!"

FIFTEEN

The May morning had done an about-face from yesterday's spring flowers, white clouds and encouraging sunlight. Today's sky was filled with dark clouds, threatening a rerun of rain as chill winds mercilessly whipped blossoms from their branches. Spring was fickle in its willingness to delay any preview of summer, Dana decided as she fought to stay awake during their drive to Arques.

The storm had begun last night, flashes of lightning and peals of thunder accompanied many dramatic conversations which continued into the early morning. The focus was on Benjamin's search of their gite. Eric had assured her he'd safeguarded their manuscript. He'd patted his secret pocket to reconfirm that the flash drive remained, nervously quelling his doubts.

Dana still had a difficult time shaking her fear. Exhausted, she sank deeper into her voluminous wrap-around sweater and closed her eyes, longing for a nap before their arrival.

"We're here." Eric's announcement startled her out of a muddled state of quasi-sleep. The braking of the car had abruptly derailed nightmarish images of caves and Benjamin, with Pierre beckoning them to follow.

Concerns about the security of their gite or Eric's flash drive took a back-seat to her sudden focus on calling Giraud. Pierre was out there somewhere and finding him remained uppermost in her mind. Before she got out of the car, she closed her eyes, trying to will Giraud's response: "*This is definitely* Pierre's cave."

"Dana; are you coming?" Eric's question held an echo of having been repeated once too often.

"Of course," she said, staring in surprise at the umbrella he held ready to shield her from a blast of rain that greeted her exit, prompting her to wrap her camera within her sweater. As she stepped out, she gave Eric a wry grin of acknowledgment that, true, she'd spaced out, but had returned to the here and now.

"Do you think the director will let us use his phone to call Giraud?"

"We can ask." He said as they dashed for the museum's entrance. Eric gave the umbrella a rough shake and placed it in a stand as Dana checked her camera. Assured it remained dry, she looked around the quiet museum. A slow circuit of the display cases revealed one other occupant—an older woman kneeling down and staring into an exhibit case. The woman gave her a strange glance prompting Dana to dash for the restroom to repair her wild look.

The large mirror that greeted her entry was not her friend. Wet and wild came to mind as the perfect descriptors—but definitely not like the glamorous-female ads. *No,* she thought as she frowned*: more like a windblown harridan.* Fishing within her purse, she dug out a hairbrush, makeup and a hair clip. To control her dark hair which tended to curl in the rain, she used the clip to tame it into a more professional look, following it with a touch of pink gloss to lips that had been well-chewed over these past few days. Last, but probably the most effective, she brushed on a bit of mascara to open wide her sleep-deprived eyes. *Almost there*, she thought as she shed her soggy sweater. Brushing the remaining drops of rain from her tan pants, she buttoned her rust-colored jacket and turned full-circle. Reassured by the mirror's reflection of a classically-garbed professional woman, she strode through the door.

Finding Eric nowhere in sight, she headed upstairs as she heard voices , their language indeterminate.

Entering the spacious upper room, she spotted Eric at the far wall, deep in conversation with a short, gray haired man. Eric's expression matched the seriousness of the director's response. "Of course, Monsieur, we have a copy of "Foxes Christian Martyrs of the World." The unctuous tones of his voice rang out, reminding Dana that she'd arrived just in time to stroke a man Barry had described as "a peacock in a guinea hen's body" as he added: "I can let you have a look at it, but that particular book will be picked up by another researcher later today."

Eric smiled as Dana neared, the appreciative look in his eyes doing homage to her revamped appearance as he turned to introduce her. "Monsieur Arlet, it is my pleasure to introduce the photographer of our team: Dana Palmer. Dana, this is Monsieur Arlet, the new administrator of the Arques museum."

Dana smiled as she extended her hand. "I'm delighted. As an expert on the history of the area, we look forward to your wisdom. Your predecessor had so kindly helped us with our research on our earlier article about the Cathars." She paused, noticing a slight "humph", if not verbally expressed, coloring his tones as he replied.

"To the extent he could, I'm certain, Mademoiselle. His knowledge of both Cathars and English is, I'm afraid, rather limited." The director returned his attention to Eric, his manner betraying his belief that, as the male, Eric was the proper person to address. "Mr. Taylor, your request for an interview concerning the Templars and the Merovingian dynasty—he glanced out the window—should, due to the storm, allow us ample time to explore such topics." He moved to the stairway, directing his instructions to Eric. "Let us adjourn to my office."

His office was more spacious than Dana had recalled and far less sparse. Replete with mahogany bookshelves, black leather furniture and interesting sculptures, the atmosphere was inviting. Not so the director's attitude. He pointed to her camera bag. "Feel free to take your photographs now, Miss Palmer." He walked over to pose between the books and the display case, one hand pointing to an object inside. "I find this a most appropriate photo to highlight our rare artifacts. This is an especially rare find—a complete clasp used to secure a Cathars' Gospel of John within their garments."

After she'd taken a few photos of the director with his treasure, Dana preceded her request with a few strokes to his feathers. "Monsieur Arlet, that pose is perfect. You will be pleased when I've developed the photos. I'll see that you receive a set. Perhaps one would be suitable for our article?"

The look in his eyes told her he was basking in thoughts of added prestige; time for her to ask: "Might I have the use of your phone for a brief call?"

Doubtless he thought she wanted to pursue such an eventuality. He nodded and pointed to a phone on the credenza, speaking in a little less officious tone. "Mademoiselle, feel free to make your call and to continue with your photographs as Monsieur Taylor and I conduct our private interview in my inner office.."

Eric, positioned out of view of the director, winked as he chimed in, "Good idea, Dana. I know you hate to have your creativity confined. Let me know later the results of your call." She shot him an "I'm out of here" look and turned away. as Monsieur Arlet led Eric toward his inner sanctum. Eric called back: "I'll find you when we're finished."

Dana took a deep breath, feeling exhilarated as the door closed and she was alone. She removed a scrap of paper with Giraud's phone number and anxiously dialed. "Giraud, thank goodness you're there. I'm in the Arques Museum where Eric is interviewing the director." She nodded, her response impatient. "True. You were right. But that's not important. I couldn't sleep waiting to learn what you thought of the cave map." With each second that passed her mouth turned into a deeper frown at Giraud's words: *"Impossible to know which cave Pierre would have chosen."* She gripped the phone tighter as he continued. "Yes, I understand and. I suppose you're right. He'd never use a commonly known cave for its hiding place." After a stretch of time while Giraud tried to console her, their conversation came to a close. She hung up the phone, refusing to let tears flow as she glanced around the museum.

There were no added visitors. Not even the woman she'd noticed earlier. After a few token shots of the main floor, she deliberated over going upstairs. She'd been in the museum before and had many copies on file of the Deodat Roche photos. Still, as a photographer, his face mesmerized her. So much so that she found the pull of the photos irresistible and hurried upstairs.

Nearing the photo display, awe deepened at the image of the aristocratic man. Deodat Roche was considered the Expert of

Experts on the Cathars, Templars and Merovingians. She regretted not having an opportunity to have known him. He died in Arques in January of 1978 at the age of 100. Fortunately his writings on the Cathars, their reputed relationship to Manicheism, their spirituality and their religion, remained. All had been devoured by her, leaving her still grappling over the segments on dualism.

The Cathar concepts of Good and Evil and God and Satan had always confused her. In reading Roche's works, however, she discovered a framework within which to hold such a philosophy. He explained that the Cathars believed that as newborns our souls became enshrouded in a physical reality whose temptations were of the Devil. Through food, sex, wealth and power, our real nature—that of being one with Spirit—was obscured. The Cathars, who traveled with a companion, prayed unceasingly, fasted regularly and, certainly as Parfaits— priests of their religion—remained celibate as a powerful means to overcome physical temptation and retain their Souls connection to God.

What is it to feel connected to God? Dana wondered as she remained fixed on Deodat Roche's photos. She'd never really asked that question before, trusting her soul—once filled with the passion of a Cathar Believer—to retain such faith throughout lifetimes. And yet, apart from her love of justice, nature, wisdom, friends and Eric, she rarely entered a church except to photograph them. But she often felt connected to…everything. *Is that God, she wondered?* A smile rose on the heels of the question, accompanied by her recognition of the element of prayer in posing such a question to—God? A rush of warmth and love filled her, followed by an image—not of God, or even of Deodat Roche—but that of Mary Magdalene.

The image didn't linger long, but the strange sense that remained as she walked past the last of Deodat Roche's photos—one taken as he neared his 100th birthday—was that of a room suddenly filled with a powerful feminine energy.

Heading down the stairs, Dana felt blessed by Deodat Roche's wisdom and the Magdalene's love. It helped to counter-balance her disappointment at Giraud's news. Unfortunately, the positive feelings faded as she walked out the door. So bereft did she feel at having her hopes of finding Pierre's cave disappear, she decided to retreat behind her lens and focus on exterior shots.

The storm had eased up, leaving a light rain creating a misty atmosphere that promised some interesting photos. She hefted her camera case on her shoulder and looked around, her eyes drawn to the only person in view—the same woman who had been studying the exhibits. She stood in the car-park across the street—the one that fronted the Mairie and Pierre's office—and stared at Dana. As Dana wondered if should cross over, maybe even enter Pierre's office, the woman called out: "arrêt mademoiselle!" She dashed across the road, arriving out of breath when she reached Dana.

"Mademoiselle, I must give this to you." Her English was labored and her words accompanied by an anxious search within her large bag until, with a sigh of relief and a swift look up and down the street, she shoved an envelope into Dana's hands. Ignoring Dana's questions, she rushed back to her car and noisily sped away.

Dana clutched the plain white envelope until, assured no one watched, she removed the single sheet and read the English words. "Meet me at the boules court in the park." It was signed: "Yoda". Her eyes filled with tears as she murmured a fervent "Thank you!" to a God she'd questioned only a few moments ago. Stuffing the envelope within her camera bag, she hesitated, wondering if she should run back inside the museum to tell Eric. A glance at her watch told her he'd be much longer, leaving her plenty of time and bigger news to share upon her return.

Arques was a small village and, true to design, she knew the park was by the church. Oblivious to the mud puddles and the strengthening of a light rain, she practically ran—would have ran if she hadn't been so wary of attention—in that direction. With every step, questions pushed up against abundant feelings of gratitude and relief that flooded her from the second she saw her wise French gnome's secret signature. "*Pierre is alive*" was the silent refrain that accompanied each step.

The park was farther than it seemed. Out of breath and rain-damp from the steady drizzle, she crossed saturated grass to the ball court, trying not to attract attention with her frenzied scrutiny. Seeing no one, she felt relief and anxiety. *Where was he?*

Nervous at being observed—a solitary woman standing in the rain and staring about—she headed for a bench with a view of the boules court. She reached it, sat down to catch her breath, and waited. It seemed forever but couldn't have been more than ten minutes before she noticed someone approaching. A heavy sigh of disappointment escaped as the person neared. *Another woman; could it be the same woman who gave me the note?* Dana wondered under her breath. *Probably not. This woman is much too small.* She felt frustrated at not being able to make out the figure. It was hidden beneath a flowing rain cloak with a large umbrella covering the face. Dana wiped away raindrops to clear her vision as the person neared.

"Dana, walk with me." The woman's whispered words—in English and much too guttural to be feminine—astonished Dana. A closer look revealed Pierre's eyes. Large and liquid, they restrained her natural impulse to hug him with a sudden narrowing as he whispered "act natural." He held out the umbrella to shield her and they strolled on. To anyone's eyes they would appear to be two foolish women, intent on ignoring the rain to persevere with their morning constitutional.

"What happened?" Dana's voice was soft but her question blended worry, confusion and relief.

"I must be brief." His words held anger. "Someone followed me and as I left the cave, assaulted me." He removed the hand that clasped Dana to his side and lifted it to draw aside his headscarf, .revealing a fleeting glimpse of an ugly gash, its scar yet to heal. At her gasp he said, "It looks worse than it is. I came around quickly, as my assailant doubtless intended. He marched me back into the cave, a gun in my ribs as he commanded I hand over the manuscript."

"No!" Dana felt his anguish. Her heart started to race until he replied. "My manuscript is safe. I prepared for all eventualities, my dear Dana. I had designed a hiding place, an offshoot of the main cavern, with a tunnel that led nowhere. Within that cave, I inserted an artificially aged parchment which I promptly led him to." Sorrow filled his voice as he continued. "He was so eager to examine it that he rashly withdrew his attention from me. Briefly as it turned out, but time enough for me to bash him over the head with a boulder. That too, I had made ready nearby." She could feel Pierre—whose reverence for life required he save all injured creatures—shiver with disgust, his eyes filling with tears at having to take such an action. He let out a long sigh. "Even though he'd confronted me with his gun, I despaired at having to harm him. My only rationale was one of knowing that his soul now spends eternity with his treasure, walled within an arm of my cave. One, of course, whose entrance I carefully concealed."

They had completed their first circuit of the path which encircled the park when Pierre halted and looked around. "We are blessed with this rain. No one has ventured out. But it is slacking off. One more lap will be all the time we have."

"All we have? But how can we reach you? Did you come by car; are you nearby and…?"

Pierre gave her arm a squeeze as he uttered "Shush. I'm here. That's all that matters. As to where, it's much too dangerous to come to me." He stopped to bend down, seemingly adjusting his stockings but using the motion to scan for signs of onlookers. Resuming their walk, he squeezed Dana's arm as he spoke. "I knew how worried the team must be, so I took this chance that the storm would keep others at bay."

"How could you know we'd be at the museum?"

"I didn't; but I knew that one day soon you would approach my office or the museum in your search for me. I spotted your car."

"You spotted our car! But that means you're here in Arques?" Dana looked shocked at his choice.

"It's the territory I know best; every secret hiding place." He paused as his eyes scanned the horizon. "From all signs my assailant had neither time nor ability to inform anyone of his destination or his discovery. The most they know is that one of their team has "gone missing" as Eric would say." He shook his head. "He simply followed me. How, without my seeing him, I'll never know." The puzzlement in his voice lingered on the air, but his certainty grew as he drew his rain cape around him. "This experience convinced me that each member of our team needs to know where all other manuscripts are." Even with no one in sight, Pierre lowered his voice. "Should anything happen to me—no contact for over a week—ask Beatrice where the dead fig tree blooms and you will have a pointer to my cave." His voice took on an added level of worry. "Please inform Beatrice that I am fine and will contact her when I return from…he hesitated…a research project in London."

"Of course; she will be so relieved." She hesitated at using her precious time to describe Beatrice's knack for surveillance.

"As to the manuscript, it's reachable but its entry requires one no larger than me." He slowed as they completed their second circuit. The rain had stopped, bringing a few children out to play.

Pierre's expression so transparently announced his departure that Dana rushed forth her concerns. "Eric is having all the manuscripts digitized and put on encrypted flash drives. Do you understand? He'll need your manuscript. How can we reach you?" Dana's frantic concern grew.

Pierre lowered his umbrella. "I must go. Assure Eric I'd just completed exactly that. But I cannot waste another precious minute. My disguise is fragile. Just look at this stubble." He pulled at his capacious headscarf to obscure his hairy chin and cover all of his face except his magnetic dark eyes. His words were muffled. "Let the team know I'm alright. I'll make contact within the week. I've discovered an interesting clue to translating the manuscripts.

"Then you *must* rendezvous with our team right away."

"As long as they are searching for me, it's too dangerous. In the meantime, my lair is well hidden and my larder well stocked." Concern gave an abrupt reach for his skirts, lifted them slightly and turned to go.

"Wait! There is so much more to tell you. Benjamin is..." Dana's words were silenced as he lightly covered her mouth with a gloved hand.

"Goodbye, my dear. Thank you for a lovely walk." He turned and, blowing a kiss, walked away, his pace giving no sign of the anxiety he felt as two men approached.

SIXTEEN

Dana's heart threatened to pound though her jacket as the men neared. Trying not to seem too anxious, she turned and began to walk at a normal pace in the direction of the Mairie. With every step, she listened for footsteps. Unable to determine if the men followed, and unwilling to tolerate the fear that they may have gone after Pierre, Dana bent as if to remove a pebble from her shoe. Turning, she raised, shoe in hand, giving it a shake as she scanned the area. The men were nowhere near. They had left the path, one bent over examining the wet lawn and the other scanning the clearing sky. A sigh of relief escaped as, oblivious to her, they began to unload a set of boules.

She moved like Mercury, winged feet scarcely touching the ground as she headed back to the museum. Her steps were accompanied by a silently repetitive prayer of thanks. Her gratitude was mixed with awe at having set her intentions on making contact. Finding Pierre alive had stirred a sense of invincibility. All four members of their team were alive and all four manuscripts safe with both Pierre and Eric onto a key to translating them. A goal that had seemed remote suddenly seemed obtainable. She couldn't wait to tell Eric. Knowing Pierre was safe would free him up to decipher the manuscript's message.

She dashed through the museum door, shouting: "Eric!" A scowling Monsieur Arlet rushed out of his office, one finger against his mouth as he hissed: "silence."

"Pardon, Monsieur." Dana said as she glanced into his empty office and scanned the lower level of the museum. "How long ago did Monsieur Taylor leave?"

"He is…" Before the director could complete his sentence, footsteps sounded on the stairway, followed by Eric's lanky legs, broad shoulders and inquiring grin.

"There you are." His look wavered at the undercurrents in Dana's expression. "I figured you had roamed further a field for your exterior shots." Eric turned to the Director, hastening their farewells. *And not a moment too soon*, he thought, as he caught the director's expression—a blend of impatience and dismissal. He fixed the man with a look of sincere appreciation. "Our time was well spent." He smiled. "Thank you again, Monsieur. Your information will prove invaluable. I appreciate your letting me examine these." Eric handed the books to the director, noticing that the man's frown had given way to a look of self-satisfaction.

"Yes, well, if you could read French…" The director glanced at the books and back to Eric. "I'm certain such information will counter the rash theories being popularized today. Now I must get back to my schedule. Good day, Monsieur Taylor." His dismissive glance at Dana was underscored by his words. "I trust your assistant's photographs will properly highlight our museum."

Dana thrust her hand out, her smile wide and her thanks so effusive that Eric's eyebrows raised in shock. "But of course, Monsieur Director." She withdrew her outstretched hand, swung round and headed for the door.

The brief time it took Eric to join her seemed an eternity. She could see his puzzlement as he neared. "What on earth has put your knickers in such a knot? I know Arlet was tedious, but you …"

"Pierre is safe! I saw him. We walked. He said…" The words rushed out faster than Dana could form her thoughts; clearly too fast and too much for Eric who looked alarmed as he raised a finger and pressed it gently against her mouth.

Dana instantly realized her faux pas, but before she could apologize Eric bent over as if to check for air in their car's tires. His scrutiny was more thorough than usual. After circling the vehicle, opening the hood and examining the interior, he let out a sigh of relief, his voice raised as someone neared. "I thought we may have picked up a nail in one of the tires. It looks OK."

"Great!" Dana's response held an impatience impossible to control. "How about we take a little stroll?"

Eric glanced discreetly around, his eyes evaluating the few cars nearby. His reply was hesitant. "OK, but I suggest we look for a park bench or perhaps a café."

Dana let out a long sigh, unable to digest even the thought of food. She took his hand and hurried him off in the direction of the boules court. "We'll find a bench up ahead." She nestled closer until she was under his arm. "I'll have to talk or I'll explode."

Due to their brisk pace they soon reached the park. Dana squeezed his hand, yanked at his arm and pointed. "Look, there's a bench, away from anyone."

As they sat down, Dana drew a long breath as. Eric smiled. "I take it you're willing to forgo a café?"

Dana nodded. "For now. I can't eat, drink or breathe until I've told you my news—and not within a public place."

"Be quick then." Eric pointed overhead. "Someone is sure to want to picnic beneath this great fig tree."

Dana's eyes widened as she looked up. "Fig tree! Oh my God, Eric! Pierre said, if anything should happen to him we should ask Beatrice where a dead fig tree that bears fruit is. That's where we'd find his cave with his manuscript.."

Eric looked up at the sheltering tree and back to her. "Why is it that Pierre can't take us to his cave?"

"Much too dangerous, he said. If you let me talk, you'll understand why." Dana pursed her lips in impatience.

"Sorry. Continue." Eric waited as she shook her head.

"I have to start at the beginning." She rushed on. "I was standing outside the museum, looking across at the Mairie and wondering if I should chance going over to Pierre's office, when a woman—the same woman who was in the museum earlier—walked across the street and handed me an envelope. Before I could question her, she dashed away.

One glance at the message: "Meet me at the boules court in the park" signed, "Yoda", and I hurried to the park. No one was at the boules court. It had resumed raining and I was afraid he wouldn't show." She smiled. *"He"* didn't. I wish you could have been there. This tiny lady, swathed in a rain cape and carrying a huge umbrella in one hand and an oversize market basket in the other, made her way toward me. She was so camouflaged that it was hard to make out her age until she neared. The voice gave her away." Dana's eyes were moist as she continued. "It was Pierre, safely hidden away in an abandoned property somewhere near Arques." She paused, her expression betraying fear for him.

"What happened to him…and his manuscript?" Eric's tone of voice anxious. "Where is it?"

"Not to worry; it's safe and it's reachable." Dana squeezed his hand, seeing his relief as color returned to his cheeks. "In fact, that's where the fig tree comes in. Wherever the dead fig tree that still bares fruit is located—and Pierre says Beatrice will know—that is where we'll find his cave." Dana drew a deep breath and glanced around before continuing. "Apparently he'd already copied the manuscript onto a floppy disc. But he visits the cave to examine it as well as the original. On his last trip he was making his exit when someone assaulted him." Dana paused, her phrasing hesitant. "Pierre is confident his assailant hadn't had time to reveal any information about the cave or its location."

"If he hadn't yet, he soon will." Eric's expression was as dark as the cloud that neared.

"Wouldn't and couldn't—Dana let out a long sigh—Pierre's assailant knocked him out, but he came around rather quickly; probably intentionally, Pierre thought. The man was so impatient to claim the treasure that Pierre led him right to it."

"No!" Eric shook his head, his face turned an ashen pale.

"Hold on. You know Pierre. He considers all the angles." She shook her head. "Even knowing that, I was floored by the safeguards he'd taken." A blend of admiration and sorrow colored her words. "He created a fake manuscript and placed it in a small arm of the cave. His assailant was so eager to examine the manuscript that he took his eyes off Pierre." She shuddered. "Not a good idea. Pierre picked up a boulder, and—she grimaced, unwilling to picture such an action—bashed his head in."

Eric let out a long breath. "No! Not gentle Pierre."

"I know. His rationale was self defense of course. The man had a gun and…" She shook her head. "Pierre chose an unwilling act of sacrificing one human for the sake of many."

"At least he could take some comfort in knowing the intruder—so eager to possess the treasure—would remain with it for eternity." Eric shook off the image and returned to his larger concern. "What about his real manuscript; where is it?"

"Securely hidden in another offshoot of the cave—one that is not only secure, but Pierre said that, should anything happen to him, access to it will require someone as small as himself."

Eric let out a withheld breath, his expression one of growing anxiety. "Back to his manuscript. Copying it to a CD isn't enough. Did you tell him that his disappearance decided us that we need to place each manuscript in safe deposit boxes and work from an encrypted flash drive?" Eric shook his head in annoyance at their not having done it earlier. "If even one manuscript goes missing, our task in translating them could be useless." Eric leapt to a stand and looked around. "We must tackle their translation immediately. I feel the Vatican's breath on our necks."

"Pierre agrees. He said he'd make contact within a week."

"That's too long. Where is his hideaway?"

"He wouldn't say."

"Sorry to bark at you, but I don't understand. If his assailant can't reveal the cave and the manuscript, Pierre is as safe today as he was before this incident."

"Except for one thing. Whoever sent the assailant knows their man has vanished." Dana fell silent, her frown deepening.

"Got it. And it's as you suspected. Having Pierre and his stalker gone missing explains why we're under such close scrutiny." Eric looked deeply introspective before he continued. "They won't keep toying with us like a cat with a mouse." His voice held a level of alarm that sent a shiver through her. "Given they sent a hit man to follow Pierre and their man hasn't returned, I'd say our orange alert has suddenly moved to red."

Dana looked around as if an assassin hid behind every tree. She turned back, her throat constricted with fear of failure.

Eric softened his words. "I don't mean to panic you, but this incident with Pierre underscores our need to get the manuscripts translated." He looked at Dana. "Only then will we have any power to defeat them."

Dana nodded slowly "I'm convinced the manuscripts' power goes beyond defeating to transforming."

Eric took her hand. "That's you, my love; always thinking beyond the box—into the heavens." He tilted her chin and planted a light kiss. "That's only a small part of what I love about you. But , let's hope that, whatever the treasure is, it will prompt humans to cease destroying other humans, animals, the planet—themselves." Eric let out a long sigh. "The kid in me holds a secret desire that the treasure may be like the Genie's lamp." He paused to ponder such possibilities. "My first wish would be that everyone could forevermore only speak the truth."

Dana laughed. "I can see it now. The President telling how it really is; scientists and drug companies revealing all, sociopaths expressing the true motives behind their actions—not to mention husbands and wives! It would create havoc."

"Or silence." Eric grinned. "I jest, of course. I just felt a need to lighten up." His expression did a 180 degree return to solemnity. "It's OK to fantasize and to allow ourselves a mini-celebration at Pierre's safety. It points in the direction of our success, but..."

"I know. It's part success and part cautionary reminder."

Eric bit back a comment on their increased danger, knowing that in order to get the manuscripts translated all would have to place themselves and the manuscripts in jeopardy by coming together. Instead he pulled Dana to a stand, saying, "I'm famished. Let's head over to the far side of the park. I think I spotted a café."

She let out a gasp as they walked on. "We need to let everyone know that Pierre is safe."

"Not so fast. Maybe we do and maybe we don't. Bear in mind that our pursuers are going to intensify their dragnet. We can't chance a tapped phone, or anything that will tip them onto Pierre. It may be better to let them think that Pierre's disappearance remains a mystery to us, at least until we've found a safe place to gather the team together."

Dana slowly nodded as they neared the café. A bright banner was posted, announcing an upcoming exhibit at the museum. She pointed to the announcement. "That reminds me. You could go back to the museum and insert in that book a note saying "P.OK" and put poor Professor Marty out of his misery."

Eric glanced in the direction of the museum and their car. "I know it's cruel to let the Professor remain in a state of anxiety, but it's only until Pierre contacts us. By then we'll have brainstormed a safe strategy to meet and begin the treasure's translation."

"Speaking about meeting, what was it you said? I vaguely remembered your whispered words last night—something about your donning a priest disguise and meeting Veronique at the Cathedral in Albi. Did I dream it?" Dana waited for Eric's reply.

Taking her arm in his, he stopped. "No. She suggested such a meeting. At first, I considered it implausible. But I need to run an idea by her. Veronique may hold the key to working on the manuscripts. Her job gives her access to research facilities with state of the art scientific equipment. I'm hoping we can find a way to utilize such wealth." He halted, his expression uncertain.

Dana shook her head as she tugged him along. "Let's pause with that topic for a moment, maybe even take a little time to celebrate Pierre's safety over a proper lunch. I've been so worried that I've scarcely eaten, but I intend to make up for it."

Eric broke into a grin. "Good idea. Let's eat." He quickened his pace to the café, opened the door and inhaled heavenly aromas.

Hesitating as they entered, they did a discreet scrutiny of their fellow diners. Dana had nearly completed her full scan, studying two tables of women, their lilting voices discussing the menu. As she moved on to the table in the darkest corner, she froze. A scarcely audible gasp escaped as she spotted two men deep in conversation. One was Benjamin, alive, animated and intent. The other man was even taller and, although only briefly observed and in profile, exuded power. Thankful for their attention being focused on the waitress taking their order, Dana gripped Eric's arm, swung him around and out the door where she whispered: "Benjamin. Let's get out of here fast."

SEVENTEEN

Their silence was illusory as they hurried away, pulse rate increasing as they spotted a black sedan parked just down from the restaurant. Discarding any thought of reentering the museum, they bolted for their car, making periodic checks for anyone following.

If solcmn, racing thoughts could be ranked as to volume, Dana knew that theirs would be off the charts as Eric drove away. Careful not to go too fast or too slow, Eric's thoughts, nevertheless, raced with questions concerning whether or not Benjamin had spotted them earlier, if he had waited for their exit from the museum or, an even worse scenario: had he followed Dana to her meeting with Pierre. Confident in their having done a thorough inspection of their car for recording devices they both tacitly observed silence, communicating their concern via occasional glances at one another.

As the kilometers passed in a haze of highway hypnosis, they continued their drill of observing any strange cars on the roadway, particularly any black sedans. The distance seemed to disappear so quickly that both looked surprised as they neared their gite.

After they parked, they remained semi-paralyzed. Eric was the first to speak. "I don't think they saw us. If so, Benjamin would have left the café and followed. What concerns me almost as much is our not seeing the black sedan parked near the restaurant." He fell silent when they reached the doorway. "To be continued outside?"

"Right. But I'll run in and get some food to replace our missed lunch and stash these." Dana took her camera bag and briefcase and headed inside.

"I'll check for email while you're doing that." Eric headed up the stairs, the strength in his steps communicating his anger. After being gone no more than ten minutes, he raced back down. His look held a fierce mix of rage, anger and disbelief. With clenched teeth, he steered her out the door before he whispered, "Someone's been at my computer."

"What could they have gotten?" Dana looked around, her expression a mix of rage at being violated and fear at their increasing vulnerability..

"Nothing significant, except for my articles an the outline for the Magdalene segment."

As they reached the arbor Dana turned and stared back at their open door. "Damned if I'm going to forever bolt in fear. I'm going back in and get us some food."

"Bring something with maximum alcohol content." Eric said, suddenly storming off toward the back of their gite. While ransacking the fridge, Dana fully expected to hear a burst of expletives. They never came.

Within minutes she'd put together a tray piled high with an assortment of leftovers: baguettes, fig jam, goat cheese, ratatouille and tarte tartin. she headed for the table underneath the wisteria before going back for a bottle of wine *and* a bottle of brandy. After arranging everything—and with still no sign of Eric—she walked toward the pool, the mystery of Eric's fate causing her hear to race.

She found him floating—completely nude—on his back in the swimming pool. He was staring up at the sky, giving every indication of ease except that, on coming nearer, Dana could read his actual state. The look in his eyes screamed: "Enough!"

Lost in his anger, he didn't notice her until she walked to where she shaded him. He leapt to a stand and grabbed for her, nearly yanking her in. "God, Dana, you should have called out. I could have..." He got out briskly, giving a shake of his head. "I'm ready to do battle with someone...anyone."

"Even after an icy dip? I can see by your goose-bumps that the water is cold!"

"Cold be damned. I took one look at the pool, stripped down and jumped in. I needed someplace where I wouldn't have to watch for strange cars, whisper, or don a disguise." He grinned. "It worked at first—until the clouds began to look vaguely like Benjamin."

Dana smiled. "I'll grab you a towel off the line." She walked back and tossed it to him. "Food is ready when you are. Although I must say you look most enticing."

"My venom is so off the charts that I'd surely poison you." His words were tinged with wry humor as he dressed and joined her.

Scarcely sampling their food, they settled back in silence, wine in hand as Dana spoke first, her expression bewildered. "I thought no one could access anything without your password."

"It beats me how they over-rode it. Thank God I'd removed anything connected to the manuscripts." He downed the rest of his wine before slamming his fist down. "They took away a floppy disc." Dana's eyebrows rose. "Not to worry; it was the one with photos that you'd decided not to use for our last article." She let out a sigh as she poured them both a dash of brandy.

Eric stared into his glass for a long time, his eyes flashing with fury. "Damn it all; it isn't the robbery as much as the violation." He jumped up with energy unslaked by his swim. "No! That's not it. It's their power. They're shoving it in our faces. I feel like Jack and the Beanstalk, looking for an axe to fell what I hate to admit is a giant foe."

Dana looked taken aback to discover that, Eric, a former priest whose persona was logical, calm, encouraging and often tinged with a teasing wit, should be capable of such rage. Her reply blended acceptance with reason. "It's understandable that we feel vulnerable and unprepared. Rome's original backlash lasted six hundred years of the Church suppressing all heretics. But we are meant to prevail this time."

Eric began walking circles around their table, scattering gravel as he turned. "I'm as angry with myself as them. I've been living in a fool's paradise, believing that since we seemed to be staying one jump ahead of them we'd prevail." He looked at her untouched food.. "After you've eaten a few more bites, I'd like to go over something that occurred to me while I was in the pool. Try to listen with Benjamin's ears." He sat back down, slathered a mound of goat cheese and fig jam on a baguette, and halved it with her. "I know you love this. Eat up so you can handle my ranting."

Although Dana thought that she couldn't possibly eat, she did. The baguette disappeared. Washed down with wine, a mellow mood began to slow the nervous swinging of her foot.

Eric mindlessly pushed one bit of food into his mouth followed by another, his focus light years removed from his actions. When he finished eating the vagueness of his stare gave every indication of uncertainty as to where he was.

Dana reached for him. "Where did you go, Mr. Taylor?"

"I got lost in cyberspace, reviewing how they overrode my code and accessed my computer.." He shook his head, reaching over to brush a smidge of fig jam off the corner of Dana's mouth. "You did eat; good! Are you ready to listen?"

"I'm ready when you are." Dana waited as Eric resumed his circular pacing.

"I've been consumed with our greatest enigma. How to get around the translation of manuscripts when they and their translators can't risk coming together. Even after protecting the originals by copying them onto flash drives, the danger of translating them in that format remains formidable." He spun around, wiping his wet hair from his eyes as he shrugged his shoulders. "I'm stymied as to the key to translating them, one we'll never discover until we get together, chain ourselves to desks and go to work."

Dana's response was halting and barely audible. "Knowing you, I suspect you have some idea as to where the team could meet."

"I've been doing nothing else but brainstorming a safe haven. I came up with an off-the-wall scenario—a cruise ship, large, crowded and sailing the Mediterranean." He laughed. "I'm tempted to drop them that clue and hope they head for Turkey."

Dana let out a half laugh-half sigh as she moved her empty glass idly back and forth, staring at the table as if at an invisible Ouija Board. "I can't think of even one place where we'd be safe from Benjamin's and his Vatican allies."

"True. That leads me to my latest idea and why I jumped at Veronique's suggested rendezvous. "

Relief filled Dana's voice. "I knew you'd come up with a safe place to assemble and begin the translations."

"It took me awhile. I ran through a wide spectrum of scenarios, from my heading-out-to-sea-scenario to gathering in a cave. But I finally decided upon a more pragmatic solution." He swallowed the last dregs of his brandy before continuing. "Hear me out." Eric took a deep breath and continued. "Veronique has begun working on a super-secret archeological dig in Vals. She claims the place is more heavily guarded than the London Tower's Royal Jewels. Her lab is in charge of examining a find which she describes as 'tres extraordinaire'." He shrugged—his voice dismissive. "The find doesn't interest me; but the setting does. Vals is an ancient oppidium, tucked away in a remote rural area, a perfect place for our team to disappear within its troglodyte caverns underground. They've sealed off the entire site with guards posted to disallow access to all but those with proper clearance."

"So that leaves us out." Dana sighed as she waited. Eric's solemn expression was replaced with a smug smile.

"Not necessarily. That's what I intend to explore with Veronique. Who vets the 'experts' in terms of their qualifications to enter, how many, at what time and for how long? If she has the clout to arrange for even a brief stay—say a week—from a special team of four experts who work exclusively with her, I figure it might just work." He stared, waiting for her response. "I know it's a leap. But what do you think, especially concerning the safety issue?"

Dana chewed the information over, literally biting down on her lower lip as images flew through her thoughts. "It sounds better than your cruise ship idea, but…"

"But what? Give me one reason why it can't work—beyond the obvious one of Veronique not be able to assure our using it." Eric waited.

Dana hesitated, trying to express her concerns completely. "Risk is the lens I'm using to examine it. We're up against some big guns. Even should Veronique pull it off, Vals is part of the Catholic Church. How much of this dig is funded by the Church? Or, to put it another way, how many Vatican experts are onboard?" Dana shook her head. "We don't want Benjamin's teammates looking on."

Eric nodded vigorously. "Glad you spotted that. When Veronique first got the assignment, she was so relieved to learn that it was a purely scientific one and not a church sponsored venture." He hesitated as he registered Dana's look. "Don't worry. I'll reconfirm any Church involvement if it looks as though she can allow us entry for any length of time." Not getting any response from Dana, he switched to a more pointed remark. "Any questions you can think of for my rendezvous with her in Albi."

Dana, still lost in thought, looked up slowly. "Vals is definitely worth considering. As to questions for Veronique, if I had a photo I'd ask if she recognized Benjamin's lunch date."

"I'll do my best to describe him, although I had less of a glance at him than you do. Whoever he may be—and I'd bet he's a Vatican serf of some sort—he's the least of our concerns. My focus will remain on Vals being approved as a safe place for our team to work on the manuscripts." Eric released a long breath. "If it can work—even for a week—we may discover the key to what they contain." He hesitated, studying her silence. "As for your mystery man, whoever he is, it's an indication that we'll soon have more than just Benjamin's hot breath breathing down our necks." Eric resumed pacing, teeth clenched as he paced to the end of their driveway and headed back. He stopped in front of her, shaking his head. "I don't know how to explain it, but I know that, once translated, the treasure will eliminate all adversaries."

Dana mustered as much assurance as possible. "I agree. I'll pray for right action that it all works out to give you a go at it soon."

Eric smiled. "Good. Something still bothers you. What is it?"

"It's the fellow you think is a Vatican flunky. Something about him reeked of power. I know I've seen him before."

"Power or not, we managed to get under their radar unnoticed." Eric shook his head. as he looked up and saw that Dana's silence indicted that she'd remained lost in thought..

"Are you still grappling with your mystery man?" .

His question startled her back to awareness. "No. I've put aside, for the moment anyway, Benjamin's strange partner." She hesitated, knowing her next words to be controversial. "I keep feeling a strong pull to be going somewhere, doing something…else.

I was trying to stay with such feelings and get a better sense of where they were headed." She studied his reaction as he responded..

"I don 't know where such feelings are from, but I'd be totally useless—as would the team—if you headed off somewhere on your own." Eric pinned her with his look.

"I understand. But whenever I tried to dismiss their urgency, something would resurrect them—a nagging something that says I must take a different path." She shrugged, looking sheepish. "The more deeply I ask for guidance, the more she'd appear, like a tour guide for the wrong tour."

"She?"

"Mary Magdalene, quite clearly. But looking more practical than beatific. In fact, the tour guide analogy is an accurate one. She was forever insisting that I follow her." Dana studied Eric's reaction before continuing. Curiosity was warring with his stubborn resistance. "I get a feeling of urgency that I should quickly pack up and follow her the trail of her life in France." Dana paused before dropping her bombshell. "Given our experience today, I think we should consider separating. It would make it harder for Benjamin to track us, right?"

Eric rapidly shook his head before she could continue. "How am I going to focus on the manuscripts when I'm worried about you?" His response threatened to unleash a fervid rebuttal. "Let's agree to sleep on it, Dana. For now, I want to keep my focus on Albi. I'll phone and confirm the meeting with Veronique. A walk up to the phone booth will give me time to think about your little bombshell." He headed off, turning as if with an afterthought. "You can come with me if you want."

Dana laughed. "Not a lot of encouragement in your offer." She waved him on his way, a teasing hint of laughter in her farewell. "It was me that suggested we divide for safety; remember. So, off you go, on your own. I'll have a pot of tea ready when you return."

Dana couldn't see his expression, but he turned and threw her a kiss. As she reentered their gite, her eyes were caught by the Rennes brochure on Mary Magdalene. She whispered a silent prayer to the bright colored image. *Guidance please. For me, for him—and for whatever it is you expect me to do.*

EIGHTEEN

"Where have I seen that man?" Like a kid with a kite, Dana couldn't let it go in spite of it soaring out of sight. She'd gone through a litany of movie actors, discarding all. *Logically,* she'd decided, *he must be with the Vatican.* But his image—even though only seen in profile—nagged at the edges of her memory. She smiled as she heard Eric's approach, shaking her head in irony at the refrain he was whistling. "Memory". As he entered she said, "Wow! Whatever your conversation, it's lifted your spirits."

He swept her into his arms, lowering his voice to barely a whisper. "Veronique took the number and called me back. I explained that the focus of our rendezvous had changed and I'd feel more comfortable discussing it in person." He swung Dana around and drew her over to the door. "Speaking of more comfortable, let's continue outside."

Resuming their usual chairs, Eric took up where he had left off. "When I even hinted at our need for a safe place to work, she cut me off by reconfirming our meeting at 10AM tomorrow at the Albi Cathedral and hung up. That's Veronique—order, organization and minimal discussion."

"Few words or not, you sound relieved enough to have actually been whistling."

"I choose the song so you'd know it was me approaching."

Dana smiled. "Our trip to London seems so remote now. But the time, the show and the song remain my favorites."

"Good. I'm glad it made you smile. By the way, while walking back, I reconsidered your leaving to do the Magdalene photo-shoot.." Seriousness replaced Eric's lightness. "I know you can't discount what's coming through. But you must know our separating pushes all my buttons."

Dana nodded. "Of course I do. I tried to resist the urgency of the message." She bit back on the "but" word that wanted to appear. "I know I shouldn't run off when we need to get the team together."

Dana stopped as Eric let out a long sigh that didn't begin to ease his tension. "It's the old fear of separating, wanting to keep you where I can be certain you're safe." He swallowed hard. "But I gave it more rational thought." He looked up in time to catch the glimmer of hope in her eyes. "I decided there really isn't any reason you *need* to be at the team meeting.

She hesitated, giving it what she hoped was enough time for solemn consideration. "Right. You could represent both of us. I can't help with the translations and…" After a pause, she abandoned reason for truth. "I must go. I know that by following the Magdalene I'll find the real source of my value to our team."

Eric tried one more bit of reasoning. "Even so, I worry about you. Remember your last independent jaunt to photograph the Templar ruins? You're lucky to have come away with just a few scrapes and some missing film."

"Hold on. It wasn't my last independent jaunt. That one—successfully and safely—ended up linking me back with Pierre. And the Templar trip provided a guardian in Monsieur Dissell." She smiled. "You must admit that I couldn't ask for a better guardian on this trip than the Magdalene." As she waited for Eric's response, she stared at their gite. "Plus, I started to consider the vulnerable target we make. Having me go one direction and you another makes it harder to track us down."

"Logic doesn't erase my fear." Eric took Dana's hands. "When we separated in the past you were killed. That reality remains imbedded in every cell." As Dana's mouth opened to respond, Eric shook his head. "Let me finish. Understand that I can't bid you farewell without alarm bells going off."

"I do understand. But we can't live as Siamese twins either. I promise I'll keep you posted daily as to where and how I am." Dana watched as he struggled with such a compromise. "Trust I'll be safe, whether on my own or at your side."

Eric looked up with a wry grin. "Not fair, pulling out the old "we're being guided" rationale. Guided or not, I'll hold you to a phone call a day—minimum."

"Agreed. Then, unless something indicates otherwise, I'll intend to get underway as soon as possible." She rushed past the "soon" emphasis. "We'll deal with that after your meeting with Veronique." She stepped away and studied him from a distance. "I'm trying to picture you as a priest." Dana looked stymied. "How in the world are you going to come up with a priest's costume?"

Eric's eyebrow lifted. "Beats me. If I were back in London, I'd have no problem. There's an old set of robes packed away somewhere in the apartment. But, since it isn't Mardi Gras time and I doubt our little village has any costumes even then…well…" His expression brightened. "How are your talents with a needle?"

A peel of laughter escaped at such high volume that Dana looked over at Barry's house, certain it would bring him out. She lowered her voice. "You've chosen the wrong partner, Eric Taylor, if what you need is sewing. My Mother must have been frightened by a needle before my birth."

"Some help you are." Eric frowned at the sound of footsteps. They let out a sigh of relief as Barry approached, balancing large sacks in each arm.

"I picked you up a few essentials at the farmer's market." He handed each of them an equally large parcel. "Voila! I got a few of our best local cheeses—a lovely brie, a conte and a camembert. I hope you like paella. A friend has a stall there. Without question, he makes the best paella for miles around. You mustn't leave here without sampling it."

"It smells wonderful, but we've eaten. How about joining us for dessert; some of these great cheeses?"

"Thanks, I'd like that. But I can't stay long. I'm the director at our local playhouse and must get to rehearsal—he looked down at his watch—in one hour. We're doing "The Man of La Mancha."

Dana found it hard to restrain a chuckle as she gave Eric a broad wink. "Sounds interesting, Barry. Tell us all about it."

After plates of cheese and glasses of wine, a lot of light conversation followed by a mesmerized state of staring into the fireplace, Eric broke the ice, prefacing his special request with a bit of history of his former career. "Look old chap, I realize that all this may sound strange, but I've a meeting tomorrow at the Albi Cathedral, one which requires my wearing priestly garb. Any chance you could loan me your show's priest outfit?"

Barry, although raising an eyebrow, both at Eric's revelation and at his strange request, never questioned it, so natural was his perfect-host tendency to be as accommodating as needed to a favored guest. "Anything for you, old chap. It's a bit dated, but it should fill the bill. I won't need it back until dress rehearsal next Friday." He looked at his watch. "I must rush off. I'll leave your costume on your doorstep. But don't wait up. Rehearsals will be running a bit late, so I doubtless won't return home until dawn."

Eric smiled and turned to Dana after Barry's car had disappeared in a cloud of dust. "Can you beat that?"

Her look matched the smugness of her words. "Are we or are we not we being guided?"

Eric responded by sweeping Dana into his arms. One long, deep kiss and they headed up the stairs for the sanctuary of each others arms. Sleep followed an intense bout of lovemaking, fierce, tender and endlessly headed for the oblivion that burns away all fear and doubt, leaving both consumed by heavy sleep and delicious dreams. At the point at which darkness gives way to dawn, Dana stirred, thinking she'd heard a sound. Before she leapt up on high alert, she remembered that it must be Barry leaving the parcel that contained Eric's priest robes on their doorstep. She closed her eyes.

NINETEEN

Sunday dawned bright and breezy, matching Dana's tone of voice as she sat a carafe of French-press coffee under Erik's nose. "Wake up, love. There's a croissant with your name on it."

A low moan came from the depths of the bedding. Eric, who could work through the night, wasn't a morning person. While she, the moment light hit her cornea, was raring to go. Dana played her wild card. "I ran you a nice tub. Don't let it cool down."

That did it. With eyes half shut, grasping a cup that was slopping its contents, he staggered toward the bathroom. "Maybe I'll be human when I exit."

The bath duration was shorter than expected. The bather exited so alert that Dana knew his mind had switched into high the moment his body hit the water. "I've been reconsidering and…"

"Great. I'm anxious to hear. But over petit dejeuner which awaits you out on the table under the wisteria." Dana brought their coffee as she led the way out and into a day whose skies radiated the blue of a Gauguin painting. Birdsong filled the air at the likelihood of adding a few croissant crumbs to their worm menu.

It was only as they were settled at the little patio table Dana registered the absence of any parcel on their doorstep. "Eric, did you get up early to retrieve your costume?"

Shaking his head, Eric walked over and scrutinized the entire area before returning. "No sign of it. Perhaps Barry got home late and worried about waking us." He looked over at the chateau. "It's too early to wake him. Before we leave for Albi I'll stop by." As he sat back down he caught Dana's expression. "What's wrong?"

"I heard a noise last night and assumed it. was Barry."

"Damn! Let's hope it was." Eric looked over at the big house. "I'm tempted to go find out—early or not."

Dana reached to halt him. "Let's give it awhile. I need to discuss your 'reconsidering' remark. If we don't sort things out now we'll get lost in Barry's response, Veronique's meeting, and…"

His forehead furrowed in deliberation as he stared at his watch. "About your going off on your own..." He sat back down, angling his chair away from the view of either their gite or Barry's doorway. Dana waited. "I think it may work…" He hesitated. "Not being with the team makes you less of a target." He took her hand. "I 'd be more relieved having you miles away."

Dana bolted upright, eyes wide with alarm. "Suddenly I'm the one frightened. Four of you confined in one place makes a perfect trap." She slammed her fist on the table. "You must make sure, wherever you decide to work, that it is safe. "

Eric took her in his arms, his response directed at the top of her head which lay nestled against him. "It's your turn to trust me to use every means to safeguard our team, our manuscripts and our destiny." He turned her face up to his. "As strongly as you feel compelled to follow Mary Magdalene's trail, so do Veronique, Pierre, Professor Marty and I feel compelled to translate those manuscripts. Therein lies our safety."

Dana drew away and they both resumed their chairs. "I understand. But I'll hold you to making contact every day."

"Best it's you that phones since you'll be moving around." Eric stared into his empty coffee cup as if it could reveal the future.

Dana spread her croissant with as much fig jam and goat's cheese as it could hold, stuffing a generous bite as if to quell her anxiety. "My feelings are so muddled. I feel anxious over you and the team, frustrated that I'm of no use in the translations and, at the same time, eager to follow the Magdalene. As if, as if…" A far away look came over her, unabated as she turned to Eric. "It's as if

I'm chosen to be in a film but I'm searching for my character, unprepared with my lines, fearful of failing the cast…" She tried for levity. "Bloody bollixed" as you would say."

Eric watched her humor erase the glistening sheen in her eyes. But he also saw that she didn't need him to reach out for her. "I understand completely. I wake up feeling like a tightrope walker—uncertain of my balance, but aware there's no net below."

"What a pair we are!" She grinned as she pushed away her e uneaten half of her croissant. "Finish this. It will give you strength."

Eric's solemn tones seemed to echo from a sepulcher. "Our strength lies with the Lord," as I so often was reminded of—or reminded others of." He buried the trailing tone of disenchantment with a large bite of croissant.

"Well, mine seems, for the moment anyway, to lie with Mary Magdalene. I've decided to get under way as soon as you've decided on a safe workplace and an invisible-man strategy to assemble."

"Both will be discussed today." Eric turned toward Barry's door as they heard it open. Barry stepped out, garment bag in hand.

"I decided not to risk leaving this outside." He said as he walked up, held out his hand and glanced up at a few dark clouds.

"But I thought I heard you outside around two o'clock."

"I got in before then and decided to bring the costume by this morning." He noticed not only the silence, but the concern in both Eric's and Dana's eyes. "You must have heard my car and assumed I'd left the garment at your door."

Eric was the first to speak. "Most likely. Seems Dana and I have developed a case of the delivery-man-wobblies. Thanks ever so much for your loan of the costume. I'll make certain it's returned as spotlessly as the souls of my erstwhile parishioners."

Barry nodded, but his expression held a residue of perplexity at the air of mystery that seemed to follow his tenants. "Very good. I'll head back to bed then. I just wanted to get this to you before you take off."

As he walked away, their expressions multiplied the very same questions Barry's expression had held. Eric turned to Dana. "Let's conclude you awoke to the sound of his arrival."

"My logical-self concurs, but…"

"Enough "buts" for now. I must get ready for the meeting with Veronique." Eric gathered the remains of breakfast and they headed back into the gite.

"Before you change into your priest garb, I need to know where you want me in this rendezvous scene."

Eric hesitated on the stairway. "Best you aren't beside me. You could wander the square or check out the museum." He glanced around. "Anything but stay here in the gite."

"Right." She looked around and gave a little shudder. "Staying here isn't an option. You can let me off at the museum."

"Good." He grinned as he hurried upstairs to change. "My disguise may be outed with you by my side."

Dana was lost in thought and sudsy water as she rinsed their few dishes and placed them in the dish rack. She jumped as Eric said, "Well, I don't feel genuine; but how do I look?"

Dana held a hand to her mouth, speechless at the priest who stood before her. No hint of a man, only an asexual being—known as God's servant—stood before her. She had intended to laugh, but something in the command of his pose, the rightness of his garb and the solemnity in his eyes had her look down to be certain his feet didn't float slightly above the floor.

He raised one hand in a pose of benediction. "Peace, my child. Trust that all things shall work together for Good."

That did it, along with his broad wink. She smiled, her eyebrow raised as he aborted a move to grab her. "It's convincing?"

"I bought it. But I can't say that I've ever actually studied a priest's garments up close." She walked around him. "It seems a bit dated—more like a story-book priest."

"Agreed. I removed the antique sash, but I can't really alter Barry's costume." He smoothed his skirt-front as he studied his impact in the mirror above their fireplace. "I think that, once I'm in the pew, it will pass nicely. Most of the parishioners won't notice. They either avert their eyes from priests or aim them up at his invisible halo. Anyone questioning my outfit will assume I'm from a parish in Ethiopia or some such exotic locale." He grinned as he reached for a tea towel. "Let's be done with that and depart."

Dana yanked the towel away. "Sacre blue, Monsieur, priest or no priest, dishes dry best in the rack." She smiled as she hurried up the stairs. "I'll be down in a flash."

Time seemed to have eclipsed during their drive to Albi. Dana, automatically observing the traffic around them, remained lost in thought. The skies, although now more clouds than blue, held no hint of imminent rain. As they approached the 11th Century Bridge over the Tarn River, Dana was jarred back to reality at the sight of the imposing facade of St. Cecilia's Cathedral. Soaring heavenward, its awesome splendor would have stunned those in the thirteenth century. Its power to impress remained. Nestled at the entrance to the structure, like a pup alongside its mother, was a once-fearsome building, the La Berbie Bishop's Palace. Now an impressive museum dedicated to Toulouse Lautrec, its colorful posters nearly erased the buildings history as the site of judge, jury and executioner of so many Cathars.

Albi, a bourgeois town, flaunting its middle-class comforts and ancient beauty, now bore little resemblance to the days of the Cathars. Although synonymous with their destruction, 'Cathar' had become, incorrectly, eponymous with 'Albigensian'. Dana knew that the town was predominately Catholic, not Cathar, during the thirteenth century. It's Bishop, Guillaume Peyre, however, was zealous and ambitious in using his castle to oversee the trials and destruction of many Cathars from throughout the Languedoc..

Albi was so camouflaged by modern prosperity that Dana found it hard to feel the level of deep sorrow that dependably overcame her at the ruined castles in the heart of the Cathar country. Albi's posh shops and bright banners, announcing current art displays and events, had successfully overlaid the energies of the past with the commerce of the present.

As they neared a parking lot located at a distance from the lot which fronted the cathedral, Dana glanced down at her skirt, questioning its Sunday appropriateness as she watched fashionable matrons hurrying for the service. Deciding that twenty-first century garb was anything from jeans to glitz, she turned to Eric and confirmed that she'd meet him back here after the service. A sudden frisson of intimidation filled her at his solemn demeanor. More intense than ever, he seemed weighted by the past, somehow jinxed at having donned the once-familiar, now fearsome, garb.

"I'm off, my..." Cowed by his priest pose, she bit back 'my love', giving him a little bow as she exited. "Good luck!"

Her words seemed to puncture his reveries. "Righto. I'll meet you back here around one o'clock." He remained in the car as she walked away without looking back.

Dana's inclination was to head for the museum, but caution reared its head. *I'd best avoid a destination that close to the cathedral,* she thought. Fortunately there were plenty of shops to explore. Some closed on Sunday, but others, more capitalistic, remained open to catch the tourist crowd. Dana darted across the square and rounded the corner into a prosperous avenue of shops, one more intriguing than the other. She stopped to look at a window display of colorful table-linens and tea towels.

Her focus was drawn to a cloth with a lovely pattern of rich blues and gold's. She deliberated about whether or not to go inside, examine it more closely, and buy it for her mother. With so much time to kill, she decided to enter the shop. As she turned to glance around before entering, she froze in place, her thoughts frantic. *There is a man, standing near the corner across the street, staring at me.* She returned her gaze to the window, studying his reflection. *No question about it. He is looking at me.*

To confirm it, she shook her head, glanced both ways along the street, and crossed over to look into a chocolate shop. Out of the corner of her eye, she noticed him dart around the corner just as she crossed. She entered the shop, hesitating for what seemed ages in front of an aromatic display of chocolates before buying a small assortment. Her exit from the store was as natural as she could make it. She glanced around, as if deciding which shop next, while covertly studying to locate the man among the growing crowd.

The man was apparently doing the same. He stood in front of a tobacconist window, his position allowing him full view of the chocolate shop. Dana remembered that just behind the street of shops lay many intricate alleyways. *Should I chance losing him in the labyrinth of passages?* No sooner had the question surfaced; she made a decision to go for it. It would force him to be much more visible in the less-trafficked back alleys. *Surely he wouldn't attempt anything ominous in such a busy city center as Albi?*

TWENTY

Eric felt anxious at the subtle stares from the growing crowd of parishioners that greeted his entrance into the Cathedral. The scent of the incense and the macabre paintings of writhing souls suffering in hell reminded him of how difficult he had found such a religion of fear and punishment.

He was relieved to locate Veronique so quickly, saving him from having to parade—antique garb on display—up and down the vast aisles as he scrutinized every likely-to-be-in-disguise-female.

It was undoubtedly true that her partner, Claudia, excelled in the dramatic arts. Veronique was clothed in solemn black, a scarf veiling her head. She'd added twenty years and as many pounds to her barely-thirty youthfulness, disappearing into the character of a grieving woman deep in prayer. It was her eyes—wide and blue and filled with flashes of intelligence impossible to hide—that drew him.

As he entered the pew, she removed her missal, allowing him to sit alongside her. The temptation to engage her in conversation was curtailed as she immediately returned to her penitent posture, lips softly moving in prayer. As Eric tried to focus on the young priest who was preparing to conduct the service, his thoughts returned to: C*an we pull this off?*

He'd rehearsed all the issues: the safety of Pierre, the need to identify the location of each manuscript, the hoped for use of Vals as the location for their teams meeting, the likelihood of Benjamin's involvement and, most importantly, the critical necessity for the team to get at the translations. Hesitant, he nevertheless had written the topics on a tablet the size of the pages of a missal. As the service began, he turned and, giving a slight nod to acknowledging her lack of a missal, placed his, its delicate contents visible, in her hands.

She whispered a polite "merci, pere" and began to read his script. A long sigh escaped, although no turn of her head or spoken words accompanied it. She studied the pages, closed the missal and resumed the posture of prayer.

A service that could seem interminable, today seemed too swiftly to draw to a close. As it did, Veronique passed the missal back to Eric, but not before covertly scribbling a hastily written note on the margin of his page. *"Meet me at the confessional in the rear of the cathedral."*

Veronique was the first to depart, handkerchief to her eyes. Eric, not wanting to chance being greeted by a fellow priest, moved quickly in her wake, joining her as she entered the confessional.

Isolated by a design calculated to respect the privacy of both, she began—her voice as soft as a confession, but far more rapid and deeply intense. "We must be brief so as not to be discovered. I am relieved about Pierre and trust he is safely hidden. Vals is a good choice for our gathering. It is as intensely guarded as the Pope himself. I am now in charge, however, and can grant the team special documents to enter—even, should you feel it safe enough, to remain for work on the translations." Her concern wavered at her next words. " I trust the original manuscripts will remain in bank vaults and not caves."

Eric whispered. "Quite so. Even having encrypted copies in Vals, puts all of them, and us, in great danger."

"Torture can accomplish all that our adversaries seek." Veronique's voice was barely discernable. "As to Benjamin, I know his methods. He is undoubtedly involved. But he doesn't act alone."

"We've proof of that. Be certain to destroy any notes, as will I. Will you arrange for 'clean' phones at Vals?"

"D'accord." Her voice lowered. "Contact me tomorrow regarding confirmation of each team members arrival in Vals."

"Right. By the way, Dana won't be part of the team at Vals."

Veronique's "where will she be" response was followed immediately by: "Never mind. Best I do not know. Offer my good wishes to her." A noise outside the cubicle silenced them. Eric waited as she parted the screened curtain, shook her head and put a finger to her mouth.

"Bless you, my child." Eric's whispered phrase accompanied her pious departure, head down as she vanished into the still-milling crowd headed for the doorways. Erik delayed his exit to burn his notes over a votive candle and allow time for Veronique to vanish before he Followed. Sweat trickled down his back as, looking neither right nor left, he proceeded with measured steps to the door.

Where is the nearest loo where I can shed this costume?." Eric remembered a WC in the museum. Memories returned as he neared. *This is where I listened to Benjamin announce his discovery of the Holy Grail.* The image brought back their unholy mix of intimacy—given they were staying at his home at the time—with the recognition of Benjamin's duplicity and the evil that lurked behind his seductive façade. *How enraged Benjamin must feel at the destruction of his reputation— and his once-handsome face?*

A quick glance revealed all urinals occupied, with no place to shed his robe. He headed for the car. A sense of urgency had him almost speed-walking as he reached the parking lot.

It wasn't hard to spot the bright red of their car, but he shook his head as he neared and saw no sign of Dana inside. He settled into the car, hunched down as he shed his priest robe and looked at his watch. 1:10. T*en minutes isn't unreasonable in this town. Its maze of streets could delay her.* The thoughts reassured him for all of ten minutes before they had mushroomed to: *Where could she be? Should I go after her? I never should have let her out of my sight.*

Glancing from one corner of the square to the other, he scanned the entire circumference. Unconvinced he'd observed it thoroughly, he left the car and walked about, staying within a reasonable circumference of the area. Just as he thought he couldn't bear the suspense a moment longer, he caught sight of her as she dashed from an alleyway across the road.

"Quick! Let's get out of here." Her voice broached no delay as she opened the door and slid below the dashboard, out of sight.

Eric's follow-through was as speedy as any chase scene in a film, worrying him that they'd surely be stopped by the local gendarmes. A swift glimpse at Dana convinced him to maintain his speed. Her duck-for-cover positioning was held until Eric gave her the all-clear. "We're well away from Albi. It's safe to unfold."

She eased herself carefully upright as she scanned all traffic to the right, left, back and front. Her hooded eyes, like a camera, kept everything and everyone in focus. It wasn't until they were nearing Revel that she responded to his question. "What happened?"

"I was followed. I decided to outsmart him by heading down an alleyway behind the main streets. After zigzagging through a maze of alleyways, I thought for sure I'd outmaneuvered him. But when I spotted him again, I dashed into a phone booth, crept down below the window and remained there for what seemed ages. My heart stopped when someone tugged at the phone booth door and I had to get up. I pretended that I'd dropped a coin, wanting to kiss the angry woman who stood outside. When I looked around and didn't see him, I made a mad dash, hoping I was headed for the parking area." She let out a long sigh of relief. "Never has anything looked lovelier than the red of our Twingo."

"How could I have ever agreed with your going off on your own?" The tension in Eric's voice underscored his question.

"But I'm fine." Dana panicked at his tone more than the words. "Stop and think about it. It's just another sign of our being guided." The caustic "humph" of his response, told her he wasn't convinced. "Eric, you can't really think I'd be in any less danger as a twosome? Capturing us together would be far more attractive and much easier a goal than having us go our separate ways. Plus, having us remain separate assures one of us coming to the aid of the other." She waited, uncertain as to her powers of persuasion as she studied him. The rigidity of his chin and the tightness of his lips wasn't encouraging.

"I hear the logic in what you say, but my emotions are running the show right now. I can't let you down as I did in the past. Can you understand?"

"That you're overcome by emotion, yes. But that you won't see the logic of my going, no."

A pall of silence fell over their journey. Dana's thoughts ran with certainty. *I must go. I will go.* She hoped, with a little time and distance, Eric's resistance would soften by the time she took off. It would free both of them from the heavy emotions of a contested departure. *Tomorrow*, she thought, *after Veronique's confirmation of the team's meeting place and time, she'd pack. That should give Eric time to reconsider.*

To block such emotions, Eric had pragmatically returned his thoughts to his list of to-dos. He scrutinized steps needed to notify Professor Marty that Pierre was safe. He suddenly remembered Pierre's request to notify Beatrice and reassure her that he was safely away at a convention. Marty could be contacted via a call to his neighboring phone booth. While public, it was actually located a short walk from his front door. It was making a connection with Pierre in time to schedule the team's meeting that frustrated him. *Perhaps*, he thought, *if I returned to the Arques Museum he'd spot the car and make contact. Why didn't he reveal his hideaway*?

Eric spun the car around, looking over at a bewildered Dana. "I decided to drive to Arques in the hopes that Pierre sees our car and makes contact. I know of no other way. We can't convene at Vals without him."

"Wouldn't our circling the area be a red flag to Benjamin or anyone else trailing us? They're bound to be watching Pierre's home and office. Professor Marty goes to the museum regularly. You could ask him to leave a note in the bus-stop box."

Eric took a deep breathe, slowing both his thoughts and the car. "You're right. But how about we head for Coustaussa, maybe find the little restaurant Pierre took us to when first we met? I don't want to return to the gite yet and Coustaussa should be safe. It's near enough to Arques without being on the main road. We then can weigh our odds of proceeding any further."

Dana nodded, darting her gaze around for a thorough scrutiny of their route as they neared the cut-off for Coustaussa. "I hope you get inspired as to where that restaurant is." Eric said. "I m feeling a need to talk through some ideas, but not at the gite." Her silence prompted him to slow down as they neared the intersection. "The turn is coming up. Are you game to look for the restaurant?"

"My stomach votes yes." Dana's nod of her head, along with her lets-make-up-smile, seconded it. "After Albi, I too could use a cool-down period."

As they made the turn and neared Coustaussa, Dana found her eyes magnetically drawn to the ragged remnant of its castle ruins, sparse evidence of its once great power and enduring mystery. She wondered if the restaurant, like Coustaussa castle, only existed in memory. Eric seemed more confident as he made a sharp turn down a narrow road. Slipping into low gear, the Twingo cautiously navigated a rocky creek-bed with water flowing across the roadway.

Once on dry ground, they rounded a narrow passageway overhung with tree boughs and saw the little café tucked along the creek. Its' moss-covered-cottage-look appeared like something out of a fairy-tale. They parked the car at a distance, obscured under a grove of trees and trudged along the riverfront until they reached the restaurant's entrance. The smell of heavenly pea soup, the crackle of a welcoming fire and the smile of the owner greeted them. Once at their table, they both grinned at the perfection of their decision.

Enchanted by the atmosphere and impressed by the superior skills of the chef, they ate with gusto, silent except for the initial clink of wine glasses. "To our success!" Of the four other diners and two dogs, only the dogs raised their ears in attention.

An after-dinner Armagnac helped loosen their anxiety and their tongues. "Dana, my love," Eric began, "I know how much you want to begin your Mary Magdalene shoot." He studied her silent poise of expectation. "As for writing my article, I don't need to accompany you to gather research." Her silence remained. "I've already read the biblical account, as well as books expanding on her possible relationship to Christ. But…"

Dana raised her glass, nervously downing a healthy swallow.

"Images of you going off on your own, perhaps followed by Benjamin, were tough to handle." He stared into his glass. "However, I'm persuaded that you'd be safer away than here and….He shook his head. "…I suspect you'd go anyway. So…"He drew a deep breath. "The bottom-line is: I'm willing to deal with my anxiety as long as you make contact daily."

Dana reached across the table and took his hand. "You'll know my whereabouts as reliably as if you were at my side." She let out a long sigh before adding, "I'll be just as eager for word of you and the team's success."

"Translating our manuscripts is crucial. Once accomplished, no matter the power of Benjamin or the Vatican, I know they will be defeated."

Dana gave a firm nod. "And I *know* that the treasure, the timing, the translations and my Mary Magdalene tour are somehow all connected." Dana's pensive look accompanied a shrug of her shoulders. "Beats me how, but the feeling is intense—a real "follow me" command. I'm convinced I'll soon discover my role in this."

A renewed sense of rightness—more sustaining than food—was followed by an awareness that their fellow diners had departed. Reluctantly, they paid the check, turned for a lingering look at the fire's dying embers, and walked out to their car.

As they reached the bottom of the hill, they stopped to study a lone woman bending over her hoe as she worked away at what looked to be a row of early-spring peas. Dana smiled as she turned to Eric. "Looks like it's the wife that keeps the restaurant supplied with fresh vegetables." No sooner had the words left her mouth, Dana whipped around to stare intently at a shape that suddenly stirred memories. Her eyes widened and her mouth opened. Before she could shout "Pierre!", the figure put a finger to its' mouth, followed by a beckoning motion.

Eric hesitated until Dana tugged his arm. "It's Pierre. Let's go!" They dashed across the tilled ground, with Eric stopping abruptly to assure himself that the garden area was out of sight of the restaurant and the dirt path revealed no dust-clouds of approaching cars. As they neared, Pierre vanished into a copse of trees that paralleled the rear of the garden.

Hop-scotching between rows of peas, they quickly joined Pierre under the tree's dense screen.

Pierre, finger to his mouth, silently led them over to a pile of boulders which effectively screened a small cave. Bending down, he beckoned them to follow. *Not so easy*, Eric thought as he tried to collapse his over six foot frame to squeeze through the opening. Dana fared a bit better, managing to avoid smashing her head against the ragged rock ceiling. Pierre led them about twenty feet into the farthest corner of the cave, pulled out a small flashlight and whispered, “Pull up a chair”, shining the light across a rock slab.

Dana perched alongside Pierre. “Is this *the* cave?” Her words were accompanied by a mounting sense of claustrophobia as the light went out, leaving them in the dark.

Pierre’s voice held a familiar touch of wry humor. “It’s good to see you too Monsieur Taylor and no, far from it—both literally and actually. This is the anteroom to my current hideaway, my bolt-hole in a pinch, so to speak. Whenever I get cabin fever, I don my matron gear to get a breath of fresh air and slip into my cave if I suspect anyone approaching.”

“Like our arrival. Coincidental or not, it’s timely, given we need to gather *all* the team together.” Eric’s tone held censure.

Pierre’s soft eyes and voice answered. “First things first. This meeting wasn’t planned. I didn’t expect you to remember the restaurant, let alone to return today. As your car approached I recognized it, confirmed its occupants and followed my instincts.”

“You call it instincts, Pierre, but I call it “guided.” Dana’s conviction echoed around the cave, prompting Eric’s response.

“Whatever led us to you, we need to take advantage and bring you up to speed.” Eric waited for Pierre to respond.

“Quite true. So on with the order of most importance.”

Eric began. “Number one was to locate you in time for our team meeting.” He reached for Dana’s hand. “I suspect that my intuitive partner must have put a whammy on fulfilling that request.”

After Eric explained their great good fortune in having Vals as a safe “office” for their work, Eric waited for Pierre’s response.

“We need to begin work, most definitely. Vals sounds compelling, but I’m concerned at having copies of the manuscripts *and* all of us gathered together, no matter how strict the security.”

“*All* gathered together, that is, except for me." Dana added. "I’ll soon depart to photograph our Mary Magdalene article.”

“*Very* interesting, my dear." Pierre’s soft emphasis held excitement. “Before I was accosted I made a provocative discovery. Woven among my manuscript’s text is an unusual reference to the Magdalene. I’m anxious to see if the other scrolls add to the mystery.” He turned to Eric, his voice more animated. “There’s something I need to show you. I believe I found a compelling theme that just may be linked to all four manuscripts."

Eric's "Really?" was matched by Dana's long "oh". It filled the cave, prompting Pierre to pat her cheek, a benediction coating his words. "If possible, we'll keep you posted of such ah-ha discoveries, my dear. Meanwhile, it is most important that you follow where the Magdalene leads." They felt him slide from his perch and stand. "Careful now. We must depart."

As all three exited the cave, Pierre brushed away a cobweb from Dana's hair before turning to Eric. "Don't chance coming back here. Let my cousin, Giraud, know when, where and how we convene. By the way, I contacted Giraud this morning and asked he notify Beatrice I'm attending a London conference. He knows how to safely relay a message—to her and to me."

Before stepping into a stretch of forest nearly as dark as the cave, Pierre planted a kiss on each of Dana's cheeks. "If all else fails, contact me via your psychic phone line, my dear. May God and the Magdalene watch over you." Before they'd cleared the forest and entered the sunshine of the field, Pierre had vanished, like the Cheshire cat, leaving only his smile to lead them deeper into their Alice in Wonderland labyrinth.

TWENTY-ONE

Eric's nerve-wracking pacing of their minimal living space underscored his anxiety. He looked from his watch to the clock on the wall. "It's ten to nine. Let's head over to the phone booth and give Veronique a try."

"I'm ready when you are." Dana was more than ready. *Anything to unleash my tiger from his cage,* she thought. She'd removed herself from his path by remaining upstairs to sort through all she needed to pack for the Mary Magdalene shoot.

She's decided to take her far more practical, and much less cumbersome, digital-camera, along with jeans, shirts and sweaters—and books. Her eagerness was, she knew, a response to a call that reached beyond photography.

Eric registered her state as Dana settled herself into the car, aware he now had a captured butterfly as a partner. He reached over and gave her the thumbs-up sign. "As soon as I get confirmation from Veronique that Vals is ours, you can pick up your rental car and be on your way."

As they neared the phone booth they noticed the village was unusually quiet for a Monday. Even the phone, well used by the villagers, had no one in sight. Eric didn't match such calm. He turned off the ignition and dashed for the booth. Dana sent up a silent prayer as he placed the call to Veronique. *Let the arrangements work perfectly.*

Waiting was difficult for Dana. She'd discovered early on that Eric was slow, thoughtful and deliberate—to the point of exasperation at times. She was impulsive, active and ten steps ahead of him, with the energy of a racehorse bolting from the gate ahead of the bell. She was learning to avoid frustration by taking brisk walks, a solution tempting her as she waited. But she decided against it as Eric hung up the phone and raised five fingers to signal his wait for a call back. He waited. She waited. An interminable eight minutes later, it rang. Dana cursed the move that angled Eric's expression out of her view.

As he replaced the receiver and turned to open the door, his jubilation radiated like a halo as he neared, pulled her out of the car and into his arms. "Never again will I question your belief that we are guided. Veronique, thanks to her recent promotion to head up the Vals project, has arranged for our team to appear tomorrow. She'll introduce us as experts who will allot the next two weeks to examining archaeological finds. She's not only assigned us a work area that mimic's a Brinks vault, but equally secure quarters with four bunk beds. Two whole weeks and the ideal safe-house for analyzing the manuscripts." His expression lit up with excitement as he turned back to the phone booth. "I'll give Giraud a call to let Pierre know we're on for tomorrow."

As he returned, a smile relaxing his features, Dana let loose an impossible-to-restrain: "Hooray! It feels as though a log-jam has given way."

"Right. With Giraud's contacting Pierre and Veronique notifying the Professor, all is moving forward." Eric started the car. "Speaking of moving forward, let's head for the rental agency and get your car. When we get there I'll fill you in a bit more." Dana nodded, relieved at the thought of soon getting underway.

The rental agency in Gaillac was efficient, the car perfectly matching Eric's request for a dependable car, no bright color. He smiled as they brought round a grey Peugeot. His actions took the dealer by surprise as Eric all but tore the seats apart in doing his inspection of the car. When the dealer went into his office to prepare the documentation, Eric drew Dana aside. "You should be fine with this car, but be sure to inspect it daily. Look for anything unusual in the visor, steering wheel, glove box, underneath, the wheel wells. You know the drill."

"Aye-aye partner." Dana rushed her follow through. "Do you need me to remain until you're sure everyone is safe at Vals?"

"No. Just follow me back to our gite and, whenever you're packed, you can load up and be on your way."

Her smile twinned his. "I feel like we're birds out of a cage."

"For the moment anyway. But once you're on your way, watch for any suspicious cars, persons and events."

Dana's assurances were interrupted as the rental agent approached. After exchanging a few formal courtesies they headed out the door. Aware that Eric had double-checked the car, she got in and patted the dash. "I dub you "Grey Ghost". Take me safely to my destination and safely home."

Eric shook his head. "And I dub you "Daft Dana." Anyone who thanks her washer and dryer, names her car, blesses it, and …"

"And blesses her partner, always and forever." Dana kissed her forefinger and reached through the open window to plant it on his lips. "Anyway, who are you to protest? You've spent nearly half a lifetime blessing everyone." She winked as she put the rental car in gear and prepared to follow their Twingo.

The glow faded as they reached their gite. Hope and anticipation suddenly clouded over with concern. As Eric helped her downstairs with her photography gear and suitcase, his expression grew anxious. The minute they were both outside he took her in his arms, reluctant to release her. "Remember to call every day. Veronique has lined up a cell phone for me that she swears is 'cleaned' daily."

"I memorized it already." Her comment made him smile as he imbedded her image on his retina.

Giving himself a brisk shake, he returned to more practical issues. "Do you have all your maps? What about your route? Are you clear about the roads?" Eric kept up a steady stream of questions as they stood at her car.

"Yes, yes and yes. I've laid out as straightforward a route as possible." She unfolded her map to her outlined route. "I should arrive in the village of Les Saintes-Maries-de-la-Mer tonight. After a day or so filming the area where the Magdalene landed in Provence, I'll continue on to Marseilles and up to Vezelay, stopping overnight in both cities." She looked up as Eric stared at her route.

The deep furrows in his brow, along with the nervous twisting of his ring—an Occitan cross duplicated on her ring finger—betrayed his anxiety. "Nothing can really part us, Dana. Always remember that."

Dana nodded her reassurance. "I'll call you the minute I check into my chambre d'hote.

Eric's frown remained as he reached for her map and began doing a mental calculation of the kilometers. "It's nearly four o'clock. Consider stopping in Bezier or Montpellier. You'll have a wide choice of gites and be well rested for your drive to Les Saintes-Maries-de-la-Mer in the morning."

"Perhaps you're right. It would also allow time for a nice dinner and some reading."

Eric grinned and rushed back to their gite. "Speaking of reading, I bought you the Sunday New York Times." I know you love it." Eric returned with the bulky paper, wedging it securely on the floor of the back seat. "Now, one more thing." He held out a tissue wrapped offering in his hand.

"What is it?" She smiled as she tore through the paper which held a necklace—a large Occitan cross—matching her ring.

Eric reached over and pressed a hidden mechanism which opened its cover to reveal a miniature recorder. "It's to capture your thoughts, feelings, whatever, as you're filming." As her eyebrow raised, he added, "It's easy, powerful and it will add to my article."

She smiled as she hooked it around her neck. "Thanks. It's perfect."

"That should about do it. I'll await your phone-call." Eric said as she nodded, turned the key in the ignition, and with a blown kiss, tried not to pull out of their driveway with the impulsive eagerness she felt.

Even with her automatic surveillance of cars on the road, Dana maintained a feeling of optimism at getting underway. *To what?* She trusted it would soon be revealed.

In no time she neared the autoroute de deux mer, the main artery across the south of France. Merging with traffic from several directions, she was propelled onto the speedway, instantly caught up in a tour de France feeling of racing East-Southeast toward her destination.

I'll never be able to survey the vehicles around me and remain alive, she thought. Her concerns eased at the equally difficult task of anyone following. Dozens of vehicles merged, exited, stopped to pay tolls and veered off for the overhead cafes. Like wild Russian dancers, following such steps would prove impossible.

The sign for the off-ramp to Bezier arrived sooner than she'd expected. She didn't even consider Eric's suggestion to stop there. *He should know I'd never want to spend a night in Bezier.* One of the more horrific acts of the Inquisition was the destruction of Bezier, with the massacre—not only of Cathars—but Catholics as well.

Dana looked out at the long-ago restored town, now prosperous and peaceful. Standing proudly on a promontory of rock, it overlooked the River Orb. During the thirteenth century, Beziers was ruled by Viscount Raymond Roger Trencavel, a valiant young Lord. Believing that the occupants of Bezier—a predominantly Catholic town—would be safe, Trencavel returned to protect Carcassonne.

The attack of Bezier, led by Arnaud Amaury, a henchman of Simon de Montfort, was merciless and undiscriminating. When asked by his soldiers how they might discriminate between Bezier's Catholics and Cathars, Amaury replied: "Slay them all. God will recognize his own." The hundreds that took refuge in the Cathedral of St. Nazaire—gathering around the Catholic priest—all met with hatchets and swords.

Dana sighed as she recalled the young Trencavel. Although offering himself to save Carcassonne, he died betrayed by his captors. The tragedy of the young lord's death haunted her as she gave one last glance over her shoulder before leaving Bezier behind.

As the speedometer exceeded the posted limits, she slowed, glad to be entering countryside. The vineyards dotting the route were bright with spring green, catching the rays of a setting sun. She glanced at the time, pleased to see she'd made a good distance in the two hours since leaving their gite. *I should get to Montpellier at about seven o'clock. Eric's right. I'll stop there. A good room, good meal and time to catch my breath.*

In less than an hour she pulled off of the autoroute and headed into a city which was larger than it looked on the map. Not needing petrol, she headed for a supermarket parking lot to review her list of chambre d'hotes. Maintaining her vigilance, she had scrutinized the cars that had exited with her, paying particular attention to any who continued along the route she'd chosen. Relief flooded her at the discovery that none had followed her into the supermarket lot. Such a level of surveillance, she discovered, was daunting, especially without Eric.

No one looked suspicious, she thought as she focused on the hotel listings for Montpellier. She noticed a starred entry for a chambre d'hote on the southeastern side of the city. *Good, she thought, closer to the autoroute and away from the city traffic*. A few minutes of calculating her location in relationship to the hotel and she prepared to drive on. She balanced watching for anything unusual with looking for the turn-off to her inn.

Two kilometers later she spotted a sign. "Château de Nuit--un kilométrer a droite." Dana was reassured by the semi-rural nature of the road as she made a right hand turn that soon led to a Swiss chalet-style building set off the road. She smiled to see a restaurant prominently anchored at the near side. As she entered the concierge smiled, practicing his minimal English as he noted her accent. "One room for one night. Very good, mademoiselle. I have a special one. Tres charmant."

As he led her up a short stairway, he mentioned that dinner would be served until nine o'clock in the café. She thanked him and her luck at finding a perfect chambre d'hote. Her room was perfect. It looked out onto the back garden, a willow tree etching its graceful fronds against a background of darkening sky. The room's interior contained a desk and chair opposite the double bed. She sat down on the bed, testing its comfort as well as that of its generous feather pillows. The pillows prompted a sudden rush of ten month old memories. She frowned, remembering her previous habit of traveling with her favorite down pillow and a photo of her fiancé,

Alex, in a silver frame that usually held a romantic note he'd tucked inside. The pain of his infidelity had destroyed two significant relationships in her life—Alex and Evie—her best friend and Alex's secret lover.

Angry at the strange resurfacing of a pain she thought she'd long dealt with, she chalked such thoughts up to her brain somehow needing to distract her from far more crucial concerns. Smiling, she withdrew her few clothes, hanging up her jeans, tops and sweaters, and the one skirt she'd packed for church visits. She tossed her favorite yoga outfit under a pillow where it did double duty as pajamas. Checking her camera bag, she reached within an inside pocket to retrieve—not the silver-framed dazzle of a photograph of a jerk—but a snapshot of she and Eric, smiling against a backdrop of the spires of Carcassonne.

She glanced at her watch. Seven thirty. Her anticipation was fast fading into tiredness. She decided to go down for dinner, trusting a glass of wine to mellow her into an early bed and some reading. After freshening up, she laid out her clothes for an early departure tomorrow and headed for the restaurant.

A lovely trout, broccoli, potatoes, camembert and a glass of Beaujolais to toast her solid beginning, primed her for what lay ahead. On reentering her room, she called Eric and reported her safe arrival in Montpellier. More than that they couldn't discuss, but their confidence came through. After hanging up, she reached for the New York Times. She decided to treat herself to one section a day, starting with the front page. Eager to catch up on world news—last Sunday's or not—she scanned the first section. A photo jumped out at her, turning her cat at the cream smile into a gasp. It was the man with Benjamin. The article described him as a U.S. politician—not just *any* politician, but a front runner in the 2008 race for President. His upcoming trip to France and Italy was undertaken in order to enhance his international expertise.

Dana shivered as she put the paper aside. "What is he doing visiting Benjamin Carter?" She tried to put the question out of her mind. Grabbing the books she'd brought, she continued immersing herself in the life of the Magdalene—prepared for whatever awaited.

Reading until the threshold of dawn, sleep finally descended, bringing—not a beatific blessing from her tour guide—but a cascade of nightmarish images of duplicity and doom.

TWENTY-TWO

As he replaced the phone, the Overseer stared off into the distance, his look one of satisfaction at having put into place a contingency team as well as having check-mated Cardinal Ezerski.

The young cardinal was one in a long line of priests who felt they could bring a fresh breath of air and a new direction to the Catholic Church. The Overseer shook his head at Father Bruce's lack of wisdom. A conservative foundation is what the Church and its parishioners depended upon. It was a workable formula that had established the Church on the solid foundation that had allowed it to endure for centuries past and centuries yet o come. *I for one,* he thought, *shall bring all my power to bear to make certain that the Church continues to prevail throughout history—without brash newcomers with inclusiveness on their minds.*

He knew that the Vatican had experienced more such free thinkers of late; but after a few setbacks they all seemed eventually to fall into line. Ezerski was different. A rebel, he'd even had the audacity to question the Overseer on the nature of his projects. *Too big for his britches, he'd bear watching,* the Overseer thought.

He returned his focus to more important things—the manuscripts. Convinced that the fastest way to obtain them was through Dana Palmer and Eric Taylor, he knew he had to establish a strong back-up team and strategy to succeed if—when?—Benjamin Carter failed.

The Overseer let out a long sigh. *As with Ezerski*, he thought, *emotional men were more apt to trip over themselves with their uncontrolled passions.*

He considered the tenuous alignment with Benjamin Carter. He'd recognized quite clearly that the man's passion was definitely uncontrolled. He was so focused on revenge, so filled with hate that he thought too little, acted too fast and promised too much. The Overseer poured himself a brandy, sipping it slowly as he thought of the hit-man team—known unofficially as The Invisibles—waiting in the wings to clean up Benjamin's messes. He'd agreed that they could begin to target the prey and be prepared for the day when the Overseer let them off their leashes and bid them bring in Dana Palmer.

Using such a team was always his ace in the hole. Their skills were so finely honed that they came out of nowhere, knowing—like a lion targeting its prey—when to pounce, when to wait, when to lure their target away to an unprotected area and when to complete the kill and vanish safely without even a rumor of their existence.

Expensive yes, but worth every million they required. The Overseer gave a slight shiver as his thoughts toyed with just what countries, individuals and assignments they were responsible for and whether or not he might someday be in their sights. Not possible, he concluded, no one in the Vatican would have any reason to destroy the one individual that assured the Church functioning so perfectly that no matter what the latest scandal—he gnashed his teeth at the pedophilia uproar—the Church managed to surmount it at the least and prevail victorious in many cases.

He looked forward to the successful outcome of what would go down as one of his most remarkable undertakings—the "Q" Project. The quest had gone on for centuries, with rumors of the manuscripts having shown up in Jerusalem, Rome, Rennes and, of course, with the Cathars. Even the Inquisition hadn't been able to ferret them out. But he, the Overseer would prevail—at long last succeeding in unraveling a mystery that had forever baffled history's wisest.

Dana would be the perfect bait, he thought. *Like a rabbit, she'd bounce along unaware of her pursuers.*

TWENTY-THREE

Traffic was already heavy at 6 A.M. Dana noticed that most cars were headed toward the west, leaving her lanes just busy enough to keep her alert. Dana had followed Eric's reminder by inspecting her car thoroughly before taking off and maintaining a regular scan for suspicious vehicles. As long as the traffic wasn't increasing, she found she could do the latter almost automatically, allowing her mind to review last night's readings of the life of Mary, called the Magdalene—the watchtower.

The Mary Magdalene of the Bible was—or at least had been created to be—a rather indeterminate figure. Mentioned several times, her role was officially discounted in the year 591, when Pope Gregory I proclaimed her to be a sinner—having grappled with seven devils—and confirmed her character as that of a prostitute. His powerful edict intentionally obscured any valid scrutiny of evidence for her more significant role. *Why such fear?*

Dana let out a long sigh as she watched the sun come up and framed a special request of her trip: *At the very least, don't let me leave this assignment still feeling as though Mary Magdalene was a cardboard character, dismissed by the Bible and now made so much of by current fans that she remained as someone apart.*

A sign shifted her thoughts: N313 up ahead. She slowed, entered the right lane and exited to the toll booth. Three cars and one truck followed suit, but two made the next turnoff. Two cars followed, but a few kilometers later, at the point at which she turned onto N572, they continued south. Although she'd considered taking more direct country roads to her destination, she balked when she saw how little were the lanes and how many perplexing offshoots. Staying with the manageable highway, she continued toward Arles. A growling stomach decided her to stop there.

An hour later, as the clock neared 8:00 she pulled into a little café. No followers, few customers and great coffee, it gave her a quiet space to revisit her notes from last night. Her reading clarified the Church's decision to take drastic measures to shield any close scrutiny of Mary Magdalene's true role—Jesus' devoted consort, companion—wife.

What evidence pointed to such a conclusion? Dana reviewed some of the damning evidence: It was unheard of for a Jewish man—let alone an heir to the House of David—to remain unmarried; the Messianic line of the House of David dictated marriages and procreation times; Jesus' mother, Mary's, behavior at the Wedding of Cana, when she asked Jesus to provide more wine, were actions to be taken only by the groom. In all important respects, both the role by Jesus' mother at the festive occasion and the behavior of Mary Magdalene, were those of mother of the groom and bride to her husband, Jesus; Mary Magdalene's regular presence with Mary, the mother of Christ, Martha, the sister, and Lazarus, the brother; her vigil at the crucifixion; her singular appearance at the tomb. All were actions of a wife.

Dana sighed, checking her watch to confirm that she'd best finish her petit dejeuner. She'd soon arrive at the little village of Les Saintes Maries de la Mer.

Much evidence indicated that Mary Magdalene landed there, living her life out in the Provence area. As Dana devoured the last few crumbs of her croissant, she remembered how convincing an ancient manuscript—*The Life of Mary Magdalene*–written by the Catholic Archbishop Rabanus Maurus, proved to be. He described the Magdalene's journey and her arrival at Les Saintes Maries de la Mer as well as many of her actions during her lifetime in France. As persuasive as the account by the Archbishop was, it was only one of many books which described Mary's dangerous journey. A Ninth Century account was reputed to have been copied from a Second Century original, most likely written—according to the best historical data— by Hegesippus. All tell of Mary's departure in 42A.D. Traveling by way of boat—most likely stopping at Alexandria—she arrived at her destination—a landing place a little west of Marseilles. *Why had I never heard of such a thing before?* Dana kept asking as she learned that, in addition to written accounts, there existed equally as much validation in the art world, which illustrated scenes from Mary's arrival and her active life in Provence.

She hadn't arrived alone. Many accompanied her on her journey: Mary, Martha, Simon-Lazarus, Joseph of Arimathea, Philip, the Apostle and his companion, Trophimus—later to become St Trophimus—the Bishop of Arles. In addition, there were Jesus' sisters, Sarah-Salome and Mary Jacob Cleophas, along with Helena-Salome, the consort of Simon Lazarus. *How then can so many remain so ignorant of such information?* Dana carried that thought with her as she returned to the car, shaking her head over the Church's success in erasing the evidence available. *What were they afraid of?*

Somehow it was easier to examine that question in the shelter of her car. She began by addressing some provocative but less incendiary evidence. The Gnostic Gospels of Mary, Thomas and Peter provided a flurry of debate over their description of Mary Magdalene as a woman revered for her wisdom as a disciple, along with evidence of her fellow disciple's jealousy at seeing her husband, Jesus', devotion. "He was always kissing her on the "mouth" (presumably; the word was illegible) and Mary's ultimate escape to France, accompanied by Jesus' family. She continued long years of teaching and preaching throughout Provence. While controversial, the most alarming evidence in answer to her question lay within the various accounts indicating that Mary Magdalene had borne children by Jesus—*as he was destined to do.*

John the Baptist, in Acts 5-7, proclaimed: "Jesus must increase, but I must decrease." The translation of the Hebrew text meant that Jesus must have a son.

It was just such evidence of his human nature that had kept her awake last night. Such speculation grew, compounded by the special mystery of one of Mary's fellow passengers—a daughter, born in A.D.33. Reputed to be the offspring of Jesus of Nazareth, Mary would ultimately give birth, some records indicate, to a second and a third child—both sons. *How could this be if Christ died on the cross in AD33?*

He didn't die on the cross, Dana thought, having grappled with evidence which suggested a different scenario. Pilate wanted to free Jesus, but the Jews cried, "Crucify him!" Documents from Nag Hammadi explain that there was a substitution made of one Simon the Cyrene. Jesus is quoted: "As for my death—which was real enough to them—it was real to them because of their own incomprehension and blindness." The Islamic Koran states: "Yet they slew him not, neither crucified him, but he was represented by one in his likeness…they did not really kill him." A 2nd. Century historian, Basilides of Alexandria, wrote that the crucifixion was stage-managed with Simon the Cyrene used as a substitute.

To understand his ability to survive, Dana investigated the many records that suggest a likely strategy. Because of the approaching Sabbath, Christ was on the cross for a much shorter period of time; a potion was administered via a sponge; he alone escaped without having his legs broken. Removed from the cross by Joseph of Arimathea—early due to the Sabbath—Christ was placed in a tomb Joseph had prepared. When Mary Magdalene met Christ in the sepulcher, Jesus was recovering from an antidote, "a mixture of myrrh and aloes, about a hundred pound weight, a purgative to counteract the poisonous venom which had been administered in order to replicate death."

And what became of him? Dana wondered. *Many theories existed as to Jesus' ultimate journeys in India and Egypt—but what of his fathering children—and might he have accompanied Mary Magdalene to France?*

Her last question was followed by an awareness of having lessened her scrutiny of any suspicious cars that might be following. After redoubling her task, she returned to thoughts of whether or not Jesus accompanied Mary to Provence, smiling at a whimsical thought. *Since there wasn't any such thing as a photo ID, possibly an escaped Jesus could have posed as Lazarus, or?*

She tentatively turned to the more serious issue of Jesus' lineage. Information indicated a birth of Jesus' daughter in A.D.33, followed by the birth of Jesus' first son, named Jesus II, in A.D. 37, followed by a third son, Josephus, in A.D.44. By Hebrew law, the lineage of the House of David strictly dictated the sequence of births: the second child was to appear at the Time of Restitution, AD 37—which must be followed by six years of celibacy before the birth of the third child in A.D.44.

Dana gave a vigorous shake of her head, feeling an unbearable state of theory-overload as she thought: *No one can ever know the whole truth about whether Christ survived the crucifixion, was married or fathered children. Or for that matter*, Dana decided, *whether his lineage continued through the Merovingian rulers of France and beyond.* She decided that Jesus, as a physical human, ate, slept, wept, defecated and, in all probability, engaged in sexual union—and that it didn't really matter. *What matters*, she thought, *is what he learned and what he taught about the nature of Spirit and our connection to God. Only by living his teachings could one hope to penetrate the divine wisdom he tried to communicate.*

Replacing conjecture with practical actions—*and just in time*—Dana thought as she spotted a sign indicating Les Saintes Maries de la Mer was just ahead. She slowed at the exit, whispering: "I'm here, MM. Whatever your reason for my urgent arrival, I trust it will include fewer questions and more answers."

Dana studied the few cars that followed. She decided to stay with her strategy of pulling into a public place—this time a petrol station—and watch for any cars that may have followed. A sigh of relief escaped at no sign of suspicious vehicles. Before departing, she studied the location of the hotel she had chosen. It was fairly close to the sea and, blessedly, only a short distance from the highway exit. Eager to check-in early, she wanted to get started on perfect sites. Not only for the best photographs, but, hopefully, those that would capture an echo of the woman who arrived here.

She drove slowly, glancing out at the sea while thinking, *Les Saints Maries de la Mer, resting on the shores of the Gulf of Beauduc, would have provided a natural harbor—even in the days of Christ.* It took her awhile to turn her focus from the harbor to the village streets, eyes widening in astonishment at the bright banners and notices posted everywhere. "You brought me here in time for the festival!" Dana exclaimed, in shock at only now registering the coincidence of her arrival on May 23, the beginning of three days of an annual Festival honoring the young girl, known as Saint Sarah, the Egyptian, and her companions, the three Mary's that had arrived in AD 42.

Legend suggests that the young Sarah, the designation referring to "princess" in Hebrew, was no more than ten, a child of Jesus born after Mary's flight to Alexandria. Sarah, like the princes of the Davidic line, is symbolically black to indicate the state of the Sangraal's bloodline: Mary Magdalene, the *chalice,* along with her progeny, all represented as "unrecognized."

That would account for the many black Madonna's in the South of France as well as throughout Europe. Dana thought, mulling over one more piece of the growing puzzle of the Magdalene as Holy Grail, the Merovingians, Rennes le Chateau, the Cathars and the Gnostic teachings in general.

As she drove into the hotel's parking area, she knew the mysteries were all connected by a threatening "secret of secrets" that would surely undermine the established religious world. A colorful poster of the Magdalene greeted her as she entered the hotel's lobby. The smile seemed to beam a message of even more colorful mysteries ahead.

TWENTY-FOUR

Eric stared at his cell-phone, feeling reassured, having de-bugged it every day, but frustrated at its silence. *Dana should have arrived in Les Saints Maries de la Mer by now,* he thought. From the moment the team halted for lunch he'd waited for the phone's ring.

Glancing around their subterranean "office", Eric reexamined Dana's belief in their being guided. He'd have to agree that his being able to contact everyone and their being able to arrive safely, each with flash drive copies of their manuscript, was a miracle. Even with preliminary attempts at translations, the team had come up with some provocative clues.

Among the most baffling was the fact that each contained a prologue in a different language: Greek, Hebrew, Aramaic and Coptic. Translations of the prologues seemed to parallel one another in their message, which described the contents as being meant "only for those who can hear." The prologue ended with a string of symbols found in all four manuscripts. The continuing text of all four manuscripts were written in Ancient Greek. *Truly all Greek to me,* Eric thought. *But even baffling to Pierre and the Professor as they labored to translate them.*

Eric recalled Pierre's frustration as he worked on comparing the other manuscripts to his, confident that the theme of "light" would appear throughout each and thereby lead to enlightenment as to the nature of the treasure.

Instead, the other three manuscripts seemed to contain a different element as their theme: earth, water, fire. Suddenly any hope for a straightforward formula for translation became mired in an alchemical mix that made the "recipe" indigestible. "Merde", "damn" and other expletives peppered the air. Professor Marty had finally tempered the atmosphere with what was meant to be an off-handed comment to his teammate.

"I've seen this before in an ancient codex that was saved from the Library of Alexandria. Whenever something was too incendiary for direct discourse, they buried it in symbolism. It looked a whole lot like this."

Pierre smiled and headed back to his computer, eagerly and endlessly searching for clues to the encoding..

Eric mindlessly continued chewing on a croque monsieur sandwich. He stared into a space created as an office-cum-home for the team for the next two weeks. Their cramped quarters in the bowels of Vals were so filled with computers, books, equipment for translating ancient texts and other more sophisticated scanning methods, that they scarcely had space for the lunch Veronique had just brought in. It had served to break the intensity of everyone's focus except for Eric's.

Eric's pensiveness was penetrated, not so much by Pierre's voice as by the hand placed on his shoulder. "What's the news from Dana? You're staring a hole into that cell-phone."

"It should ring any minute." His look held concern. "I'm anxious at how to communicate some sense of our status—but safely."

"Avoid anything that puts our manuscripts and ourselves in danger." Pierre studied Eric to see if his words had penetrated. "We can't be overly cautious."

A frown accompanied Eric's nod of agreement. "I know; as does Dana. I've come up with phrases such as: "My work is proceeding well. I hope yours has been equally successful." He looked at Pierre for confirmation. His teammate's frown revealed uncertainty.

Professor Marty joined them, having caught the nature of their worried expressions. "I agree with Pierre. The least said, the greater the likelihood we have of pulling this off. Not to mention surviving long enough to do so." He sat down alongside them. "My excitement is so intense that I can't eat." He patted his once-expanding waist. "What a way to diet—digesting only the content of the manuscripts." Professor Marty rose and gave a little salute. "I'm back to my favorite repast."

Eric and Pierre echoed their intent to join him soon. Their antidote to worry was work. Eric envied Professor Marty and Pierre's knowledge of Hebrew, Greek and Latin. Veronique's strong suit was her understanding of the archeological significance and the scientific techniques. She was currently busy comparing them with some original texts dating back to the same period—the first or second century AD. Eric's focus wasn't the language translation, but the methods used to bury information between arcane symbols appearing in all four manuscripts. While Pierre and Professor Marty were frustrated at their baffling presence in what they'd hope would be straightforward text, Eric was as excited as a kid gifted with a train as he tried out various codes that might provide the key to a meaningful sequence.

His fascination with ancient methods of imbedding arcane information began early, ignited by his father's work hiding critical information during World War Two. For awhile Eric became steeped in Egyptian manuscripts, attempting to understand their hieroglyphs and fascinated by the comparison with the languages on the Rosetta stone. Their manuscript's prologue seemed to contain a mini-Rosetta stone he determined to break. His current passion was so keen that he was trying to learn, not only ancient Greek and Hebrew, but a smattering of the ancient Coptic language—an unusual translation of the spoken Egyptian language. Its etiology fascinated Eric when he learned that Coptic was a melding, using the Greek alphabet for Egyptian symbols which were, of themselves, representations of various vocal sounds.

Although Eric had no ability translating ancient Greek, Hebrew, Coptic or Aramaic, the deciphering of the mixture of strange symbols related to no known language was right up his alley. Their mystery had him resurrecting information on a means of deciphering the symbols that the treasure was imbedded in and determining which codes may be applicable. He'd burned the midnight oil—eyes and brain on burn-out from his painstaking review of complex codes.

Initially, partly because of his research on the Templars and their tie-in with the Rennes le Chateau treasure, he considered the code that had helped to translate the inscription on the tomb in Rennes. It was a complex decipherment using the key, MORT epee, followed by a knight's tour of two chess boards. But, given that the inscription and the translation method were in French, and the message proved impossible to retranslate into more ancient languages, he soon moved on to other codes.

The Atbash Cipher next drew him, especially due to the fact that it was in Hebrew, one of the secondary languages of the manuscripts. Seemingly less complex, it consisted of a folding in half of the Hebrew alphabet—twenty-two letters—so that Aleph comes opposite Taw, creating a completely different message. He held its possibilities in great awe and considered it worthy of a try. But other even more elegant codes had arrived in latter years, such as the Visigoth decipher used in Henrri Boudet's book. Eric felt its application warranted consideration, but only as an alternate choice.

And yet, despite many geniuses working diligently on complex codes, Eric felt daunted by his awareness of the many texts that, to this day, remained untranslatable: Linear A, the Etruscan alphabet, the Phaistos disc and various ancient texts which had no Rosetta stone to aid in solving them. Eric shuddered. *Don't let our manuscripts fall into the "untranslatable" category.*

Pierre had tried to shore his teammate up with his belief that, since the text was predominately written in ancient Greek, they surely fell within one hundred years fore or aft of the First Century and, like much of the writings of the Essenes, used allegorical codes, often positioned as parables and, as was theirs, prefaced by "*...known only to those who could hear*:"

"We'll find a way to "hear" the right formula, Eric my friend." Pierre and Eric had agreed to "listen as well as look." Overnight it seemed to have become their credo.

I'm ready to listen. Why hasn't she called? Eric thought, his attention returning to a more pressing mystery. No sooner had it been formed than his question was answered with the sound of a Bach refrain. He yanked the cell phone open, calling "Dana?" before she had a chance to say "Hello".

"I'm here and all is going well. There's is not a lot to say for the moment. I'm about to begin my photo-shoot soon. Hopefully the shots will capture exactly what our article needs. That's about it. My journey thus far has been uneventful."

Eric could tell from her matter-of-fact account that she too was avoiding any mention of specific names of towns, times and outcomes. As limited as that made their conversations, his main focus was on hearing her voice and knowing she was alive and well

He tried to replicate her neutral manner as he relayed his prepared text. Hearing his anemic tone, he added a lift to his voice. "That's about it. Now that I've heard from you, I can return to work with renewed inspiration. This article is shaping up to be the most successful of the three."

"That sounds great, Eric. If my photos match your text, I'll be pleased."

"Just keep well and call me daily."

Their loving sign-offs sounded frustratingly incomplete, Eric thought as the call ended. But the sound of her voice had renewed him enough to return to work with added vigor.

As Eric approached, Pierre could tell that Dana had called and all was well. "Now let's get down to business. I've found some interesting connections within the manuscripts." He reached out to scroll down until his computer screen highlighted a few pages of diagrams on the screen in front of them. Pointing to some highlighted Hebraic text, he moved down to a segment designated *Manuscript Two* which had the same curious diagrams. "We've transcribed some of the Greek text—not that it has revealed any epiphanies thus far—so we've begun to try to coordinate the Greek text in one manuscript with that in the other three. We've started with a comparison of references to some known names: Herod, Torah, Moses, and—as Dana would appreciate—Mary Magdalene. Problem is, the names we could puzzle out, but the method of connecting the names with any meaningful message was a different story. It had us coming and going until Professor Marty mentioned the possibility of trying equidistant letter sequencing used in deciphering buried messages in the Torah." Pierre watched as Eric remained silently fixed on the text, his eyes widening. "Since arcane codes are your baby, Eric, we're hoping you've heard of that one."

"The Bible Code" is what you're referring to. And yes, I've heard of it, first as a skeptic, but I was converted into a believer when I replicated the computer programs using the technique both on the Torah and on *Gone With the Wind,* among other books. Only the Bible revealed clear and verifiable information, unobtainable with any other publication. Back in 1997, Michael Drosnin came out with a very thoroughly researched book: *The Bible Code*. It hit the best seller list. The author was acclaimed for his thoroughness. Given his reputation as a skeptical reporter, he approached it in an unbiased, pragmatic and rational manner, focusing only on corroborating the facts." Eric frowned. "The use of the Code—as amazing as the examples were—actually revealed future events as amazing as the assassination of Israel's Prime Minister-Yitzhak Rabin." Eric paused, his pursed lips revealing his doubts before he spoke. "However, Drosnin's efforts to prevent such an outcome proved unsuccessful. Fate and Rabin's determination fulfilled the message."

"Are you saying, it isn't worth a try?" Pierre looked incredulous.

"No; but Drosnin's application was focused on using the Code on the Torah—the first five books of the Old Testament—a much older document, believed to have been authored by God himself. I suspect ours weren't so divinely inspired." Eric stared off into space. "It doesn't even reference the name Jesus. It will prove complicated to try it on four different manuscripts but, if you insist, I'm willing to give it a go. If it works at all, it should have some provocative messages."

Pierre's usually unshakeable expression of calm, had turned into a mix of excitement and concern. "You're saying that Drosnin's book described the translation of a message hiding for three thousand years and that by using the Bible Code, clearly indicated the future assassination of Prime Minister Yitzhak Rabin." Pierre let out a long sigh, followed by clenching his jaw as he stared at the computer. "Given that extraordinary example, we must at least try it on our four texts."

"Look. No promises. But I actually have the program loaded on my computer, which, by the way, was the invention that finally allowed for the discovery of the Bible Code." Eric gathered up the print-outs of pages of the manuscripts. "Are these all that we have printed of the existing text?"

"They're just the one's I've been working with. We've loaded our encrypted manuscripts on each computer but have only managed to examine the first six pages of each manuscript. I've taken manuscript two as my primary focus. Veronique has done a preliminary review of three, the professor four and you have manuscript one. After copying the manuscripts we each have approximately twenty two pages of text to review. Right, Professor?"

Pierre looked over at Professor Marty, huddled over his work with such intensity that he hadn't registered his teammates excited dialogue. "Right. I'm about ready to throw up my hands. My text isn't getting me anywhere." As Eric and Pierre moved to have a look, the Professor sighed as he scrolled down his pages, shaking his head. "I might as well be trying to translate a nightingale's song."

"I hear you." Eric smiled as he examined the Professor's text. "A good analogy and, speaking of which—I may be barking up the wrong tree—Pierre here thinks we should try the Bible Code—adapting its procedure for a trial run on the combined texts of all four manuscripts."

"The Bible Code, huh. From what I've heard of it, you have set yourself a daunting task, I'd say—with or without that state of the art computer program of yours." The Professor walked close enough to stare down at Eric's computer screen. "You do understand that the successful application of the Bible Code requires, not only all the text to be in ancient Hebrew, but every Hebrew letter must be linked together." He looked up at Eric and shook his head. "I'd say you're in for the most complex acrostic puzzle times four—with a translation level at *x* times infinity. But, dead-end as it may prove to be, I'll volunteer to help you set it up."

Eric smiled. "What better focus could we apply ourselves to than to test its value, one way or the other. At the same time, we can proceed to examine a couple of other codes that may fill the bill." Eric smiled up at Pierre. "Thanks for your inspiration." He then turned back to the Professor. "I'll help you get the copies ready, Professor. Let's hope that, when I've run them, the Bible Code may give us some intriguing melodies."

Eric was so consumed that around minute, long after the others had adjourned to their cubicles for rest, he remained at his computer. Print-outs of text floated across, around and beneath his desk. At the first light of dawn he must have fallen asleep at his desk. He jerked upright, coming out of a heavy dream with the words "...for those who can hear" and "in the beginning was the Word" ringing through his mind.

TWENTY-FIVE

Standing outside her chambre d'hote, Dana looked down the village street, scenting, if not seeing, the cool, briny bouquet of sea. Too eager to consider eating, and relieved to have had her conversation with Eric, she felt anxious to get started with her photo shoot.

As she confirmed her gear: lenses; telephoto zoom, wide angle, and macro; tripod for special shots; flash cards—each one capable of hundreds of shots—and extra batteries, she gave thanks for the invention of the digital camera. Not only had it eliminated heavy cameras and so much of the paraphernalia that accompanied them, but it allowed for greater flexibility and speed. She could, and did, take unlimited photos, uploading them to her laptop computer for late hours editing. For extra safety, she even uploaded them to a master website as a back-up holding tank.

After securing her priceless—literally and figuratively—Nikon, she set her steps due south. Her walk wound her through the village and brought her quickly to the sight of the sea. Like many small seaside villages, its beachfront wasn't conducive to magazine shots of swim-suit clad models. A fishing harbor, lined with boat-landing slips, little cafes, rocky sands and not much warmth, had few bathers. *Probably tourists from Denmark who think our May breeze an arbiter of suntans,* Dana thought.

The thought took her by surprise, not the logic of the conclusion, but her use of the word "our". Dana smiled, knowing that it went beyond her label as a "Francophile". *But few knew just how much beyond; certainly not her more accurate descriptor: "Cathar".* As she reviewed her thought, an added dimension insinuated itself; the possibility of the "our" referring to Mary Magdalene. "Are you here?" she whispered as her smile brightened. Apart from the celebratory banners, she'd not felt any strong evidence of the Magdalene's energy in the village. Lots of outward and visible acknowledgement, but no "chicken skin", as her Hawaiian friends called it. No prickling sensation of being enveloped in the Magdalene's energy.

A group of revelers greeted her as she neared the sea. Caught up in the lengths of streamers they'd been hanging from light post to light post, they saluted her as she approached. "Bon jour, mademoiselle, soyez le bienvenu a terre de la Magdalena! How lovely, she thought, was their sweet welcome to the land of the Magdalene. Dana took out her camera and with her basic French asked if she could take photos of them.

As she shot from various angles, the three young men and four women got into the play of it, assuming multiple poses—banners affixed to brows, swinging around the lamp-posts. It reminded Dana of a long-ago photo shoot she had done of Mardi Gras in New Orleans. One of the girls, proud of her proficiency in English, asked if Dana had come for the festival and why she took so many photos.

As Dana explained her assignment to photograph the realm of the Magdalene for a series of articles that explored a connection between the Cathars, Templars and Mary Magdalene, the girl brightened, raising her little fist into the air as she shouted in delightfully accented English: "Girl Power!" She then turned to her compatriots to explain. Completing her enthusiastic explanation, she turned back to Dana. "Our celebration of Saint Sarah and the three Mary's is not to be missed. Tonight there will be something very special. You must be ready with your camera."

When Dana assured them she would attend, they returned to their decorative tasks. Two hours later Dana had covered the entire village taking over a hundred shots. Retracing her steps back toward the hotel, she heard her name called out. Turning, she saw the girl who spoke fluent English running up to her.

"You must be certain to go to Marseilles before the festival concludes. The Feast of Pentecost at Saint Victor's Abbey is too beautiful to miss." At Dana's nod, she rejoined her friends.

As they faded from view, Dana admired the banners and posters, this time from a more direct vantage point than behind the camera lens. She shook her head, smiling in appreciation of the great honor in which Sarah, the Magdalene and the Mary's were held. Dana was astonished at the abundant proof of Mary Magdalene's having lived long and active years in France.

The supporting information was incontrovertible. Mary Magdalene continued to be venerated as an important personage in France, held in honor by the Templars, who were dedicated to her. There were numerous published accounts that recounted her life in France, some written by renown French Bishops. Apart from books, the plethora of art, images, celebrations and cathedrals dedicated to her, left little room for doubt as to her life in France.

And as for her death, the Tomb of Mary Magdalene at St. Maximin la Baume in Aix-en-Provence continued to have a steady stream of visitors. The Magdalene's relics, however, long sheltered in a splendid casket of quartz, were honored with reverence and zealously guarded as they had always been throughout their long and fragile history.

Monastic scholars were highly regarded for their accurate recording of events. When Charles, Prince of Salerno and Count of Provence, opened the Magdalene's tomb, he removed a parchment placed there in 710. It read: "The year of our Lord 710, the 6th day of the month of December in the reign of Eudes, the most pious of France. When the Saracens ravaged that nation, the body of our very dear and venerable Mary Magdalene was very secretly, during the night, removed from its own alabaster tomb and placed in this one which is of marble, whence the body of St. Sidonia had been previously taken, in order that the relics of our holy saint should be more secure against the sacrilegious outrage of the perfidious mussel men."

Louis XIV was one of many kings who honored the Magdalene's grave with a special visit to place Mary's casket of small relics into a crystal urn designed with gold lions supporting it. However, during the French revolution, although the relics remained safe, the crystal urn was somehow lost.

Dana felt a shiver, not from the clouds that were forming, but from a resonant connection to the Lady. Suddenly images and emotions, not her own, rippled through her—a mix of anxiety over having journeyed so far from her homeland, excitement at bringing her children to safety, honor at accepting the mission to safeguard the lineage of the House of David, sorrow at her husband, Jesus, absence and a solid commitment to spread his wisdom in this land.

Although lonely for him, she must have experienced gratitude at the many family members that attended her journey, Dana thought. Once that last lingering echo of emotion faded, Dana tried to separate her own feelings from Mary's. Hers seemed so much more ignoble, a blend of confusion, awe, anticipation at what her journey held and a growing sense of fear. Shaking her head, she banished such feelings and continued her walk back to the hotel, detouring to take additional shots of the surrounding hills.

The afternoon had passed swiftly. As always, while she was photographing what she'd felt to be the most perfect shots, she lost all track of time, anyone around her, all sounds and sights apart from those captured in her lens. Even Mary Magdalene thoughts and emotions were walled away as Dana's professional persona focused on capturing perfect shots for the third article of their series.

Surprised by the sun lowering in the sky, she felt she'd completed a good day's work as she neared her hotel. Eager to give Eric a call and registering her stomach's plea for food, she decided that after their call she'd have dinner before the evening's events.

Their conversation was extra-stilted. Her words sounded beyond blah in their emptiness. "Right, my love; work goes well here. Interesting but not terribly exciting thus far."

His response held a faint excitement, hard to erase even with his mundane account. "Mine is also going well. I'll fill you in more as circumstances allow. Take care, enjoy your work. I'll look forward to your call tomorrow."

After she hung up the phone—their "love you-goodbyes" the strongest communication—she ran his words over in her mind, convinced that whatever was going on had energized him She savored that thought over dinner.

The local fish dish was heavenly, she decided as she waived away a choice of delectable desserts, attracted to the sounds of revelry outside. Remembering the English speaking girl's comment on the surprise of the evening festivities, she was impatient to be out among the celebrants. A fleeting doubt as to whether the parade warranted a costume faded as she walked out and met with a crowd dressed rather wildly, but not all in costume.

It could almost be any Mardi Gras type of celebration. Wildly colored costumes and banners, loud music and masses of people. The difference was that many carried poles which were topped by images of Saint Sarah - the Egyptian. Held high by gypsy men in vivid costumes, the masked men were mounted on beautiful white horses, all chanting loudly in full-throated unison: "Vive Saintes Maries, vive Sainte Sarah!"

Dana smiled, knowing that there was some confusion over the label, "Sarah, the Egyptian". The parade replicas were an attempt to faithfully illustrate the dark coloring associated with her. Sarah was described in some records as a servant of Mary Magdalene; although records exist that describe Sarah as the first born child of Mary Magdalene and Jesus. Born in Egypt, the country where the pregnant Mary had fled before deciding, as her daughter grew, to seek safety in southern France.

"Black" Madonna's, Dana thought as she took a series of shots of the vivid characters, were being paraded about irrespective of the misunderstanding that so closely associated this parade with the gypsies. The Egyptian part of Sarah's title was translated as "gypsies" and associated with black for two reasons. One the dark magic believed to be practiced by the Romany gypsies, the other the false belief that Egyptians were very much darker than the French.

Misunderstandings or not, all celebrations incorporated such incongruities, many varying wildly from any of the accounts that began them. The parade's inception—accurate or not—was alive with energy. The colors, music and revelry increased, creating a level of joy and celebration that felt addictive. Dana tried to maintain her professional role but, having taken countless photos, she stashed her camera deep within her camera bag, letting herself be swept up in the excitement of the crowd.

Costumed figures swirled her about in a snake-like parade through the streets and along the harbor-front. Any attempt to remain apart was impossible. She gave up any resistance to the increasing excitement and the joyful beat of the music.

As the groups rounded the far side of the harbor, they made a swift swirling movement turning them, in unison, back in the direction of the village. She felt herself swung so wildly—a crack the whip motion with her at the whip's end—that she spun away, unable to halt the wild momentum that landed her forcefully at the foot of a small group of on-lookers.

Before she could rise—or even check for signs of injuries to her or her camera—someone yanked her to her feet. She glanced up to see the costumed figure of one of the gypsies who had earlier paraded in on horseback. Her blood turned to ice, not by the roughness as he spoke—"So, we meet again, dear Dana"—but by what lay behind the slits of his mask, eyes that the Devil himself would covet.

TWENTY-SIX

Emotional tension filled their cramped underground quarters. Eric's excitement was multiplied by that of Veronique, Professor Marty and Pierre. Such heightened energy impelled each of them to continue working with such intensity that time meant nothing. Food lay untouched and silence prevailed—a silence that was filled with eager, focused confidence.

Although no "Eureka's" had floated on the air thus far, Eric felt, as they all did, that they were on the trail of something that suggested such an outburst may be imminent. He'd tried to caution, if not pessimism, at least rational, scientific neutrality in a belief that the Bible Code would produce useful information. Even Eric's enthusiasm was salted with doubts as to any likely success, especially with those involving the cross-linking of all four manuscripts.

After having dealt with the translation to Hebrew, Eric had run endless computer searches, hours and streams of names and dates. He'd added "Cathars", the names of several Popes and Kings, "Moses", the names of the presumed children of Christ and even the names of his teammates.

He'd covered the birth date of Jesus, Moses, Abraham, on up to modern dates, beginning with 9/11/01 to the present. He stopped to rub his eyes, convinced he'd burn out his eyesight from ten hour stints at his computer. Eric sighed, his frustration at the increasing fragments of dubious data convincing him to bring his search to a temporary halt. He got up and walked over to the coffee pot—the extent of his minimal daily exercise. Fortunately there wasn't a mirror in their quarters, he thought as Professor Marty walked up and Eric noted the blood-shot, tearing, raggedness in his eyes.

"Anything new showing up?" The Professor looked over at the bright screen of Eric's computer—his optimism undimmed.

Eric shook his head. "I'd hoped the scan of dates would prove helpful, but using them seemed only to make things worse. I'm about ready to disregard that avenue."

"Let me pour another cup of coffee and I'll give it a closer look." The Professor poured an overfull cup and walked gingerly over to Erik's desk.

"Let me see one of your data streams." Professor Marty rushed over, waiting until Eric retrieved the last sequence and held up a pointer to illustrate his worthless output.

"I see one of your problems. You've been submitting dates using a modern dating system. The Bible Code uses Hebrew designations for dates as well as words." He shook his head, raising his hands at the empty nature of Eric's efforts. As he caught Pierre watching him, he muttered, "Il a fait une betise."

Pierre frowned as he hurried over to join them, grateful Eric couldn't translate the Professor's "He did something stupid" comment. Pierre gave the Professor a penetrating look before examining Eric's computer's unintelligible text. "I guess we didn't do such a good job—the Professor and I—in our attempt to create a workable program for you. In fact, I'd say we were the stupid ones."

Professor Marty shrugged, his look revealing his mea culpa as he and Pierre examined even more closely that which they were all shaking their heads over. After a period of "hmms", Pierre looked up in disbelief.

"Sorry Eric. Thanks to us, you've been laboring with a bastardized translation. *If* anything ever showed up, it could define the treasure as a cocker spaniel dog in Asia!"

Pierre smiled as he met the Professor's eyes and tried to explain. "We both overlooked the dating change in replicating the

Hebrew wording." He began a slow pacing of the limited space, his fingers stroking his chin. Within less than ten minutes the silence was broken. "Trying dates in English simply isn't going to work. What we need to do now is to work on putting them into ancient Hebrew. And that may be only the beginning. After last night's reading of your literature describing various codes, I decided we probably should run any dates, names and phrases through the *Atbash* Code." Pierre stroked his chin. "Once again, using Hebrew as our language."

Eric heaved a sigh of relief, wishing he'd recognized the oversight himself, but excited to correct it. The Professor shook his head as he looked from Pierre to Eric.

"What on earth is the *Atbash* Code? I'm familiar with several that you've mentioned—he turned to look at Pierre—but I've not heard of that one."

Pierre began the explanation. "It's rather a simple code but the preparation in advance of applying it takes some time. The techniques the scribes used to tie Old Testament revelations to the New Testament—while disguising prophetical information—were carefully concealed via the use of Eschatological Knowledge."

Professor Marty shook his head. "You're implying that certain words and phrases were given special meaning known only to insiders?"

"Right you are, dear Professor. With the use of dual layers of meaning used throughout the Gospel texts, it placed them beyond Roman interpretation. The code was discovered when the Dead Sea Scrolls at Qumran were published." Pierre looked at Eric. "I can't recall the chap who discovered the code. Somebody who won a Nobel Peace Prize—was it not?"

"Dr. Hugh Schonfield stumbled across it while studying the scribal codes used in the scrolls and relating it to the Old Testament. The cipher, when he arrived at it, was simple. Using the Hebrew alphabet of 22 letters, the cipher replaced the first 11 with the last 11 in reverse order."

"You mean Z with A and Y for B?" Professor Marty shook his head at Eric's explanation. "Simplistic is right!"

"Yes, well, if it were English, your example would be correct. In Hebrew it would be aleph=tau and bet=shin, leading him to label it as the Atbash code." Pierre turned to Eric for confirmation.

Eric slapped his forehead. "I should have thought of the code all along. As I was writing the article on the Templars, I came across it again. The Templars were accused of worshiping a strange God called "Baphomet". When Baphomet is translated into Hebrew and the Atbash code is used, its actual translation becomes: "Sophia" or "wisdom."

"Wow; so the use of the code not only fooled the Romans but the Inquisitors as well." Professor Marty smiled.

"Wait, there's more to the Baphomet image." Eric paused as the Professor hung on his words. "Dr. Schonfield arrived at an interesting conclusion: 'There would seem to be little doubt that the woman's head, revered by the Templars, represents Sophia in her female and Isis aspect, and Mary Magdalene in the Christian interpretation."

Pierre nodded as the Professor began to smile and shake his head. "Right; the Templars mystery figure—buried under the word Baphomet—was the very person that the Templars had dedicated their service to: Mary Magdalene. Such a code seems pretty simple, but quite effective at burying information within dual layers of meaning."

"Simple. Yes and no, as I've learned. It's not so simple when it comes to translating information into the original Hebrew and then viewing it through the lens of the code." Eric sighed, got up, did a few stretches and sat back at the computer. "We'd better get to it."

"Pierre, I'll create a list of the names, terms and dates I think Eric should check. I hope this won't throw you off schedule on your current project?" Professor Marty waited aware that Pierre was lost in thought. The Professor turned to respond to Eric's comment on the complexity of translations. "We're moving along pretty well with our project." The Professor hesitated. "Our dilemma lies in the area of the proper sequencing of the manuscripts and…" he halted as Pierre's attention returned.

"Sorry; I was thinking it through. You'll have what you need to get the Atbash ready to go, Eric. We should be able to translate your dates into Hebrew in no time." Pierre turned from Eric to the

Professor, his glare conveying: *later on about our manuscript headaches.*

"Right, the Professor agreed. "We'll get to it and have the Hebrew version of the dates on the list you provide us." Pierre nodded and both returned to their desks.

Eric frowned as he scrutinized all the dates and names, shaking his head with uncertainty. *Will our attempts to apply the Atbash Code allow for the successful application of the Bible Code— or will it simply produce a similar "garbage in-garbage out" response?*

Such concerns kept him up all night reviewing the computer's information on the Atbash application as well as the history of the Bible Code as he searched for support that it could work with their manuscripts.

The next morning it took him awhile to get past his frustration at having failed to consider the Atbash application and to spot the fact that such dates as the Rabin assassination were reflected not as September, 1995 but as 5756. When he did, he found the date part of their list moving quickly. Just as he was about to complete it, Veronique walked up with a slight smile on her face.

"They told you, didn't they?" Eric's guilty look segued into a smile as he added, "I suppose I can't plead exhaustion as an alibi for overlooking the Atbash code?"

"Eric, my dear, put it behind you." She glanced over at the other members of their team as she lowered her voice. "We've all found ourselves chasing down unlikely rabbit holes. The difference is that many of our errors have been unnecessary to reveal." She held out a sheaf of papers. "Look. I just got back a good reading on a carbon dating of the manuscripts. They are definitely from the first Century. The closest we could get to an exact date would put them around 44AD, definitely in the days of ancient Greek. But equally obvious is that whoever created the manuscripts took great pains to disguise their information. God help us that, when you've searched using the Atbash code, it or the Bible Code will produce something. We need the key to defining our treasure—and quickly." She sat down on the chair beside him and stared at his computer screen.

"Right." Eric said, his thoughts doubtful. *Not likely that our manuscripts are from the hand of God, meaning that they, like Gone*

With the Wind, may prove immune to the Bible Code. But, they may well prove subject to the Atbash Code.

Veronique hesitated, head turned to one side as she waited for Eric's faraway look to subside. "From the studies I've made of the manuscripts, I wouldn't rule out the possibility that they could have been encoded by as equally a sophisticated designer as whoever created the Bible's hidden messages."

"Sophisticated is right. But it's a stretch—time-wise and author-wise. Especially if the Bible Code's creator—as the Jews believed—was God—or some sort of Gods." Eric scratched his head. "The breadth of information is beyond any human author's knowledge. Although during my last night's reading I came across some sage in the eighteenth century—called the Genius of Vilna—who actually understood the secrets hidden in the Bible well before the invention of the computer. He claimed the implanted code accounted for all that was, is and will be until the end of time. Not only in the general sense, but including details of every species and all individuals; with a full account provided of all that happened to each from the day of our birth until our death."

Veronique shook her head. "I'm not up to that big of a stretch." She shook her head. "For that matter, nor is the Bible. But I do know that Newton believed in the Bible Code. After his death, his notes were examined and shocked everyone. Millions of words—not about astronomy or math—but about esoteric theology were discovered." Veronique frowned as she continued. "And much of his research was threaded through with symbols. Whatever they obscured, he definitely believed that, hidden in the Bible, there was a complete prophecy of history."

"True. I've read about Newton's obsession." Eric stared down at his erratic computer-run and shook his head. "If Newton had had a computer in those days, he wouldn't have made such a goof as mine. In fact, I have no doubt that he would have translated our manuscripts in short order."

"Quit knocking yourself, Eric." Veronique stood up. "You discovered the glitch and will be back on track in no time." She looked down at her watch. "Speaking of time, I have a meeting in Toulouse to discuss the results of our digs around Vals." She saw his raised eyebrow. "As leader of this dig—as hard as it is to tear myself away—I must put in an appearance on behalf of the job that provides for our safe space." She glanced down at the carbon-dating report she'd brought with her. "I thought you'd want to see the results." She held out the report, turning to see both Pierre and Professor Marty watching, their glances quizzical. "I was headed for you two next." She walked over until she stood between Pierre and Marty. Both let out matching "ah-ha"s as they examined the report.

"Be careful Veronique." Pierre said as she turned to go. "Even with our copies of all four manuscripts secure, thanks to your guards outside, bear in mind that not one of their translators is expendable."

Eric nodded, followed by Veronique's smart salute of agreement as she briskly walked away. A pang of cabin fever descended as she left. Eric anticipated being able to travel further a field than their current practice of waiting for the darkest part of evening to take a limited walk around the walled-off grounds. With a sigh, he picked up a computer print-out and headed for Pierre and the Professor's desks. "Here are the dates, one copy for each of you. You'll probably come up with a few more names and dates to translate as well."

Professor Marty took the list and gave it a serious scrutiny. "Hmm. How about we add the 44AD date—the closest we've arrived at— as that of these manuscripts?"

Eric shook his head in the affirmative. "Put it on your list and whenever you two are ready to input the corrected Hebrew dates let me know. I'll stand by for the results. I'm trying not to hold out much hope, given the Bible Code's only meaningful output came from a much more ancient document—all of which was divinely dictated. Anything at all, however, could give us a shot in the arm."

Professor Marty grinned. "I love such Americanisms. If "shot in the arm" means success with this Bible Code business, then I'm in agreement."

Eric couldn't muster more than a faint grin before turning away, feeling at loose ends as the other two worked at reviewing terms and names while converting dates to Hebrew. He sat back down at his computer. Suddenly something he'd read last night renewed a spark of excitement. It was the Israeli mathematician, Eli Rips, who created a scientific paper on the Bible Code after his theories were questioned by leading mathematicians and scientists. They insisted on having a peer review to validate his results. Rips welcomed any and all such reviews, relieved, but not surprised, to find that all had substantiated his claims, with odds so high as to be incontrovertible.

Eric took in a deep breath, shaking his head, astonished that the Bible should have been constructed in a manner far beyond the most intricate than any New York Times crossword puzzle. But that it had in common a similar sort of puzzle was indisputable. It used words densely scattered within the text, interweaving a hidden story of past, present and future.

Eric had started off with Rips basic explanation of the technique in applying the code: adding every fourth or twelfth or fiftieth letter to form a word. But even using this basic approach, Rips had discovered it was more than just a skip code. Woven throughout—underneath the original Hebrew—was a network of phrases and words that created revelatory information. Eric clicked on Rips initial computer program, the one that had convinced Rips that the Bible wasn't only a book, but a most sophisticated computer program. *Powerfully convincing,* Eric thought, *but could it possibly work on our texts?*

Once the team had installed the program, they used the Rabin example as a test case, asking the computer to search the Torah for the name "Yitzhak Rabin". It appeared—once—after a skip sequence of 4772. That number had been arrived at by the computer program dividing the entire Bible into a single strand of 3041805 letters with 64 rows of 4772 letters each. The center of that matrix represented the Rabin snapshot in the Bible Code, a snapshot of interlocking information that included the name of his assassin, the place and the time it would occur: just after the Hebrew year beginning in September 1995. Rabin was assassinated in 1995 on November 4th.

Eric continued to scroll through pages of Hebrew, following Rips application as he searched for confirmation of other predictions of future events. He shook his head as names, dates and places began to appear, predicting, in advance, the collision of Jupiter, the start of the Gulf War and others.

Eric's excitement grew at soon being able to apply the same technique to their manuscripts. Although he liked to think of himself as an ultra-pragmatic realist—a label Dana would find absurd—he didn't try too hard to soft-pedal his air of anticipation.

As he looked over at his teammates, raptly involved in organizing the proper input, he noticed their exhaustion. Replicating Rips process of eliminating all the spaces between the words, although time consuming, had been less of a tedious task for Professor Marty and Pierre than converting the Greek to Hebrew before linking the letters. Eric wondered how such an application to the modified four manuscripts might differ. In using the ancient Hebrew Bible with spaces removed, Rips hadn't been surprised to see the ancient Hebrew text of the Bible turn into the original Torah. Such a format was understood, by most sages and scientists, to have existed throughout the ages. It resulted in restoring the Bible to the form in which Moses had received it from God. Eric sat up in bed, utterly shocked to realize that his years in the priesthood never revealed such information. *What an intricate web,* he thought, *but even more complex was the skill of the webmaster—surely God.* He suddenly recalled the phrase running through his mind this morning: "In the beginning was the Word". *One long word,* he thought, *a string of Hebrew combining all words and all fates.*

Fearing his personal internal program may be threatening to crash, he felt relieved to hear Pierre and Professor Marty calling him. He shook his head as he neared, trying to brush away the incomprehensible—a hidden code revealing that God had a pattern for the planet, its people and all of life.

"We're making headway." The Professor's words seemed reenergized.

"True." Pierre's rational tones balanced the Professor's optimism. "We're nearly at the point of testing whether our manuscripts were Bible Code encoded and, if not, whether the Atbash Code can tell us anything." He looked from Eric to the Professor. "By anything, I mean the key to understanding the Inquisition's description of the treasure as: "... so powerful as to change the world."

The three continued to work throughout the afternoon and, with Veronique's return, all four continued well into the evening, eager to reach the starting point for testing the Atbash Code as well as the Bible Code. "Which should we try first?" Pierre's question met with a chorus of unanimity. "The Bible Code first."

Veronique, the team's skeptic, explained her conversion. "I couldn't believe that this program revealed specifics of Rabin's assassination, Bill Clinton, Saddam Hussein, the Gulf War—all by searching the ancient Hebrew text of the Bible. But I began to reserve judgment when other books showed nothing compared to the Bible's distinct revelations." She held both hands out. "I'm a scientist and need something concrete to grasp.. Confirming the vast statistical probability against such an outcome convinced me.."

Pierre tried to moderate any undue confidence. "Until we test enough phrases, words and dates, I suggest we restrain our excitement." He looked around the room, noticing that his teammates were focused—like race horses nearing the starting gate—on getting back to the data they were fast preparing.

The Professor seemed to have almost completed the Hebrew translations and Pierre was tweaking the input, readying the program for testing the newly compacted—sans spaces—data contained within the four manuscripts. Pierre looked up to see a frown on Professor Marty's face. "Out with it, Marty. Now what has you fretting?"

"I'm nervous about the manner in which we removed all the spaces in the four manuscripts. How do we know what sequence the manuscripts should be in? There's nothing to indicate their order. Not 1, 2, 3, 4—or even any logical text that suggests a sequence. Our arrangement could result in output as senseless as: 'Twas brillig and the slivey tove…'

Pierre gave a sigh of impatience. "You're quite right, my dear colleague. We may have to rearrange the sequence as many times as necessary." Pierre could see the mental calculation Veronique had begun. "Yes, dear lady; it is a daunting task. But not for the computer." Pierre looked around the room. "Are we ready?" As all heads shook in the affirmative, Pierre looked at Eric. "Well, what's it to be? Any favorite choice for the first name or date to input?

Eric looked around the room. "How about this for our beginning name. 'Benjamin Carter'?" Surprisingly, it met with nods of agreement from everyone.

"It gets the vote." The Professor said as he pulled out a piece of paper. "We also agreed on a date to check—the day Benjamin was presumed to have died in a fall from Montsegur."

Eric watched as Pierre—using Rip's translation technique on Eric's computer—walked them through the steps he would take. He hesitated, his expression reflecting an even deeper layer of concern than did Professor Marty's. Pierre shook his head vigorously before he began the run, looking from one team member to the others. "As to the value—should *anything* appear—I understand that the reporter, Michael Drosnin, went to Israel to try to forestall the predicted death of Rabin. In spite of convincing his prime minister, Rabin decided to follow what was meant to be his fate."

Professor Marty picked up the thread as Pierre fell silent. "I see what you're getting at, Pierre. What if our manuscripts reveal key information and the parties involved choose not to act upon it? Is there free will or is there a destiny that we must live out?"

"Exactly!" Pierre remained with his fingers poised above the keyboard, prepared to discover the outcome; but wary of its inevitability. *If,* he thought, *the treasure has the power to change the world, is God rewriting the script at this stage. Or did he plan the changes for a particular time in a particular way, with us as the door-keepers?"* Pierre looked up at Eric. "You've had more time to study this thing. Is fate alterable?"

Eric shook his head. "Newton may have been hard-wired to answer that question, but as for me, I'm baffled by the whys, wherefores, or reasons for such a code and awed at its implied inevitability." Eric took a deep breath and shrugged before he continued, his teammates raptly hanging on his every word. "As to the Great Director in the sky, I am speechless, deaf, dumb and humble to believe that I could know even a crumb of His purpose."

Pierre nodded solemnly. Professor Marty, however, was growing impatient, his words distinctly irritable. "All right you two, we can philosophize forever. But before we get into the odds on changing our fate, I want to see if the program reveals anything."

Pierre reminded him that should the Bible Code prove to be meaningless, they still had the Atbash translation to apply met with a muttered, “shush” from the Professor. Pierre took a deep breath and inserted the name, Benjamin Carter, along with the date of death—in Hebrew. The Professor stood, chin in hand, staring fixedly at the screen. Veronique paced back and forth.

The first pass resulted in nothing intelligible. After more than three hours of shuffling the series of manuscripts and resubmitting—only to get repeated mish-mash—tempers were starting to fray. Professor Marty paced to and from Eric’s computer screen, cursing under his breath. After long stretches of time and repeated scrolling through endless screens, Pierre let out a prolonged sigh, followed by hesitant words. “My Hebrew may be a little rusty; but have a look and let me know if you see what I see.” The Professor studied the screen, looked away, rubbed his eyes and looked again, only to do a little dance, his shout of “Yes!” startling Eric, who peered even more intently at the text.

“Oh, my God! There it is. “Benjamin Carter”, crossed by “Montsegur” and then crossed in an X pattern with the word, “Overseer” at one end, and ...” Eric’s account had mesmerized the team, staring as he leaned nearly into the computer, searching for any other strange words, muttering in tones of awe at each new piece of the puzzle; until he shouted. “Dana”!

Like some danse macabre, Eric’s eyes burned into the screen as he studied the words, turned away, turned back, swung his chair out and away from the desk, bolted upright and headed for the door, followed by both Pierre and Professor Marty, who, in close synchronization, kept him from opening the door and dashing out.

“Eric, my boy, slow down and let’s figure out what this is telling us. There are no dates or “assassin” words in the acrostic. You must admit that Montsegur, Dana and, an apparently alive, Benjamin, *are* connected.” Pierre drew Eric back over to the screen. “The word, “Overseer” is the most perplexing part of the puzzle.”

Eric stared at the screen again, giving it a lengthy study before turning back to the others. “It must be somehow connected to both Benjamin and Dana. Although it doesn’t indicate Benjamin’s death at Montsegur, it certainly links the location with him.” Eric’s look of confusion grew.

"But….remember that it was Giraud that pushed Benjamin off Montsegur. If Benjamin actually died, Giraud's name would appear and not Dana's." Pierre's words echoed through the room leaving a sudden silence as the darkening of night deepened.

Eric's expression turned ashen as he withdrew to an even darker place. Although his teammates knew his anxiety was tied to concern over Dana, they also knew that it would be many hours before Eric heard the ring of the phone. With each passing hour, Eric went from fidgeting to pacing, to sitting down in front of his computer, only to jump up from his staring-without-seeing-pose and return to nervously consuming cups of coffee as he waited for dawn.

One by one his teammates took turns remaining with him as the others slept. Each tried to involve him in some of the more exciting aspects of their discovery. Pierre's was the largest bombshell. "Such output is phenomenal! We were so excited that names appeared, that we totally overlooked an amazing outcome. Our manuscripts, converted to Hebrew with all words linked, provided the same sort of revelations as did the Torah."

"Right." Professor Marty's eyes widened. "And that, in spite of the fact that our manuscripts were written far more recently. What do you make of that?"

Pierre shrugged, bafflement in his voice as he turned to Eric. "I'm speechless. Besides the time difference, we had to ignore the untranslatable symbols scattered throughout our four manuscripts. I know you think they have more to reveal than even the words."

Although Eric showed faint interest, his response focused on Dana. "I can't focus on any of that until I'm sure she's OK."

"Eric, Dana was fine when you last talked with her. My guess is that she will call on schedule tomorrow with a rather routine account of her day." Pierre's assurances didn't penetrate Eric's pall of worry. "If there *is* a problem, you need to get a good night's sleep in order to be of any help to her."

Eric looked up. Pierre's words had penetrated. *He definitely would be no good to Dana*, he thought, *if he remained paralyzed by fear and exhaustion*. Nodding agreement, he allowed Pierre to lead him over to his sleeping cubicle. Long after Pierre had bid him "Goodnight", Eric stared inwardly at the disturbing conflux of words, their acrostic image taunting him with a conviction that all was definitely not right with Dana.

TWENTY-SEVEN

Dana screamed for help as Benjamin tightened his grip and pulled her away from the midst of the crowd. Explosive fireworks drowned out her cries. She fought to free one hand and yank away his mask. His expression was frightening—as much for its determination as its disfigurement. The anger in his eyes increased the volume of her screams. "Help!" she cried, each repetition louder, forgetting, in her fear, to call out the French word, "aide."

"Help" was clearly understood. Suddenly another hand grabbed at her, yanking her away from Benjamin. A voice rang out. "Let her go!" A gendarme, hearing the cries, came running over, stick at the ready.

Dazed, Dana attempted to pull herself up from the ground as Benjamin turned away with a chilling curse. "I *will* have you, Dana—friends be damned!" He disappeared into the crowd, accompanied by the shrill whistle of the gendarme racing behind.

The English-speaking voice that had challenged Benjamin, belonged to the girl Dana had met this morning. Her companion was the burly man she'd introduced as a farmer from the Camargue. Dana remembered the girl's added descriptor. "My Jacques can toss a bull." Dana felt grateful for man's verification of such talent in wresting her from Benjamin's grasp. Both the girl and the cowboy were now inspecting her scrapes and bruises. Concern was written on the girl's expression. "They are not so bad as to warrant a hospital. But please come to my home. My mother is a healer. She will surely have a potion for your wounds."

"I must return to my hotel and…" Dana halted, her mind running with images of Benjamin. *He may know exactly what hotel I'm in, as well as the car I'm driving.* "You are so kind. Perhaps I shall take your advice and not return to my room quite yet."

The girl's generous mouth widened, causing her cheeks to reach for the blue of her eyes as she turned to her friend. "Jacques; we go to my home. Would you please drive?"

He shook his head, whispering something in French that Dana translated as, "Could I deny you anything?"

Helene turned from her besotted admirer, her long auburn hair swaying like a horse's tail as she took Dana's hand. "Over here is our car; go slowly now." Her little hands were strong but gentle as she guided Dana through the milling crowd and over to a side street where they had parked their car.

The drive to the girl's home took scarcely five minutes. Situated at the edge of town, near to the highway, it was located in one of the older sections on a street cobbled with well-worn stones. A shutter opened and a curtain was drawn back as they parked and began their approach to an old house, its ancient stonework resting for support on that of its neighbors.

The girl gave a little knock and opened the door, calling out: "Maman! It is I, Helene, with Jacques and a friend."

The woman who entered the living room was unexpected. Youthful, attractive and sharing the color of her daughter's russet hair. She was rubbing her hands with a towel as she neared. "Forgive me. I was lost in my sculpting." Her English was flawless, only the lush lilt of French identifying her nationality. Reassured that no bits of grey clay remained, she leaned over to plant light kisses on Dana's cheeks as they exchanged names.

Claude frowned as she took a closer look, noticing the rip in Dana's tee shirt and the ugly bruises. "Dana, my dear, what happened to you?" The mother looked up at her daughter. "Did the evening turn rough?" It wasn't her daughter's "No, but…" response as much as the look in her eyes. Claude squared her shoulders and turned back to Dana, gently drawing her down onto the sofa as she knelt in front of her. “Please roll up your sleeves. I would like to examine those bruises.” Total silence filled the room as Claude looked, touched, pressed and shook her head before turning back to her daughter. “Helene, bring the arnica please.”

Helene soon returned with the ointment. Her mother began to liberally spread it over Dana’s abrasions. “This should have those bruises healed in no time.” She shook her head as she looked from Dana back to her daughter. “This was not a fall. Look at the purple of these bruises, like handprints. How did this happen?”

As Helene and Jacques rushed to describe the situation, Dana felt grateful for a moment to contemplate her next words. As they finished with their stories, Claude returned her attention to Dana. “Who is this beast of a man who attacked you?”

Dana deliberated, opting for minimal disclosure. “He is an evil man who is determined to harm me.” Her audience remained silent, eyebrows raised and head’s shaking as they waited for her to continue. Dana let out a long sigh. “I know he is following me.”

Helene rushed over to the door, pulled it open and scanned the area. “I don’t see any strange cars outside. But if he is following you, you can’t return to your hotel. Where were you planning to go after leaving here?”

Dana recapped her assignment for Claude’s benefit. “I am a photographer, working on an article about Mary Magdalene. I have finished all my shots of your village and planned to leave in the morning for Marseille and, after staying overnight, continue to Vezaly, photographing areas involved with the Magdalene.” Dana hesitated, her deep sigh betraying that which her confident account attempted to obscure.

Claude’s eye widened as she walked over and took Dana’s hand. “If this man is after you, my dear, he knows your hotel and your car.” Claude looked over at her daughter. “Dana must not return for them. We must make other plans.”

“But I could accompany her.” Jacques responded, his words nearly as hearty as his physique as he walked over to Dana. “Please consider me your body guard until we can get you to a safe place.”

“That is very kind of you. But even for one as strong as you, I dare not risk exposing you to this man’s rage.” Dana looked from

Claude to Helene. "You are quite right, however. It's best I don't go near my hotel."

"Very well. Then we must develop another plan." Helene turned to her mother. "Is it alright that she stays here for the night?"

"Of course. You may stay longer if you wish." Claude nodded toward Helene and Jacques. "These two are leaving tomorrow to drive to Marseille for the Magdalene's celebration."

"That's right. You can come with us. Marseille is a big city. We can find a place where no one will find you." Helene excitedly reached for Dana's hand. "Please say yes."

"I must return my rental car, pay my bill at the hotel, and..."

Claude spoke before her daughter, open-mouthed, could get a word out. "This bad man does not know me. I shall go to the hotel, ask to pay your bill and explain that you have been injured and have returned home. I shall do the same tomorrow when I take your car to our local Euro-Car Agency. That will free you to go to Marseille with Helene and Jean tomorrow. Once in a safe hotel, you can decide as to continuing your trip." Claude turned to Jacques and Helene, her look as powerful as her words. "Do not let Dana out of your sight until you are sure she is safe."

"Maman, please..." Helene frowned as she shook her head. "I learned everything from you. You must stop treating me as a child. I am soon twenty-one. We will be very careful with this game of "cops and robbers" do you say?" She grinned at Dana..

Claude smiled at her daughter before turning back to Dana. "You are in good hands, my dear." She walked to a closet, opened it and pulled on a jacket. "I am off to handle your car and room." She extended her hand. "May I have your keys, please?"

Dana felt things were moving a bit too fast, but she couldn't come up with any better plan. She reached into her handbag and withdrew a key-ring with two keys attached and enough euros to settle the bill in cash. "My rental car is a gray Peugeot parked in space A26. And would you please throw my clothes and camera gear—whatever I've left behind—into my suitcase and bring it." She studied Claude. "It's not a lot. But it may be too heavy to manage." Dana looked over at Helene and Jacques. "Maybe..."

Claude shook her head. "Not necessary. I can sling a hundred kilos of clay from table to shelf. I'll be fine. If I do need any help, the aubergiste will assist me in getting them into the car." Claude pursed her lips. "As for your car, shall I drive it over here for the night or would you rather I return to deal with it tomorrow?"

Dana hesitated. "Best you chose to err on the side of caution. I can't risk your being followed back here"

"Nor I." She smiled. "It would put our brilliant plans for your journey tomorrow under a cloud of scrutiny. We cannot have that." Claude turned toward her daughter. "If, for any reason, I am delayed returning, I will call you. You will be here, d'accord?"

"Of course, maman. Dana and I will work on our strategies."

Claude gave Dana a long look. "Not by the look of her. I must insist you get right off to bed, my dear. Prepare the blue room, Helene." As Dana prepared to decline, Claude choose a more reasoned approach. "Getting a good night's rest is your best strategy." Waiting until Dana nodded; she turned, and with a "very good", headed off for the hotel.

The blue room was small but with its own little bathroom and a little bed whose blue comforter and matching pillow enveloped her in the softness of down. Initially her thoughts were of Benjamin's voice, eyes, words and, most of all, his intentions. But the anxiety such thoughts brought was erased by her focus on Eric. Grateful for having spoken with him earlier, she wondered how to explain her circumstances tomorrow without alarming him.

In spite of the drama of the evening, or perhaps because of her complete exhaustion, she was surprised at how quickly she fell asleep. The room's seductive soothing eased her into deep slumber, broken only by dreams of someone beckoning her to follow. She wanted to go; if only the path hadn't been covered in hot coals.

The next morning vanished in a swirl of activity that soon saw Dana settled into the backseat of Jacques's old Fiat as they skimmed along toward Marseilles. Claude had been so efficient in settling her hotel bill and her car rental account. Jacques and Helene so vigilant in keeping a watch for anything and anyone at all suspicious that Dana felt confident at having out-foxed Benjamin.

Helene kept up a cheerful patter of commentary on the places they were passing, reiterating her mention that Dana shouldn't miss the services at the cathedral. "The presence of the Magdalene is even stronger in Marseille and the area around it. She traveled, taught and preached throughout the area." Helene stopped her account to turn and look at Dana, studying her expression as she added, "We shall arrive soon. All will go well. You need not fear."

Dana smiled. "I have mixed feelings. This man knows that I am a photographer and will consider that I may remain in this area in order to photograph such sites. So…" She hesitated, her mind racing to fill in the blanks as to whether or not Benjamin would anticipate her destination.

Helene's eyes widened. "I understand. Whether he follows or not, he could decide to be at the cathedral and examine all professional photographers in the vicinity." She turned away, directing her questions to Jacques. "What do you think? We must come up with a strategy to prevent this awful man's plans."

Jacques took a minute to think it through. "I would like to think he believes Dana has left the area. But it's equally likely he will come to Marseilles." He turned to Dana. "As you suggested, I have kept watch for all black sedans with their windows obscured. Although I have seen none as yet, I have concerns that his transport may be quite different." He paused, obviously deep in thought and hesitant at expressing it in English. Both Helene and Dana waited. "I don't think he knows of Helene's home and our car. But, if he suspects that you may go to Marseille, he can arrive at any time, in any car and be there waiting for you." Jacques let out a deep sigh as he darted a shy glance at Dana. "Do I make sense in English?"

"You make perfect sense, Jacques." Dana frowned. "So my choices seem to be to go without a camera to the event, buying postcards or some such visual aide for my article, or, two, not go at all. Perhaps I shouldn't even stay in Marseille. Help me consider the "what ifs?" For example, if I were to miss the celebration, where might I go that he wouldn't expect?" Dana fell silent, meditating on the right choice, asking the Magdalene to give her a clue. Both Helene and Jacques remained quiet, reviewing options. After long minutes of silence had passed, Dana formed her thoughts into words.

"I'm choosing an option that protects you two as well. Obviously that means I don't accompany you. But, even without my being at your side, he may recognize you and approach you to find out information about me. He could attempt to do you harm."

Helene swung around with a smile of relief on her face. "I feel better at your avoiding the ceremony. As to risk to us, we will be in costume. Have no fear for our safety."

Jacques nodded in agreement. "That man seemed like a mad dog. Best you not bait him by being visible."

Helene smiled as she reached over and touched Jacques's arm. "I agree." Her voice raised in volume as she turned around to Dana. "I have a solution for your photos. My second best subject in school was photography. We brought two cameras—one a digital SLR and the other Jacque's old Leica. I know they are not of the quality of your expensive camera, but we can take many photos for you and mail them to your magazine."

Dana leaned up closer to the front seat. "You are remarkable, my friends."

Helene's smile turned to a frown. "I want to be careful so that, if he is at the cathedral, he wouldn't notice us. Especially Jacques; he would stand out taking many photos." She fell silent as they all mulled the situation over.

Helene broke in with an idea. "Wait. There will be many more revelers than in Les Saintes Maries de la Mer. Most will be in costume, just as we will. But I will pick up full masks and capes that completely conceal Jacques and my features." She grinned at Jacques. "Maybe a wig for us both—blond like Galahad and Guinevere. I've always wanted to be a blond."

Jacque's response blended caution and excitement. "That could work. But, even so, we shouldn't make a big production of taking an unusual amount of photos. We'll share them between us, taking only the amount tourists take."

Dana released a sigh of relief. "Good idea. It should work." She hesitated, knowing even more than they just how dangerous their game could become. "Promise me you won't take any risks. If you see him—or anyone you think may be him—do everything to make a safe exit."

Helene got the message more from Dana's fear-filled eyes than her words. "You have our word." Her solemnity switched to smiles. "But, if all goes well, we shall have some photos for you."

"I'll look forward to receiving them." Dana reached into her handbag for a tablet. "Here's information as to how and where to send them."

As Helene took the note, Jacque's expression returned to worry. "More important than the photos, Helene, is a plan to get Dana away from Marseilles and its cathedral,"

Dana's response held a mix of anger, frustration and disappointment. "I had planned to head for Vezaly after Marseilles. It seemed the logical next destination for my Mary Magdalene photo-shoot. But Vezaly may prove to be just as vulnerable a choice as the cathedral at Marseilles." Dana paused only long enough to let out a strong expletive in English followed by the French, "Merde! So where do I go from here?" Dana fell silent, as did her companions—all in quiet contemplation as the kilometers sped by. Dana's silence was so deep and her question so single-minded that she found herself falling into a meditation, her silent plea reaching out. *Help me, Mary Magdalene. You have drawn me here. Tell me where I should go?*

Suddenly her whole being was filled with a sense of light and a sweet presence, accompanied by the scent of roses. A message came, rippling through her mind with the clarity of a fast moving mountain stream. *"Go to my cave. Find it and you will find me."*

TWENTY-EIGHT

Benjamin Carter squirmed with discomfort as he lay on the simple bed the abbey had provided for him. As exhausted as he was, his racing thoughts and his never completely healed body prevented sleep. *The fact that the Overseer could provide accommodations at a moment's notice,* he thought, *was one more bit of evidence of the man's power to have his slightest wish accomplished instantly.* Benjamin glanced at his watch, registering not only the early hour, but the date. Beads of perspiration formed at the reminder of how little time remained for him to accomplish that which he had agreed to—the capture of Dana.

Benjamin leapt up, feeling a sudden claustrophobia in the cell-like room. He moved to the window, throwing open the shutters to draw a deep breath of the pre-dawn mist. The fact that he wore only shorts didn't account for his sudden chill. His mind began to race with the evening's frustration. *Damn you, Dana Palmer,* he thought. *I would have you now if not for those stupid kids.* He'd checked the town's few hotels, only to finally locate the hotel where she was registered—and find she had checked out. The concierge presumed she had returned home. *I don't trust her,* Benjamin thought. *I believe she created a ruse to put me off her trail. What a waste of so little remaining time if I race back to Toulouse, only to find no sign of her. And yet...* He stared around the silent grounds of the abbey outside of Marseille, thinking of what she would have done. *If I guessed wrong in coming here, I could end up squandering precious hours, even days, in searching Marseille to pick up her trail.*

He sat at the little table, pulled out his notebook and pen and began to lay out a strategy for his search that would cover all possible options. The watery dawn light was filtering through the room, highlighting its meager decorations before bouncing back from the mirror on the opposite wall. Benjamin's focus was drawn by the sunlit mirror as it reflected his image back into the room.

He winced at the gargoyle look of his scarred face. Even now, over eight months since his narrow brush with death, he couldn't believe the change. Bitterness rose, the taste of bile becoming his steady diet. Revenge kept him going.

He ran a finger along the ragged ravines of what so recently had been smooth cheeks highlighting a strong jaw. Coupled with his abundant dark hair and unforgettable eyes, he had turned many a woman's head. Evie had teasingly chided him about his movie star image. *"George Clooney had better watch out."*

The memory of her words added salt to his wounds. The outward and visible destruction took a back seat to the anger he felt at the destruction of a career poised on the brink of fame. He remembered his state of exultation at his discovery of a manuscript that he'd long sought. Convinced it was the real treasure of the Cathars, he'd had his plans threatened by the arrival of Evie's friends, Dana and Eric. The humiliation he'd felt following his announcement of what he'd claimed was the Holy Grail, was minor compared to the realization that Dana and Eric, along with a few French compatriots, were on the trail of the true Cathar treasure. "Damn them! They have the treasure now. But not for long." His words reverberated through the room.

Benjamin turned away from the mirror, letting his mind design a future that was nearly in his grasp. His thoughts savored every image of his victory. *I'll have the surgery completed first, before my announcement. When I am confident that I am ready to return to my office and resume work, I will have my revenge when I announce that I have found the real Cathar treasure. As to placing it in the hands of the Vatican...*

He paused, his expanded state of euphoria fast fading. *What the Overseer has in mind as to the treasure,* he thought, *is a decision I must overturn. My alignment with the next U.S President, will assure me all the power and support I need to dictate my terms.* He congratulated himself on his skill in using the perfect bait. "…so powerful as to transform the world." It had hooked the power-hungry Senator. Benjamin sneered as an image of using such power to puncture the Overseer's pomposity appeared. *I will, of course, keep such a discussion under wraps until my surgeries are successfully completed and I'm ready to resume my post.*

Irritatingly, the image of the Overseer remained long after he'd tried to erase it from his mind. *The man is not to be dismissed lightly—even with my alignment with the soon to be U.S. President, Even so, I shall outmaneuver him. After my capture and delivery of Dana will come the easy netting of Eric as he follows her. They will turn over the manuscripts and...*Before he could complete his thoughts a knock on the door startled him. He leapt up and away from the table.

A priest stood outside the door. Not the humble sort at all by the impatient urgency that coated his words. "The Cardinal is waiting to speak with you. Come along."

"The Cardinal is here?" *Why would the Overseer show up now? It is almost as though the bloody bastard can read minds.*

"No. Excellency is holding on the phone. We mustn't keep him waiting."

Benjamin grabbed his pants and shirt, pulled them on and was led at a fast pace, down one floor, across the inner courtyard and into an antechamber of the abbeys' office, where he was handed the phone.

"I understand there was a mishap last night. Your report please, Professor Carter." The Overseer's words were, as usual, minimal. However, the implication of the breadth of his information, was massive. Behind his terse responses to Benjamin's nervous account of his next steps was the even more deadly—from being unspoken—edict. *Do not delay. The time is near. Either I take possession of Dana Palmer and the manuscripts—or...*

TWENTY-NINE

Professor Marty walked over to Eric's desk, concerned that he'd not spoken, hadn't turned his light on, ignored completely the scent of paella permeating the air, and remained fixed in a frozen stare at his computer screen—not even looking up as the Professor extended, in one hand, a tray with a hearty serving of paella. The other held a glass of one of the Corbieres best red wines. The Professor shook his head as he placed both on the table alongside Eric. "Eat something. You look a far cry from the confident, debonair Eric I first met, the chap who could pose for an ad in a men's magazine. Who drug in this unshaven, haggard and as antsy as a druggie-without-his-fix excuse for a human being?" As the Professor turned, his question unacknowledged, Veronique walked over to try her approach.

"Look Eric; it's going on seven o'clock. I doubt you slept last night, but how about getting a little food in you before Dana calls?" Her question was met with a vacant stare. "You've been at the computer all day. Take a break or you'll be no help to anyone."

All nodded their agreement as Pierre walked over and placed his hand on Eric's shoulder. "She's right you know. Dana wouldn't want to see you in this state. And as for working on fear, here's your chance. You either defeat it or it will defeat you."

Eric blinked, seeming to respond to the mention of Dana's not wanting to see him in such a state. He stood up, stretched and looked around, stopping to register each of his teammate's expressions. All solemnly studied Eric, their searching eyes scanning for what they hoped would soon be a sea change.

"Quit looking at me that way. It's the old bugaboo of my having abandoned Clotilde to die in the flames. I should have saved her instead of running off to save these blasted manuscripts." He picked up his notebook and tossed it against the opposite wall. "And I'm bloody well doing it again. While she faces danger, I sit with my cronies and play with puzzles."

As if through some subliminal communication, none of the team rose to the bait. They remained silently fixed, patiently staring at Eric. Their looks held not a hint of censure as they waited and watched, sending in silence their combined message: *Get it out. Blow off steam and come back to having faith that this time around is a chance to deal with fear*.

The slam of the notebook as it hit the wall had penetrated. Like a sleepwalker, Eric fought to overcome a fugue state filled with fear and flaming-rage. As he met the eyes of his team a sheepish look stole over his face. "What an ass I've been. This code business is a two-edged sword. The minute it revealed Dana linked with Benjamin—and whatever "Q" is—I fell apart. All I can think is that she's out there alone. Until I get her call, I'm going to be useless."

"So eat. It'll keep your energy high for whatever comes." Pierre gave him a pat on the shoulder. "We need you alert if we're to get the job done this time." His words seemed to penetrate. Eric nodded, sat down and began to eat. Pierre sighed as he walked back to his desk to join the others in a silent prayer for the phone to ring.

An hour passed as the entire team, including Eric, immersed themselves in testing individual sequences of connected data, hoping one of them would hit on a trail that could reveal the manuscripts secret. Pierre's voice broke their hypnotic focus. "Eric, what do you make of this? Come have a look. I added another piece to "Montsegur" and "Cathars" and the word, "Treasure" appeared, crossed with the words, "Baphomet, Temple and Light".

Eric leaned over Pierre's shoulder as he watched the program input the words, search through the text, and suddenly reflect an acrostic illustrating the connection Pierre described.

"I'll be damned. If the letter sequencing is producing anything it tells us we've finally got the manuscripts in the right order: light, water, earth, fire." Professor Marty said as he joined his smiling team mates crowded around to examine the puzzle. "But what is this "Baphomet" reference? Let's try a date to see if it gives us more information."

Eric looked up at the others. "Good idea; but which date should we try—a date for Cathars, Temple or Treasure?"

"Let's try the Temple." Pierre looked up at the others. "So what'll it be—953 BC when Solomon's Temple was completed or one of the dates it was destroyed? I vote for trying 1126 first. That was when the Knights Templar occupied quarters in the Al-Aq Mosque—right above the destroyed temple."

"It's worth a try." Veronique sounded hesitant as she looked over at the Professor. "All I know about Baphomet is that it was a head, supposedly worshipped by the Templars."

The Professor snorted. "Nonsense! When we used the Atbash Code, "Baphomet" translated to Sophia, meaning wisdom, and not just any old wisdom but that which held a secret depth attributed to Mary Magdalene. "

"It's that aspect that intrigues me, given Dana's urge to follow the Magdalene's energy." Eric's voice held a shade of fear.

Veronique put her hand on his shoulder. "Go for it, Eric. Run the combination. I'm curious to see what shows up."

Eric began the search of data streams as the Professor turned toward the coffee area, returning with cups of coffee for all. "We'll need this. Something tells me we'll be up till dawn."

Eric's nod was accompanied by a glance at the clock and a long sigh as he muttered, "Come on, Dana. Why haven't you called? Are you waiting until we have Big News for you?" As he reached for his coffee, his phone rang. His leap from his chair knocked his cup to the floor.

Eric's anxious, "Dana?" had an audience gather round as they struggled to keep one eye on the computer screen while keeping all ears on the conversation.

"You've had a change of plans? What…you're at a phone booth where? How in the world did that come about?"

Eric fell silent as he listened intently to Dana's white-washed account. "Don't worry, Eric. I'm more than ever convinced that I've been guided." After her positive preface, she went on to describe her adventure with Benjamin in Sts Maries de la Mer, highlighting the drama of her new friends boldly coming to her rescue, their help in checking her out of the hotel, taking her to their home for the night and driving her to Marseilles."

"So that's where you are. Did you reserve a hotel room and another car?"

An array of wide-eyed, open-mouthed listeners greeted his steady stream of questions. "Are your friends with you? Why do you hesitate? Are you sure you're using a safe phone?" He let out a long sigh of relief as he repeated her assurances that she was using a phone booth in a little village north of Marseille. A look of relief filled his listener's expressions as he gave them the OK sign.

"You're where?" Eric grabbed a pen and tablet. As his eyebrows rose and his mouth turned down, his audience remained transfixed, straining to translate what sounded like major changes to Dana's plans.

The team's curiosity turned to concern as they heard Eric begin to explain his panic at code results linking her with Benjamin and the letter "Q". The worried looks on his teammates faces silenced Eric's further discussion of such results.

When he'd completed his call, he hung up the phone, shook his head and turned, rapidly spewing out Dana's incredible account to his wide-eyed team. "Things are heating up. Benjamin is definitely alive and somehow managed to follow her to Les St Maries de la Mer, roughing her up as he yanked her from the carnival crowd." A gasp went up from his audience. "She managed to escape, thanks to the help of some adventuresome new friends."

"I take it she's heading back here?" Pierre's anxious expression revealed his hope she'd do just that.

"No. She intends to remain, but not in Marseilles. She's avoiding Mary Magdalene's famous sites where Benjamin would expect her to show up and be lying in wait for her." Eric shook his head as though only now fully incorporating her choice. "Instead, she's headed for some remote village surrounded by grottos and caves. She believes one of them to be the cave of Mary Magdalene."

"Is she sure the area won't draw Benjamin there as well?" Veronique waited, concern clearly evident in her expression.

"Dana claims its far from being known—and certainly not a tourist area. It's somewhere northeast of Marseille—near Aix en Provence. She managed to find a gite just outside the village of—he looked down at his notes—"Nans la Pins" in the Massif de la Saint Baume". Eric looked worried. "I'm not convinced she'll be any safer there, but…" He pursed his lips, a frown deepening as he ruminated over risks. His teammates relaxed when he resumed speaking with a touch of confidence. "Dana claims she was drawn there. Ever since she arrived, she swears she feels a strong connection to the Magdalene." He looked up at his audience, a mix of awe and concern coloring his words. "Increased by the gite owner regaling her with tales of Mary Magdalene's teaching and preaching in the area. The man seemed to know every cave she'd ever occupied."

As Eric paused, he caught Veronique's raised eyebrow and the look in her eyes that said, 'enough of such fuzzy logic.' "How long does she intend to remain there?" Veronique's pragmatic question held overtones of worry.

"Her plan is to hike the area and take lots of photos. She should have a better idea tomorrow as to her return. For now, she said she was headed for bed—guarded by the Magdalene." He smiled as he shook his head. "Get this. Her bed faces a work by the artist, Rene de'Anjou. Painted in 1460, it is *Marie Madeleine Preaching to the King and Queen of Marseilles.* "

"You've had your phone call, heard her voice and come away with a detailed account of her status." Pierre grinned. "As usual, our Dana is being guided—and by the Magdalene, no less. So why do I see your mouth returning to a frown?"

Eric reluctantly grinned. "You're right, of course. In spite of near-misses, I have to remind myself that she has succeeded in outwitting Benjamin, meeting up with allies, and is now tucked away safely in her bed with the Magdalene looking down." He turned from Pierre to glance back at his computer screen. "My frown was due to my having discussed the Code's results linking her with Benjamin."

"It's not apt to lull her to sleep." Pierre agreed.

"She seemed to take it alright, assured me she'd keep an eye out for someone named "Q" and even suggested that maybe his connection was what saved her." Eric raised his cup of cold coffee in a toasting gesture. "Whatever the beneficent influence, I'll drink to all's well that ends well—for Dana and for us." He sat back down in front of his computer screen, his enthusiasm restored. "Now let's see what turns up when we convert our word search to Hebrew." He shook his head. "I'm baffled by the fact that, despite our manuscripts having no connection with the authorship of the Torah, we seem to be getting results. But I do think we should now refer to our code as the Cathar Code—or simply, the Code."

"Agreed, but putting aside the Code and its prophetic aspects for the moment, the Professor and I have come up with some provocative revelations in working on the manuscript translations." Pierre's voice held a mix of awe and excitement, seconded by the Professor's outburst.

"He's right. The implications are powerful!" The Professor walked over, excitedly turning to Eric. "We wanted to tell you but not until Dana had called." He pointed to Pierre. "You tell him."

Pierre began, slowly and deliberately, his words accented with awe. "In essence, we find that each manuscript seems to be a tutorial or instruction manual, using the sounds of the language—how the letters combine to create words—to understand the mystery of how alchemical transmutation of energy is accomplished when different elements are combined."

"Wow!" Eric shook his head. "How exactly?"

"Divine, or spiritual energy, light, is 'lowered' through mental, air, emotional and water energetic frequencies, to become physical (earth). Spiritual evolution—essential for our planet—must be mastered by reversing the energetic flow back to enlightenment."

The concept rang in Eric's thoughts throughout the night, especially the frightening conclusion, "...those that can accomplish it must accomplish it in time to transform the planet."

THIRTY

Dana stopped to catch her breath after rounding a rough stretch of upward climb and arriving at a plateau. She felt elated at the perfect blue skies and mild temperatures, at the gite owner's sharing with her the route to Mary's special places, and, most of all, at being alone. She hoped her luck would hold and that no one would be poking about when she finally reached the remote caves. As she resumed her climb toward the grotto, she gazed full circle to assure no one neared. *Well*, she thought, *not entirely alone. Just before falling asleep—perhaps in a dream—Mary had come to me, saying I should trust in her guidance.*

With each step, Dana silently thanked, not only the Magdalene, but the gite owner. His directions were as perfect as his inspiring tales of the Magdalene had been. Before Dana had left this morning, he'd provided her with information and maps of the area. He'd also lent her a knapsack, a water canteen and a coffee thermos. His wife had even packed a picnic lunch. She shifted her backpack and glanced down at her tennis shoes, hoping they would hold up for the rugged terrain. So far so good, she thought, resuming steps which felt as light as her spirits as she drew near to the first of the special areas indicated on the map. "This her private place", the gite owner had said. "She teach, preach and pray many hours, many days until the last years of her life." *Now,* she thought as she stopped to remove the tiniest of her cameras, *let no one else appear.* To capture the special mood of timeless endurance, she needed every shot to count. Thankful that her digital camera's sophistication and its special lens should result in quality shots, she almost lost herself in the magic of capturing the views. Suddenly she remembered Eric asking her to capture her adventure on tape as an aid for his article. It was easy to forget his recorder, so small that she'd inserted it behind the slot on her camera case that held her business card.

She smiled at her resistance and his response. *'I don't want to think about shouting into that thing as I film.'*

'No worries. It'll pick up a whisper.'

She began an account of the setting as she snapped dozens of shots. Her excitement grew as her attention was drawn to what looked like the perfect setting to capture on film. Just up ahead she could make out a wall of tumbled boulders, concealing what she could identify as cave openings. She hesitated, taking plenty of time to scan for light, angles and distance. Reassured at the solitary setting, she blessed the remoteness of the area as she clicked away, whispering her emotion of excitement as she previewed the results.

A long sigh escaped at the glory of the special morning light. *Perhaps*, she thought, *the lack of other explorers was due to her 6:30 departure. It was early even for her.* She looked at her watch. 8:30. A *perfect time and a perfect light.* After inserting her long-distance lens, she took many distance shots before moving closer. As she contorted herself to capture certain angles, she regretted having left her tripod behind.

Each series of shots brought her closer to the caves. More grottos than caves, she decided as she neared. Their subterranean caverns appeared large enough to provide shelter from the elements. Some were spacious enough to provide a hideaway for anyone seeking solitude. As she entered one of them, she glanced overhead and discovered what had created such a special dwelling. Carved by the power of water, that element still continued its sculpting, as evidenced by the slight sheen of moisture nurturing a ceiling of green mosses and ferns.

As Dana captured the scene and her mood in a series of photos, she felt a growing sense of not being alone. Responding to the strong presence, she stashed her camera, deciding to bask in the energy of the place and of the soul who had once occupied it. A rocky outcrop within the grotto provided a perfect ledge on which to perch. Settling herself atop it, she smoothed her palm over the slightly indented surface of the worn granite. As she did, she closed her eyes to meditate. A series of visions formed accompanied by a subdued light. It filled her interior landscape with the shadowy outline of a face—soft, wreathed in smiles and framed in a mass of russet colored hair. The eyes radiated a love that brought tears to Dana's own. Feeling anointed with bliss, she understood for the first time the meaning behind the word. The familiar scent of roses brought tears to Dana's eyes and a smile to her lips as she waited, content to remain in such a state.

The image faded. Before any distress could surface, the image resumed, this time less a static profile than a series of active scenes. They reminded her, not of photos, but while similar to a film, communicating more than objective scenes. As she watched she had a sense of inhabiting Mary Magdalene's life, thoughts and emotions. Waves of experiences and relationships washed over Dana. She relived Mary's early life—not as a prostitute—but as a well-to-do woman of vast intelligence and a seeking heart. She more than "saw" Mary's early contact with Jesus, who guided her in vanquishing her "demons"—not those of a crazed state of mind, but those of ego, doubt and despair. A multitude of scenes revealed Mary's zealous support of Jesus as she preached, taught, wrote and traveled beside him—ultimately becoming his beloved companion and primary disciple. Dana felt the joy and passion of their wedding at Cana and Mary's warmth and closeness to Jesus' family. As the scenes rapidly moved forward to images of the crucifixion, Dana experienced Mary's deep pain and despair, as well as her intelligent complicity—with the aide of Joseph of Arimathea—in assuring Christ's survival.

Dana, although transfixed by the emotions of the images, could feel a trace of surprise ripple through her as the scene of the crucifixion soon was rapidly followed by the birth of Mary's and Jesus' first child, their journeys away from Jerusalem seeking countries of greater safety, her sorrow at parting from Jesus to undertake the journey to Marseilles with Joseph of Arimathea,

Jesus' sisters, brother and Mary's firstborn child. Suddenly the scene shifted from a boat. Dana recognized the countryside of southern France, startled at the images clearly resembling this very grotto. Many experiences of Mary's life in France streamed past—images of her teaching, preaching, praying and fasting, her home these caves and grottos. But such images faded as that of Mary returned, looking directly at Dana and beckoning her to follow.

Dana strained to make out any path as she scurried behind the ethereal image moving her effortlessly away from the grotto. Although there was no path and no indication that there had ever been one, Dana seemed to glide effortlessly over the ragged terrain. She slowed as they neared an area increasingly thicketed and densely covered by massive walls of overgrown scrub and ragged spills of rock. So daunted was she by the physical reality of the terrain that she hesitated, replacing her effortless movements with a sudden stumble as she lost her footing. The energy seemed to pause and wait. Dana regrouped and pressed on, catching her breath as she felt the Mary energy grow. Somehow a thick stand of dense brush parted, unaided, as a large boulder behind it, seemingly imbedded for eons, effortlessly moved. A swirl of a wind that wasn't a wind sped toward an entrance, as if motioning Dana to follow.

Dana cautiously entered, remaining in a semi-stooped position as the Magdalene compelled her to move deeper into the darkness of the cave. What little air it held was overhung with the silence of centuries. Unable to see, Dana followed in the wake of she who had preceded her. In spite of her growing claustrophobia, Dana moved in pitch dark, guided by trust in the Magdalene. A pause, a slight movement and a sudden turn indicated that Dana should follow an offshoot of the cave. Narrow and furnished with many boulders filling its cramped interior, navigating it proved daunting. A rustle of sound accompanied the sensation of the Mary energy having elegantly removed all obstructions. Her energy expanded with a definite sense of purpose, as though searching for a specific cluster of boulders. Dana suddenly felt enveloped by the energy form which compelled her to kneel down and touch a strange "boulder". Obscured by eons of encrustations, Dana could tell with one touch that it's shape resembled that of an ancient amphora.

A sudden rush of power descended and Dana found herself easily removing the amphora's seal and reaching within. As it opened, an unearthly light filled the cavern. She removed a parcel wrapped in a dirt-caked fabric. Rotting and falling away, it enshrouded a rolled parchment. As Dana held it up, the Mary energy radiated with urgency as a message filled, not only Dana's thoughts, but her entire being. *My Christ has told me to fulfill one last mission. The time is now. Do not hesitate.* As Dana formed a question as to what it was she was meant to do, the energy compelled her to reach deeper into the interior of the small, vault-like extension of the cavern. Dana's hands touched a different container—this one even more substantial than the other. Smooth and cool, it felt as though it was made of crystal with stiff protrusions—legs?—extending from its corners.

"The Redeemer lives." The words resonated within every cell of Dana's being, as well as externally. They filled the cave, bringing an acute ecstasy that brought Dana to her knees.

"What am I to do?" She asked, her words echoing through the cavern. An impulse directed her to place a hand on the crystal casket as a response resounded. "Your answer lies within." It surprised her by opening easily. Dana reached inside and gently explored what appeared to be someone's relics—a collection of bones and a skull with hair attached. Dazed, Dana forced herself to look up—straining to define Mary's energy. It took shape, moving from energy to a misty outline of a beautiful woman convulsed in tears. The figure looked up from the casket's contents, her tears flowing unrestrained as she lifted the skull to the heavens. "He lived. He lives—forevermore." The powerful pronouncement reverberated through the cave and into the heavens.

Dana shivered with a chill greater than any she'd ever felt before. Suddenly another energy filled the small space, an energy with such massive power that Dana felt as though she weighed a million tons and would sink through the planet. As it slowly left, the image of Mary—bathed in bliss—turned to her and placed the manuscript, resting alongside the skull, into the crystal casket. Her voice sounded like ethereal music, each note imbedding itself into her very soul. "Keep it safe. It, and your manuscripts, must return the light of the world now—when it is most is needed."

THIRTY-ONE

Benjamin waited, like a cat at a mouse-hole, knowing his prey would have to make her exit. His recent debacle had to be countered by his capture of Dana—soon. He had done everything but peer under the masks of anyone with a camera at Marseille. Empty-handed, he feared the repercussions after his report to the Overseer.

He drummed his fingers against the table, his rage off the charts at the thought of the finality of his future should he not succeed. But he would succeed. It was all that mattered now. He held fast to the image and the emotion as he waited for his meeting with the Overseer.

And waited—and waited. The devious Overseer was letting him stew in his juices. He resumed rehearsing his high-card, trusting that, when introduced, it would counter-balance his temporary loss of his prey. But first he'd need to get support for an instant counter-attack and personnel to accomplish it.

He'd thought it through, convinced his logic warranted an immediate full-court press to assure her capture. She had remained somewhere in Provence, he felt certain. Equally certain was her need to return to Eric. To do that she would be limited in her choice of the a few main highways headed west. She'd almost certainly take the faster autoroute de deux mers. With enough personnel, he'd have lookouts posted at Montpellier, Bezier, Carcassonne and Toulouse exits, as well as at all the cafes along the highway. He smiled at his cleverness in having checked all car rental agencies, finally coming away with a description of her car. Unfortunately, they could give no information as to Danas direction, but only that she intended to return it in Toulouse within the week. Knowing the foolishness of trying to search for her—with all the country roads and directions impossible to explore—he came up with his plan to identify the moment she joined the main highway heading west. Now to have the Overseer agree to his request.

As the minutes passed he felt a trickle of perspiration carving a path down his spine. *Should he play his high-card first?* He wondered. It had taken a great deal of persuasion to convince the next President of the U.S. that he should be in on sharing a treasure so powerful as to transform the world. His response—laughter and dismissive words—rang in his memory:

A pipe dream. Manuscripts that could transform the world? The Vatican controlling them? Now, the Midas touch with unlimited gold would get my attention. But you must be joking to think I'd waste time on an undefined "treasure" that may never materialize and, if it were to, would disappear in the labyrinth of the Vatican. Why ask me to get involved? I intend to get elected and if it doesn't assure me votes, don't waste my time."

Benjamin remembered pulling out all the stops to keep his attention. He highlighted the power of this treasure—so significant as to start the Inquisition and destroy all "heretics" who might possess it. The Templars may well have discovered its power, as evidence by the unceasing wealth in their coffers. That was the point at which his ears perked up, his entire demeanor changing as Benjamin mentioned the Rennes treasure and the magnitude of riches that would assure him the Midas touch he needed.

"Why should the Vatican need a partner in this endeavor?" The senator's words rang in his ears. He'd prepared his response both to the senator, as well as to the Overseer.

Benjamin replayed every moment, savoring the memory of his concluding argument, considering it his finest hour. He let it run through his thoughts, a smile as his confidence grew. *This is a treasure so powerful that it cannot be hidden away, nor can it be understood or implemented without the cooperation of the most powerful government in the world. We no longer live in a primitive world such as existed in the thirteenth century. Such a treasure cannot be kept under wraps. Once the magnitude of its potential becomes known, countries will fight to possess it.*

It was at that point that the Senator began to lick his lips, firm his posture and take the bait as he replied: *"I'll agree to a meeting with your Vatican contact, but it has to be soon."* He'd pulled out his card, hastily jotting his local phone number. "Have him call me soon."

Benjamin felt adrenaline surging through him. He had rehearsed his presentation all night long, hoping its logic would be as equally convincing with the Overseer. *Where is he?* He thought as he jumped up and began to pace the office, looking out into the distance at the spires of Fontfroide Abbey. *I need to get the surveillance team in place immediately.*

Footsteps sounded behind the door. Unrushed, firm and as confident as the man who entered. Benjamin remained standing, trying to read the emotion behind the Overseer's eyes. It was impossible. His composure was that of marble—fixed, solid, enduringly impenetrable.

"I understand your prey has outwitted you once again." He looked at his watch. "Time is running out, Mr. Carter."

"Yes, but…" He proceeded to present his plan and request the Overseer's allotment of personnel to assure its effectiveness.

"You at least had the intelligence to come to me before initiating an action that would prove, once again, to backfire." He walked to his desk, picked up the phone and after a brief conversation ending with, "Very good. Report to me at its implementation." He turned, nodded and said, "It is done. I will inform you of when and where an opportunity presents itself. The rest is up to you." The look in his eyes was dispassionate but deadly.

Benjamin rushed to frame his more significant proposal. He began by describing his relationship—a white sheep cousin in Benjamin's black sheep family—with the Senator. The Overseer seemed well aware of the man, his goals and his likelihood of taking the helm of the U.S. in the upcoming election.

Benjamin rushed forward the rationale of the man and the country's power to aid the Overseer in accomplishing his aims with the treasure.

"You did what?" was repeated more than once.

The Overseer's look of incredulity struck terror in Benjamin as he realized what a terrible gamble he had taken. So heinous that, not only could he be living on borrowed time, but so could his venerable cousin, the senator.

He had no choice but to press on. He rushed forth all the logical reasons why such a treasure couldn't be hidden away this time around. And that, given that fact, the Vatican could not be assured of controlling it without an alignment with the world's most powerful country; one whose soon-to-be-president would like a meeting to discuss the benefits of such a partnership.

The Overseer fell silent. His focus, while seemingly out the window, actually was directed to the dissecting all of the pros and cons of such a meeting. He turned back to Benjamin, his look of assurance much more commanding than any President's. "Call him. I will meet with him now."

Benjamin was shocked to even reach the Senator, but more so to have him agree to join them shortly. Such an unexpected response puffed him up with a confidence he'd not felt for some time. *I must have sold him. Soon the Overseer will follow.* He was left alone with such satisfying thoughts as the Overseer left the room—not hurriedly, but with power and purpose in his steps.

Thirty five minutes passed before the Overseer returned with the Senator in tow. Benjamin had never seen his cousin display anything close to modesty before, knowing the word "genuine" wasn't in his lexicon. However, as a politician he could read his adversaries and choose his posture to accomplish his ends. Clearly the brief introduction was all it took to tell him the Overseer was not one to be messed with.

Their meeting as a threesome was brief—barely enough to go over a bare bones outline of 'how powerful, how soon, how shared' issues surrounding the possession of the treasure. Once having the direction established, the Overseer dismissed Benjamin.

An hour and a half of cooling his heels elapsed before the senator exited. Benjamin tried to interpret his look but it remained neutral until his cousin began to speak as they headed for the car.

"The Vatican wouldn't be involved if this treasure wasn't massive." Benjamin remained silent, noticing the look in his cousins eyes—a look that dismissed Benjamin's need to respond as inconsequential. "My interest is definitely piqued, but only if the timing works out." The senator ran his tongue over his upper lip at an image of the outcome. "It's the old 'bird in the hand' rationale. I'll need a big bird guaranteed to buy me enough votes to cinch my election. A treasure that might take forever to manifest—and that must be shared by others—isn't at all attractive right now." His stream of consciousness faded as he turned to look at his cousin. "Now, my dear Benjamin, if you could sweeten the pot with a sure bet that would buy me ample voters I'd definitely be interested enough to make it worth your while."

THIRTY-TWO

Jubilation rang throughout the room as Professor Marty, his massive bulk suddenly as light as a feather, glided about the room, repeating, "This is it! I swear we did it!" He stopped his victory dance to clasp arms with his teammates who, although trying to retain a veneer of scientific doubt, shared his exuberant excitement.

One by one they turned back to their computer screens, fearful that either the information had disappeared or they may have overlooked some important piece. Pierre was the one who pointed to a stream of data and sounded a note of caution. "Look, I agree. It's beginning to reveal something provocative. My concern is that it seems pretty farfetched as the treasure's secret. But, as researchers, we must confirm such incredible output." He shook his head as he looked up and Professor Marty responded.

"Even I can't absorb its magnitude." The Professor spread out their latest run using the Code. "If what we're beginning to see occurs, then the Church wasn't overstating it when it described the Cathar treasure as "....so powerful as to transform the world..."

Pierre looked over the Professor's shoulder and gave a shudder. "True. But bear in mind the results when they used the Bible Code to verify prophesies of Isaiah concerning Armageddon. Three years showed up as probable: 2000, 2006 and 2014. Each was encoded with 'atomic holocaust' and 'World War'." Pierre paused, holding his teammates hypnotized as he continued. "Remember, as provocative as what we're getting may seem, we have to conclude events aren't entirely cast in stone. 2000 has passed without 'the ultimate terror', the year 2006 seems poised to do so and, as for 2014, we have a few years to, hopefully, moderate its fate."

"Agreed. But the issues of 'for certain', 'probably' and 'subject to change' will keep us burning the midnight oil trying to differentiate." The Professor's excitement had gradually diminished as he looked up at Pierre. "But you could at least let me bask in my 'ah-ha' moment a bit longer, my dear Pierre. The indications are overwhelming, true. But we mustn't discard them." He scowled as he looked at Pierre and waited for his response.

Pierre tried to soften his explanation. "Have a look, my dear friend." He held out some computer printouts filled with data. "So far, the Cathar Code keeps pointing to revelations so profound that, if applied, will transform the world. But such a transformation seems to entail a 'for better or for worse' option, transforming not only individuals, but—if accurate—their universe as well."

The Professor raised his eyebrows. "What are you getting at? Do you mean that certain individuals, who subscribe to specific religious tenets, will claim Paradise while others experience being allocated to the grim reality of life on a changed earth? "

Pierre tried a different tack. "Not exactly; but the indications point to the treasure needing to be revealed now because, unless certain changes are made, the code indicates 'world-brink-disaster'. And right above it is 'religious war'."

Eric, listening as he paged through charts, looked up. "We're beginning to get more information around the word 'Light'. I reread your manuscript translations. Their revelations indicate enlightened beings will begin to move toward a transformed world—free of war, greed or environmental destruction." Eric waited for a response.

Pierre was the first to nod as he picked up on Eric's train of thought. "I think you were getting confirmation when you used the Code to run further programs around the word 'Light'. All indications are that the treasure's operant concept may be 'enlightenment'. It reminded me that our earth was formed by the proclamation: "Let there be Light. If Light formed matter, then…" Pierre fell silent as the Professor picked up the thread.

"It may mean that those whose light has increasingly darkened by falling away from the spiritual and deeper into the physical are going to find it impossible to co-exist if we are in for higher vibratory fields. On the other hand, those whose energy fields have been increasingly refined, i.e., 'enlightened', will be able to exist as the planet changes its vibratory rate."

A silence fell upon the room until broken by Veronique. "As a scientist I'm aware that we humans vibrate in perfect synchronicity with the earth's vibration—but trying to understand the implications that some could and others couldn't adapt to its change, confounds me. If so, who falls into which category?" Her expression darkened. "And if such a division—what would become of less enlightened souls?"

Pierre let out a long sigh as he gathered together the latest pages of his and Professor Marty's translations. "We've just begun to open Pandora's Box. Such profound references surrounding the word, 'Light' have sent us off on a wild goose chase of esoteric scenarios. Let's keep such speculation at bay for now. "

Eric looked solemn as he stared at Pierre's print-outs of data. "If there is going to be some Big Bang, let's reserve judgment as to how that might play out until we get into the specifics of what lies ahead. Fantasizing about Good Guys, Bad Guys or any such theories as parallel universes will distract us from seeing, hearing and interpreting the manuscripts' full message."

The Professor sighed as he turned to examine the expressions on the faces of his teammates. "I don't know about the rest of you, but I was just getting into the theory of the treasure actually transforming the world by getting rid of those who have been increasingly committed to anger, hate, greed, warfare and the rape of the earth's resources. Finding their energy fields too dense to fit the evolving planet, they can simply move on and…"

Eric put his hand on the Professor's shoulder. "That's a scenario we might all enjoy, so suited is it to any scores we might want to settle. Like 'bye-bye Benjamin' for one. But tantalizing as they may be, as Pierre said, they stand in the way of understanding the true teachings."

Pierre opened his mouth to add his comments. Before Pierre could speak, Veronique, so excited that she broke into French, responded. "Alors la…" Veronique halted. "Well then, I for one am relieved not to have to contemplate any parallel universe. What would happen, for example, if you and I", she pointed to Eric, "are working on a project, and boom, I'm in a room alone and you are goodness knows where? I'd much rather an outcome where we all go boom or we all go bliss." She smiled as she looked from one teammate to another.

"I'm with you—I hope." Pierre winked as he tried to wrap it up. "Let's give ourselves a little rest"—the looked at his watch—"before we return to a scientific analysis of the manuscript's.

It was growing dark before any of them took any sustenance beyond frequent cups of coffee. Eric continued to scrutinize the code, puzzled even more by the results from his last submission. As he entered the area, date and the group having hidden the treasure, the Code provided an acrostic which included, 'Light, Vals, Mary Magdalene, Dana and 'Q' again—along with Vatican'."

Eric had just returned from a refill of coffee when he looked over Pierre's shoulder to see that he was continuing to examine the manuscripts for every appearance of the word 'Light'. "OK", he said—startling Pierre out of his focus—"whenever we come on the word 'Light' it links us to one or more of the other manuscript's references to 'Light'. What do you make of it?"

"I'm discovering, gradually, that the four manuscripts seem to be shaping a collective meaning. Granted, their surrounding symbols are still enigmatic. It makes it harder to understand what I'm convinced is an important overlay of esoteric wisdom. But the word 'Light' seems to be our flashlight in this tunnel."

Pierre grinned up at his teammate. " 'Curiouser' and 'curiouser' as Alice would say. But powerful beyond expectations."

Eric placed his coffee down on the far end of Pierre's desk and drew up a chair. "Where do we go from here? We need to understand these arcane symbols—and, more importantly, the direction such knowledge may lead to."

Pierre looked over Eric's shoulder to scan the screen. "I see you're about to expand your word search. As profound a concept as Light appears to be, it occurred to me we might want to add sound to the mix.

Overhearing, Professor Marty walked over. "As in, for example, 'In the beginning was the Word.'"

Eric matched the Professor's grin with his. "Do you think we're ready for what may show up? Look what 'Light' triggered."

The three scanned the room for Veronique. Although within hearing range, she was so totally absorbed in one of her Vals project reports that she scarcely stirred when Eric called out. "We need your opinion, Veronique. Pierre just made a suggestion that we input 'Sound' or 'Word' and see what it produces."

Veronique shook her head as she walked over. "Enough of these esoteric word bombshells. I say we examine the 'what-now' and 'what-next' area, using a present or near-future date."

That turned everyone's heads. Eric studied their expressions as they all stared at Veronique and the room fell silent. He finally spoke. "Let's take a vote. Are we all game for running such a search? Hopefully it will lead in a more pragmatic direction."

It took a moment for each to detach from his present bias. Pierre waited as one by one they nodded. "I think I speak for all when I say that we're open to trying it now."

Veronique put her report aside as she busily turned to preparing their work stations in a configuration that allowed all four of them to cluster around the computer, provide input and await output. But before sitting down she headed over to the coffee station. "For this I need to be hyper-activated with plenty of caffeine." She stopped before pouring and turned back to her teammates. "However, my stomach is rebelling at what must be my tenth cup of coffee today. Hold everything while I go search the little fridge. I need solid sustenance before getting lost in cyberspace." Without waiting for a yeah or nay, she bolted through the door, returning in short order with cold paella, two slices of left-over pizza, a large chunk of dried gruyere cheese and a box of not so crispy wafers to put the cheese on. In a matter of minutes, Veronique had transformed the food to actually resemble something edible as she arranged it in a manner suggestive enough of actual dining to activate their long-ignored taste buds.

As they made short shrift of their repast, their eyes actually brightened. This time not from excitement but from having enough calories to fortify them for a task expected to last until dawn. "The first step is to decide on the right combination of words for meaningful results." After much comradely contentious discussion they decided to add a new addition of words: danger, treasure, and Magdalene. Eric felt a ripple of anxiety.

Just as they'd completed inputting the new data, Eric's eyes fixed as tightly on the output as his ears fixed on the phone to ring. His teammates would monitor him from time to time, knowing the results were likely to renew his apprehension.

Everyone jumped at the sound of the phone's ring. Eric nearly fell over himself in the rush for his cell phone which he'd left on the coffee counter. Time seemed suspended until they heard Eric's shout. "Dana! Thank God!"

After assurances that Dana was using a phone booth on the outskirts of a miniscule village and, knowing his cell phone had been 'cleaned', he gave her impatience a green light as he rolled his chair off at a distance to avoid distracting his team. They could hear Eric discussing something that prompted frequent outbursts of "No!" Even such dramatic asides didn't interrupt the intensity of their focus. Not until, that is, Eric shouted. "You found another manuscript?!"

All activity stopped as all eyes and ears turned to follow his conversation. "A crystal container with what—are you sure—the bones and hair of who? No! It can't be possible. The bones must be the missing relics of Mary Magdalene. I read about a crystal casket holding some of her relics that disappeared during the 1700s. She said what? You saw who? No! They're *not* Mary's missing relics? Whose?" Color drained from his face and fear filled his eyes. "Don't even whisper such a thing!" Eric jumped up, shook his head and began to pace as he listened. His open-mouthed audience strained to catch every word. "That manuscript must be used alongside our manuscripts in order to understand the treasure?" He listened for awhile longer before repeating with even greater intensity, "No names!"

By then Eric had a semi-circle of three teammates trailing his steps, hanging onto every word of the unbelievable dialogue. "Dana, you're in great danger. Our recent results connect the treasure with 'Baphomet', or Mary Magdalene, linked with the words 'danger' and 'skull'". A gasp accompanied his words. "The scene you described seems beyond belief. Are you sure you haven't gone off the deep end due to the strain of your past few days?" Eric held the phone away from his ears; the sound of Dana's wrath filling the room. "Calm down. I want you back as soon as possible. If you leave in the morning and drive straight thru…" Is your rent-a-wreck up to such a journey? What if it breaks down? And what if you're followed?" He hung on Dana's response.

"Right; maybe it's me that's going off the deep-end. But whatever you do, given your cargo, don't stop! It's much too dangerous." A heavy sigh preceded his swift turn, an action that clipped the Professor, only inches away. "Of course I'm anxious to see it. That is to say, "*we* are anxious to see it. But I'm more anxious to see you arrive in one piece." A long silence filled the room. Eric's set jaw, deep breaths and anxious pacing were the only communication for what seemed to his audience to be achingly endless stretches of silence. "All right Dana. Go for it." More silence and a deepening frown. "Make sure you won't need to stop except for petrol. Ask the gite owner to pack you food for your journey. If you decide, for any reason, to stop for the night—call and let me know!"

He halted, listening intently to Dana's reaction. "Whatever happens—relics be damned—don't take any risks!"

He sighed as he turned and ran into a wall of teammates. Eyebrows raised, he tried to describe the teams' reaction, adding, "You realize we'll all be on tenterhooks until your arrival. Your manuscript may be our missing lynch-pin. Drive carefully and give me a call whenever you stop for petrol." He listened intently before repeating his concern. "Should anything—I repeat anything—happen to your car, or should you discover anyone following you, find one of the busiest motorway cafes, remain there and call me. I'll be there as fast as our Twingo can go." After a series of "um-hums" and "you're sure" types of comments, Eric added heightened reminders of his concern along with fervid assurances of his love.

Dana must have given a response of a different kind. “I know. *She’s* guiding you.” Eric’s voice radiated impatience. “But I’m not confident her guidance could prevail in the face of Benjamin or the Vatican’s team.” He softened his comment as he aired a sudden decision. “It’s tempting to head for the gite, or for me to head for where you are—but that would take too long.” He paused, focusing on her response. “So come ahead as far as Arques. I’ll meet you and escort you to Vals.”

As Eric listened, he smiled. “Of course. I remember it well. I’ll be waiting at the abandoned bus stop.” He hesitated. “Try to make it as close to seven-thirty as possible, but take whatever time you need. I’ll be there.” Drawing a deep breath, he listened closely as Dana repeated the time and place. “Exactly. Call me should anything delay you. I won’t relax until you and your cargo are safely here in Vals.”

As Eric hung up the phone, he shook his head, a look of shocked disbelief in his eyes as he turned to his teammates. They ignored the results of their latest word input, so impatient were they to listen as Eric began to discuss Dana’s extraordinary account. A hushed air, mixed with doubt, awe, wonderment and increasing fear for Dana’s safety, enveloped the room. Hours vanished as the discussions continued into dawn, deflecting their focus from the output of their recent entries. Fortunately, since a scrutiny of the code’s new output would have instantly escalated Eric’s fears for Dana beyond his—or his teammate’s—toleration limit.

THIRTY-THREE

Dana departed laden down with tokens of her hosts' generosity. The front seat was filled with a basket brimming with foodstuffs sufficient to sustain three people. As she waved one last farewell, she turned and headed down the country lane. Her emotions were as brimful as the basket beside her. She felt unbearable excitement at heading back, compounded by acute anxiety at the safety of the parcel entrusted to her. Never a pill taker, she suddenly wished she had some medication guaranteed to mute her growing apprehension.

Eric's phrase, 'soldier on', came to her as she got behind the wheel of her car. Repeating it, sotto voce, she reached up to touch her Occitan cross necklace that concealed Eric's miniature recorder. Touching it as a talisman, it helped to reconfirm her vow to accomplish her mission.

She drove with one eye watching for any strange cars, one eye on the highway ahead, and one hand periodically confirming the safety of the parcel she'd carefully wedged in front of the passenger seat. It looked so cheerful in the brightly colored gift wrapping her hosts were eager to provide. Dana smiled at her reply when her hosts asked who the present was from. *It is a gift from a special friend.*

I wonder what they would they have said if I had told them that it was a gift from Mary Magdalene? Dana shivered at the enormity of safeguarding such a profound gift to the world. Her heart skipped a beat, forcing her to take a long, slow breath. *Anxiety clouds the strength I'll need for my journey,* Dana thought as she glanced at the clock on the dashboard. It was nearly ten o'clock as she turned onto the motorway and headed southwest. *Not as early a departure as I intended*, she thought, *but it was important to take time to say farewells, fill the car with petrol, check the oil, water, tires and scan for anything tampered with.* She gave an appreciative pat on the car's dashboard before accelerating into the fast lane. Encouraged at a mileage sign indicating the distance to Aix en Provence and Arles, she did a rapid calculation. *I should be in Arles by noon, take less than an hour for lunch, Montpellier by three, Bezier by four- thirty, putting me at our rendezvous spot in Arques a little before dark.*

As noon neared, she spotted a sign indicating Arles just ahead. She shook her head to dislodge the highway hypnosis that had overtaken her. So many miles had flown by without her awareness. Even so, she'd managed to check for any strange cars keeping pace with her and confirm that the parcel hadn't taken any wild shifts. A stretch of light rain required wind-shield wipers and a glance down at the gas gauge, thinking, *It's time to look for a gas station-café stop.*

Within ten kilometers she saw the first exit, meaning a petrol station ahead. Soon she was parked in the petrol bay, filling the tank and admiring the old car's dependable service. The tank full, she pulled over into an area of picnic tables alongside the petrol station. A thorough scrutiny revealed several vehicles in the campground. She studied the two large semi-trucks and the four sedans with families spreading their picnics along the greensward of grass. Dana decided to remain in her locked car and explore the contents of her picnic basket. *But first* she thought, *I must use the ladies room.*

She gently retrieved her 'birthday gift' and made her way toward the WC. Glancing at each closed latrine door, she worried that one of them may harbor someone suspicious. As she neared the last empty stall, a little girl of about eight years rushed up, having spotted the bright parcel in Dana's hands.

"Tres beau!" She reached up to touch it.

"Non, Amie. Ne pas toucher le cadeau!" The mother rushed up and pulled the child's hand away, frowning as she turned her child and herself toward the exit.

Dana dashed into a cubicle, her heart racing as she clutched the parcel. Minutes went be as she waited for all sounds to cease before she pushed the door open, washed her hands and dashed back to the safety of her car.

After locking the door, she tucked the parcel securely in front of the passenger seat, feeling her heartbeat return to normal. Assured no one suspicious lurked nearby; she opened her basket.

A chunk of Gruyere cheese, an apple, a flaky croissant and a long drink from the carafe of coffee, restored her. As she pulled back onto the motorway, she felt a renewed sense of confidence in the Magdalene guiding her safely to her destination.

The kilometers must have flown past without my registering them, Dana thought as she saw the fairy tale towers of Carcassonne shining in the setting sun. She moved the car to the right, following the sign indicating D118, her exit for Arques. Heightening her attention on any strange cars that followed, she nearly plowed into the car ahead of her at the exit's toll station.

As she pulled away, heading for Arques, she felt a surge of energy triggered by the familiarity of the road. A sense of being on the homestretch prompted the release of a long sigh. Silently, she repeated an heartfelt prayer of thanks to the Magdalene. A beautiful and very distinct sense of energy—not the masculine 'can do' type of energy, but a deep infusion of feminine wisdom—descended, leaving her with an all-encompassing sense of her own power. She marveled at never before having recognized, so directly, her strength. As the thought entered her mind it met with an unspoken, but distinct, internal response. *Such energy is returning to the world. The feminine power is sorely needed to revitalize the light which is the heart and soul of your planet. I am honored to contribute to such a treasure.*

Dana held the energy of the message close to her heart, feeling it radiate through her, infusing the car with waves that seemed to radiate to and from the precious package lying innocently on the floor. She was in such a state of bliss that she took extra care as she made the turn to Coustaussa. Bringing herself slowly back to the physical present, she kept a look-out in the distance for the towers of Arques Castle

As she neared the castle, its rural serenity was highlighted in the twilight, the glow of still-visible fields of yellow encircling it within a blanket of spring flowers. Rather than perched majestically high on a mountain-top it sat securely, yet rather forlornly, on flat ground at the outskirts of the village. It owed its intact status to having been built during the fourteenth century, soon after the terror that destroyed the Cathars.

Dana recalled her surprise at her first visit to Arques Castle. It had provided the most complete illustration of life in a castle in the thirteenth century. As she'd taken the spiral stairway that led up through all four floors—each level intact with spacious rooms—she remembered thinking that, with the addition of a few Persian carpets, she could move right in, snuggle into one of the window seats, and admire the courtly carvings on the walls. She'd not felt the usual grief and rage that would have prevailed had Cathars been killed within—only admiration at the castle's state of preservation.

She pondered such emotions as she drove by, aware that admiration wasn't the same as love. Peyrepertuse or Queribus, virtually any Cathar castle, all in crumbling stages of destruction, filled her with a passion beyond expressing.

Her reveries faded, her heart beating fast as she neared the abandoned bus station. The small brown building, surrounded by a fallen veil of wire intended to wall off entry, looked rather sad, as if mourning the loss of its once-familiar gaggle of passengers.

She strained to see through the darkening skies, her vigilance at the highest level. But this time her focus was searching for their familiar red Twingo. She slowed down, peering intently for any sign of people, movement, anything unusual at all before she even considered stopping. *Parking alongside the old bus stop for any length of time is chancy*, she thought.

Dana drove past, puzzled at no sign of Eric approaching. She decided to reverse direction and return to the bus-station.

Chancing a brief stop, she turned off the ignition and glanced at the dashboard clock. *It's our agreed upon time. What's keeping Eric?* As she looked up, she saw a car parked at one of the pumps of the little petrol station across the street, just down from the bus station. She stepped out to get a clearer view. Although darkness was descending, she felt certain it could be their red Twingo. *Eric must be filling up the tank for the drive back to Vals*, she thought.

Dana debated whether or not to reach inside, draw out the parcel and cross the street for their rendezvous—or risk sounding the car's horn to alert him she was there. She strained for a closer look, trying to be certain it was Eric before she crossed the road or drove away from their agreed upon meeting place. Out of nowhere, a car—moving much too fast—nearly ran her over. Dana froze to the spot, suddenly riveted with fear as the black sedan slowed to a halt. A man leaped out, his arm darting swiftly to yank her near. Dana screamed: "Eric!"

Before she could tell if Eric heard and followed, she looked up at her assailant. "Benjamin!" Dana's adrenaline soared. She fought like a wildcat, kicking, scratching and hanging onto the Magdalene's gift with a grip that would never let go. Her screams were equally powerful. "No! Never! Mine!" She yanked at the precious package whose wrapping seemed to get caught on the car's door handle.

"Damn you Dana!" The angry words were her last memory as Benjamin thrust something into her neck that felt like a very painful bite. Raging at her dwindling focus, she did her best to remain upright but found herself falling to the ground as the deadly elixir sent her into blackness.

THIRTY-FOUR

Dana fought to free herself from the depths of a painful haze pierced by flashes of lightning. Although her vision was slow to return, her ears registered a cacophony of voices as if she were being questioned by a band of demons. Individual sounds pierced her pain, their rolling tones ranging from harsh declarative statements to softer, but no less urgent, questioning. As hellish as her mental landscape felt, she fought to remain within its maelstrom rather than awake to the reality of her questioners.

"Come on. You should be coming out of it by now." The voice's familiarity, accompanied by a firm shaking, prompted her to wince as she slowly raised her eyelids to the sight of Benjamin. Not the slick Benjamin Carter of dark, handsome, honored researcher fame. But his antithesis. His clouded image recalled the portrait of Dorian Grey at the end of his life—grotesquely ugly, etched by eons of his soul's evil deeds.

"I see the famous photographer has decided to join us." Benjamin's voice was all that remained of the Benjamin she'd first met. It's rich tones coated a delivery that had increased its arrogant smugness. "Don't try to retreat into unconsciousness." She felt a prick of her arm, accompanied by a hot flush. "This should bring you round."

It did exactly that. She experienced a surge of energy beyond anything normal, prompting her to attempt to rise. Energy aside, it wasn't enough to break the bonds tying her to a chair. She shook her head, the only part of her free to move. Encouraged by the faint sliding to and fro of her necklace, she blinked to clear her vision, spotting three men in the background.

One of them was clothed in the garments of the priesthood. She frowned, puzzled at his garb's flash of red. *More than a simple priest,* she thought. Another man stood near the door, his bulk alone declaring his role.

The third man, although dressed conservatively, seemed somehow out of place. He spoke, his voice carrying arrogance and urgency, coated with the honeyed twang of the South. "We need the manuscripts. Ask her where they are."

Dana watched as the more-than-a-priest person gave him a look of contempt scarcely softened by the neutrality of his firm response. "All will be accomplished in good time, Senator."

As the confident words left the mouth of the person who was obviously the leader, Dana watched as he turned his focus from the Senator to the third man in the room. His size and strength weren't disguised by his unassuming garb as he stood guarding the door. It was the look that passed between them that curdled Dana's blood. The look heightened the vigilance that flashed in the guard's eyes, as alert and challenging as to preclude the devil himself escaping.

Questions fought for priority in Dana's consciousness. *Where was this room*? With no easy view out the widows, nor any décor identifying it as a home or a cell, she had only one clue—a large desk. *So it's an office*, she thought. *But where? And how long had she been out?* Her watch was missing, but her ring and necklace remained. *Was she still in Arques?* Suddenly an image returned that caused her to gasp, biting back her biggest question. *What became of the Magdalene's gift? Had she dropped it as...?* "Eric—where is Eric? What have you done to him?"

Benjamin sneered. "The idiot actually thought he could outrun us. He will soon take the bait and join us." The confidence in his tone was like bubbling acid, reminding Dana that Benjamin lived to extract justice from those responsible for his physical and professional destruction—Eric and herself.

As if he read her thoughts, Benjamin glanced from Dana to the guard at the door. "And when he does, I assure you he will not leave." Benjamin's steely statement was emphasized by an addendum. "My friend will see to that."

"Enough. Your role is not to instruct the guard at the door." The ecclesiastical man's tone was so firm as to send chills down Dana's spine. He turned on Benjamin a gaze that instantly halted any presumption of seniority.

As the most powerful person, Dana directed her comment to him, hoping his status in the Church assured compassion. "How can a priest go along with such evil?"

The man drew himself to an even fuller stance, erasing Dana's 'priest' descriptor with the overweening majesty of his powerful presence. His pale complexion matched his white hair, both of which were belied by the vigor of his posture and the power in his voice. His tones were as deep and as assured as if they ushered from the mouth of God himself. Their imperious message broached no challenge. "My role is to guard the treasure—for the good of the Church and the world." His eyes punctuated his tones as they glared in emphasis, stabbing his mission, like an icicle, into her heart.

As he finished speaking, Benjamin couldn't restrain himself. "The Overseer has spoken. I vow to put the treasure in his hands, with you as the bait. But while we are fishing", chuckling at his metaphor, "you are going to tell us the precise location of your colleagues and the manuscripts." His certainty prompted her to clench her teeth in rebuttal. He read the message in her expression. "Oh, not willingly, I'm sure you are thinking." The emphasis in his words raised the color of his furrowed complexion to a reddish purple. "But I assure you, dear Dana, that we have the means to make you talk." He turned to his colleague.

His power filled the room as the Overseer turned, steel flashing behind his dismissive glance at Benjamin. His motion to the third man at the door brought an abrupt change in Benjamin. Like a dog about to be whipped, he flinched as the guard approached.

He passed Benjamin to stand in front of Dana. His massive hands yanked the tapes that had pinned her to the chair as he drew her to a standing position. For all the energy coursing through her,

her legs must not have gotten the message. They threatened to collapse as she reached out one bleeding palm to balance herself.

"There is nothing…" Dana slurred her speech and sank to the floor.

"She hasn't fully come around." The syrupy voice of the Southerner penetrated, his tones filled with urgency as he knelt beside Dana, who lay on the cool tiles. His breath felt fetid, but heavily camouflaged with the most expensive cologne overlaying its rottenness. He flicked her hand back and forth before standing. "She's out of it."

Dana was grateful for her yoga flexibility which gave her ability to assume the inertness of a rag doll. Her body may be loose enough to feign unconsciousness, but her mind actively fought for clarity. She needed to buy time. Solemn tones—confident, clear, broaching no debate and obviously issuing from the man she'd dubbed 'Monsignor Icicle'—reached her ears.

"Contact headquarters and arrange for a supply of sodium pentothal to be sent. Mere torture, I would venture to say, will be inadequate. Maintaining Mademoiselle Palmer with a clear mind, ringing with total recall, is mandatory in order to access our information." His voice rose, not so much in volume as in authority, as he ordered Benjamin, an underling, to get the serum. "Now."

Dana remained, eyes closed and body still as her mind ran with questions. *Where am I and where is Eric? And where are the relics and Mary's scroll? Might I have dropped them at the bus station?* Dana felt encouraged at the thought that Eric may have retrieved them since the leader had never once mentioned them. *How can I escape before they return with the truth serum? What role does this Southern Senator play?* Dana tried to restore her confidence that the Magdalene would not abandon her, but concluded that, *If all else fails, I've gone to my death before and I'm willing to do it again to carry the secret of the manuscripts with me.*

Not knowing how long they would accept her unconscious state, she did a mental review of what 'truths' they may be able to pry from her with the serum. *At this point,* she thought, *I know there are four manuscripts, each requiring the others to reveal the treasure. I know that Eric and the team, sequestered in Vals, were decoding the manuscripts and seemed to have achieved some validation that it was working. As for the Magdalene's gift—oh, my y God,* she thought, *whatever they suspected so far, she did not want to reveal the full extent of their discoveries.* While estimating the degree of danger such knowledge represented, she decided it was much too risky to undergo the truth serum. *How can I resist it? I must not expose Eric and our team. If the truth serum pries out their location, will they...?* Her thoughts spun, searching for a reason for hope—to no avail.

A soft knock on the door was followed by Benjamin's voice as he reentered. "Here is the serum you requested, Monsignor Overseer."

"Tie her to the bed." The Overseer's instructions were promptly undertaken. As the voice of the guard affirmed the strength of her bonds, he remained alongside, awaiting further orders. "That will be all. Except, as you leave, order dinner to be brought in."

As the guard departed, Dana heard the Overseer address Benjamin. "If she weakens, it could impact the effectiveness of the serum. I must have the full truth."

Benjamin, of all people, failed to comment. Suddenly a harsh blow struck her. "You won't outsmart me again, dear Dana." The shock of its fierceness nearly prompted her outburst. She prided herself on maintaining a feigned stupor.

The Overseer's response was closer, clearer and caustic. "Such rashness concerns me, my dear Benjamin. It is the sort that could hinder a task that must not be compromised."

His emphasis on *must not* extinguished Benjamin's hubris. "Forgive me. I assure you that I won't let such emotions overstep your strategy again, Monsieur Overseer."

Overseer? Dana puzzled at the repeated title, never having heard of such a rank in the Catholic Church.

His response was like ice running down one's spine. "Of course you will not."

Benjamin's obsequiousness revealed his knowledge of how far he'd overstepped his role. "I assure you that my actions will lead to complete success. Soon I will be kissing your ring as the next Pope." So strong was the sudden fear that filled the silence that Dana knew Benjamin had overdone his apology.

Dana was shocked by the Overseer's long silence. It seemed so extraordinary a reaction to Benjamin's gall that she felt tempted to open one eye. *Might the Overseer had silently snuffed Benjamin into eternity?* The silence hung in the air with the brittleness of steel, its sharpness matched by the Overseer's ultimate response.

"Do not doubt that your loyalty shall be rewarded, my dear Benjamin." The slickness of his sentence segued into a threat. "But, if you—or your cousin, the senator—betray me, or, in any way, jeopardize the Church, well…" He let the unspeakable consequences echo on the air as she felt him stride away. As the door opened, the deadly weight of his words hung like storm clouds.

"Good day, Mr. Carter. The Senator and I have other business to undertake. Your business is to never forget my words." The Overseer's comment, although as smooth as syrup, was uttered with a level of threat that prompted the guard to whisper as Benjamin neared the door, "Take it from me; don't ever think of betraying the Overseer."

THIRTY-FIVE

Surging waves of anger, frustration, terror and a level of pain beyond that of his physical injuries, threatened to unhinge Eric as he replayed the image of Dana being swept into a speeding car. He'd sped after them in such haste that he'd yanked the gas pump's handle from the station owner's hands, leaving him staring in disbelief at a chase reminiscent of a movie.

"Damn!" was Eric's last word before losing consciousness when a car entered the roadway ahead of him, forcing him to spin off the road into a rock wall. Eric recalled his anxiety as he came to and wiped away a smear of blood on his watch. *Twenty minutes. Dana could be anywhere.*

He recalled the sounds of sirens filling the air as he was making a painful effort to pry the driver's door open—with no success. The passenger-side door protruded inward as if determined to meet its partner.

A police car, accompanied by a fire truck and an ambulance, had drawn alongside. A flurry of activity ensued as men pried at the door soon having it give way. They'd been careful—too careful for his anxiety level. Two men from the ambulance and one from the fire truck cautiously removed him and placed him onto a stretcher.

"No! I'm fine. I have to find Dana." The memory of the words recalled the even sharper pain that seemed to originate in his forehead and was echoed by a matching pain radiating from his right leg. He remembered thinking that it looked strangely crooked as they eased him onto the gurney. Analyzing his condition had ceased soon after someone injected him with an elixir that carried him into unconsciousness.

Darkness had fallen by the time he awoke. His leg was in a cast, but thankfully not one of heavy plaster. He looked around the room and found a pair of eyes meeting his. "Tres bon, Monsieur. Comment allez-vous?"

Eric's tongue felt heavy with its efforts to form any words, let alone in French. He managed to get out: "En peu de mots—terrible." The nurse nodded and rang a buzzer attached to the wall. Within seconds a man arrived, accompanied by a woman. The first person seemed to be a doctor, but the woman was definitely not a nurse. *Why her?* Wrapped in a cloak that enshrouded her to the eyes, she reminded him of an article he'd written on Mexican cuanderos, prompting puzzlement that French medicine should combine Latin America's herbal witchcraft. Eric's confusion heightened as the doctor said, in perfect English, "Your mother is here to see you, Monsieur Taylor. I shall leave you for awhile. When I return we shall discuss your condition."

As the door closed, his visitor neared and lowered the face covering, prompting Eric's shattered emotions to overflow and unexpected tears to start. They were followed by a rush of relief and fear. Relief at the gentle wisdom in Pierre's eyes—and fear at the likelihood of his having been followed.

"Don't exhaust yourself by speaking." As Eric shook his head and opened his mouth, Pierre covered it gently with his hand. Carefully removing his hand, he peered about the room, examining any and all outlets in his scan for a planted 'bug'. Satisfied with the visible, Pierre got down on his knees and examined the underside of Eric's bed. Rising, he entered the lavatory and repeated his search.

As he returned to Eric his usual soft-spoken voice was now barely distinguishable. "We must make use of our little time. As to what brought me here, Arques is a small town which immediately buzzed with word of a woman's abduction and a man's injuries. Word reached us in Vals and I volunteered to come, in disguise of course." He paused as the sound of footsteps outside passed on by. Releasing his breath, he smiled. "God willing, my luck—and skill as an actress—seems to have remained."

"Dana, a black car…" Eric's words were soft but frantic. His anxious stare at the door signaled his urge to bolt away and find her.

"Don't do anything foolish. We're all concerned, but we have a strategy to find her. Not one of running around willy-nilly looking for her. The black car was undoubtedly a Vatican vehicle, unmarked and untraceable. We know they are not commuting back and forth between Rome. They have her somewhere around here, hoping to bait us to reveal ourselves in our efforts to find her."

"Yes!" The look in Eric's eyes begged Pierre to do just that.

Pierre held up a finger. "We will find her' but we must proceed carefully. I trust they've set up a safe haven for their operations, a spot so inviolate as to prevent Dana's detection. But near enough to draw us."

"We must…" Eric's panic grew as he stumbled over his words, "…find her. The manuscript and the relics…" Exhausted, Eric slid back against the pillow, his face ashen.

"Let me finish." Pierre looked anxiously toward the door, lowering his voice even more. "I've spoken with Giraud. He has a cadre of discreet people investigating all likely churches, abbeys and museums. In the first cut he's targeted several abbeys within the surrounding area."

"Abbeys…?" Eric frowned. "Aren't they too touristy?"

"Some have properties removed from their public areas. Giraud's contacts will target all Church-owned properties within a radius of 200 kilometers."

Eric attempted to rise. "Don't expose Dana to danger."

"Remain calm. Our helpers don't know the real purpose of their search. They think its part of the research Giraud is doing to create a new museum brochure. No one has mentioned Dana, but a key focus for his new brochure is availability for lodging. Giraud himself, intends to investigate any such candidates.." Pierre smiled.

"As a priest. He claims he looks even better in priest's garments than I do in a woman's." Pierre smiled.

"They'll suspect…"

"True. I don't deceive myself. They'll expect such actions and anyone involved, disguised or not. With Dana missing, they know we'll be up to something soon. Any ploy we use will play into their desire to gather us together." Pierre frowned. "However, the team has discussed some strategies to give us the upper hand." At Eric's raised eyebrows, Pierre continued. "Without spelling them out, let me say that our safeguards would deceive any pursuers."

"I must be part of the search team." Eric replied.

"Of course; but just how quickly you're able to participate will depend on your doctor's approval. He assured me your leg wasn't broken, only dislocated. Rest so your general condition will allow for a swift release." Pierre looked around. "For two reasons. One, they know you are here and may have, or soon will have, bugged your room. Two, our team needs your help.."

"We must save Dana. She's…" Eric's voice faded.

"They won't harm Dana. They need her as bait to get us and our manuscripts. Don't worry. Use your confinement to come up with a plan to outwit them."

"It had better be damn soon or…" Eric's response was interrupted by an opening door and Pierre's firm pressure on Eric's arm.

"I know, my son. But you must rest and follow the doctor's orders." Pierre swept his cape up around his face, hands to his eyes to shield mock sobs as the doctor neared.

"Visiting time is over. Please give us a call tomorrow. If his progress continues to improve, you may be able to take him home." The doctor turned to hold the door for the old woman's departure. Pierre used that brief turning away to give Eric a thumbs up sign.

Pierre's departure, undertaken with the slow gait of the elderly, didn't match his racing thoughts. *Was the room bugged? Was he followed? How safe are the others? Where is Dana and what are they doing to her?* He scanned the exit, twenty feet away, its doors swinging to and fro as a solid stream of white-garbed staff and visitors ebbed and flowed. Given the newspaper's account of Eric's accident, he knew the hospital was being watched. He'd only dared his entry disguised and as part of a teeming crowd of visitors arriving to attend the opening of the new psychiatric ward. There was no such crowd now, Pierre thought, deciding to avoid so visible a means of exit. He glanced around, spotted a sign for a Ladies Room and headed in that direction, pleased to find it lay in the far corner of the building, alongside a stairway.

With no one in sight, Pierre slipped through the stairway exit, walked two floors down to the hospital's kitchen area and, giving thanks that all were too busy preparing dejeuner to notice a lost little old lady, grabbed a cook's outfit from the dirty clothes bin. Darting under the stairwell, he donned the garb of a kitchen worker, the overly-large uniform skillfully concealing his little old lady disguise. Pulling a grease-stained head cover down over his eyes, he made his exit via the loading dock area. Seeing no one in view, Pierre stepped down the ramp and crossed to the parking lot.

His heart was beating and his hands sweaty as he arrived at the beat-up car he'd long owned—tinkering with restoring it as a hobby—but kept hidden within the abandoned property just beyond Coustaussa. If they'd identified 'his' car by plates or registration, this one wasn't it. Settling himself behind the wheel was easier than settling his thoughts as he surveyed the roadway, trying to disguise his scrutiny. *I'm not destined to be a Poirot*, he thought, such a career light years away from any he'd ever envisioned.

Chosen profession or not, he felt confidence grow as he drove off with no indication of being pursued. Even so, he decided he wouldn't return directly to Vals, especially if there was the slightest chance Eric may be released from the hospital tomorrow. He decided instead, to return to his little hideaway near Coustaussa, confident no one had identified his safe haven.

A slow, steady drive down the lightly traveled back roads, with no one suspicious in view, decided him to find a phone before reaching his turn-off. He needed to update the team on Eric's status and he wanted to phone his cousin, Giraud, and quiz him about his success in pin-pointing any likely places Dana may be held.

At the sight of a roadside phone booth ahead, he pulled over and dialed Vals. Veronique answered—the team gathered around her—eager to learn of Eric's prognosis. A collective sigh of relief went up at the possibility of his being released as early as tomorrow.

"Ask him what about Dana—any word?" The Professor's loud voice in the background was filled with anxiety.

"I'm about to give Giraud a call. He's been working on identifying where they may be holding her."

Reassured, their conversation concluded with a chorus of "We need you back here soon. Things are even more provocative."

As they concluded their brief call, Pierre let out a long sigh, primed by anxiety over Dana that he couldn't release in front of Eric or their team. As he dialed, he prayed Giraud would have targeted likely sites where she might be held..

Giraud said he'd call him back. After five minutes had passed, the phone rang. "I'm taking a page from your book and using the public phone booth. Good timing, your call. I've refined the most likely Catholic sites in the area down to four that allow for *special* accommodations."

"Hold on while I get a pen and paper." Pierre poised his pen. "Let's have them."

"The Benedictine abbey in Lagrasse has some outbuildings capable of housing guests. Although I wouldn't start with it. It's focus is on Byzantine services. Saint-Polycarpe abbey near Limoux might be worth a look. Not much in the way of outbuildings, but it has an interesting aqueduct as part of the property. The third, Villelongue abbey, is privately owned and, since it isn't connected with the Catholic church, is probably a long-shot. But it does have accommodations and is remote. Last, but unlikely due to its throngs of tourists, is the Fontfroide abbey. It has extensive grounds and outbuildings that are worth at least a closer look."

Pierre felt unable to restrain his excitement as he told Giraud he may head for Limoux the minute he hung up.

"Hold everything. You'd be at risk. I've arranged for a chap to head there this afternoon and interview them for a prospective listing in our museum brochure. Wait until I receive his comments."

Pierre reluctantly agreed. After a few minutes of update on Eric and the team, Giraud said he must return to his office. "Contact me tomorrow. I should have targeted Dana's most likely location." After the call Pierre continued toward his remote hideaway, a mix of anxiety, encouragement and urgency making it hard to handle his impotence at waiting.

As he neared the country lane he removed the white butcher's robes in order to be garbed in his matronly persona on reaching his 'home'. The restaurant was closed so no cars were in view. He was careful to hide his vehicle in the fallen-down garage that was tucked well behind his part-cavern, part-shack abode. As he neared he suddenly remembered that he'd left a few books there—one in particular that covered a translation of the alchemical notes that Newton had so valued. Both nervous to verify that no one had found his lair and books, and excited that, with them, he wouldn't waste the hours, he quickened his steps.

Hours melted away. As dusk descended he withdrew to an interior room with no windows. While the meager illumination couldn't betray his presence, the book's illumination was so blinding that it kept him reading long into the night, thinking with the turn of every page: *Eric must look at this as soon as possible.*

THIRTY-SIX

The Overseer stared down on his captive. "She hasn't come around enough to swallow any food." He looked up, addressing the guard. "Could we have overdosed her?"

"No, your Excellency. The dose for her weight should have brought her back to full consciousness by now."

"Then it's time—food or no food—to see what the truth serum will reveal. Notify Professor Carter to join us now. I'll let you know when we need you." As the guard promptly exited, the Overseer turned to find the Senator looking down at Dana.

"No more stalling. This bitch is stonewalling, hoping we delay questioning her." The Senator yanked her hand, digging his fingernails into Dana's palm—with no reaction.

The Overseer's voice was icy. "*Never* initiate such actions."

The senator's attempt at an apologetic demeanor revealed his lack of experience expressing humility. "Whatever you say; it's your playground."

Benjamin arrived one minute too late to observe his cousin's comeuppance. He entered and, without any greeting, walked straight to Dana, watching her breathing intently before he looked around and met his cousin's brimming with exasperation-gaze,.

"We'd better get *all* the information she has to give the moment that serum is administered." The senator turned his challenge from Benjamin to the Overseer. "If you don't find the manuscripts, we have nothing further to discuss."

On hearing the words "*all* the information" Benjamin blanched, his thoughts agonizing over the risk he was taking in keeping the relics and the latest manuscript to himself. *I'm damned if I trust the Overseer having all the control. As to my dear cousin, Frederick, at least blood is thicker than water if I decide on a side agreement with him. What I possess may be more powerful than the manuscripts. Partnership or not, I intend to keep it well hidden.* Conviction turned to fear at the Overseer's response to the senator.

"As to your getting *everything* you need, senator, that will be determined after the Church has done its due-diligence. The manuscripts will undergo a thorough examination using every scientific analysis available." A silence descended for so long that Dana decided to risk a narrow peek. Her focus targeted the Overseer's scarcely detectable glance at his credenza.

The senator finally responded, his face flushed with anger. Like the parry and thrust of two fencing masters, his tone was equally pointed and deadly. "You claimed the Catholic Church wanted the manuscripts and that, once translated, a powerful treasure would be revealed." The senator met the Overseer's silent, granite-like gaze without flinching. "In return for my support when President of the United States, I expect to share in such power well in advance of the Presidential election. Without such assurance, I leave you to your task."

The Overseer remained unmoved. "A web of power is in place. I've had established a secret lab with the world's most renown experts awaiting the manuscripts As partners, you will be kept abreast of our strategies, but..."

The interruption was like lightning out of a darkening sky. "I repeat: all that concerns me is knowing what it is and whether its power can impact the votes I need. Given it can, you shall have the power of the U.S. to aid the Church's interests. If not..."

The Overseer stopped him with a look resembling that of a scientist studying an insect under glass. "*Interests*" is too mild a term to describe the Church's involvement, especially if the translations prove detrimental to the future of the Church. I shall determine the nature of the impact and, like a meteor, deflect any damage."

The senator moved closer to the Overseer, deliberately invading his intimate space. "Don't waste my time, Monsignor. I shall expect to know soon what the treasure is and if it has the power to get me elected. If so, you'll have the weight of the U.S. to deflect any damage to your Church."

The Overseer was unmoved by the Senator's heightened intensity. "May I remind you, dear senator, that any such agreement will call for the Church's step by step analysis of the manuscripts and their impact. We have ultra-sophisticated methods to translate the manuscripts expeditiously and will take action should their power prove detrimental." He paused, studying the impact of his next words. "They may well prove to be insignificant."

The senator glared at Benjamin and back to the Overseer. "I've been assured that the Church has known of their power for centuries. Your records of the Inquisition attest to their power to transform the world'."

"True. But to transform the Thirteenth Century world or the Twenty-First Century world? Such a determination is part of the studies the Church shall undertake." The Overseer waited to see if his words had registered with the senator, adding, "Our preliminary agreement states that at various stages of the testing of the manuscripts, and before any announcement is made, the Catholic Church shall agree to the appropriateness of going forward."

The senator's face moved from red to purple as he exclaimed: "You're telling me that at any stage you may stop it?" He looked over at Dana. "When you don't even know where the manuscripts are?" He sneered. " I don't need this."

"I suggest you reserve judgment until after we've learned what Ms Palmer shall reveal." He walked over to the intercom and rang for the guard, who instantly responded. "Now, my dear senator and you too, Professor Carter, please be assured that we shall soon learn the whereabouts of the manuscripts."

Dana's heart pounded. The Overseer clearly knew nothing of the Magdalene's manuscript and the relics. *Either they fell as Benjamin grabbed me or...* As she heard them addressing the guard she risked a quick glance. Benjamin was wiping away streams of sweat. *The truth was in those rivulets,* she thought. *He's hiding the Magdalene's treasure for himself. Knowing Benjamin's ego, she should have known he'd never let go of his find.* Such a thought compounded her fear that while under the serum's influence she'd reveal their existence. Her throat locked, causing a choking sound.

The guard's voice seemed to originate from directly over her face. "She's coming around just in time." Dana was careful not to exhibit anything beyond a preliminary stirring, faking a return to unconsciousness.

"See if you can bring her around." The Overseer's command was instantly acted upon. Dana felt like a rag doll as the bodyguard jerked her upright, shaking her enough to rattle her teeth.

"Wake up. It's time for your medicine."

Dana slumped from her forced stand to a limp pile sprawled out on the cold marble floor. Eyes shut, a soft groan emitted from her parched mouth. "Water."

"Bring her some water." The Overseer waited as the guard returned, yanking her to a stand and held the bottle to her mouth.

"Wake up, Dana Palmer." She recognized the voice of the Overseer. "We shall provide you with food. After you've eaten, we insist on a full disclosure." He paused as he took her hand. "Wake up now!" His words shocked her, not at their message, but at their power. His touch felt like that of a zombie, cool, confident and with the capacity to take life without hesitation.

She finished drinking, her eyelids wavering with effort as her lashes lowered. Her intent was to give every indication of a struggle to come out of an unconscious state so deep as to have precluded any ability to have overheard their conversation.

"Here's her tray of food." The bodyguard placed the tray on the table, hefted Dana upright and placed the spoon in her hand.

"Thank you, Leon. We shall proceed after she has eaten." The Overseer took the vial in his hand and peered into her eyes. "How fortunate for you that you decided to come around. Eat."

"Thank you." Dana muttered her response as she met the Overseer's eyes, searching for how much sympathy, if any, he might be capable of: none. Ditto from the senator. Standing behind the

Overseer, the senator's stare was veiled from long practice. But it couldn't totally obscure a growing rage toward the Overseer.

As the Overseer turned, the senator's expression startled her at the swiftness with which it resumed its poker-faced blandness.

"The food will counterbalance the earlier medication. Force feed her if need be." The Overseer removed the spoon from Dana's limp hand and gave it to the guard.

That explains the generosity of the food, Dana thought as the guard pried open her mouth. She gagged. "More water please. My throat is too dry to swallow."

"Get her more water. We need answers now!" The voice of the senator filled the room, impatience breaking through his façade and threatening to dislodge the vial of serum as he bumped the table

The look on the Overseer's face as he retrieved the sodium pentothal was like a wall of steel. "Perhaps you should leave us, senator." The voice mirrored the look. "Never again give directions to my staff, nor strong-arm them, verbally or otherwise. Any infraction and I shall be forced to terminate our meeting."

And that isn't all you'd terminate, I'd dare say, Dana thought as she drank from the water bottle. She finished it in one long draught. "More please. My mouth is so dry." Her voice faded into a laryngitic silence. Dana gambled that lots of liquid might dilute the results of the serum. After drinking the third bottle, she noticed the Overseer's look. Its power dared her not to chance requesting more. It filled Benjamin with fear and impotence.

She took a few bites of the cold fish and potatoes before putting her spoon down and retching. "I'm going to be sick." She bent over, clutched her stomach and vomited up her food.

"It's the effects of her earlier medication. Take her into the lavatory." The Overseer studied Dana as the guard led her away.

Dana was grateful the bidet was isolated behind its own full-length door. "Please, I must use the toilet." She lunged for its seclusion, continuing to retch as the guard waited outside.

A sound of chimes caused her to look up and notice a partially-opened window. *The window's mottled glass obscures visibility, but the opening may*, she thought, *give some idea of where I am.* She strained to see out the narrow slit as she pulled the toilet handle. The noisy cascade of water disguised her "oh" at the barely discernable outline of an abbey in the distance. Craning her head along the width of the opening, she peered intently, hoping for a clue as to which abbey. A shout startled her.

"Enough. Come out or I come in."

"I'm coming." Dana took one last look, thinking she'd spotted poplar trees in uniform rows. *Fontfroide Abbey!.*

How could she relay her location to Eric? Impossible. But she could record it, she thought. Before exiting she remembered her concealed recorder in her Occitan cross necklace. She turned it on, grateful she'd know what she had revealed under the serum. The thought of Eric's nearness eased her fear as the guard led her back.

The Overseer studied her as she neared. The food had been removed, the vial missing from the table. As the guard lowered her down onto the divan, the Overseer nodded. "Very good, Leon. You may leave." With his departure, the Overseer turned to Benjamin and the senator.

"Refrain from either questioning her or responding." The senator's eyes were as clouded as ice as he reluctantly nodded. *Benjamin's were far more expressive*, Dana thought. *His panic was transparent as he kept mopping his brow.* Dana relished his discomfort, while at the same time praying to Mary: *Please do something to prevent my revealing your treasures.* She briefly considered one more try for mercy from the Overseer. *Mercy isn't an option*, she thought as he neared. *This man will do whatever it takes to protect the Church. If it means administering illegal methods of interrogation or—even more heinous—the death of the innocent, he would never hesitate.*

Dana stared as the Overseer removed a key from under the Christ statue, unlocked his credenza and removed the vial of serum. Before turning the key in the lock, he released a soft sigh—a mix of satisfaction and*...something more*, Dana thought. *It was impossible to decipher.* Any clue vanished as he replaced the key.

Vial in hand, he bent over Dana, as did the senator and Benjamin. Suddenly Benjamin bolted upright, knocking the vial onto the marble floor where it shattered.

"I…I…I thought…" Benjamin's stuttering finally found a rationale. "I heard something or someone." His expression blended relief and fear.

The Overseer's look was that of one bothered by a pesky fly, threatening to squash the irritant. Instead he pressed the intercom and summoned his bodyguard. At no response, he opened the door, his call for Leon answered by a strange guttural sound which prompted him to rush out, Benjamin and the senator following.

Heart beating, Dana dashed for the statue, withdrawing the key before they returned, leading a dazed Leon.

"Someone rough-housed me before they drove away." The bodyguard's eyes were filled with disbelief and shock "I was hanging on the car door as he drove off. I'd have killed him if I caught him." He waited for the Overseer's response, his repeated "Sorry, sir", expecting similar consequences as his punishment.

Always an enigma, the Overseer's response was unexpected. "Leon, please order another delivery of serum and double lock the guard gates after you take Ms. Palmer to the meditation chamber. See to it that she has water and is secure for the night." As the bewildered bodyguard tried to absorb such a reaction, the Overseer knelt in front of Dana.

"Tomorrow the new serum will arrive. You shall remain in isolation until then, when, I trust, you shall prove cooperative."

The Overseer had turned his focus away from the senator and Benjamin. The senator shook his head and frowned at such a charade, while Benjamin seemed almost giddy with relief. As the bodyguard led her away, Dana overheard Benjamin's whisper to the senator. "We need to talk."

Roughed up or not, her escort rallied to his master's voice and led her to safekeeping before addressing his other duties or his own injuries. The look in his eyes was neither pity nor sympathy. More like one taking the garbage out—a messy, but necessary, task.

The 'meditation room' was set apart from the main building. Its ancient structure contained no opening other than the door. Dana was familiar with such a building. A pigeonaire, it originally housed pigeons or chickens. Its conical tower was a familiar part of the Languedoc's landscape. But what looked quaint at a distance seemed a dungeon as the bodyguard switched on a solitary light bulb and pointed to a severely plain cot tucked into the far corner. "Bonne Nuit, Ms Palmer." His words rang in her ears, as did the rattle of chains and the turn of the lock as he departed.

THIRTY-SEVEN

Eric was elated to hear he would be released from the hospital. Like a race horse at the starting gate, he was focused on reaching the finish line and finding Dana. But by the time he had dressed, submitted to being pushed in a wheelchair to the hospital entrance and paid his bill, he found even such minimal exertion had sapped his strength. If he had any intent to override it, he gave it up as the sound of footsteps approaching caused him to turn abruptly and let out a sigh of relief.

"Very good, my son. Your Mother has come to take you home." Pierre smiled as he placed his arm in Eric's. Speaking several decibels higher than usual, he said, "Before we leave, dear, I must use the ladies room." Pierre steered him away from the entry and toward the restroom. As they neared, he looked around before lowering his voice. "They'll be watching the front door, waiting for you. Whether they suspect a little old lady as well is uncertain."

Pierre studied Eric. His pants, shirt and sweater seemed to hang loose on his once-athletic frame. "Since we can't have you walk out as Eric, I brought you something—courtesy of Barry—that I hope will work." He paused at the entry to the Ladies Room. "I'll check inside." Pierre returned quickly, shoving his large purse into Eric's hands. "Go put this on."

Eric returned within seconds, enshrouded in familiar garb.. Pierre nodded as he led him down the back stairwell. They passed the entrance to the busy kitchen unnoticed and headed for the loading dock where Pierre motioned Eric to halt.

"Let me check it out. It's risky having a priest and an old lady exit via the loading dock. But not as dangerous as leaving via the front door." He was gone a couple minutes before returning. "No one is in view. One long step down and we're on our way."

Eric's skirts didn't handicap him, so energized was he at the sight of Pierre's car in the parking lot. Honoring his wincing leg, he carefully let himself down from the loading dock and headed straight for it. Pierre was already in the driver's seat as Eric entered, buckled up and joined his 'mother' in a scan for any signs of being tailed as they pulled away..

After a few kilometers passed with no one in sight except local service trucks, busses and family sedans, Eric looked at Pierre and smiled. "I suspect you're growing fond of your alter ego."

Pierre glanced down at his skirt. "It's given me more respect for the feminine, but I'll be glad to shed it." Pierre watched closely as a car passed. "It's the detective side that's demanding." He frowned. "I wonder if I'll ever cease watching every car."

Eric nodded. "God willing, we shall soon shed such roles." Pierre's solemn surveillance was interrupted as Eric asked, "How are the translations going? I'm so anxious over Dana, all else has left my mind." He let out a long sigh of anxiety mixed with hope as he added, "I count on the treasure's power to change the playing field."

Pierre turned and gave a firm nod. "Absolutely. When I update you, you'll see how Dana's find fits into the treasure.."

"Dana's lost find, you mean. Until we find her, I'm useless." His impulsive grasp at the door handle startled Pierre, reminding him that reining in Eric's panic would be his chief task.

"I've some interesting news for you. Our chap was greeted with open arms at the first three abbeys. Actually the fourth as well. That is, until he drove away from the main Fontfroide Abbey to check on some outlying buildings and met with violence." Pierre grinned. "But the guard didn't realize he'd be tackling a former heavyweight fighter. Our fellow came away with few scratches compared to his opponent."

"Sounds like they must have something to hide." Eric gnashed his teeth. " If that something is Dana..."

"Maybe. But right now we need to focus on something else. Don't make your look too obvious, Eric, but watch that laundry truck. He's been following us since we left the hospital. I'm going to pull off onto one of the side roads and see what he does. If it's a genuine laundry van, he should continue on. If not, hold on!"

Pierre swung the car hard left onto a country road and the van followed. Increasing its speed to the maximum the car could handle, Pierre turned to Eric. "I'll try to outrun him. We've been headed for the autoroute, but I'm staying with country roads—especially these country roads. I know them like the back of my hand." The little car sped along the until they approached a sharp curve where Pierre shouted: "Mon Dieu! Say a prayer."

Eric stared ahead as a farmer and his tractor entered the road. Pierre swerved the car, barely missing the tractor. The laundry van, which had been following at an equally wild rate of speed, turned, twisted and spun out of control, circling into the farmer's field before turning over on its side.

"I'm not stopping." Pierre accelerated as he glanced into the rear-view mirror before returning his focus to the road. Any pangs of guilt he felt at not stopping were assuaged by Eric's comment. "The farmer is helping the van driver out of his vehicle."

"Good! With the van out of commission, we may have outmaneuvered them." Pierre shook his head. "Even so, we won't return to main roads in case this fellow radioed our description. I'm going to use some pretty rough country roads to route down to Alet-Les_Bains, heading for Coustaussa." He noticed Eric's paleness, his right hand holding his injured knee. "Hang on as best you can. There's an extra cot in my hideaway where you can rest tonight. Tomorrow we'll strategize our visit to Fontfroide."

Eric gave his partner an OK sign. "You should reconsider a career as a detective."

Pierre frowned. "That remains to be seen. As long as this road remains clear, I'm going to keep my foot firmly pressed to the accelerator. I suggest you shed your disguise. If their description is a priest and a hag, we'd best leave that image behind."

Eric carefully shed his priest's garb before Pierre turned off at a little unmarked dirt road. The road, although less curvy, was much rougher. They let loose sighs of relief when no other vehicle materialized out of the dust cloud behind them. Pierre slowed, pulled over and stopped. "I'd best hang onto my disguise. They know me as a Ms. in the hinterlands of Coustaussa. "

Pierre sped away while Eric kept a look-out. After a few more bumpy kilometers with no sign of any following vehicles, Eric picked up the map and did a rough calculation. As he replaced it, Pierre noticed Eric's white-faced expression. *He won't admit it, but Eric needs to rest,* he thought.

"Hang in there, my friend. Soon we'll reach our turn-off. Once we've phoned our team, we'll have a bit of rest and a meal."

The noise of the car slamming up and down the corrugated road—not to mention the impact on Eric's leg—made Pierre give silent thanks at the sign indicating Coustaussa five kilometers away. He drove in silence, knowing a phone booth was just ahead. "The gang will be relieved to hear your voice." Pierre said as they reached it. "But keep it short. Best we get our car and ourselves out of sight."

Eric did just that, his brief message that of resting before heading to Fontfroide tomorrow. It wasn't until he said, "Once we get Dana, I'm ready for anything," that energy returned to his voice.

As they neared the dusty lane leading to Pierre's hidey-hole, relief filled Eric's face. *A rather too pale one, I'm afraid,* Pierre thought as his shaky partner entered the cabin. He wondered what the likelihood would be of dissuading Eric from charging off to the abbey? *Certainly no discussion tonight*, he thought as he searched his larder for the minimal food remaining.

A glass of wine, a chunk of cheese and a reaffirmation that he would be up early and ready to drive to Fontfroide Abbey tomorrow had scarcely left his lips before Eric fell into bed. Pierre heard him cry out in his sleep: *Dana!*

THIRTY-EIGHT

Dana wasn't about to spend the night in sleep. She had the key to the credenza, determined to use it and find out if the Overseer may have discovered and locked away her treasures. Mary had entrusted them to her. Damned if she would let the Overseer, the senator, Benjamin or anyone, have them. Rage filled her as she scanned the room, searching for a way out.

Minutes dragged on as she studied the ancient walls, finding them impenetrable. She moved her gaze up, staring at the ceiling, knowing that behind what seemed to be a solid wooden covering soared the conical top of the pigeonaire. If she could access it, there should be an empty space with openings once used by birds.

Deciding it to be the only possible way of egress, she searched for the wall that had the most protruding blocks of stone alternating with the old wood, allowing her some chance of scaling it. She pulled the table over against the wall and began a tentative survey of possible hand and footholds. A beam that crossed just below the ceiling could provide a spot to rest while she probed.

Her body loved to move. Thanks to years of yoga and gymnastics, she was physically fit. She climbed like a fly, each step cautiously adhered to the wall. She soon reached the crossbeam, resting as she used one hand to push against the ceiling, relieved as it began to give way. *It was designed to give access to the birds,* she thought, grateful it had been only lightly sealed. After the first segment of wood gave way, she worked on the adjoining one until it too gave way enough to allow her to squeeze through and land in a dust and dung-filled space. She let out a sigh of relief to see something else filled the room—moonlight—coming not just from the wire-covered bird openings, but from an entry door. It's warped wooden frame yielded easily to her shoves.

Scaling the outside was a different story. The clinging vines covering the wall gave the illusion of support. But her grip soon failed, plunging her down to a ground softer than expected. After she'd gingerly examined her limbs, she stood and looked around. However long ago the chickens had departed, there remained heaps of straw piled around the rotting remains of what appeared to have once been a chicken coop. Staying in the shadows to avoid the bright moonlight, she searched for any sign of movement. Her heart raced. *Had anyone heard her? Dare she attempt to cross the courtyard to the Overseer's office?* She sent out a prayer as she headed for the dark building, using surrounding hedges as cover.

The door would surely be locked, with the bodyguard—injured or not—somewhere nearby, she thought. She cautiously moved to the back of the building, seeking a window where the Overseer's office would be. She began prying at the shutters of what she hoped was a right guess. The shutters opened. As she stepped into the darkened room she smiled at the image of the Overseers overweening confidence in his invulnerability. *Stupid man!*

She felt the cool of the marble as she moved across the floor, her heart beating in fear. A sudden scent of roses empowered her to move to the credenza and open it. She discovered, not the Magdalene's gift, but a leather-bound tablet clasped with an ornate closure. She removed it, carefully locking the credenza as she wedged the case into the waistband of her jeans before returning the Overseer's key and letting herself out the window.

Moving toward a willow tree's boughs, she paused, hidden behind its spring-green veil as she reviewed her strategy. As much as she wanted to head for the nearest phone—unlikely as she recalled the remote and empty countryside around the abbey—she remained. She sighed, knowing that if she left she'd never see the

Magdalene's precious casket of relics, nor the manuscript, ever again. *I must stay*, she decided as she reviewed the equally daunting consequences of staying: *the truth serum would reveal the existence of the Magdalene's treasures; the Overseer will claim them via a method of torture Benjamin couldn't endure; the senator—what's to become of his partnership with the Overseer?*

Lost in what seemed an insolvable dilemma, she began to carefully retrace her steps, suddenly halting at the sound of voices coming from a small building at the far end of the courtyard. As she neared, holding close to the cover of shrubbery, she could make out the voices: *Benjamin and the senator*. Their conversation seemed urgent, heightened not so much in decibels as intensity. She knelt within a cluster of peony bushes below the shutters of the window.

"I say we get them and leave now. She's bound to reveal all under the serum." Dana could detect the level of anxiety in Benjamin's voice as he added, "Once she does, the Overseer will have manuscripts, relics, everything. He won't need you and, as for me, I will…" Benjamin choked, unable to envision his fate.

"You will vanish, not a noticeable event given you are presumed dead anyway." The callous response of his cousin, the senator, angered Benjamin.

"If so, I'm determined never to reveal the relic's location."

"What's so important about a bunch of bones? Don't tell me that they too are 'powerful enough to transform the world.'"

"It's not their use to the world but their value to you that could prove important." Benjamin's voice lowered. "Let let's go outside and I'll explain."

Dana panicked. Hidden at the door-less rear of the cottage, she knew they'd exit on the opposite side of the building and, God-willing, remain there. She moved to a massive stand of old lilac bushes, ducking out of sight. As her breathing calmed, she watched as they drew out patio chairs, sat down and resumed their dialogue.

As soft as his words were, smugness coated Benjamin's statement. "So much for the Overseer bugging the place."

The senator's impatience was mounting. "Out with it. What's so important to me about these bones?"

Dana bit her lip to keep from choking in horror as Benjamin began by describing the wrapped 'present' Dana had been holding when he captured her. He quickly moved on to an explanation of just what these bunch of bones could mean to his cousin's presidential campaign.

"Bear with me, Frederick. I'll start by bringing you up to date on DNA research. It's come a long way during the past decade. With those bones, scraps of skull, flesh and hair, we can determine whose they are." He paused for dramatic affect. "If my hunch is right, they're not Mary Magdalene's—but those of Jesus Christ."

"Christ!" The senator's response was too loud for Benjamin. He whispered a harsh 'hush" and halted further conversation until he felt confident no one had overheard. "Yes, Christ himself. And as advanced as our DNA research is, it's matched by our success with cloning. Can you imagine the benefit to you in announcing the Second Coming as your calling card for the election?" Benjamin fell silent as he waited for his venal cousin to work out the numbers.

"Oh my God. Sam Wallace would pee his pants to announce such a thing." The senator didn't wait for Benjamin's response. His voice filled with urgency. "Of course, not for nothing. His followers votes would assure my win. But I need verification before I go out on that limb. It'll take a lot of time, money and trials before I know if it can be pulled off by the election." Dana watched as the senator stood, drew himself up into his full six feet four stance of the picture-perfect-president-to-be and began pacing..

"How soon could I guarantee Sam that he and his followers can count on it being their baby, so to speak." He'd halted, his mouth in a sneer. "It will be a baby, will it not?"

"Easy now, the potential *is* there but…" Benjamin's words were overridden by Frederick's excitement.

"My God, Benjamin, if we succeed—with seventy million evangelical parishioners in the USA—you're looking at the country's next leader: President Frederick Walter Evans. Sam's here in France now. I'd love to take advantage of his barn-storming mission throughout the first-world countries. A perfect opportunity to prepare them for the return of the Messiah." Whispered or not, Dana thought the senator's words sounded like someone on amphetamine. "He can ignite the Christian community in advance, using all sorts of Biblical revelations as a preamble to the actual announcement." As the senator's words seemed to fall on deaf ears, he halted and stared at his cousin. "What do you mean, 'the potential is there, but…'?"

"Whatever it is and however it is accomplished—cloning, stem cells or the like—it will take time."

"How much time ?"

"Perhaps not as much as you think." Dana recognized power returning to Benjamin's voice. "As to the actual birth, if all goes well, it could occur on the eve of the elections."

Dana gasped, but stayed focused on the senator's response.

"I can see it now. The Evangelical American Ministry could proclaim the momentous event. Sam Wallace came over with me to help strategize my campaign. How about you meet with him—let him know we're pregnant?"

Benjamin shook his head, returning to his earlier "but", his tempered tones trying to bring the senator back down to earth. "*But,* my dear cousin, *everything* depends on what happens when Dana goes under the sodium pentothal and spills the beans. "

Dana froze, aware it was her main sticking point as well.

"Where are these relics? After all the pie-in-the-sky antics over the 'supposed' manuscripts, I insist on seeing them. We'll need to get them squirreled away before the Overseer hears about them." Something in the senator's voice caused Benjamin to fall silent as he listened. "Once I've seen them with my own eyes, you and I can create our plan for them. We'll cut the Overseer out entirely."

Dana waited for Benjamin to reveal the relics hiding place. She needed to know. But another part of her couldn't risk revealing—under the truth serum—their location. Minutes passed before she heard Benjamin's response.

"Once I'd captured Dana and discovered what was in her parcel, I was a nervous wreck, knowing my quarters would be bugged and my actions watched closely."

"So where'd you put them?" The senator's impatience grew.

Just as Dana felt sure Benjamin had decided to stonewall, he resumed his account. "Fortunately the container was wrapped in birthday paper, causing scarcely a glance from the guard."

The senator sneered, "appropriate," as Benjamin pressed on. "I had to hide them somewhere near my room, but not in it." Benjamin hesitated. Dana could feel the war going on between his sharing and not sharing his find. He must have decided his survival may depend on his cousin. "An old well caught my eye. You can't quite see it from here. It's between the back of the pigeonaire and a storage building with an old tractor sticking out." A brisk movement from the senator revealed his intent to head for the well. Fortunately, at the same time, a light came on in the Overseer's office building.

"The guard is making his rounds. We can't risk being caught removing the top off the well in the middle of the night. I guarantee the relics are there and, whatever Dana's revelations under the truth serum, she, at least, has no idea what happened to them."

"Good. If she does reveal them, you can buy time by accusing her of having hidden them before you snatched her, or some such thing to put the focus back on Dana and her team."

"And where will you be? Gone with the relics, I assume."

"I'll be with you, of course. It would look strange if I traipsed off. We're a good team, my dear Benjamin. You have the scientific know-how to pull this off and I have the clout to cover your rear. Trust me, the relics will be safely re-hidden before our ten o'clock meeting with the pompous Overseer."

Benjamin uttered a soft "hush" as the Overseer's office lights went off. "I know Leon's routine. He'll be headed this way any minute now.. Let's call it a night."

"Right you are. We have a big day ahead.."

As much as Dana loved lilacs she never thought she'd be grateful to them. She curled motionless in their midst, watching Leon's flashlight dart about as he made his rounds, thinking: *Please don't let him see me—or look up at the pigeonaire.*

He continued his move from building to building, shining his light around the periphery, including the surrounding bushes. But never did its beam fall on her.

As he neared the pigeonaire, his beam targeted only the hefty lock. With a sigh of relief, she continued observing his midnight patrol, waiting long after all signs of the flashlight's beam had ceased. Finally, unfolding her limbs, she tentatively retraced her steps, remaining against hedgerows until she neared the pigeonaire and darted to the back of it where she stared over at the well.

Her heart threatened to beat right out of her. The well was twenty or so feet away, between her and the storage building.

Drawing a calming breath, she weighed the risk of nearing it, knowing her vulnerability crossing an empty space. The upside was the fact that the moon had gone behind clouds and the well was shadowed by the hulking mass of the derelict building. *Help me, Mary Magdalene, s*he repeated as she moved.

Sinking into a puddle of fear, excitement and exhaustion as she reached the well, she knelt behind it and watched for any movement before easing herself to a stand.

She studied the well's covering, a circular wedge of wood that fitted the circumference. But how tightly, she wondered as she wedged her fingernails around the edges, seeking a section that would allow her to pry up the lid. She found it—giving thanks to Benjamin for having so recently eased its fit.

She bit back on the jubilant '*Ohs*' that wanted to escape at the sight of the torn but still remaining colored wrappings. *Before lifting the casket out, however, I need a safe place to hide it—and fast.* The moonlight, she feared, would soon give way to dawn.

Later, covered with straw, chicken dung and scratches, she silently congratulated herself on her inspired choice of a hiding place that secured the treasure and the Overseer's precious notebook. Climbing the wall had been the harder accomplishment. The old grapevine's heavy trunk gave support half-way up, but the fragile ivy of the last few feet made for a frightening one step up and two steps back climb that threatened to dislodge her at every step.

Once safely inside, she sat at the little table, calming her breath as she eyed her hodgepodge job of repositioning the ceiling back into some semblance of its original condition. She wiped away at her scratches and gulped the remaining water. A rush of fear overcame her. She'd reveal all under the serum.

THIRTY-NINE

A sound at the door caused her to jump up from a dazed dream, her head on the table. Like a drowning person, between the sound of the chains and the opening of the door, the night's events flashed before her eyes, leaving her heart racing in fear that her actions would prove her and the treasure's undoing.

The first sign of 'normalcy' was the look of disdain on the bodyguard's face as he entered. She darted a glance at the ceiling, aware that, to anyone looking up. it might look slightly askew. The bodyguard didn't look up.

"The Overseer is ready for you." His words were as firm as his grip as he guided her out into the daylight. Dana avoided looking back toward the garden shed as she watched a gardener pass in front of them. The bodyguard gave no sign of having experienced serious repercussions over his debacle at the hands of yesterday's visitor. Dana wondered what that was all about. *Probably one of the senator's people*, she thought.

Leon announced Dana's arrival on entering the Overseer's office. A nod from the Overseer and he led her over to the divan and secured her arms. Dana stared around the room, meeting the anxious eyes of Benjamin and the smug eyes of the senator, before coming to rest on the vial of sodium pentothal in the Overseer's hand.

At a word from his master, the bodyguard turned to leave. The Overseer carefully plunged the syringe of serum into Dana's arm, his look unreadable. Dana closed her eyes, praying she'd avoid revealing where the relics and manuscript were hidden.

The 'Q' Project must succeed, thought the Overseer as he watched and waited for Dana's response to the drug. *It's the biggest challenge of my career. Soon I shall possess the manuscripts and, once again, secure the Mother Church.*

He closed his eyes and silently recommitted himself to returning the treasure to a place of safety known only to the Church. Opening his eyes, he looked down at Dana. It had been more than a minute since he'd administered the serum. He trusted a night spent in isolation and the impact of the sodium pentothal would prompt a full revelation. He drew a long breath, anticipating her information.

Dana's eyelids began to flutter, a strange half-smile on her face as the Overseer leaned over her. She tried to focus, but her words slurred like someone under the influence of far too many glasses of champagne.

"'Overseer.' What a funny name. As you lean over me like that, what do you 'seer'?" She began to giggle before breaking into a ragged cough. "Water please, Overseer. Please to oversee my request, see-er of souls."

"As long as you oversee my requests and give me answers." The Overseer released her bonds, pulled her to a sitting position and waited for her to stop coughing. She didn't. He walked over to his credenza, returning with a carafe of water and a glass. "Drink." As she finished, he took the glass from her hand. "Enough. Let's talk."

As though the water had lubricated her vocal chords, Dana began a voluble outflow of muddled communication. She squinted, holding her hand up to her eyes as if to measure the distance to the credenza. "How perfect the light! Stand over there while I capture your photo." Dana pantomimed a click of a camera, looking astonished. "You mustn't frown. Such perfect light reveals your soul." Dana raised one eyebrow. "Don't you agree?"

"I think you are toying with me." The Overseer yanked her to a stand. "I will be enlightened, not by any shutter lens but by your answers to my questions." He looked in her eyes. "Do you remember how you got here?" He waited.

Benjamin made a sudden shuffling motion, nervously catching Dana's eye as if in challenge. "Here...?" She shook her head. "In this room?" Her head moved from side to side. "Where is here? She pursed her lips in thought. "I was in a car." Dana's voice increased its anxiety as she took a few tentative steps. "Where is my present? Have you brought it?" Her face filled with alarm that matched that in Benjamin's eyes as she stared at him. He glanced from her to the senator, who returned his glance with a fierceness that dared him not to faint dead away.

The senator stared at Dana with a different look, one of puzzlement as to when and whether she would mention the relics. *If not, why not?,* he wondered.

Your *present"*. The Overseer snorted. "I'm out of patience with nonsense." He lowered her back onto the divan. "Sit down. I want answers now. Where are the manuscripts? You know full well what your team is up to and where the manuscripts are. Think. How many are there? Where are they hidden?"

Images of last night's drama filled her thoughts, not in any coherent order, but with a distinct sense of fear. "We take it to be examined—the museum of course." A pouty look, mixed with stubbornness resembled that of an eight year old, especially when Dana drew herself into a 'so there' posture.

The Overseer studied her statement, a shadow of hope emerging. "You were meeting Eric Taylor. Had you taken the manuscript to the Arques museum? And, if so, is that where the other manuscripts are?" His voice rose. "Answer! Now!" He waited, his expression light years from an eight year old.

Dana prayed the impact of the serum would soon begin to diminish, taking with it the reguritive rush of 'truths' she'd so precariously attempted to sort out and offer, giving thanks, once again, for her passion for keeping abreast of the news. (Eric swore she'd read the cereal box if nothing else was available.) She'd spent the night anguishing over the truth serum exposing the Magdalene's treasure. Suddenly she'd recalled having read something—back during the Gulf War—about the CIA's lack of success using truth serum on terrorists. *If the Overseer isn't aware of such information*, she'd thought, *I may fool him into accepting different 'truths'.*

"Ms Palmer, I recommend you quit resisting." He stood over her with a calm, curious and steady scrutiny that held about as much compassion as a scientist examining a bug. "You can give me the answers to my questions—quickly and completely—without my using other tactics, or you can be made to answer in a way far less comfortable."

Dana knew he meant it. She attempted to square her shoulders, still feeling too loopy, but meeting his eyes with firmness.

"The manuscripts are separated. Each is in a fool-proof hiding place." Unable to control it, she felt a giggle surface, thinking, *this drug may not produce truth, but it does produce a strange high.* "Like Pierre's, each manuscript is hidden in a place only its owner knows." Dana watched the Overseer's expression. *He bought it. Probably because of his man who vanished while pursuing Pierre.*

He studied her for what was beginning to seem too long before he responded. "Now we shall begin to draw each rat out of his hole—using as bait the others—starting with you. The Church *will* obtain those manuscripts, my dear Dana." He turned a look of disdain on Benjamin. "Professor Carter was too lenient in his tactics. I won't make that mistake."

His scathing glance at Benjamin was extinguished and replaced by a long moment of silence before he turned to the senator. "You've been exceedingly self-contained, dear senator. Have you reconsidered your decision to align with my efforts?" The way he said it, although sending a shiver through Dana, seemed not to have ruffled the senator's equanimity.

"I am still in a data-gathering mode, dear Overseer. Time is of the essence. If an actual manuscript shows up soon and the translation indicates power of the sort I seek, well then..." He opened wide his hands. "At that point, I'm more than interested."

The Overseer looked from the senator to Benjamin. Dana watched bug-eyed, thinking, *maybe it's the impact of the serum but I see trouble ahead for those two.*

The Overseer withheld any response to the senator as he turned back to Dana. "I can see you are not going to reveal the location of the manuscripts. Starvation isn't an easy death, my dear.

I trust, after another night, you will be more forthcoming concerning the location of your cohorts." He scrutinized her expression.

Dana fought to retain some semblance of being under the impact of the truth serum. "I don't know. I don't know. I don't know. Each one is different. Only it's caretaker knows." She ended her sing-song refrain with a big smile. "The Shadow knows. I just take pictures. Mr. Taylor won't tell me anything. He travels from place to place." She smiled. "But I know he'll find me."

"Precisely—you will draw him and his manuscript and he draws another and so on. Soon the Church—the treasure's rightful owner—will reclaim the manuscripts." The Overseer walked over to his desk and returned with a sheaf of papers. "For the moment I shall postpone a more intense type of interrogation." He studied her. "In fact, delaying such tactics until Mr. Taylor is here will, I feel certain, guaranty both his and your full disclosure." The ring of the phone startled everyone. The Overseer answered impatiently. "I ordered no interruptions."

"He did *what* last night?" The incredulity in the Overseer's tone set Dana reviewing the drama of last night, hoping none of it was caught on tape as the Overseer said: "Bring me the tape."

His expression of disbelief was mixed with determination, further heightened by shock as he walked over, removed the statue atop the key and let out a long sigh. Dana studied his next move, praying he wouldn't test the key out on his credenza and discover his notebook was missing.

Beneath the statue that covered the key, she had fully expected to see a religious shrine. But the white cloth, embellished with threads of gold, enclosed, not a cherished icon but a state of the art television. *Seems fitting, if not appropriate,* she thought, *at his combining the worship of God with that of mammon.*

The Overseer was oblivious to her stare, so intent was he on the bodyguard who was inserting the video tape.

"Push the Play button and withdraw Leon. I shall notify you of any further need." As the bodyguard completed his order, he departed, looking surprised that Dana remained on the divan, her bonds in place.

Dana felt angry at being restrained, surprised at having been allowed to remain and curious to learn what it was that had prompted deep shock on the Overseer's face. Such emotions lasted less than a minute before Dana shivered, suddenly aware of why the Overseer had disregarded her being there. *To understand all on your deathbed would matter not*

The Overseer looked stunned as he watched Sam Wallace address a large audience. The French translator was doing his best to translate his sonorous ranting. Suddenly a hush fell over the audience as the minister held up his hands for silence. With a solemn expression he announced that soon he would have an earthshaking revelation about the End Days—something that would confirm what he had long preached: Armageddon approaches and Christ shall soon return. After long minutes of a tumultuous response from the audience, he added, "I am being prepared to make the Divine's announcement of exactly when and where Christ shall return. Soon—so stay tuned." Bedlam broke out.

The Overseer's focus was so intense that he remained oblivious to anyone's presence as he moved to the window, staring immobile for long moments before he turned back and met with Benjamin and the senator's stares. Both tried for a believably awed look but bewilderment was on the face of one and smug satisfaction on the face of the other.. Dana studied them, knowing full well that the senator must have primed the pump with a phone call to good old Sam, providing him with a preview of coming attractions.

"How can they be so smugly confident?" The Overseer shook his head. "For Sam Wallace, saying the End is coming is old news. But to announce he knows and will soon reveal *exactly when and where*, is quite another." The Overseer's words accompanied a fumbling with his key as he stooped to unlock his credenza, reached inside and knelt to anxiously confirm it actually was there. He let out a low-pitched cry: "No!"

Head down, his grim look, Dana thought, *suggested that of Hamlet meditating on a skull.* Dana amended the tribute. *"Alas, poor Benjamin, and dear Senator, I knew them well."*

His outburst prompted Dana to struggle to rise, capturing the Overseer's returned concentration. He looked over at her, neither surprised nor concerned by her presence, apart from the continued likelihood of its interrupting his far more important thoughts. He reached for the phone, pressing an extension that brought the bodyguard swiftly through the door.

Before any mention of escorting Dana elsewhere, the Overseer immediately challenged him. "Did you let anyone into my quarters last night?" The look on the man's face moved from astonishment to terror as the Overseer added, "Someone removed a priceless item from my credenza."

Dana thought the bodyguard's words held the panic of one being led to the hangman. "The senator returned to retrieve his briefcase. His airline tickets were inside and he needed to reschedule his flight. You were at prayers and…"

A gasp went up, undisguised, from the senator. "I took my briefcase, and only my briefcase, and left. The guard remained with me. Whoever raided your credenza, it wasn't me."

Benjamin chimed in. "Right, he left with the guard and returned immediately."

"Someone got inside and removed my journal. Dana was locked away, so that leaves Benjamin, the senator and you." He stared at Leon. "Might the man who attacked you yesterday…? But you are the only one with duplicate keys." Dana registered the guard's fear. Another emotion suddenly stirred, gratitude that she had beaten the senator to the punch.

"Take Ms Palmer back to her room and return immediately."

Dana's bonds were yanked off and she was led away. Leon looked as though he would choose eternity in her quarters instead of returning to his master.

FORTY

Pierre reviewed a night spent in a state far from restful. He knew Eric would resist taking another day to rest. Therefore he'd kept busy preparing for a trip to Fontfroide Abbey, knowing it could prove even more dangerous than his employee had experienced on his visit. As he reviewed various scenarios: what if Dana were held captive there; what if Benjamin is well armed; what if Eric and I are captured? He felt uneasy.

Giraud was an ace in the hole. He would act as a back-up, ready to descend at any indication of foul play. He and his cousin had always made a good team—Pierre's blend of logical, methodical and mystical balanced his cousin's earthy, active and impetuous qualities. Pierre grinned as he thought, *I wouldn't want anyone else on my side, even if he does arrive like some comic book hero. Giraud's last reminder had been: "Load the trunk with everything from brickbats to bullets."*. Well, the trunk was loaded

And just in time, he thought as he heard Eric approach, a cup of coffee in hand. "I can't believe I actually slept in." He stared at the clock as he shook his head. "It's ten o'clock already. Let's work out our strategy and be on our way."

"You really could use another day to heal. How about we let Giraud make an exploratory visit to the abbey before we put our strategy in place?"

"And meet with the same greeting given to his cohort? No. With you or without you, I leave for the abbey *today*." Eric put down his coffee cup and gave every indication of bolting away.

"Alright, but not without a bit of food in you. My larder has little left but I do have cheese and eggs. You need some protein for stamina. While you eat we can review our strategy."

As Pierre whipped up a perfect omelet and put it under Eric's nose, Eric seemed to revive enough that their discussion of strategy heated up. Both agreed it was a waste of time to visit the main section of the abbey. "The mystery is in the outbuildings—where Luis was attacked." Eric looked over at Pierre. "Luis noticed only his attacker, the guard. But we should plan on their having backup troops. Can we handle it?"

Pierre masked a budding frown. "Any other time I would feel myself to be well guarded with you along, my friend, but today…mon Dieu…you may be the one that needs protecting."

"If Dana is there my adrenaline will shoot up off the charts. I'm like one of those Olympic athletes that crash, get up out of a hospital bed and win a gold medal. Trust me. I must go."

Pierre let it drop.

"OK, so let's go over our plan." Pierre's words met with a sudden finger pressed to his mouth as Eric reached for Pierre's TV and turned up the volume. Pierre had automatically turned it to the morning news channel for an update. "I've seen that fellow before. He's a religious zealot with millions of followers. He calls down the wrath of God on anyone that doesn't see eye to eye with his and 'God's' will." Eric put his hand to his head. "But this is way over the top. He just announced he'd soon reveal Christ's return—precisely when and where."

"Tres fou, if you ask me—the ranting of a crazy man."

"He's crazy all right, but not stupid. He dare not hold out that promise and renege."

"So he scours the Actors Guild for a stand-in for Christ to pull off his charade." Pierre turned away from the television as the interview ended, surprised to see Eric deep in thought.

"Follow me with what may also be the ranting of a mad man." He lowered his voice. "We know that Dana met MM, who entrusted her with *His* relics—and another manuscript. They were undoubtedly taken from her by Benjamin.' Eric paused, letting out a long exhalation. "Could Benjamin or his cousin, a presidential candidate, now in France, possibly be involved with Sam Wallace? Or does Wallace's revelation have nothing to do with the relics?"

"How? Nothing could possibly assure the timing of Christ's second coming. Maybe they intend it to be spiritual; something to be experienced only by his favored few million followers?" He turned to a silent Eric. "Out with it. Let's hear your theory."

"I may be suffering delusions as a result of my accident, but hear me out." He drew a long breath.. "Dana had both manuscript and relics with her when she was kidnapped." Pierre's look blended skepticism with neutrality as Eric continued. "Given Benjamin kidnapped Dana, he now has the manuscript and relics. The manuscript may expand on the Gospel of Mary Magdalene—or on the relics."

Pierre interrupted. "But what possible connection could there be to Christ's return?"

Eric shook his head. "Come on, Pierre—think. Those relics are those of Jesus Christ!"

Pierre let out a low whistle. "Oh, my God, the cloning of his DNA!. You're really stretching it. Now if Benjamin or the senator were at Wallace's speech, but…"

Eric rushed on. "Let's return to my 'what ifs'." Eric's excitement heightened as he recalled his years in the priesthood, steeped in solid research into religion, history and science. "What if Benjamin aligned with the Senator and his rabid friend, Sam Wallace in manipulating those relics to manifest Sam's claim?"

Pierre released a long breath. "Brilliant, mon ami—as in move over Dolly the sheep and make room for Christ the Savior."

"Exactly!" Eric stood. "We don't have a minute to lose. Let's strategize on the way."

Intense as the atmosphere was that permeated their car, Eric drifted into sleep. "Why didn't you wake me?", he mumbled.

"You've just gotten out of the hospital, been bombarded with information and activity and have a dangerous enemy awaiting. I wanted you fresh for the charge." Pierre shook his head. "Besides, it gave me time to review our strategy."

"Good. Let's have it, but..." Eric frowned as he turned to study the car in his rear-view mirror. He drew himself into a greater alertness as the car neared and passed them, the driver giving a little salute. "Giraud?" As Pierre nodded "yes, I thought he may be a good addition to our force", Eric released his breath. "Right. Giraud is like a cannon. The sight of Benjamin will inflame him. But it's the sight of Dana that I'm counting on."

Pierre tried to ease Eric's fear. "Don't worry. They're using her as bait, trusting we'll do what we are about to do—join her. But let's plan beyond our first sight of Dana. We arrive, unarmed, at least in any real sense of the word. I threw in a hunting rifle..." He shuddered. "My soul already has one death to account for. So, into the charge we go, minimally armed., uncertain of the lay of the land and quite certain that if Dana is there, she is not alone."

"You're right. With Vatican sedans aplenty and with Dana held at an abbey, the Church is definitely involved—big time. So, I take it we try diplomacy and if all else fails, I'll handle the gun. I'm not a marksman, but we need something if things heat up."

They both fell silent, scanning the road for any other cars than Girauds which had long shot out of sight. Clearly on their own, Pierre pointed up ahead to the faint outline of the abbey in the distance. "To battle we go, Three Musketeers, swords at the ready."

"More like the Man of La Mancha tilting at windmills."

FORTY-ONE

Dana knew it was a little before ten o'clock in the morning when they returned her to the pigeonaire. *Now what*, she wondered. She was fired up and ready to take action beyond that of her frantic circling of the limited floor space.

The longer she paced, the more anxious she became over the safety of the Magdalene's treasure. *Should I chance a quick trip down the wall,* she wondered. She tried to remember what Eric had explained of the Catholic liturgy. *It must be close on to eleven now and I think that's when they have morning prayers.*

"I can't stand being cooped up and not knowing." Her words, although uttered through clenched teeth, acted to recharge her energy as she pushed the table back up against the wall.

Entering the dusty chamber above, she was careful to peer through the window opening and be sure the coast was clear before making her exit. *I can stay hidden under the piles of straw in the wreck of the old chicken coop*, she thought as she prepared to drop to the ground, praying to the Magdalene to guide her and prevent Leon from returning to lead her away.

She kept a steady look-out while hidden in the wreckage of the coop. *I need to confirm that everything is still where I hid it.* As she moved cautiously to its special hiding place, she remembered the Overseer's treasure—his notebook. *I can't possibly scale back up into the building carrying the casket with Christ's relics and Mary's manuscript—but I can see what's so powerful in his book.*

With her heart in her throat, she moved the short distance required to confirm that the treasure remained safely hidden. *The notebook, however, is easy to retrieve,* she decided as she reached for it. She backtracked carefully, staying in the shadows until she reached the broken down coop and paused to scan the area before ascending back to her cell.

As she snuggled within the straw she was suddenly aware that darkening clouds were threatening rain. Before she crammed the notebook into her jeans and resumed her upward climb, she opened it, elated to see that it was written, not in Italian but in English. She looked forward to interesting reading once she returned to her prisoner status. Just as she placed her foot for her upward climb, she shook her head and slid back down. *I can't take this book with me,* she thought, *and have it discovered..*

But I can't return it until I have some idea what makes it so important. She slid back down and into a nest in the straw while she scanned the words for a sense of what made it so important. Minutes passed as her grip on the book increased, along with the lines of fear that etched her face as she whispered: "Oh, my God!"

Her hands were clammy with fear as she closed the book knowing she had to secure it with the Magdalene's treasure. She eased up from her nest, tucked the book into her jeans, surveyed the landscape and began her path to return it to its hiding place.

The old lilac bushes were a blessed refuge, she thought as she hid within them, thinking she'd heard a sound. She froze in place, her eyes straining to see who may be near. Suddenly and silently, a hand reached out and covered her mouth. She tried to spin around and confront her captor, thinking, *Oh, no! They've found me with the book and...* Her head was slowly turned around to meet that of her attacker. Her eyes widened in disbelief. *Giraud*!

"Hush," he whispered as he slowly released his hand . "What are you up to?"

"I'm their prisoner...she saw him grin..."At least they think I am. I've hidden the Magdalene's relics and..." He returned his hand to her mouth. "Not a word. We must get you and them away."

"It's not easy. If they find me gone they'll tear up this place. Benjamin knows they're too heavy for me to lug about in broad daylight and…"

"Benjamin!" Giraud sneered. "I get to finish my job."

Dana grinned at the memory of Giraud's having pushed Benjamin off the heights of Montsegur and down to his 'death'.

"And I best get back into my lair before we are caught out and the treasure is found." She looked down at the book. "Certainly this part of it."

"Give me the book and let me know the relic's hiding place. I can certainly hide the notebook and may be able to figure a way to get the relics away."

"You're in danger, Giraud. The Overseer is powerful."

"The Overseer?" Giraud's whisper fell silent. After agonizing minutes passed and a light rain began to fall, Giraud spoke again. "The coast seems to be clear. But whisper in my ear everything I need to know." As she did, she added: "Where is Eric?"

"Off with you now, and suffice it to say, I won't be your only visitor."

Her feet seemed, like Mercury, to sprout wings as she easily made what had seemed the most dangerous part of her climb back up and into her captive role.

Her churning thoughts were matched by a churning stomach as she replayed the last scene, her fear heading off the charts. *We blow this and we destroy lifetimes.*

Eric slowly turned his attention from the road ahead to glance at Pierre. "We'll soon be at the exit to the Fontfroide Abbey." Suddenly Pierre became consumed with thoughts of Giraud. He'd expected his cell phone to ring, confirming his location after he reached the Abbey. Anxious at no word and aware he hadn't told Eric of Giraud's mission, Pierre grabbed for the map of the abbey and its outbuildings.

"Two kilometers, Eric said; let's review our strategy."

Pierre nodded, knowing he must share the fact that Giraud was doubtless already at the Abbey. His worry turned to conviction as they reached the turn-off they would take to bypass the main abbey buildings and head for the area where his friend had met with a rough welcome.

As they turned, Eric looked over at Pierre. "I saw your reaction. What's worrying you—the lameness of our strategy?"

"Giraud went on to Fontfroide Abbey ahead of us—part one of our strategy. He wanted to investigate before calling us to do a full court press. I haven't heard from him."

A dark cloud covered Eric's expression. Pierre waited it out. "Now we have to rescue two instead of one. But whatever lies ahead—as long as Dana and Giraud are alright—I'm ready for it." Eric slowed as they reached a barely perceptible lane..

"Continue on up ahead and you'll see another turn-off coming up. Turn left. It's a back road that leads to the outbuildings." Eric put the car in low gear, grateful that the rain would prevent the car stirring up dust clouds. His silence was hard edged with intensity as he stared ahead.

A goat gamboled about a fenced off cottage that paralleled a sizable kitchen garden at the entry to the property. A little further on they spotted the pigeonaire in the distance as Eric slowed nearly to a stop and turned to Pierre. "I'd better park before we're discovered."

"Too late; look." Pierre pointed up ahead where a man began walking down the road to meet them. "Impressive, but old and not so formidable that we couldn't take him." Eric stared as the man neared and motioned them to park alongside the building.

As they moved slowly, Eric whispered to Pierre. "I know a Church big-wig when I see one. This guy is one of their biggest guns. But his ease and self-confidence makes me think we may be barking up the wrong abbey." As Eric parked, he whispered to Pierre: "Keep a keen eye out nevertheless."

Before Eric turned off the ignition the man had positioned himself directly outside the parked car, not smiling, not frowning; simply waiting. As both Eric and Pierre exited, wariness in their stance, the man approached. He paused briefly, as if expecting a sign of recognition or honor. At no such response, the man extended his hand. "I'm Cardinal Vicenzo; how may I help you?"

Pierre met the handclasp and turned to Eric. He remained immobile, looking stunned as he repeated, "Cardinal Vicenzo? I've heard of you. Aren't you headquartered in Rome to aid the Pope?"

A faint smile seemed to flicker on the Cardinal's face, but vanished so quickly that Pierre questioned having seen it.

"True. My goal is to aid him in assuring the needs of the Mother Church. For the moment, here is where I can best be used—and you two are here to assure my success." As Eric and Pierre turned in alarm, the Cardinal nodded toward a man who, gun in hand, was fully prepared to block any rash moves. The Cardinal pointed toward the building. "Please enter. We have other guests awaiting your arrival." He began a slow walk, the guard following behind. As Pierre and Eric entered, the guard, with a subtle nod from the Cardinal, remained poised for the slightest signal.

Eric and Pierre could do nothing but glance around as they entered. The interior was surprisingly cool and inviting. A cage of canaries sang somewhere near the entrance.

The Cardinal spoke to the man who waited at the door. "Please show Mr. Taylor and Monsieur de Lahille into my office; and bring us a tray of tea and coffee."

"What is going on here?" Eric whispered to Pierre as the guard led them into a large office and pointed to chairs clustered, theater-fashion, in a semi-circle around an ecclesiastical-looking alter. "Be seated. The Overseer will be with you shortly."

As the guard left the room, both Pierre and Eric turned to one another, matching looks of bewilderment filling their expressions. "The 'Overseer'?" Eric gave Pierre a look of bewilderment. "I've never heard of that honorarium. But whoever he is and whatever he intends, this killing us with kindness ploy is wearing thin. The second this Cardinal or Overseer, returns, it had better be with information about Dana's whereabouts—or else!" Eric's emotions had grown with his voice's volume. When the door opened, Pierre prepared for fisticuffs between the Overseer and a former priest.

Instead, Eric's jaw dropped and his rage surged at the arrival of Benjamin Carter and a man he recognized as a powerful senator. *What a deadly triumvirate,* he thought. *The Vatican, lusting after the manuscripts for centuries, Benjamin, seeker of vindication, and the senator, a man who'd stop at nothing to become the next president.*

"Sit down." The Overseer's expression and tone of voice remained veiled. Only the others instant response reflected his power. *The proverbial 'if looks could kill' stare that Benjamin fixed on Eric held added bile,* Eric thought. *I've got to hand it to the senator. He's assumed an impenetrable façade of honored guest.*

Pierre leaned in and whispered, "What gives? A team, or master and slaves?"

"Let our meeting begin." The Overseer turned to Pierre and Eric. "I trust you know the purpose of our mission." He pointed to Benjamin and the senator.

Eric responded. "We saw this morning's television program announcing the coming of Christ." He turned a scathing stare on the senator who hardly noticed, so fixed was he on the Overseer. "What a diabolical purpose—the cloning of the Second Coming."

"We saw right through it." Pierre glared at the Overseer as Eric added, "I know the Church has been involved throughout history in the dirtiest of scandals. But to attempt to clone Christ's relics—this tops them all. How could you support such a circus?"

"Obviously they doubted—and rightly so—that I would do so." The Overseer glared as Benjamin and the senator whispered a nervous dialogue between themselves. "I assure you that your tenure as guests is certain to be most uncomfortable unless you produce these relics—now." The emphasis in his tone was chilling.

The senator looked at Benjamin as a wealth of conjecture passed silently between them. The senator knew, if Benjamin produced the relics the two of them were done for—cut out of a triumph of a lifetime. But, that lifetime could be minutes if Benjamin didn't produce what the Overseer requested—quickly.

Benjamin's look left not a shred of any option other than cooperating. "Yes, they were with Dana and I hid them. But I would have told you and…" His effort to modulate his feelings of confusion, anger and fear was unsuccessful.

"Get them. Now!" He turned a scathing look at the senator. "Dear senator, you obviously are in collusion with Professor Carter. You returned to my office alone, with a ruse of reclaiming your briefcase and removed my notebook. While the Professor goes for the relics…".He looked at a paralyzed Benjamin. "Under armed escort, I expect you, dear senator, to return my notebook—immediately." He waited and watched as their faces turned white, confusion in their eyes.

"I entered your office briefly and took my briefcase—that and nothing more." The senator turned to Benjamin, confusion filling his stare.

The bitterness in Benjamin's response was at an all time high as he glared at Eric. "Damn you and damn Dana Palmer. It's not the senator and it's not me who messed with the relics. I'm sure Dana's behind this." Making a swift turn, he faced the senator, looking for support in such a conviction.

The Overseer gave an incredulous look. "Ms Palmer was locked away during the time it was stolen." He retuned to the senator. "If I do not have it in my hands in ten minutes, begin your prayers." The Overseer's voice fell silent as he fixed an X-ray gaze on Benjamin and the senator—a focus immediately shattered as Eric leapt from his chair.

"Damn you—I insist on seeing Dana now! Get her out of that prison or ..." His clenched jaw and clamped teeth reflected his intent to rip the Overseer out of his robes and his life. Pierre chimed in.

"Where is she? We're not leaving without her." His slight form seemed to expand to fill the room.

"In due time, Mr. Taylor and Monsieur de Lahille. Do have a chair. If our discussion goes well, I shall invite Ms. Palmer to join us." He turned to the senator and Benjamin, who looked as though all the air had gone out of their balloons. "Please follow Leon. He will escort you to retrieve that which I requested."

Eric and Pierre remained standing. The Overseer smiled. "Take your chairs. We have much to discuss before Dana arrives."

Once all eyes were focused on him, the Overseer began, his questions revealing he'd learned almost as much as they. "You've translated the manuscripts. They predict, as the Church suspected, massive changes. How massive?"

Pierre looked at Eric, both of them sensing that their fates, and that of the world, hung on their answer.

Gambling on minimal truth, Eric began, simply confirming that 'Yes, there were changes ahead—with Earth-changing impact. What their exact nature was and how, if possible, to counter it, had yet to be determined'.

The Overseer's intensity heightened. "The Church has long suspected that such information was contained in these manuscripts. We fought for years to capture and conceal such information." He looked around, his shoulders firmed as he continued, "I am dedicated to that which is best for the Church. Should such information as appears in the manuscripts be distorted by avaricious servants of the Devil, using it for venal ends"…He gagged before continuing. "Such as Frankenstein attempts to clone Christ, I would fail in my duty if I did not protect the Church."

Eric rushed in his heated rebuttal. "Whether you would or would not participate in the cloning of Christ, you still want the relics and the manuscripts. Given their revelations, the time ahead won't allow for such religious circuses or devious secrets."

The Overseer fell into a solemnly pensive state before responding. "I anticipated such a reaction. I will not stand for anything but full cooperation. You will hand the manuscripts over. They will rest hidden once again, along with the relics."

"You don't understand, time is..."

"Time is certainly running out for you—and for Ms Palmer. She dies if you don't comply immediately." He turned at the sound of someone approaching. "Ah, they return with the relics and my notebook."

Leon entered, his expression filled with flashes of confusion, fear and anger, his gun arm held steadily in the direction of his captives: the senator and Benjamin. "They had me haul away the lid to the old well, swearing that's where they hid what you wanted." Before the guard could go on, Benjamin turned to the senator.

"What did you do? I told you where they were. You must have come back to get them. Where are they?"

As the senator shook his head the Overseer responded. "Yes, where are they—and where is my notebook? One of you had better tell the truth in the next five minutes." The Overseer waited as sweat began to pour down both Benjamin's and the senator's faces as the minutes ticked away.

"Thirty seconds remain. Where are they?"

The door opened and a hand flew out, knocking Leon's weapon across the room. No one reached for it as Giraud held up an equally powerful weapon. "Don't move!"

As Pierre and Eric shook their heads and smiled, Giraud grinned, looking down at his watch as he shouted: "Time's up. You can come in now."

Dana walked in the room and into the arms of an ecstatic Eric.

"More of that later." Dana sighed as she straightened up and turned to the Overseer. "Where are the relics? Safely hidden away from you and the Church forevermore."

The Overseer sneered. "That remains to be seen. I am relentless in achieving the Church's aims. You may have one victory— but you'll lose the war.

"I don't think so. Not after the Pope and the world press learns of the contents of your notebook."

The Overseer's face went white. He reached for a chair to keep from collapsing. "Where is it?"

"Safe and secure—and copied. It remains ready and waiting to bring you down—and your Church with it."

"No, no, nooo…" The Overseer looked like the end of his world had arrived already.

Eric clasped Dana close. "Good on ya, mate." He turned to the Overseer. "A pity, old chap. We could have used your help to prepare your Church's faithful for ways to handle the manuscript's predictions."

Giraud and Pierre were beaming; but Giraud never once lowered his gun which was now aimed more pointedly at Benjamin. "Seems we have a score to settle, my friend. "As Benjamin cowered, Giraud smiled as he said, "No. You, my dear Benjamin, shall reap the consequences of kidnapping Dana, as well as live knowing your chances to restore your career are ended. Foolish, foolish man."

Eric walked over to the Overseer, shocked to see how diminished he looked, his expression ghostly. "We shall take our leave now. Remember our insurance policy. Don't even think of getting in our way ever again." Turning back to the senator, he shook his head. "You can say good-bye to the presidency, senator."

FORTY-TWO

As Eric, Dana and Pierre drove to Vals they automatically scanned for any cars following, relieved to realize that only Giraud kept pace. Eric shook his head. “Good old Giraud. He saved the day, both atop Montsegur and today when he rushed those relics into a safe-deposit box, along with the Overseer’s notebook.” Eric’s voice rose as he reached over to pat the briefcase Dana clutched on her lap. “It’s your manuscript from Mary that excites me. The team will have a field day trying to decipher it.”

Dana smiled. “Mary assured me that it will provide a crucial key to understanding the others.”

“You are the crucial key, my love.” Eric took her hand. “I hope the last few days convinced you of your important role?”

“So true, my dear.” Pierre reached over from the back seat and added his gentle touch. Your kind of energy—the feminine energy—is bound to be an important component of the wisdom in the Magdalene’s manuscript.”

“She did imply that developing that quality—she referred to it as the Christ quality—is what must come to pass for our world to prevail.”

Eric shook his head. “Pity the Overseer couldn’t really help prepare the Church and the Pope for what lies ahead. It will be crucial that all faiths unite in echoing the same message: "Change is coming. Enlightenment must occur if humanity is to prevail."

Dana, secure alongside Eric, began to stir at the thought of the Overseer. "Why in the world would the Overseer keep a journal of everything he'd ever done to 'protect' the Church? Such a horrendous account, if revealed, would surely destroy it and him."

"He knows that." Eric sighed. "His fear at ever having it revealed may very well finish him up."

Dana sighed. "Well at least it will keep him off our backs. Now let's move on to a more positive topic. "Can you at least give me a hint of what the team has learned of the manuscript's revelations before we arrive in Vals?"

Pierre smiled. "Much would be lost in translation without your actually looking at reams of reports. Veronique and Professor Marty were working non-stop to put the indications in some sort of order that will be far easier to understand than anything I could relate." Pierre, seeing protest form in Dana's eyes as she turned to stare at him, reached out his hand. "Hang in there. Another four kilometers and you'll get to see it for yourself."

They all fell silent as the kilometers sped by and they neared Vals. "We're here." Pierre's announcement interrupted Eric's parking as Giraud's car draw up alongside them. Pierre got out. "Wait here. I'll see about getting Giraud in."

As the guards neared Pierre spent a few minutes in conversation before waving them all to come ahead..

Eric's excitement at being back at Vals was such that he rushed through the door and shouted—"We're back!" All heads turned as Dana repeated his greeting.

The sound of her voice caused both Professor Marty and Veronique to shout in excitement as they lionized her and Eric. "Thank God you're back. Out with it. How, when, where?" Veronique looked up at the broad smile of victory on Giraud's face. " I think I can guess that you played a role in the 'how' part, but…"

After a lengthy account, punctuated with bursts of shock, excitement and hearty congratulations, Veronique and Professor Marty turned back to their desks.

The Professor had a look of awe on his face as he shoved a ream of paper into Eric's hands. "Welcome back, one and all. Now read this. We need clarification of what's been showing up. After submitting non-stop strings of words, names, dates and connections, we've finally had a sense of threading the text together to create a sense of its core message." He let out a deep sigh. "It should rock the earth to its core."

"Great; let me at it. At last I can see what you've been up to." Dana joined Eric as he unfolded the lengthy cover sheet. "I take it this is the summary page."

"Right." Veronique chomped at the bit to have him begin to read it so they could discuss it. "You'll see. Any feedback you might have on how much to tell, when to tell, who to tell and how to proceed ..." She fell silent, gazing in anticipation.

Professor Marty looked at Eric. "How about reading it aloud? We think we've arrived at a cohesive sense of what we've learned from the manuscripts thus far. We attempted to create a more sequential arrangement of our word input and their response in a more understandable flow. For example; "treasure", "world", "transformed" in one sequence and so on. But it would help to hear it read aloud." He turned to Veronique. "Agreed?"

At her nod, Eric glanced down at the papers in his hands and began to read:

"WORLD: There is much negativity impacting Earth's environment, governments and humanity. Crisis looms.

TREASURE: The wisdom teachings of Abraham, Moses, Buddha, Mohammad and Christ must be understood at this time. The manuscripts hold the message to restore hope. They shall unfold a treasure so powerful as to transform the world.

TRANSFORMED: A dimensional shift shall take place so overwhelming in its implications as to shake up the planet and all on it. It shall be preceded by chaos as wars in the Middle East. Earthquakes, hurricanes and comets near.

ARMAGEDDON: Israel, Japan and Syria are seemingly implicated in some way. Nuclear holocausts prompt fear. Christ and other spiritual masters are used to counter other faiths in asserting that only certain religions know how to prepare for world's end. No end. No past or future. All is one. Only change. Enlightened souls prevail. Dense souls depart."

Eric paused and shook his head as he muttered: “Some treasure. Let’s get to the hope part.”

Pierre responded. “Hold on; the good news is that after such catastrophe comes cleansing and enlightenment. Read on.”

"LIGHT: Profound change will occur. Position of planets produce a new vibration of light. In the beginning was light—forming sound, creating matter. Cells increase their ability to hold light. Many shall adapt and will prevail. More will not.

CODE: A history of all actions taken by all of Earth’s peoples, throughout all times. The Creator mapped all in the Bible and other divinely created manuscripts, such as ours—written by Christ while in Egypt. Enlightenment is encoded.

MARY MAGDALENE: Wisdom throughout all time. Her manuscript shall reveal more about the evolution of women’s love and light and its ability to bring transformation to the world.

CATHARS: The Cathars knew souls to be sparks of God, Love and Light. Physicality clouds such knowledge. Cathar souls have returned to help others hold the changing light."

Eric reached the end, drew a long breath, looked up and stared at the team. “Wow, if this is how much you’ve learned *thus far* “I’ll be anxious to hear your comments when you’ve translated this.” He turned to Dana who extended her precious manuscript, a gift from her beloved Mary called Magdalene.

“Seems we have a lot of work to do.” Veronique said.

Dana smiled. “And so does the world.”

EPILOGUE

And so it came to pass that a new Golden Age appeared. Beyond even the memory of the time of ultimate changes, unfolded a time of radiant transformation that spread great Light throughout the planet Earth.

Man was truly man 'kind', his soul blended with the female to create a race of beauty and sublimity. Humanity fully expressed its divinity and connectedness to all that is. And as it did, the soul energy of plant, animal and human vibrated in harmony, manifesting a life of great beauty.

Honoring the environment resulted in an abundant cornucopia of fruits and vegetables laden with only the highest energy of LOVE. Honoring the young sponsored the fullest expansion of their God given divinity, their talents expanding and resulting in great gifts to all. Respecting the elderly added many decades of added longevity, health and contributions of great wisdom.

Plenty abounded and as the connection with all life grew the ability to survive below the ocean, commune with the majestic sea creatures and expand a philosophy that radiated into the universe prevailed.

Chivalrous and courageous, with a depth of passion unimpeded, men and women developed to the fullest many aspects of their beings—artists, scholars, scientists and all manner of the creative arts blossomed fully. The alliance of science with philosophy incorporated a full understanding of the connection with physics, metaphysics and spirituality. All was GOD.

Not only were the enlightened races filled with delight at their differences but, along with their ever-expanding wisdom and Spirit, they were playful and forever looking forward with joyful anticipation of waking up to another day.

Gratitude rippled throughout the world, the words "Thank You" ringing not only in the many languages that yet remained in the new world, but in the common language whose sounds carried an enhanced energy of all-encompassing Love.

Religion was expressed in many ways but always from an inclusiveness that shared a common philosophy, one to which all of humanity vibrated: "The Kingdom of God is within you." Knowing that the soul of everyone and all of creation was a perfect reflection of God made for divine wisdom and glorious connectedness.

War and the killing of anything was a concept unable to be understood on any level. Peace prompted the freedom to blossom completely. As part of their prayers, all would continue to give thanks for that time of great change and those people who succeeded in unlocking a heavenly treasure that truly transformed the Earth.

ABOUT THE AUTHOR

Nita Hughes was for many years a Vice President for Security Pacific Bank (Bank of America). As a global executive in the International Private Banking division, she provided financial advice to high net worth clients in Asia, South America, and Europe.

Nita draws on diverse passions, including her love for the South of France, speaking, singing, and traveling. Her writing includes contributions to books on autism, corporate training, and marketing.

When not involved in her personal pursuits, she is a partner with *Hughes Associates*, a team of professionals committed to helping entrepreneurs and artists profit from their creative endeavors.

Nita lives with her husband Douglas on the Hawaiian island of Maui.

For more information, visit the author's websites at:

www.PastRecall.com - or - ***www.CatharLegacy.com***

A PREQUEL TO ... *THE CATHAR LEGACY*

In the novel, ***Past Recall***, Nita Hughes blends an ancient story of terrifying persecution with a vision of hope for the world today.

The tale is told by a woman photographer who unexpectedly discovers information from the past about a spiritual secret, a treasure so coveted that an entire culture was massacred in an attempt to own it.

Her search for answers propels the characters of this romantic thriller through time as history threatens to repeat itself.

We are introduced to Clotilde and Jean de Mirepoix, devout Cathars in 13th century France. Their world of growing enlightenment is being extinguished by a reign of terror. Clotilde and Jean seek refuge in Montsegur, a Cathar sanctuary thought to be impregnable. But their safety fades in importance as they attempt to secure the Cathar treasure, described in the archives of the Catholic church as "*so powerful as to change the world.*" Vowing to safeguard the treasure throughout time, their souls commit to return and unveil it at "worlds end".

Now that time has come, as photographer Dana Palmer and writer Eric Taylor collaborate on a story whose secret may provide the world's salvation-or its destruction. For more information, or to order the book online, visit the author's websites at:

www.PastRecall.com - or - ***www.CatharLegacy.com***

Printed in the United States
151009LV00004B/32/A

9 781411 664302